FAMOUS

JENNY HOLIDAY

Edited by Tracy Montoya. Copyedited by Julia Ganis, juliaedits.com. Cover design by L.C. Chase.

First edition, July 2017

ISBN

978-0-9950927–6-1 (paperback)

978-0-9950927-7-8 (ebook)

CHAPTER ONE

Seven years ago

Sometimes a wedding was not just a wedding.

This one, in which Evan Winslow's friend Tyrone pledged his eternal devotion to his girlfriend Vicky, was, in fact, a test. It looked like a normal wedding, with white funereal-looking flowers and ill-fitting tuxedos, but it was *also* Evan's Hail Mary pass: one last attempt to hold on to his life in Miami, to his nascent career, to his entire freaking life.

His final experiment to measure how extensive—how *permanent*—the damage inflicted by his father on the Winslow family's reputation was going to be.

Evan had laid low for the past two weeks, hoping the whole "out of sight/out of mind" adage would prove true, and now it was final exam time.

This test had one question: Could Evan attend his friend Tyrone's wedding and not be recognized, not upstage the proceedings with his mere presence?

The answer was no. Fail. Flunk.

Which meant this was it. Today was the end of life as he

knew it, which sounded melodramatic but was no less true for it. Because if Evan knew one thing with certainty, down to the dusty corners of his soul, it was that he could not live with the fame—the *infamy*—his father's crimes had brought down on his head. He had already been coming around to accepting the idea that his painting career was done before it had even really started—thanks to the crimes of Evan Winslow Sr., Evan Winslow Jr. was destined to be persona non grata in the art world—but now he'd brought the goddamned paparazzi to his best friend's wedding.

He'd tried to hedge against that prospect, and he initially thought he'd succeeded. He'd spent the night at his brother's place. Evan's brother wasn't in the art world—the family business—having opted instead for life as an overgrown trust-fund baby. So he wasn't getting as much media attention as Evan. Evan had called a cab to his brother's house, timing things so as to arrive at the church just before the ceremony started.

But he'd miscalculated, emerging from the taxi as a limo pulled up and disgorged the bride and her attendants.

He'd held out a shred of hope that the flashbulbs that started going off were actually for the bride. But how many brides hired half a dozen photographers with zoom lenses to photograph their nuptials?

How many wedding photographers yelled things like "Were you in on it too?" and "Will you attend the sentencing hearing?"

So he'd hustled inside ahead of the bridal party and tried to make himself inconspicuous.

Which, of course, had set off a series of whispers among the guests. People talking behind wedding programs, some openly pointing at him. The bride's mother glaring, no doubt because he had upstaged her daughter before she'd even made an appearance.

It didn't even matter that everyone recognized him, really. The fact that he had failed his test was regrettable but not elementally important. Because even if the infamy died down, could he live with the lie? With the notion that everything he had—his luxe condo; his painting ability, honed over years of lessons from the world's greatest artists; his expensive grad school—was all built on lies and paid for with stolen money?

The answer to that question was also no.

So it was time to go. To start over somewhere else. Pack his shit up, transfer to another college to finish his degree—say goodbye to his entire life.

He had no earthly idea how to do that, but that was a problem to be solved tomorrow, on day one of his new life. Right now, the last day in his old life, he had a wedding to attend.

Thankfully, the music changed at that moment, signaling the start of the ceremony. Everyone turned, and he breathed a sigh of relief. For a few moments anyway, there were people in the room who would attract more attention than he would.

He almost laughed as the first bridesmaid appeared. The dress was ridiculous. She looked like a short, puffy, pink mummy. Evan didn't know fabrics, but he suspected that the multi-layered, shiny dress she was wearing had not been constructed from any fiber or dye that occurred naturally in this world.

And there was another one, and another. They kept coming, parading down the aisle in ascending order of height, like caricatures of bridesmaids rather than actual bridesmaids, with their identical upswept hairdos and identical pink heels.

His wrist twitched. They would make a great painting, all of them lined up like nesting dolls.

No, correction: as the final bridesmaid appeared at the top of the aisle, Evan had to revise his previous thought. They would make a great painting, but *she* would make a spectacular painting. He would title it *Bridesmaid Number Seven.*

Tall and thin with long limbs, she was the sort of person people might describe as gangly. It was like someone had taken a regular, average woman and stretched her out like taffy. But she was too graceful to be rightfully called gangly. She had an ease about her, which was rather remarkable, given the packaging and spackling she'd been subjected to.

Evan noticed those sorts of details when a painting was emerging. It was like his brain clicked into some other mode as it swept over a scene, processing, neutrally assessing everything with equal attention, waiting for the jolting spike of feeling that signified the correct take on a subject.

He was a beat behind everyone else standing for the bride because he was still looking at the last bridesmaid. She and her colleagues arrayed themselves at the front of the church and turned to watch the bride process. Her face had interesting angles: sharp cheekbones and slightly unruly brows arching high over eyes that should have been too close-set to be called pretty.

Where would he put her? In a forest, maybe? In her ridiculous pink dress in a forest, Titania styled by Barbie? No. That wasn't quite right.

As the bride passed his pew, he forced his gaze from her tallest attendant and considered his friend Tyrone's soon-to-be-wife with more attention than he had ever found it necessary to bestow on her before. Vicky had the same facial structure as the bridesmaid, but less of it. The cheekbones were there, just not as prominent. The two women had to be related. Sisters, maybe?

As Vicky's father kissed her and sat down, the bridesmaids turned their backs to the congregation, presenting the assembly with a row of identical bows on their backsides, each one a little higher than the one next to it thanks to the arrangement of attendants from shortest to tallest.

He was still thinking about her face, though.

He would start with Yellow Ochre and add tiny amounts of Cadmium Red Light to start with, and then he'd layer in the planes of those gorgeous cheekbones.

It was with a jolt, a great wrenching, invisible blow, that he realized: *no*.

Not that those were the wrong colors, but that he wasn't going to paint her.

He wasn't going to paint anything.

After today, he didn't paint anymore.

"Is that cute guy in the corner the son of the infamous art criminal?" Emmy whispered to her cousin Vicky. Now that dinner and the first dance were over, she'd finally gotten a minute alone with the bride so she could ask about the handsome man sitting alone at a table in the back of the ballroom. She figured he must be "the one" since she'd seen him intently speed walking past a clump of photographers on his way into the church.

He'd been staring at her much of the evening.

It started when she was walking back up the aisle after the ceremony on the arm of her assigned groomsman. The intensity of his gaze had drawn her attention, but he'd looked away when she caught him staring.

And she'd *kept* catching him. His appraisal had continued throughout the toasts and as she'd tried to make conversation with the rest of the wedding party over dinner. She'd glance over at him only to find him already looking at her—enough times that he'd started grinning sheepishly, like he knew he'd been busted.

But of course if she kept catching him, it meant *she* was staring at *him* as much as he was staring at her.

It was just so hard *not* to look at him. He was tall and broad-shouldered under his impeccably tailored suit, and when he smiled as she'd catch him looking, he did it with his whole face.

"Don't look!" Emmy shriek-whispered as Vicky turned to peek over her shoulder.

"I can't tell you who he is if I can't see him," Vicky declared, not even trying to make her surveillance subtle. "Oh! Yep, that's Evan Winslow!"

"His dad even made the papers in Minnesota," Emmy said. The story of the jet-setting art dealer's fall from grace had all the makings of a Greek tragedy, and it was playing out in the tabloids. It was a true-crime story that had the nation fascinated, except instead of dead bodies there were Ponzi schemes and counterfeit art.

"Yep," said Vicky. "The trial was huge. They were one of the richest families in Miami. It's been all over the place. Poor guy. Ty says he's taken it all super hard." She cocked her head. "So you think he's cute, huh? A little nerdy for my tastes, but I dare you to go over there and talk to him."

"No way! I can't just—" Emmy's objection was cut off when the DJ cued up a horrid song that made Vicky's sorority sisters scream and rise as one.

As they swept Vicky away in a tornado of pink tulle, she called, "Go over there. What have you got to lose? You'll never see him again anyway."

There was so much more she wanted to ask Vicky. How old was Evan Winslow? What was he studying? Vicky's new husband knew him from the University of Miami, where they were both grad students. Tyrone was doing his MBA, but she had a hard time imagining this guy in a business school. He seemed like more of an intellectual—a humanities type maybe. His hair, though currently slicked back, seemed like it was a little too long for him to fit in with the would-be capitalists, and his nerd-chic horn-rimmed glasses seemed more Buddy Holly than business. She started to make up a story. Something from the point of view of a sensitive guy forced into business school by his conniving, greedy father. The chorus could be the dad talking, but by the end of the song, the lyrics would be turned around, the guy defiantly using the father's words against him.

Well, hell. Emmy wasn't generally an assertive sort of person. She tended to hang around on the sidelines and make up little snippets of songs about what she saw unfolding around her. But Vicky was right. She was flying back to Minneapolis tomorrow, and she'd never see this guy again. In twenty-four hours, she'd be back doing battle with her parents, facing their perpetual and poorly disguised disappointment over her barista job and her "childish dreams." So why not put an end to their little mutual staring society and go say hi to the infamous Evan Winslow?

Gathering about a thousand yards of pink polyester in her arms, she hiked up her skirts and set off. He must have felt her approach, because he looked up from his cake while she was still a good twenty feet away, an expression of surprise seguing into another of those magnetic, self-deprecating grins as she got closer.

"Hey," she said, trying to make the greeting seem casual.

"Hey," he echoed. Then he added, "You're here," as if all this time he'd merely been waiting for her arrival, as if *she* had been the point of his attending the wedding.

He picked up a wedding program and slid it across the table to her.

"Ha!" She laughed in delight. If she'd been making up a story about him, it seemed he had done the same thing, in a way. Except where hers was coming together from turns of phrase and snippets of melody, his was composed of ink—garden-variety ballpoint from the look of it. He had drawn her on the back of the program, right on top of the Shakespeare sonnet that Vicky, who Emmy was pretty sure wouldn't know a sonnet if it bit her in the ass outside the context of wedding planning websites, had artfully placed on the otherwise-blank heavy-gauge paper. The funny thing was that Emmy wasn't wearing the god-awful dress in his portrait. He'd put her in shorts and a tank top, which was pretty much her uniform when she wasn't performing bridesmaid duties.

"You drew me! You're an artist?" She'd known his dad was an art dealer, but she didn't know that much about the rest of the Winslow family—she'd read the headlines but hadn't really followed the details of the trial.

He paused for long enough before answering that she started to fear she'd offended him somehow. "I used to be a painter."

"What does that mean?"

"It means I used to paint, but now I don't."

Okay then, that was clearly not a topic he was keen to discuss, so she tried another question. "Vicky said you're in grad school with Tyrone?"

"We're both at the University of Miami, but I'm doing a PhD in art history. Ty and I met in a campus running club."

Yes. The satisfying ping of having uncovered the truth in her proto-song echoed in her chest. An artist *and* an intellectual. She'd been spot-on.

"Are you from Minnesota?" he asked. "You look like you're related to Vicky."

"Yeah. She's my cousin. I'm Emmy."

He stood and stuck out his hand. "Hi, Emmy. I'm Evan."

She was on the other side of the table—too far away to reach his hand—so she walked around. Wanting to pretend that she was in control, she slowed her steps. But that was only because she wasn't entirely comfortable with the truth of the matter, which was that in her haste to reach him she'd *had* to slow her steps. She was a stupid, powerless fish he was reeling in.

He didn't let go when the handshake would normally have ended, just hitched his head toward the door. "Want to go for a walk?"

Of course she did.

"Aha!" Evan said, pushing his shoulder against the heavy metal door at the top of the stairwell. "Unlocked!" He held it for a laughing Emmy to precede him onto the roof of the banquet hall. She had her voluminous skirts gathered in one hand and her high heels dangling from the fingers of the other. "Be careful of your feet. Who knows what's up here."

She paused at the threshold and peered out. He looked over her shoulder. Yeah, the gravel that lined the ground was going to require shoes. Or…

"Eeee!" she shrieked, laughing as he swung her into his arms. "What are you doing?"

What *was* he doing? He was acting like the hero of some lame made-for-TV romantic comedy. Not his style at all. But there was something about being in limbo, teetering on the precipice between one life and another, that made every decision this evening seem less important, every action less imbued with its potential future consequences.

"If I'd known that 'go for a walk' was code for 'break onto the roof,'" she said, "I might have thought twice about accompanying you."

The roof had been the only place he could think to escape, where he could be sure there would be no photographers. But he didn't want her to feel uncomfortable, so he paused, wondering if he should turn around.

But then she craned her neck to get a better view and said, "It's gorgeous up here!"

So he crossed the roof and deposited her on some kind of ventilation structure that would do as a bench.

"Beautiful," she said, still talking about the view.

It was. The buildings of the Miami skyline he knew so well were jewels against the otherworldly pink sky of dusk. But so were the shining sapphires of her eyes.

And that was another made-for-TV thing he didn't do: compare women's eyes to gemstones. *What the hell?* There was limbo, and there was losing control of himself.

"Give me that," she said, grabbing the stolen bottle of champagne he had tucked under his arm and setting to work on the cork. When it popped, she squealed and held the fizzing bottle away from her for a moment before tipping her head back and drinking directly from it. The slanted pink light caught tendrils of blond hair escaping the pins that anchored an elaborate updo. He watched her throat undulate as she drank. Then she lifted her head, used her forearm to wipe her mouth, and grinned as she handed him the bottle, perfectly framed by the blazing sunset.

He was cursed with a painter's eye. He saw things other people didn't. He was never going to get over not painting her.

"What's your last name?" he asked, thinking, irrationally,

that if he knew it, he could somehow find her later. Put a bookmark in this meeting and come back to it, even though he knew that he was going to have to draw a sharp line between what he was already starting to think of as his "old" life and whatever was going to come next.

"I'm moving to Los Angeles in two months," she said.

"So it's Emmy I'mMovingToLosAngelesInTwoMonths?" He couldn't help teasing. "That must have been a mouthful when you were a kid."

"No." She laughed. "I'm moving in two months, and I'm going to change my name when I do, I think. I haven't decided to what. So it's just Emmy for now."

Ah, so he wasn't the only one on the verge of reinventing himself. Perhaps that's why he felt this strangely, strongly compelled by her. They were of a kind. "If that's how you're going to be, I won't tell you my last name, either." She likely already knew it, but she hadn't brought it up, so he wouldn't either.

"Don't tell me," she said. "Let's just be Emmy and Evan. E and E." She took another swig of the champagne. "Like e.e. cummings."

"I will wade out till my thighs are steeped in burning flowers," he said. He wasn't sure how his brain had produced that obscure line, but he knew now how he would have painted her.

She'd been looking at the skyline, but the cummings snippet snagged her attention, and she turned, eyes suddenly glazed with moisture.

"What's the matter?"

"I'm a songwriter," she said. "Or at least I'm trying to be."

Ah. The impending move to L.A., the name change—the pieces were coming together.

"Sometimes when I hear a line like that, it makes me

despair of ever writing anything worthwhile," she said, shaking her head.

"Don't despair. You can do it."

"How do you know? You don't even know me."

He shrugged. She had intelligent eyes that looked intently at the world. That's what storytellers needed. That's probably what he had seen in her, why he had picked her out from the row of identical puffy pink dresses. "I have a feeling you're going to make it."

"You're the only one who thinks so," she whispered.

"I have a good eye," he said, struck with the urge to reassure her. "I see things other people don't." He turned so they were side by side, both facing the now rapidly darkening city —which was why he didn't have any warning when she leaned over, grabbed his cheeks, and kissed him.

Her lips were soft, and pressed so lightly against his it almost tickled. His first instinct was to push her away, because what could come of it? They were both headed for new lives, both making a break with the present.

But he couldn't make himself do it. What was so wrong with kissing a pretty girl on a rooftop? It was the perfect coda, actually, to his Miami life. So he surrendered, letting his whole body relax into the soft hunger of their kiss, forcing himself to attend to every nuance of the experience, to savor the bittersweet finale, as if he could file it away somehow, and take it out and examine it again later, like he would a memento from his past.

And, oh, he hadn't felt this alive for months. It was like she was filling him with energy he thought had been drained permanently by the police raids, the meetings with lawyers and PR people, the endless court proceedings. He sipped at her lips, letting his hands frame her face, wanting to anchor her there forever. As he deepened the kiss, testing the seam of her lips, she opened for him, but there was a tentativeness there, a hesitation.

It was like she didn't really know what she was doing.

The rogue thought entered his mind as her tongue slid along his, ripping an involuntary groan from his throat as he gently pushed her away.

"How old are you?" God, how could he have missed that? Hadn't he just been bragging about how good he was at seeing things?

Her brow furrowed. "Does it matter?" She was flushed, her pupils dilated, her breath short.

She was gorgeous.

It didn't matter how old she was, not in any elemental way. But it *did* matter here on this roof, in the clumsy corporeal world. It meant the difference between continuing this spectacular goodbye-to-his-old-life kiss and *not* continuing it.

"Tell me."

She pulled back and scooted farther away from him on the bench, confirming his fears even before she spoke. "I'm nineteen."

Right. It might be perfectly clear that this was merely a casual kiss, but he wasn't going to be *that* guy. He eyed the nearly empty champagne bottle on the ground at their feet. That was all he needed—the story of Evan Winslow, Jr. getting a nineteen-year-old drunk and seducing her.

So much for enjoying his bittersweet Miami coda.

"How old are *you*?" she countered, a challenge in her voice.

"Twenty-six."

"That's not so bad," she said.

"Not so bad for what?" He was teasing her, but only because teasing was all he could do now. "You're right," he said. "A seven-year age difference is not bad at all for sitting on the roof talking about everything under the sun until someone notices we're gone and sends out a search party." He patted the seat beside him, shrugged out of his suit jacket, and held it out to her.

He wasn't a *total* saint, though. He liked the disappointment that washed across the striking angular face he wanted to paint so badly his fingers ached.

"Talking," she said, pouting a little but sliding back over to sit next to him and letting him slip the jacket over her shoulders.

"*Talking*," he confirmed, emphasizing the word for himself as much as for her.

"Okay, uh, what's your favorite TV show?"

"I don't really watch TV." He didn't tell her that he didn't even own one. Or that the glimpses of his family's sordid drama that he'd caught on CNN at his brother's house had been enough to reinforce his desire to never get one.

"Last concert you saw?"

He thought—hard—and came up with nothing. He had been to a few shows on the last cruise he took with his parents. His mother dragged Evan and his brother and their father on an annual luxury cruise and made them dress for dinner and generally fulfill her fantasy of the perfect Ralph Lauren family. But probably cruise ship bands playing Neil Diamond covers weren't what Emmy had in mind. "I'm not really one for live music," he finally said.

"Okaaay," she said, screwing up her face like she was trying to think of a new topic.

"It's no good," he said laughingly. "I'm completely pop-culturally illiterate."

"How come you don't paint anymore?"

Whoa. If her previous questions had been rubber-tipped darts that pinged easily off their targets, this one was a razor-sharp axe that sliced right through him.

"I don't want to talk about that," he said, which was the absolute truth, even if it didn't answer her question.

"Okay," she said, and he was surprised that she was going to accept his evasive answer. Maybe it wouldn't be so hard to upend his life after all. Maybe he could get used to being not-a-painter. "So what should we talk about?"

"You. We should talk about you." She was the most compelling person he'd met in a long time. And she was the *only* person he'd met recently who hadn't said a word about his father. "I want to know everything there is to know about you, Emmy NoLastName. Tell me about moving to L.A. Sing me a song." He turned to face her head-on. He would listen to her for as long as he could get away with it. He would listen and watch. Then he would say goodbye.

To her, and to himself.

CHAPTER TWO

Seven years later

It seemed like a good idea at the time.

How many of Emerson's misadventures in the past few years could be summed up that way?

She eyed the graceful Victorian as her assistant Tony slowed to a stop. With its overgrown garden, giant shade trees, and huge wraparound porch—complete with swing—it looked like a postcard from Anne of Green Gables Land. Like a place where a catalog family would pose for their Christmas card picture in front of an adorably lopsided snowman.

In other words, something out of another world. As far from her life in L.A. as it was possible to get.

Which, she reminded herself, was exactly the point.

This time it will be different.

Except, yeah, she always said that. And it never was. But to cut herself some slack, when she said that, she was usually talking about a boy. And those days were done for a while—a good long while. No matter how much her romantic misadventures seemed to translate into hit songs that made her managers swoon as the tabloids speculated over which ex-boyfriend could be matched with which song, she wasn't going there anymore. This was the beginning of a new era. Emerson Quinn: single, independent, mistress of her own emotional and creative destiny.

There was also the part where the person inside the postcard house was most decidedly not a boy.

He was a man. Just not a man who was going to have any sway over her.

"I still don't like this, Em," Tony said. "They're going to find you. You busted out, yeah, but you can't hide indefinitely."

Emerson pivoted to face her longtime assistant. Despite his tendency toward melodrama, she adored him. Hell, as her first manager, he'd been the only person in the world who'd looked at the gangly teenager and seen past the combat boots and false bravado. Who'd listened to her demo and heard something bigger than the Neko Case wannabe who hadn't quite mastered the Garage Band app on her Mac.

And when she'd insisted she was going to be a singer-songwriter despite the fact that her parents had vowed to disown her over it, Tony had shrugged and said, "Well, why the hell not? Someone gets to do it."

More importantly, Tony was the only person in the world she could really, truly trust.

"They're my managers, Tony, not the Mafia. Don't be so sensationalistic. I wasn't in prison." No, it was just a hotel suite, fully stocked with snacks, keyboards, and middle-aged Swedish songwriter dudes who were inexplicably talented at churning out pop songs designed to capture the inner life of the modern American twentysomething.

It felt *like prison, though.*

Okay, now *she* was being melodramatic. It was just that the last tour had only finished two weeks ago, and she was *done* with hotel rooms.

She simply needed…a break. People did it all the time. That it was an unscheduled one that would throw a wrench into the well-oiled machinery that was the Emerson Quinn hit machine? Well, she was choosing to make that not her problem for a while.

But she was faking all her bravado. Tears prickled behind her eyeballs. She pressed her lips together and forced them back. Emerson was *not* a crier. Emmy used to cry; Emerson did not. "I'm just taking a little vacation, Tony," she said. "Catching my breath."

"And you couldn't catch your breath in, say, New York? London? Or even back in Minneapolis? You know, somewhere with *civilization*? Lattes. Newspapers. *Homosexuals.*" His lip curled. "From what I can tell, all this place has is corn."

"You heard Song 58," she said. Song 58 was the temporary title of a tune she and a co-writer had banged out yesterday at the Beverly Wilshire, thus named because it was her prolific co-writer's fifty-eighth song of the year. The guy was a machine, and he was currently on loan to her.

"Yes," he said. "It was…"

She knew what he meant. Song 58 was fine. It was good, even. With some work in the studio, it could be totally catchy. It just wasn't…

Ugh. She didn't even have words for what was wrong with her right now. All she could think to say was, "I'm not writing the next album in that hotel room, Tony." Goddamn it, her voice had hitched a little. *And I'm not writing it with them at all.* But she didn't tell Tony that part. That part was a half-baked notion pricking at the edge of her consciousness, the idea that she could…drop out and come back a couple months later with an entire album in hand. She didn't dare voice that out loud.

"So let me tell Brian and Claudia you're taking a well-earned vacation, and you don't have to go anywhere at all. You can hide away at home in your PJs. Just you and the Hollywood Hills. I'll have food delivered daily."

They'd been over this and over this on the flight. "You know that wouldn't work. As much as you think you can just call them and…" She didn't have the heart to tell him that he didn't have a say in the matter; that whatever credit he deserved for discovering Emerson, managing her career for those critical early years, he didn't get a vote anymore.

"I know, sweetie. I know." That was the thing about Tony —he heard what she left unsaid.

The hint of sadness in his eyes was a punch to the gut. They both knew that, theoretically, he could suggest that her managers Brian and Claudia send the co-writer away and leave writing the next album for later. Or she could suggest the same thing. Insist, even—she was the "artist," after all.

But they wouldn't listen. Not for long, anyway. They never did. She and Tony had made their devil's bargain when they'd decided her career needed the power of a big creative management company behind it and left Minneapolis for California, and now there was no escaping.

Except maybe in Dane, Iowa, population 14,581. And, according to the town's Wikipedia entry, half of those were college students.

"I get it. But Em, you don't even know this guy." Tony nodded at the falling-down Victorian. "And now you're going to hole up in his house? What is this? *Notting Hill*?"

She *did* know Evan Winslow, though. It might be irrational. It might have been one night seven years ago. It might have been one night seven years ago in which *nothing happened.* But she knew him. And he knew her in a way that went beyond the brand. Hell, he was possibly the only person on the planet who hadn't heard of the brand.

And he'd offered to help. *Let me know if I can ever do anything for you,* he'd said as they'd parted ways after their night on the roof in Miami. He was the only other person in the world, besides Tony, who had ever done that. Who had believed in her.

Of course, the offer hadn't been serious. It was one of those things people said but didn't mean. He hadn't even told her his last name. She'd known it, of course, as everyone had, but officially, he'd kept it from her.

But she'd never forgotten those words: *Let me know if I can ever do anything for you.* The phrase had become a mantra during her impulsive flight from the Beverly Wilshire, a lifeline.

And today she was here to call in her chips.

So she hoisted her purse and flashed Tony a smile that belied the fluttering in her belly as she got out of the car. "Pop the trunk, and I'll get my stuff."

"At least let me come in and meet him," Tony said, ignoring her instruction and hopping out to retrieve her suitcase himself.

Slinging her guitar over her shoulder, she tried to take the handle of her bag, but he wouldn't surrender it. "You're my assistant, Tony, not my father. I'm twenty-six, for God's sake. I'm not a kid anymore."

"I know." He rolled his eyes. "Do I ever know—it was a hell of a lot easier when you *were* a kid."

"Easier, maybe, but platinum records pay several orders of magnitude better than First Avenue," she said, naming the Minneapolis club where, with Tony's help, she'd broken into the local music scene, paving the way for their move to L.A. and her first major-label deal.

He laid his hand on her arm. Tony wasn't the affectionate type. If he didn't knock it off, she really was going to cry. And that was *not* happening.

"I just think it's a little sketchy that this guy you met once seven years ago has agreed to let you stay here."

Emerson didn't bother telling him that Evan had not agreed to any such thing. That he didn't know she was coming. That he might not even remember her.

Because if she told Tony any of that, she'd be on the first plane back to Los Angeles, and by nightfall, she'd be ensconced in her hotel suite, the lock clicking into place on her gilded cage like thunder in her ears.

Before he could object again, she air-kissed him, yanked her suitcase from his grip, and rolled it up the cute-as-a-button cobblestone path that led to Evan Winslow's front door.

And crossed her fingers and rang the doorbell.

The doorbell rang.

Perfect. Nine midterms down, twenty-eight more to go, and what Evan really needed right now was Mrs. Johansen on his porch bearing yet another casserole destined to join the growing collection in his freezer. What on earth had possessed him to agree to teach a summer course?

The answer, of course, was Larry. The chair of the art history department at Dane College had the power to make or break Evan's tenure bid in September—and since he'd made it clear he was currently leaning toward "break," Evan needed to ingratiate himself as much as possible, to be a good citizen of the department. If teaching Intro to Renaissance Art to thirty-seven undergrads in Dane College's questionably air-conditioned humanities building during the summer term was what it took to lock down his peaceful, hard-won Iowa life, he would expound upon the wonders of the Sistine Chapel until he and his students were blue in the face.

Besides, Michelangelo rocked.

It was important to remember that in addition to being optimally located in the middle of nowhere, his job at Dane College was a pretty sweet gig. Much better than he'd ever imagined all those years ago when he'd stepped in front of the cameras after his father was sentenced to thirty years and panicked as a CNN reporter asked him, "How does it feel to have lost everything?"

The doorbell rang a second time.

He sighed and set down his pen. As tempting as it was, he couldn't not answer. Mrs. Johansen would only come around to the back door, and he didn't want her struggling with his half-broken gate.

He padded to the door. Probably he should put a shirt on, but it was hot as hell, and it was almost certainly just Mrs. Johansen, so screw it.

He swung open the door.

It was not Mrs. Johansen.

Holy shit.

He was like a cartoon character, utterly flattened when a grand piano fell from the sky. It was Emmy. With a guitar and a…huge suitcase?

"Hi," she said, like she was paying a routine social call.

"Hi," he echoed, frankly shocked that his voice worked.

She had changed. Her face had thinned out, making those angular, sharp cheekbones even more prominent. Her hair was different—still blond, but instead of a solid color, it was streaked with lots of different shades ranging from light ash to golden honey. And it was shorter now, chin-length with bangs, choppy, messy-on-purpose. Instead of the regulation insipid coral lipstick she'd worn at the wedding, her lips were painted a bright scarlet, which made for a stark contrast to her pale skin.

There was something else different, too. Something harder to articulate, but it was there just the same, lurking beneath the surface. It was what he would try to draw out if he were going to paint her.

If he still painted anymore.

It was a weariness. Not that she looked overtly tired—there were no rings under her eyes, and her skin glowed in the bright afternoon sun. No, it was a hesitancy, slight but definitely there. As if the nineteen-year-old who'd been so guileless, who had told him with shining eyes about her musical dreams in the hours after their ill-advised kiss, had been knocked around a little by the world in subsequent years, had some of her soft, rounded edges hardened off. It was subtle, but enough to change her whole demeanor.

But her eyes were the same. He would know those eyes anywhere. Blue, but not the clichéd blue of milkmaids and Barbie dolls. A deep, dark, soulful blue, with the tiniest ring of yellow around the pupil on one side that you had to look closely to see.

And he *had* looked closely, back then when she was nineteen and he had to take the high road, back when they were both about to embark on new lives. Looked close, as they talked through the night, then forced himself to look away.

She cleared her throat, pulling him from his trance, reminding him that he was standing shirtless on his porch in front of Emmy NoLastName, seven years and fifteen hundred miles from the wedding at which they'd met.

She shifted from one foot to the other. "So, it's too bad about Vicky and Tyrone."

Who? Oh, right. The bride and groom. Her cousin and his friend Tyrone. Though they had occasionally exchanged emails in the year or so after Evan left Miami, he hadn't seen Ty since the wedding. He now belonged squarely in the box in Evan's head marked "Before." Evan didn't like to overlap with "Before."

"Too bad?" he echoed, his mouth having gone dry from the adrenaline spike her appearance had caused.

"They got divorced?" She cocked her head, no doubt astonished that he hadn't heard the news.

All right. He'd been standing there like the proverbial deer in headlights long enough. "How did you find me?" he asked, his voice coming out sharper than he'd intended.

"Google."

"But—"

"I asked Vicky to confirm your last name, and then I *typed it into a search engine.*" She grinned. "It's almost like I'm a *spy* or something."

Right. He sometimes forgot that Dane wasn't an invisibility cloak, though it often felt that way, the miles and miles of corn that surrounded it in every direction buffering him like a verdant moat.

A horn honked. "Woo-hoo, Professor Winslow, looking go-o-o-od!" A car full of girls squealed down his otherwise-sleepy street, a couple of them half hanging out the windows. They must have startled Emmy, because she ducked her head and shielded her face with both hands—kind of like his father had done every day on his way in and out of court, hiding from photographers and angry crowds alike. Kind of like he had learned to do in the weeks that followed, before he'd gotten his shit together and left town.

His face heated, and he smiled awkwardly. "One of the downsides of a small college town."

She let her hands fall back to her sides. She was looking at his chest.

A shirt. A shirt would be a good idea.

"Did you, ah, want to come in?" he asked against his better judgment. He had never had anyone from his old life in this house. When he saw his mom and brother, it was always at his mom's place in Atlanta, where she'd started *her* life over with Husband #2.

But Emmy was apparently the exception.

Also, some ill-advised part of his brain whispered, *she's not nineteen anymore.*

He gestured into the house behind him, and she whipped her eyes to his face. A slow smile blossomed, like she knew she'd been caught ogling but didn't care. It reminded him of the way they kept catching each other looking at the wedding, except this time, the look was…more heated.

"I was hoping you'd say that, and I would love to come in." Then she sighed, and her shoulders slumped a little—in relief? Defeat? He couldn't tell. "I'm in a bit of a bind, actually."

As Evan disappeared down the hallway, calling, "I'll be right back—make yourself at home," Emerson let out a breath and peeled off her T-shirt, leaving only the tank top she had layered underneath. The Minnesota summers of her childhood had been hot and sticky, but that was nothing compared to the blast furnace that was this town—and Evan's apparently un-air-conditioned house. Other than the odd stint on her terrace perched in the hills, Emerson couldn't think when she'd spent any time recently in an environment that hadn't been artificially heated or chilled.

It was hotter than sin in Dane, Iowa.

But also: Woo-hoo, Professor Winslow. Looking go-oo-od.

He'd been handsome at Vicky's wedding all those years ago, but handsome in the way that really dressed-up men are. In their suits and tuxedos, with their close shaves and careful smiles, men like that flipped the "Prince Charming" switch that girls like her, raised on Disney princesses and graduated to Netflix rom-coms, had socially conditioned into them. Hell, hadn't she spent the last half decade going from one potential Prince Charming to another, telling herself each time that she had finally found "the one"?

But seven years later, shirtless, barefoot, with a pair of jeans sitting low on his hips, Evan was a completely different kind of handsome.

Handsome wasn't even the right word. Because who knew about the bodybuilder's chest that had been hiding under that suit and tie? The dark brown hair that, freed from gelled-back wedding guest perfection, flopped across his face, almost at man-bob length?

There was one thing that hadn't changed, though, and that was the way he looked at her with those eyes so brown they were almost black. Like he was studying her. Memorizing her. Surrendering his grasp on the material world for a moment in favor of…her. Even those nerd glasses he still wore couldn't mute the effect. In the years since she had last seen him, a *lot* of people had looked at her. She'd played arenas of tens of thousands of people and live awards show broadcasts viewed by millions.

None of that was like this. Like the way Evan looked at her.

She was immune, though, she reminded herself. That

wasn't why she was here on this ridiculous Hail Mary mission. He could look all he liked, but she was not in search of a prince, charming or otherwise. She was in search of a haven, and if the only one she had access to had a hot guy as its gate-keeper, well, she was just going to have to build a deflector shield around her heart.

She looked around for something to distract herself from thoughts of his gaze, to tip her back into the real world. The world where she had a problem that needed solving. From the entryway, she could see into a sun-drenched living room, its walls covered practically floor to ceiling with art. Photographs and paintings hung on the walls, which, she could see from the cracks between the frames, were covered in a faded floral wallpaper. More pieces sat on the floor, resting against the walls two deep in some spots. It was like a museum—a messy, willy-nilly museum with no theme.

She was drawn to it, despite the fact that she didn't really know anything about art. It was exuberant and hopeful—exactly the way Evan had made her feel at the wedding. Exuberant as they'd sneaked up to the roof, laughing, her heart as fizzy as the champagne they'd stolen. Later, hopeful when he'd asked her question after question about her musical ambi-tions, making her laugh when he denied having heard of any of the bands or singers she'd invoked to compare herself to stylistically.

"Hey."

"Oh!" She jumped. That was another side effect of life in the spotlight: every moment of her life was scripted. She was never surprised—unless Claudia was shoving a birthday cake in her face unexpectedly so one of the PR people could capture the "surprise" for Emerson's social media feeds.

"Sorry." He scraped a hand through his hair, and she was more disappointed than she should have been that he'd put on a T-shirt. A faded forest green, it was worn and soft-looking. She was seized with an inexplicable desire to rub her cheek against it, to curl up with it like a security blanket. "So what can I do for you?"

Take off your shirt and give it to me for a blankie?

When she didn't answer—she was trying to think of something a little less creeptastic to say—he tried again. "I can't imagine what brings you to Dane."

You told me seven years ago to let you know if you could ever be of any help, and now I'm here? That didn't sound any better than the more specific version, which was that as she'd been on the elevator last night up to her suite at the Beverly Wilshire, floors ticking by like a bomb timer, she'd been overcome with the wild idea that she could maybe find somewhere to hide out and write a renegade album that did not contain Song 58.

Which was obviously insane.

Some people had a devil on their shoulder, or an angel, or some combination of the two. Emerson had a fatalistic imaginary friend who could envision, in extraordinary detail, all the different ways disaster could strike in any given scenario. Maude—yes, she'd named her fatalistic imaginary friend—was good for songwriting. Being slightly obsessive about details, following ideas along to every possible conclusion: this was what made good songs. In fact, the only reason she was here today was that she had told Maude to shut up. She'd gagged her and stuffed her into a closet while she made her dramatic escape from L.A. But she probably should have spent less time on the flight here arguing with Tony and more time figuring out what the hell she was going to say to Evan.

She hadn't gotten much further with her plan than a vague hope that the art history nerd who didn't watch TV would remember her—the real her. That maybe, if she was lucky, he'd had his head in the sand deep enough that he hadn't heard of Emerson Quinn the brand.

But Maude wasn't having it. She'd busted out of the closet.

Of course he's heard of you. He's probably heard all about the scene with Jesse and that model in Central Park. He saw you fall down at the Oscars. Or those horrible paparazzi shots when you were sneaking out of Kirby's house—there wasn't a corner of this earth that picture didn't penetrate.

She cleared her throat. "I, ah, needed a little break from my life. I just wrapped a tour. I'm supposed to start working on my next album, but I...couldn't face it." There. That was true.

"So you did become a musician, then?"

"I did." Saying so made her flush with pride. Even though she wasn't necessarily thrilled with the way things were going right now, she had made it, and she was proud of herself.

"That's great. What kind of music do you do?"

Oh my God, he *hadn't* heard of her. On the one hand, she was a little disappointed. On the other: *Take that, Maude!* Maybe this insane stunt, this idea of trying to find somewhere to hide where someone actually knew *her*, wasn't so crazy after all.

"I needed a break, see," she said, ignoring his question. "Things have been...extremely busy, and I wanted to, well, hide for a while, really, and see if I could put together some new songs."

"So you came to Dane."

You said to let you know if you could ever be of help? She still couldn't make herself say it quite like that. "It, ah, seemed like a really out-of-the-way place where I might be able to lie low for a while, get some writing done."

Then he was coming toward her, his brow furrowed. He reached a hand out, and her pulse quickened. Oh my God, was he going to *kiss* her? Because as gorgeous as he was, that was *not* what she was here for, so she was just going to have to—

"Mrs. Johansen! Be careful on the steps."

Oh. Okay, then.

Brushing past her and letting the screen door bang behind him, she heard him scolding the visitor. "I told you one of my steps is loose. You've got to use the railing!"

Emerson's body automatically went into stealth mode. She didn't even have to think about it—hat on head, hair jammed up into hat. She was fumbling in her purse for her sunglasses when they came in.

"Midori Johansen, this is my..." Evan's brow furrowed.

"Emmy," Emerson said, sticking out her hand even as she avoided eye contact with the visitor, supplying the nickname primarily because giving her full first name would risk exposure...but also, now that she was here with Evan, she *felt* like Emmy again.

Evan cleared his throat. "Emmy, this is my neighbor, Mrs. Midori Johansen."

"Where are you visiting from?" Mrs. Johansen asked.

"L.A.," she answered, but then mentally kicked herself for not making something up.

"I used to live in L.A.!" Mrs. Johansen said.

"How did you, ah, come to settle in Iowa?" Emmy asked, coaching herself to produce normal conversation.

"My husband was a professor at Dane College," Mrs. Johansen said. "He was at UCLA for his graduate studies, which is where we met. We moved here in 1964."

Emmy allowed herself to relax a little. If Mrs. Johansen had moved here as a young wife in 1964, she had to be in her seventies at least. And anyway, if she'd been going to say, "Are you Emerson Quinn?" she would have done so by now. That was usually the first thing out of people's mouths when they spotted her in an unlikely place. And sometimes, if the place was unlikely enough, she could get away with the "No, but I get that all the time" deflection.

"Dr. Anders Johansen, whom I didn't have the pleasure of knowing," Evan said, "was a world-renowned linguist. He was a Swede, and he came here to study the Scandinavian linguistic traditions of the Midwest."

Mrs. Johansen, based on her first name and appearance, seemed to be Japanese. Emmy wondered how she had met her Swedish husband in L.A. in the middle of the last century. What had their courtship been like? There was probably an interesting story there, and suddenly she wanted to hear it. She felt its pull physically, like her body was starved for the normalcy of a "how we met" story that didn't involve publicists and paparazzi.

"Oh!" Mrs. Johansen exclaimed, pulling Emmy from her thoughts. "I have to go back home. I forgot my money."

"Don't worry about it," Evan said. "Tell me what you want, and I'll drop it by later."

"I couldn't do that." She started to shuffle away. "I'll be right back." Then she chuckled. "Who am I kidding? At the pace I go, I'll be back in twenty minutes."

"Mrs. Johansen, you keep me in casseroles. The least I can do is buy your veggies."

She looked indecisive, so Emmy, though she didn't quite know what was going on, said, "Mrs. Johansen, if a handsome guy like Evan was offering to buy my veggies, you can bet I'd take him up on the offer." *Buy my veggies.* Wait. Did that sound dirty?

Mrs. Johansen grinned. "You do have a point. No one has bought my veggies in a very long time."

Emmy laughed. Mrs. Johansen reminded her of her

grandma, who'd been a kindred spirit to Emmy in their family of accountants.

"Just this once, then." Mrs. Johansen thrust a piece of paper at Evan. "I'll make you an extra casserole this week."

Evan smiled. "I can't wait." When his neighbor turned to go, he followed, gave her his arm, and escorted her down the steps.

Emmy waited on the porch while the pair shuffled across their adjoining lawns and up Mrs. Johansen's porch. After he'd seen Mrs. Johansen safely inside, Evan paused on his neighbor's porch, looking at Emmy like he was trying to figure out what to do with her.

Finally he called across the yards, "Fancy a trip to the farmers' market, Emmy NoLastName?"

Did she? Probably the farmers' market in Dane, Iowa, was a world away from the West Hollywood Whole Foods. But wasn't that the point?

He started back across the lawns. "Then I can drive you to wherever you're staying."

Ouch. Okay, message received.

Time for Plan B. Except she had no Plan B.

"I hope it's not the Cornflower Inn," he went on. "Rumor has it they have bedbugs. But even so, there are a few other inns in town, so I'm sure you can find somewhere else if need be. The only time the town is booked up is the first week of classes and homecoming."

Humiliation bloomed on her cheeks as he brushed past her, scooped up some keys from a table in the entryway and... a bike helmet?

"I have an extra bike you can ride, and you can use my helmet. It's adjustable."

"Whoa." The farmers' market was one thing. *Riding a bike* to the farmers' market? "No way."

"It's a ten-minute ride. Too close to bother with the car, and parking there is a pain."

"I haven't ridden a bike in…" God. How long had it been? "Fifteen years, probably."

"It'll come right back to you." He grinned. "It's like riding a bike that way."

Emmy imagined herself pedaling down a country road under an impossibly wide blue sky, the buzzing of cicadas the only sound. Not only no security detail, no Claudia and Brian hovering, but no engine, no gas. Nothing but Emmy, propelling herself through space. Suddenly, the notion of getting somewhere under her own steam was incredibly appealing.

Then Maude cleared her throat. *Picture this: a bike mangled in a row of corn. You, in the middle of freaking Iowa surrounded by people, flashbulbs popping, without the protection of a car.*

For the second time today, Emmy told Maude to shut up.

CHAPTER THREE

And...*holy crap*. Evan was on a bike ride with Emmy NoLast-Name, cruising out of town and past farms like it was nothing. Like no time had passed at all. Like they'd gotten up the morning after the wedding and casually decided to go for a bike ride. Except of course they were half a country away from Miami, and in the meantime, his whole life had been upended and remade.

There was also the part where Emmy wasn't nineteen anymore. Now, she would be twenty-six—the age he'd been the night they met.

He adjusted himself on the bike seat. Sometime after she arrived, she'd shed the shirt she'd been wearing, leaving only a pink tank top that left almost nothing to the imagination as it hugged her curves, which were subtle, but somehow all the more affecting for it. He couldn't blame her—it was hot as hell. But damn.

Emmy's sudden arrival had him totally discombobulated. And, he would admit, totally turned on.

He needed to get his shit together, though, because what

the hell? She'd looked him up seven years later and just appeared on his doorstep? Who did that?

"Eeee!" Emmy cried, coasting down a small hill and letting loose a delighted shriek. The weird thing about Emmy was that in addition to being ridiculously attractive, she was also adorable. Those qualities were usually mutually exclusive. But if there was anything cuter than Emmy NoLastName attempting to ride a bike, Evan wasn't sure what it was. With her long, lanky limbs, she kind of reminded him of Kermit the Frog riding his bike in *The Muppet Movie*.

If Kermit had worn short-shorts, a tank top, and gold strappy sandals.

"Eeee!"

And if Kermit had been going *way* too fast.

"Watch out!" he hollered as she approached a set of train tracks as the bell that signaled the imminent arrival of a train began clanging. *Fuck.* He pedaled like crazy to catch up with her.

She came to an ungraceful stop about a foot from the tracks as the arm that stopped traffic lowered. "That was so fun!" she exclaimed. Then she had the nerve to laugh.

Yeah, if you were in search of a boner killer, there was nothing quite like imminent death. "Jesus Christ, Emmy," he snapped, rolling to a stop beside her and trying to shake off a vision of her flattened by the oncoming train. "Train comes, you stop, okay?"

"Pffft," she scoffed, raising her voice to be heard over the clanging and making a dismissive gesture with her hand. "The laws of physics are no match for me."

He took a deep breath. Okay, this was a good reality check. That Emmy was here was, in theory, kind of…interesting. But he couldn't afford interesting right now. In addition to twenty-eight more exams to grade, he had that goddamned rinky-dink town art show he'd been roped into. And of course, the ever-present tenure file hanging over his head wasn't going to assemble itself. His committee was chaired by the overtly hostile Larry, so his submission had to be impeccable. Even then, it might not be enough.

"So," she said as the train continued to rumble by, "professor in the middle of nowhere, Iowa. I have to say, I'm surprised."

He shrugged. "You know what they say. Those who can, do. Those who can't, teach."

"I don't believe that about you," she said, dismissing his deflection with an unimpressed shake of her head that ignited a spark of annoyance in his chest. "I googled you after the wedding. You were an up-and-coming artistic talent, everyone said. Poised to make a breakthrough."

"You never saw any of my work."

"Doesn't matter. I know you."

You don't, he was ready to protest, but he stopped himself because he knew what she meant, even if he wanted to pretend otherwise. They'd spent a mere six hours together seven years ago. But, somehow, they did know each other. Or they had. Maybe the past tense was the key there. "You *knew* me, maybe. I'm not the same person I was back then."

The lights stopped flashing—saved by the caboose. The mechanical arm raised, and they were off again without having to continue the uncomfortable conversation.

"After you," he said as they picked up speed, still riding side by side.

"I don't know where I'm going."

"One thing to learn about Dane is that it's all straight lines," he said. "Corn, roads, everything is straight lines and right angles." No twists and turns. Nothing and no one lurking unexpectedly behind a bend in the road. No blind spots. "The market is a little farther down this road. There's a break in the farms where there's a park."

When she nodded and pulled ahead, it gave him a moment to think, to regroup. His mind settled on that suitcase of hers currently sitting in his entryway. This "break" she mentioned. She didn't think she was staying with him, did she? That was crazy, right? People didn't just show up on other people's doorsteps—especially people they'd met once seven years ago—and invite themselves to stay.

But then he thought of her saying, "The laws of physics don't apply to me."

And eff him—suddenly, the prospect of Emmy NoLast-Name paying him a visit wasn't the worst idea in the world.

"This is the cutest place," Emmy declared as they rolled to a stop. There were all these little canopied stands where fresh-faced people were selling fruits and vegetables, an area where people with dogs were congregated around bowls of water and treats that one of the vendors had set out, and even a guy playing a guitar and singing Bob Dylan covers.

Evan shot her a quizzical look. "It's like pretty much every other farmers' market I've ever been to."

"Well, I've never been to one, so excuse me if I'm delighted."

"You've never been to a farmers' market? Aren't you from Minnesota?" He squinted against the punishing midday sun to look at her. He kept doing that—looking at her like there was something he was missing, something he was trying to figure out.

Why you're such a freak, perhaps?

"Yeah, well," she said, a little defensive, "my parents

weren't farmers' market types." That was an understatement. The pair of accountants didn't believe in paying more for food than was necessary, so groceries were procured exclusively from Costco, perishables portioned into freezer bags and frozen. The only time she'd ever had meals that could have been assembled from a farmers' market was when she used to go to her grandma's house after school. And of course, today she wasn't the kind of person who could just idly stroll outdoor markets.

"There's a sculpture garden adjacent to the market," he said. "If you want to check it out, let's do that first and do the shopping on the way out."

"Cool." She followed his lead, inserting the front tire of her bike into a rack, simultaneously impressed and appalled that no one locked their bikes here.

They skirted around the stalls lining the perimeter of the market and emerged into what seemed to be a cleared farm field. Surrounded on three sides by corn and bordered on the fourth by the road, it was dotted with sculptures, most of which were whimsical creatures made out of rusted tools and bits of metal she couldn't identify. But then there would be the odd incongruent piece—like a rainbow made of spray-painted rocks inlaid in the ground.

"The guy who owns this land is a farmer with an artistic bent. The metal pieces are his, made from old farming equipment. Some of them are quite clever." He led her to an enormous bird of some sort, perched on a piece of driftwood. It was made out of chains and what looked like gears taken apart. "This is a red-shouldered hawk, which is an endangered species."

"Is it endangered because of farming?" she asked, admiring its strange, cold beauty. That would be quite a statement to make.

"They definitely breed in wooded areas. This area has been

farmland for longer than the hawks have been endangered, though, so I'm not sure it's that simple. Still, there's no denying that its habitat is shrinking, and humans are to blame."

"Huh," she said, fingering the hawk's "feathers." It definitely made a person think.

"The others are one-offs by random people. Jerry—that's the farmer-artist—lets anyone put their stuff here. I think this"—he pointed down to the rainbow-hued stones—"was a gay pride piece from earlier this summer."

"Gay pride in Dane!" she exclaimed, belatedly realizing her surprise might be coming off as snobbish.

He shrugged, not seeming to have taken offense. "It's a college town full of hippies. Farmers and hippies."

"And this Jerry guy is both?"

He smirked. "I hadn't thought of it that way, but that's about right, though usually there's not much overlap between the two categories."

One of the sculptures was a little bridge that went nowhere. It sat on the land, inviting in its absurdity, so she mounted the steps on one side and watched him get smaller as she gained elevation.

"Jerry's a real art enthusiast," Evan continued. "He's given this field, which is adjacent to his cultivated land, over to the sculptures. He also has a barn he's renovating that is going to become an arts annex to the town's community center." He sighed. "I'm supposed to be curating a show for its grand opening later this summer, in fact."

She got the impression that the show was not something Evan looked forward to, but also that it was not something to press him about, and after their uncomfortable exchange about why he didn't paint anymore, she wasn't keen to anyway.

She stopped at the highest point of the bridge. "This place

is awesome." Not a very eloquent declaration, but it was the truth. She took a deep breath of the clean, heavy summer air and something inside her chest began to loosen. She made a slow revolution in place as if the bridge were her castle and she a queen surveying her realm. The market on one side of them was abuzz with activity—the sounds of the busker's guitar mixed with the lilt of conversation floated up into the sky. The other side was farms as far as she could see. Rows and rows of green perfection stretching out forever against that impossibly blue sky.

"…coming down?"

What? She turned back to face Evan, who was regarding her with his eyebrows raised. "Sorry, I spaced out for a minute there. What did you say?"

"I asked if you were ever coming down." He smiled, and the skin around his eyes crinkled, but the smile didn't reach his eyes proper.

In some ways, he was exactly the same as the man she'd met at the wedding, but in others, he had changed. He'd aged, of course, but it was more than that. It was like he'd shuttered some part of himself that had been more apparent, less protected, the first time she'd met him.

"But take your time," he added, his smile becoming a tiny bit more genuine. "Enjoy your Juliet moment."

"Would that make you Romeo?" she teased, wanting to draw out even more of the Evan she remembered. "Wherefore art thou Romeo?"

"Nah, I like to think I'm smarter than that punk-ass Romeo. No pointless suicide for me."

"Right," she said, "You're more of an e.e. cummings guy."

Probably she should pretend not to remember, play it cool. But he was the first guy who'd ever quoted any poetry at her— hell, he was the *only* guy who'd ever quoted any poetry at her, unless you counted her ex-boyfriend Kirby's "woo woo woo oh girl" lyrics, and she most decidedly did not. Kirby was in a boy band; the e.e. cummings-quoting Evan was…not remotely a boy.

Suddenly brave, she lowered her voice and looked into his eyes. "I will wade out till my thighs are steeped in burning flowers."

Something flickered in his expression, and that she had reached him made triumph spike in her belly.

It wasn't a love poem—she'd looked it up after the wedding. At least she hadn't thought it was. Not on the surface, anyway. But there was something about the way he had spoken the line to her back then, an intensity that had made her cheeks heat, that made them heat now, in fact, as he gazed up at her and pinned her in place with his all-seeing eyes.

But as soon as she had his attention—his true attention— it was gone, stolen by something behind her. She looked over her shoulder to see a pair of teenage girls making their way over.

The calm, grounded sensation that had been slowly unspooling in her chest since she arrived in Dane was quashed by the great big thud of her stomach dropping. Her scalp started to prickle. What the hell was the matter with her? She'd taken off her bike helmet but forgotten to replace it with her hat. And for God's sake, she wasn't even wearing her sunglasses. And she was standing on top of a bridge—the highest point for miles.

She was a sitting duck.

With hands made clumsy by panic, she dug in her bag for her hat as she stumbled down the stairs on the bridge's far side.

"What's wrong?" He met her at the bottom, grabbing her elbow to steady her.

"Nothing!" But her voice edged on hysterical. She fumbled her wraparound sunglasses on, yelping as one of the arms poked the sensitive skin near her eye. "Nothing," she tried again, willing her hand not to shake as she took his arm and angled him so he was between her and the girls.

Normally, she'd be graceful in a situation like this. A pair of girls on their own was harmless. They'd say nice things, ask her to sign something—hopefully not a body part—take a picture, and be on their way. Claudia and Brian disdained the teenage demographic Emerson Quinn had built her career on, wanted her to skew older, which she was starting to do naturally anyway. But Emmy didn't mind them. There was something comfortable about appealing to her base. And, more than that, she remembered what it was like to sit in your bedroom and listen to the same song over and over, wearing headphones for the pure pleasure of beaming the music directly into your brain, pretending the singer was talking to you personally.

But today, the last thing she needed was a tweet or an Instagram post locating her in Dane.

"What's the matter?" She could hear the concern and confusion in his voice as she looked over her shoulder. "And *don't* tell me nothing." He reached out and tried to take off her sunglasses.

"Don't!" she snapped, whipping her hands to the glasses to keep them on.

He held up his hands like she'd pointed a gun at him, and the squealing grew louder as the girls approached.

Nice job, said Maude. *You haven't even been here an hour, and you've already ruined things. You'll be back at the Wilshire by nightfall.*

Her throat started to thicken. No. She swallowed hard. Emmy *refused* to cry, even behind her sunglasses.

She looked at the ground as the flurry of girlish chatter crescendoed. "Ohmigod! Is that him?"

Bracing herself, she painted on a smile because there was nowhere to escape in this wide-open landscape.

Wait. They'd said, "Is that *him*?"

"I think they're behind that buffalo thing," one of the girls said, passing within a foot of Emmy but not even sparing her a glance.

Sure enough, a pair of boys emerged from behind a buffalo sculpture twenty or so yards away. Relief flooded her, making her limbs quiver. They were chasing a boy. Hormones: the only thing more powerful than celebrity.

Which left her standing in an open field with a fake smile on the only part of her face that wasn't obscured by her glasses and hat.

"What the hell just happened?" Evan was confused, maybe even angry. And rightly so. She had been holding out on him, partly because she couldn't believe that he really didn't know who she was.

She started walking, heading for the next sculpture. "It's kind of hard to explain."

He didn't follow right away but eventually sighed and jogged to catch up with her.

"You didn't have a TV back when I first met you," she said when he'd fallen into step beside her. "What about now?"

He furrowed his brow. "Nope."

"Still not into pop music?"

"Not unless you count Ella Fitzgerald and Duke Ellington as pop music."

She grinned. "What about your students? Don't you, like, absorb any pop culture through them?"

He didn't answer her for a long time. Then he stopped walking. "Can I ask you something?"

44

She stopped too. "Of course."

He blew out a breath. "Ahh, this is kind of awkward."

"Hit me," she said.

"This break of yours. Were you thinking you'd, ah, stay with me?"

Well, shit. This *was* awkward. The truth was because she'd stopped listening to Maude, she hadn't really thought through the details. She'd just fled, blindly propelling herself toward Dane.

"Actually," he said, "let me ask you another question."

Great. Anything to avoid having to answer the first. "Shoot."

"Are you famous?"

Here it was. He might not know who she was, but he wasn't dumb. He knew how to interpret her cryptic statements about needing to hide out for a while, not to mention the freak-out she'd had in the sculpture garden. "Yes," she said, looking directly at him. "Yes, I am."

He cocked his head. "How famous?"

She thought about it. It wasn't like she could hide the truth, even if she'd wanted to. Evan could google as easily as she could. "Extremely famous."

"And you thought you were going to stay with me."

"Yes." She closed her eyes against the shame. It hadn't been a question, but she answered it anyway. At least she could tell him the truth; she owed him that.

When she opened her eyes, his lips were pressed together, his face pinched. "This…" He waved his hand back and forth in the space between them. "You being here…is not going to work."

Of course it wasn't going to work, Emmy berated herself as Evan examined eggplants. She didn't even need Maude to say *I told you so*. What on earth had possessed her to come here? To get on a plane and clap her hands over her ears like a kid chanting "La, la, la, I can't hear you!" while Tony, ever loyal and unconditionally trailing in her wake, tried to talk sense into her? The shame that had flooded in when Evan smiled apologetically and said, "Let's get the shopping done, then we'll go home, and I'll drive you wherever you like," was not abating.

Not even a little bit.

Had she become so entitled, so indulged, that she thought she could swoop in and insert herself into Evan's life with no notice, no permission, and no plan?

Which left her...where? Where would she go? To Minneapolis, where her parents, though they would let her stay with them, would judge her every movement with a mixture of bewilderment and passive aggression? Jesse's house in Toronto? She and her latest ex were supposed to be "friends." After their very humiliating—and very public—breakup in Central Park, they'd calmed down and agreed to part amicably, and Claudia had seen to it that *People* reported as much. She should have known better than to think that she would ever be enough for Jesse Jamison, famous bad-boy rocker. The most humiliating part of the whole thing was that as usual, she'd been taking it more seriously than he had. "I didn't realize we were exclusive," he'd said, and honestly, he wasn't wrong. Jesse's manager had introduced them, they'd gone to a few industry events, and Emmy had jumped right to naming their future children. Jesse wasn't a bad guy. He would take her in, but her pride would not allow it.

She had nowhere to go.

Well, that wasn't strictly true. She could, of course, jet off to any number of secluded resorts, but she could never fully relax at any of them. Employees could tip off tabloids, and the other rich people at places like that always tried to ingratiate themselves. Just thinking about it was exhausting.

She had only wanted to go somewhere normal for a while. *Be* normal for a while.

But it was impossible. There was nowhere to go that would fit the bill.

A hard truth hit her as surely as if she'd been standing before an audience throwing rotten eggplants at her: Emmy had created a life she didn't want to live in.

The sob came out so abruptly, so utterly unexpectedly, that she didn't even recognize it as such at first. It was a ripping sensation, a strange episode of whiplash as the ground lurched beneath her while she remained in place.

But then there was Evan, steadying her with his hands on her shoulders but also with his eyes as he bent over, putting his face level with hers. He didn't say anything, didn't press her to articulate what was wrong. Just searched her face, scanning like he was trying to read a barcode that, once accessed, would project all her secrets onto a screen only he could see.

"I don't cry," she said, even as hot, traitorous tears streaked down her cheeks. She could only be grateful that her first barking sob hadn't been followed by another, that her weeping hadn't fully crossed the line from silently weak to audibly pathetic.

"And yet you appear to be crying," he said. He tugged on her sunglasses for the second time that afternoon, but this attempt was gentle. He was seeking permission.

She let him take them off this time, let him lean even closer, let him look into her eyes with nothing between them to protect herself.

But then, regrouping, she tried again. "I am not a person

who cries. I have not cried for nine years." Not since the night her parents kicked her out of the house, in fact.

"And yet you appear to be crying," he repeated, the sentence becoming a mantra in her head, working itself into her consciousness the way only the truth can. He took off her hat, too.

Again, she let him. Stood there and wept, plastic and immobilized like a doll you pour water into in order to make it shed tears, while he watched her.

Without breaking his gaze from hers, he let go of her shoulders and ran his fingers through her hair, dragging them across her scalp. The rough-gentle touch, the electric confluence of pressure and pleasure, gutted her. She couldn't look at him anymore, so she looked up, but the sky was too blue, doubling the volume of the silent tears spilling unchecked out of her eyeballs. So she looked to the side, but there was only the unrelenting corn. The other way: a pyramid of eggplants.

There was nowhere to rest her eyes.

Not only did she have nowhere to go, she had nowhere to look. She couldn't rest her body *or* her eyes.

The next sob didn't surprise her because she was coming undone.

"Omigod!"

Yes. It was going to happen now.

"Are you Emerson Quinn?"

Evan whirled like he was trying to find a heckler in a crowd.

Then another voice, distinct from the first. "Emerson Quinn is over there, and she's *crying*."

The wise, wicked fingers that had been burrowing into her scalp disappeared, and she bit back a wail. Those fingers had been the only thing anchoring her, the physical sensation keeping her self-aware enough to *know* that she was coming undone.

Just before she surrendered to the madness, sank into the warm, familiar waters of yet another public humiliation, she heard his voice, from far away, like he was talking to her through a telephone made of soup cans and strings.

"Nope, just my girlfriend, but everyone always mistakes her for Emerson Quinn." He laughed. "But damn, if we had a dollar for every time someone said that, we'd probably be as rich as Emerson Quinn."

Then he shoved her hat back on her head and planted a palm on each of her cheeks.

And kissed her.

She was crying, and Evan Winslow was kissing her.

Last time, on that rooftop in Miami, Evan's kisses had been gentle, warm, careful even, and then he had pulled away and asked her how old she was.

That control was nowhere in evidence now as his lips moved against hers, hungry and demanding, as if one of them was drowning—she wasn't sure which—and needed the other for air.

His mouth was possessive this time, even a little aggressive, as his tongue pressed against the seam of her lips.

She opened them—what else could she do?—and sighed.

As with her sob, the noise seemed to startle him, and he pulled away. She wanted to shout her protest.

"Not crying," he said, clearing his throat, straightening his glasses, and turning to smile at the teenager standing behind the tower of eggplants. "Just really, really allergic to pollen. Isn't that right, sweetie?" he prompted, handing over her sunglasses. "Also not Emerson Quinn." He grinned and shook his head at the girl. "What would Emerson Quinn be doing in Dane?"

Then he leaned in, pecked Emmy's nose with a short, staccato kiss.

Before she could blink, it was over, and he was handing the girl two dollars and dropping a couple eggplants into a nylon shopping bag he produced from his pocket.

"Wow," said the girl, mouth agape from what Emmy suspected was watching the world's most scorching kiss. "You look *so* much like her."

Blinking and a little bit breathless, Emmy put on her sunglasses and reset the "no crying" clock.

CHAPTER FOUR

"Professor Winslow!"

Goddammit! They'd almost made it. Evan hopped off his bike and turned to see Kaylee Sanders walking up the path from the sidewalk to his porch.

"Go inside," he whispered to Emmy, who was already bounding up the steps, shielding her face.

The screen door banged behind her as a beaming Kaylee approached. Smart, curious, and disciplined, Kaylee was one of his favorite students—she even helped him out at an arts program for high school kids that he ran at the community center—but it could be hard to shake her once she'd cornered you.

"Did you grade my exam yet?" she asked.

"Not yet," he lied. Kaylee was her own worst critic, and if he told her that she'd "only" gotten a ninety-two because she'd mixed up *buon fresco* and *fresco secco*, he would never hear the end of it. And right now he had to get inside and deal with the fact that Emmy NoLastName was actually some kind of famous person called Emerson Quinn.

"I was thinking about what I'm going to do for my term

paper," Kaylee said, and Evan sighed, resigned to his fate, only half paying attention as his brain continued to churn in the background, going over and over the astonishing fact that there was, apparently, a mega-famous pop star in his living room.

One that he needed to get *out* of his living room as soon as humanly possible. Because he wanted no part of fame, not even by association. None. He was allergic to it, in fact, having had more than enough exposure for a lifetime.

"Everybody knows da Vinci's *Vitruvian Man*, right?" Kaylee went on. "So I was thinking maybe I could look into some of his lesser-known anatomical studies."

"That's a great idea," he said, unable to prevent himself from getting caught up in the enthusiasm so clearly evident on her face. "You might want to narrow it down, though, and focus on a subset of his anatomical work—his studies of the skull, for instance."

She nodded. "Maybe I could find another artist who drew skulls and look at both of them?"

"Also a promising line of inquiry. Or if you want to do something comparative, you could look at a precursor to da Vinci and then compare to him."

"Like Pollaiuolo?"

"Yes! Take a look at the musculature in *Battle of Nudes* and think about how it evolved to get to da Vinci."

God, he had to get tenure. As much as he could take or leave the majority of the students who ended up in his classes because they thought looking at pictures would be an easy way to fulfill liberal arts requirements, students like Kaylee reminded him how lucky he was. At his lowest point, after he'd moved away from Florida, when he was drowning in student debt, working two crappy jobs, and still being tracked down by reporters for "one year later" type features, he had never dared hope that he could still manage to make a career related to art.

There was a little more chitchat before he could extricate himself. It was just as well, because it gave him a chance to collect himself, to prepare to go inside and kick Emmy-Emerson-Whoever-The-Hell-She-Was out of his life for good.

When he did go back inside, Emmy was waiting. She'd taken a seat in the living room at the front of the house.

She grinned, apparently totally recovered from her breakdown earlier, sprawling on a threadbare Windsor chair like she was queen of the place. "Wow, you are a *geek*, Professor Winslow."

He glanced at the open bay window she was seated next to —she must have overheard his conversation with Kaylee. Every window in the house was open, thanks to his broken AC. Her tank top was plastered to her skin, as his T-shirt was to his. You only had to be standing still in this heat to drown in sweat, but on top of that, they had busted it home on their bikes, heeding an unspoken agreement not to speak until they got back to his place. He forced his eyes up from her shirt. Her face was shiny, but instead of making her look bedraggled, she glowed.

"I think that girl has a crush on you."

"Who?" It took him a moment to catch her meaning. "Kaylee? No." Kaylee was a fellow art geek. A budding art geek.

"You must have girls falling all over themselves to take your classes. I'll admit that I was surprised about this whole college professor thing, but you're clearly a natural at it, because—"

"What the hell are you doing here, Emmy? Is that even your name? Was it ever?" He paused, taking in her widening eyes. He'd shocked her. Good. He'd shocked himself, too, with the harsh question and the piqued tone he'd delivered it in, but he found himself increasingly irritated that she wanted to talk about nonexistent juvenile crushes instead of the drama of the last hour—the drama *she* was responsible for dumping into his normally calm life. "You told me at the wedding that you were going to change it," he reminded her, but then he wished he hadn't. He didn't need her to know that he remembered every last thing she'd said to him that night.

She swung her legs, which had been extended onto an ottoman, down to the floor and sat up straight. "Emerson Quinn is my real name." She spoke in a flat tone, nothing moving except her eyes as she watched him warily. If he felt a little twinge to have inspired the sudden guardedness in her, he shoved it aside. "Emerson was my mother's maiden name, and my parents gave it to me as a first name. I went by Emmy when I was younger." She swallowed. "I didn't lie to you at the wedding, if that's what you're thinking. I was still Emmy then —that's what everyone in Minnesota called me. And I was going to change my name when I got to L.A., but they told me not to. They said my real one was 'catchy and pleasingly androgynous.'"

If only it wasn't so bloody hot. He could hardly think straight in this blast furnace of an afternoon. He ran a hand through his hair as if physical contact with his scalp might jumpstart his laggardly brain, and lowered himself to a chair opposite hers. "They?"

She popped to her feet the moment his ass hit the seat, as if she'd been on the other side of a teeter-totter from him. "My managers. And to answer your other question, about what I'm doing here..." She trailed off, drawing a circle with her toe on the threadbare Persian carpet. But then she looked up to finish the thought. "I ran away."

"How does an adult woman run away from home?"

"Not from home," she said, almost sadly. "From every-thing. From my entire life."

That didn't exactly clear things up. "And you came here because?"

She stared at him, those intense blue eyes boring into his own for a long moment before she turned away. "You know what? I made a mistake. I'm sorry. I'll go now." She disappeared into the entryway, leaving behind a room heavy with the weight of her disappointment.

The sound, a moment later, of her suitcase rolling over the floorboards made him want to scream. *Why* was it so hot?

The screen door connecting the house to the porch banged behind her. He got up and peered out the window. The sight of her standing in the dim light of the covered porch, sweating, sunglasses perched on her tussled head and guitar slung over her thin shoulders, was like a slice through his chest. That was the problem with Emmy NoLastName or Emerson Quinn or whoever the hell she was: the pure, unadulterated image of her. It was like a drug, entering his bloodstream through a sharp, jagged puncture wound she made in his chest. The same jolting attraction that had come over him when he first saw her walking down the aisle all those years ago began barreling down on him again. One part of his mind snapped off from the rest and started trying to figure out what colors to mix to get the two tones of pink of her tank top—the regular bubblegum shade of the dry spots and the darker, earthier color of the blooms of wetness under her arms and breasts.

Without even realizing it, he'd gotten up and followed her to the porch, and now they were standing staring at each other.

She was fiddling with her phone. "I assume this town is too small for Uber? But if you could tell me the name of a local cab company, I'll be out of your hair." She pulled her sunglasses down and jammed her hat on her head, shuttering herself from the world, and from his gaze.

"Where are you going to go?" He wasn't sure why he cared. He was getting what he wanted, wasn't he, which was her leaving?

"To the airport," she said.

"And then?"

After staring at him for a moment, she shrugged.

She didn't know. That's what the shrug meant.

Fuck. He was going to regret this. This went against every impulse he had. But he couldn't help it. His right hand twitched. He wasn't in charge anymore, apparently. Somehow there was a direct connection between his hand, grasping an imaginary brush, and his mouth, which inexplicably opened and said, "Hang on a second."

Disconcerted, Emmy let herself be led into the kitchen at the back of Evan's house. Let herself be handed a tall, icy glass of lemonade.

"Mrs. Johansen makes me a pitcher practically every day in the summer," Evan said, sitting at the battered farmhouse table that filled the generous space at the back of the kitchen and was framed by windows that overlooked an overgrown yard.

She nodded and, still standing, took a drink, the cold tartness sliding down her throat drawing her attention back to how amazingly hot it was. It also snapped her out of her daze. "I'm sorry I just descended on you. I don't know what I was thinking. I'll call a cab and—"

"Sit."

When she didn't, he nodded at the spot across from him, but she wasn't sure she should obey. Tony had been right.

Maude had been right. She didn't belong here. Coming here had been a mistake, and instead of providing a haven, had served only to reinforce how alone she actually was.

"Goddammit, Emmy. Sit *down*."

She sat. The sharp tone Evan had deployed a couple times since she'd arrived didn't accord with her memory of him, with the image of him she had built up in her mind all these years.

"Good. Now start at the beginning."

"The beginning?"

"Yes. You ran away, but from what? You're some kind of famous person, apparently. A musician?"

She blew out a breath. "Have you really never heard of me? Of Emerson Quinn?"

He furrowed his brow. "Maybe?" Then his nose scrunched up like he'd smelled something bad. "If I have, it's only in a generic 'famous person' sort of way. It gets confusing. You know, like Taylor Lautner and Taylor Swift. Not sure who those girls are, exactly, but I know the names."

"Taylor Lautner is a man."

He smiled then, and it took some of the heat—the metaphorical heat, because it was still an oven in his house— out of their encounter. "I rest my case. So humor me and tell me who you are. What you are."

She blew out a breath. Summarize herself in a few sentences. The *CliffsNotes* version of her life. It shouldn't be so hard. But the fact that it was might be part of the problem.

"You know I was planning to move to L.A. after we met at Vicky and Tyrone's wedding," she began. "I did, and I...made it in the music business."

He nodded. "Good for you." The praise was delivered in a matter-of-fact way, like he wasn't surprised. She toyed with the idea of telling him that at times, the confidence he had shown in her at the wedding had been the only thing keeping her going. She hadn't always believed in herself, but on the worst nights, the ones where she'd been tempted to hop a plane back to Minneapolis, beg her parents' forgiveness, and get her old coffee shop job back, she'd remembered the extraordinary man from the wedding who had been so sure she was going to succeed. She hadn't wanted to let him down, which was stupid because she'd never expected to see him again. But the memory had been enough to keep her putting one foot in front of the other until, somehow, she'd done it.

"I have been wildly successful by any external measure," she said, still struggling with how to explain things.

"But?" he prompted.

"But it's almost like there's a machine at work now. The Emerson Quinn machine. I have these managers. They're very...persuasive."

"So you ran away from the Svengalis."

That was pretty much it. She laughed, but it sounded bitter to her own ears. "I've just come off a ten-month tour."

He whistled. "Damn. You really are a big shot."

"It's time to start working on the next album, but I don't..."

"You don't want to do it."

She shook her head. That wasn't it. She wanted to do another record. The fact that she hadn't picked up her guitar or sat at a piano for twenty-four hours was making her a little crazy, actually. "I want to write the next album by myself." The declaration came out a little breathless. Actually saying it out loud for the first time was scary, but also exhilarating. "Not only without co-writers, but, like elementally by myself. Physically alone."

And it wasn't only the business side of things she was running from. She decided to be honest with him about that, too.

"Also, I've had a string of…bad relationships. I feel like there's so much noise in my life that I can't make good decisions anymore. I need to clear my head and be by myself for a while." She blew out a breath. "I want a break from my entire life, basically." Wow, it sounded pretty pathetic summed up like that.

"And you can't tell them this?"

She slumped forward and rested her head on the table. It was too heavy to continue holding up. "It's hard to explain."

"So you came here. Why?"

"Still hard to explain," she said, deflating a little bit more.

"Try."

She lifted her head and looked him straight in the eyes. No sense dissembling. He was either going to let her stay or he wasn't. If he didn't, she'd never see him again, so what did she have to lose by telling him the truth? "I was working with a co-writer yesterday. We wrote the first song for the new album. It's called Song 58." He furrowed his brow. "It's a placeholder title. Song 58 is sort of a heartbreak ballad with a twist at the end—which is kind of my thing. It was fine. It *should* have been fine. But I…freaked out. I don't want to do Song 58."

"What do you want to do?"

"I don't even know. Maybe I *can't* do anything else. But I want to try. But I feel like to really give it a shot, I need to physically get some distance. So I sprang myself from my golden cage and tried to think if there was anyone I knew who might help me. If there was a place I could go where I might be safe. It was…hard to think of somewhere. Of some*one*."

Evan made a weird, strangled noise in his throat. She might have laughed if she hadn't felt like she'd slit her wrists and bled out all her stupid, childish wishes in front of him.

"Why me, though?"

What could she do but keep telling him the truth? Keep

showing him all her insecurities? "Because you listened to me that night on the roof in Miami. You believed in me. You said I should be in touch if you could ever be of any help." She took a deep, shaky breath, forcing herself to keep meeting his gaze. "No one had ever done that before. Or has since, really, at least not without some ulterior motive. And when I ran away, I tried to think who in the world I could trust. I thought of you."

"All right." He spoke quietly, and his eyes glittered with an intensity that hadn't been there before. "You can stay a few days. A week, tops. Until you figure out something else. But I have one condition."

The hope that slammed into her was as abrupt and forceful as her fear had been at the farmers' market. The idea of a haven. A respite. A chance to breathe. It shimmered before her like a beautiful mirage. She hardly dared to blink for fear it would disappear, prove to be merely a fevered projection of her desperate, overheated mind. "What?" she whispered, almost afraid of what he was going to say.

"I hate to get all double-oh-seven on you, but you're going to have to stay in the house, or disguise yourself or something, because no one can know who you are."

She couldn't help letting loose a peal of laughter. He had no idea how on board she was with that condition.

He must have thought her laughter signified incredulity, though, because he slapped the table in front of him. "I mean it. I've done my time in the spotlight, and I'm not going back there. Not ever. Not for anyone. Besides that, I *can't* have a media circus descend. I'm up for tenure this year, and some of my colleagues already think I'm trading on my father's infamy —that I got the job to begin with because my last name is Winslow. So no one can know that you're here. *No one.*"

Her laughter died in her throat when she heard how

passionately, how urgently, he spoke. She of all people understood his wish to remain out of the spotlight. Fame did weird
things to people. For her, it was the price of doing music. For
him, there was no payoff whatsoever.

So she stuck out her hand for him to shake. "You got
yourself a deal."

By the time Evan slid one of Mrs. Johansen's casseroles out of
the oven and began to assemble a salad from the farmers'
market haul, several hours had elapsed. Plenty of time for
second thoughts to creep in. And third thoughts. After he had
driven his surprise houseguest to Walmart and trailed her
while she picked up some clothes and hair dye, she'd disappeared into one of his guest rooms for the balance of the day,
leaving him ample time to google her shit.

And what a lot of shit there was. When she'd said she was
"extremely famous," it wasn't as if he hadn't believed her. But
he hadn't been prepared for *three hundred and seven million*
Google results. Or for a cascade of photos of her doing everything from eating at a restaurant to walking a red carpet in a
ball gown to sneaking out of some boy band member's house
in the middle of the night—that last one seemed to have set
off a firestorm of gossip. God, he was glad he hadn't known, all
these years, who Emmy NoLastName had become. To know
that there had been millions of pictures of the muse that got
away just sitting there for his perusal? It would probably have
unhinged him more than his father's trial had.

Which was why he'd invited Mrs. Johansen to dinner. He
needed a buffer.

As if on cue, the doorbell rang.

As he greeted Mrs. Johansen in the entryway, Emmy came

bounding down the stairs wearing a new combination of shorts and tank top and sporting a jet-black hairdo that made her pale skin look even paler. She looked like the love child of Marilyn Manson and the Gap.

The hair didn't suit her at all. He tried but failed to hold back a laugh.

She stuck her tongue out at him, which only made the pixie/goth juxtaposition all the more absurd. "At least it does the trick," she murmured in his direction.

Proving her point, Mrs. Johansen said, "I don't think I've met your friend."

Emmy shot him a look as she sashayed past, eyebrows raised so high she might as well have said *neener, neener, neener*. It was funny—it was like now that they'd gone through the weirdness of her arrival, and the intensity of negotiating the terms of her stay, they had snapped back into the flirtatious banter they had enjoyed at the wedding.

"It's me, Mrs. Johansen. Emmy Anderson. I dyed my hair since we met each other this afternoon."

She'd handled that well, seamlessly slipping the fake last name they'd decided she should use into the conversation. "Anderson" sounded suitably generic for this part of the Scandinavian-settled Midwest—he hoped.

Mrs. Johansen curled her lip. "Why? It looked so much better before."

Evan did laugh then. Mrs. Johansen did not fit most people's stereotype of an elderly woman. Yes, she was a casserole-making machine, but she had quite a mouth on her and never hesitated to say exactly what she thought—unlike a lot of Midwesterners, who tended toward passive-aggression. Nope, Mrs. Johansen favored aggressive-aggression.

Emmy smiled and shrugged. "Sometimes you gotta mix it up a bit."

They settled down to dinner—tuna casserole complete with crunched-up potato chips on the top, which Mrs. Johansen had included in a little baggie taped to the foil pan she'd made the casserole in.

"So, Emmy. You and Evan are a couple?"

"No!" Emmy turned pink. Of course, everyone was pink because of the heat, but she turned *bright* pink. "Evan and I are…"

He waited for her to finish the sentence, but when it became clear she wasn't going to, he came to the rescue. "Old friends. We were neighbors growing up," he added, feeling like they needed a more specific backstory.

"In Miami," Mrs. Johansen said, but not, seemingly, with any suspicion.

Shit. He hated lying to Mrs. Johansen, but what choice did he have?

"Yes!" Emmy yelped, and he was thankful she had stepped up to do the actual lying. "I'm at the start of a vacation, and I decided to come see old Ev for a bit." She punched him in the arm. "And besides, I am *not* in boyfriend mode right now."

"Why not?" Mrs. Johansen asked, and he found himself interested in the answer, too.

"I'm taking a break from men for a while." She glanced at him, and he couldn't read her expression. Then she looked at her hands, which were folded at the table, and let a silent moment elapse before adding, "If you want to know the truth, I've had my heart broken one too many times in recent years."

Evan had learned during the afternoon's crash course in Emerson Quinn that she was famous for immortalizing her ex-boyfriends in songs. She had referenced a "string of bad relationships" earlier, but he was surprised to hear her suggest that she'd had her heart broken. The dominant interpretation out there seemed to be that she ate men for breakfast—and then wrote songs about them and got rich.

Emmy cleared her throat, then blew on a bubbling forkful of tuna casserole. "So, yeah, I have declared a moratorium on dating for a good long while."

"I have not," Mrs. Johansen said. "And yet I can't get a date to save my life. Which, given how old I am, anyone who went out with me might actually be called on to do."

"Have you tried internet dating?" Emmy asked before popping the cooled bite of casserole into her mouth. "Oh my God," she moaned. "This is *so* good."

"Men in my age bracket aren't on the internet."

"Well, who says you have to stick to men in your age bracket?" Emmy parried.

"I like her." Mrs. Johansen pointed at Emmy but spoke to Evan. Then she turned to Emmy. "Do you have one of those camera phone things?"

Emmy nodded. "Want me to help you set up a profile?"

Evan groaned as the two women began talking excitedly about how Mrs. Johansen could present herself to best attract would-be suitors, but nobody heard him.

As Evan cleared the table and handed Emmy a tub of ice cream and a scoop, Emmy came to the shocking realization that she was having a good time. It was an odd sensation, not having the eyes of the public on her. Not having to watch what she said, how she sat, what she wore. How she laughed, whether she had lipstick on her teeth, if anyone she had ever dated was in photographing distance.

She liked it.

She also liked tuna casserole, it turned out. *A lot*—she'd had two helpings.

And the company was first-rate. Mrs. Johansen was funny and friendly, once you got past her sometimes-brusque exterior. She made Emmy nostalgic for the years her grandmother had taken care of her after school. Emmy was looking forward to helping her try to get a date or two. She had the idea that this was what friends did—helped each other with their OkCupid profiles. Of course, most people's friends weren't seventy-nine, but hey, a girl had to start somewhere.

And then there was Evan. Nerdy, gorgeous, cranky, complicated Professor Winslow, her co-conspirator. It was a good thing she had already declared it the Summer of No Men, because—there was no point in lying to herself about it —he was a temptation. There was an air of contained strength about him that was magnetic. His movements were graceful but measured, his eyes all-seeing but slightly shuttered. It was like he was holding back some part of himself, and the longer she was around him, the more she wanted to know what it was.

"So I know you don't paint anymore," she said as she slid him a dish of ice cream. "But do you have any of your old stuff around?" His head snapped up, and his eyes darkened. Why did she feel like she'd done something wrong? She tried to clarify. "You have so much art in this house, but I'm not sure any of it is yours?"

"You paint?" Mrs. Johansen asked.

"No." Evan spoke sharply. "I used to. But not anymore. Not for years."

Emmy still didn't understand why he was so weird about this subject. He'd been the same way seven years ago. It was almost like he was talking about an addiction: *I don't drink anymore.* "He was really talented," Emmy said. "Supposedly poised to take the art world by storm, and—"

"I don't paint," Evan snapped, in a tone that brooked no opposition.

Okay, then. She was the guest here, she reminded herself, and if her host wanted to be all intense and weird over an abandoned career, it wasn't her place to poke at him.

"What do you do, Emmy?" Mrs. Johansen asked, clearly trying to diffuse some of the tension that had settled around the table by changing the subject.

"I, ah, I'm a writer." She hated deceiving Evan's friend, and she thought a version of the truth was probably safe. Mrs. Johansen would have said something long ago if she had recognized Emmy. And Emmy *was* a writer—of songs. "I'm hoping to get some writing done while I'm here, in fact."

"Oh, have you published anything I'd know?"

"No, no," Emmy said quickly. "But I'm hoping the work I do this summer will…change things for me."

That, at least, was the absolute truth.

"I think I'll leave you two to ice cream," Evan said stiffly, having ignored the half-melted bowl in front of him. "I have tons of work to do tonight." He pushed back from the table.

Mrs. Johansen smiled and shook her head. "No rest for the weary—or the untenured." Then she turned to Emmy. "Did Evan tell you he's up for tenure this fall?"

Emmy shook her head. She didn't exactly know what that meant, but it didn't seem that now was the time to ask, given how annoyed he'd been with her questions about his painting.

"Well, then he probably also didn't tell you about his villainous department chair." She grinned. "Honestly, academia is worse than a soap opera. My husband used to quote Kissinger, who apparently said, 'The lower the stakes, the larger the egos.' She set down her napkin. "So you both have summer projects—that's nice." Then she yawned. "Time for me to turn in."

"I'll walk you across the yard," Evan said.

"Speaking of internet dating," Mrs. Johansen said as Emmy followed them to the entryway, "if you're not going to take this one yourself, maybe you can set him up with a profile, too. Never met a more chivalrous young man. He shouldn't be rattling around alone in this huge house all the time lost in his work."

Both women ignored Evan's eye-rolling, and after arranging to visit Mrs. Johansen tomorrow to finalize the OkCupid profile, Emmy stood on the porch and watched the pair shuffle across their adjoining yards, Mrs. Johansen hanging on to Evan's arm like they were in *Downton Abbey*—if the young, handsome heir to the earldom had favored frayed, faded jeans and bare feet.

Emmy took a deep breath and shook off the sense of unease that had permeated the evening since she'd brought up Evan's painting. The air was heavy, sweet with the scent of the roses that covered Evan's untidy, overgrown front yard. A soundtrack of crickets gained momentum.

This was a good place. She was lucky to be here, even if only for a little while.

She tilted her head back and looked into the sky, which was bleeding from light to dark blue as the evening's first stars popped out, and tried to think why on earth Evan Winslow would give up painting.

CHAPTER FIVE

"Why don't you paint anymore?"

Evan rubbed his eyes against the bright sun as he shuffled into the kitchen the next morning to find Emmy already in it. He had avoided the question last night by going directly upstairs to his bedroom after seeing Mrs. Johansen home, and he was going to keep doing it. "Good morning to you, too."

"Coffee?" she asked, popping up before he could answer and pouring him a cup. She had made herself at home. In addition to brewing a pot of coffee, she had found the newspaper from out front. It was...oddly satisfying to see her making herself at home in his kitchen.

"Your room okay?" he asked, partly out of real concern but also as a tactic to continue delaying the discussion of his abandoned artistic dreams.

"Yes, thanks." She plunked a mug down in front of him. "How come you have so many guest rooms?"

"I bought the place furnished from an older woman who was moving to her Arizona condo full-time and didn't want to take anything with her. I haven't gotten around to doing anything with it."

"Which I guess explains the pink floral wallpaper."

He dipped his head in agreement. "It's a ridiculously big house for one person, but it was a steal. As you can see, it's pretty much falling apart, but it has good bones. I liked the look of it. I had all kinds of plans for it, but I haven't made the time."

"Yeah, like you have so many rooms you could keep a few of them as guest rooms, make one a den and still have one left over for, I don't know, a *studio*."

He paused for a moment, consciously working to tamp down his annoyance. "Hungry?"

She didn't blink. "Famished, actually."

"On Sundays, I go out to breakfast. Get dressed."

She rubbed her palms together. "Yay! I can try out my disguise!"

She had spent a long time in the clothing section on their trip to Walmart yesterday, and Evan found himself intensely curious about what she might concoct to hide her identity. He'd seen her eyeing a strapless sundress. It was pretty, but it wouldn't go very far on the whole camouflage front. She had nearly made it out of the kitchen before he called after her. "Just make sure you don't look too…"

"Too what?"

"Too attractive." He paused. "I know it will be a stretch, but try."

Ten minutes later, Emmy appeared back in the kitchen, and he burst out laughing. She was wearing a huge T-shirt that said, *Save Water, Drink Wine.* It must have been ten sizes too big for her, so it functioned as a tunic of sorts, flowing over a pair of jeans. The skinny profile of the denim couldn't hide her long, shapely legs. And even in that tent of a shirt…well, she hadn't succeeded in fulfilling his "not attractive" request.

But with the black hair, which she had scraped back into a ponytail, and the large, floppy straw hat, he was pretty sure she wouldn't be mistaken for…herself. At least he hoped.

Prayed.

Because if this all went to hell, he honestly wasn't sure he could deal with it.

She gave a little twirl, distracting him from his doomsday scenarios. "What do you think?"

"I think you're going to succumb to heat exhaustion in those jeans, but I also think you look amazing."

"If by amazing, you mean horrible, I am in complete agreement." She looked down at her body. "I tried to wear some shorts that I bought yesterday, but this shirt is so long on me, it made me look like I was naked from the waist down."

Naked from the waist down. Now there was image. He cleared his throat.

"Here's the best part," she said, walking toward him and standing on her tiptoes to get right in his face.

"What?"

She widened her eyes and leaned even closer. "Color contacts!" she said, fluttering her eyelashes, and indeed, her normally blue eyes had been transformed into dark brown.

It was…startling. More so than the hair. It was like someone had messed with some elemental part of her.

"Oh my God, I'm so excited to go out, I can't even!" she squealed, prancing over to the sink and depositing her empty coffee cup. "Don't get me wrong—I'm super grateful to you for letting me hide out for a few days, but I was thinking it was going to get pretty Grey Gardens around here if I never left the house."

He usually brought a pile of work to the diner on Sunday

mornings. God knew, he had enough of it stacked up. But apparently instead of advancing his own cause, he was going to spend the morning with Hurricane Emmy, the tent-wearing pixie goth. "Don't get too excited. I'm pretty sure Wanda's place is a far cry from what you're used to."

She aimed a million-megawatt superstar smile at him, which looked strange juxtaposed with her schleppy look. "I'm sick of what I'm used to. That's the whole point."

"Oh my God, I *love* this place," Emmy whispered once they were seated side by side on stools at the counter at the diner, and its proprietor Wanda had departed with their orders.

"It does the trick." Wanda's food was reliably good, her pie great. He favored it because it tended to be patronized by locals rather than college people, and he got more than his fill of college people during the week. He was especially glad of that fact today, because if Larry, his department chair, found out he was harboring a famous pop star, Evan could kiss tenure goodbye. Even though Evan had pretty well succeeded in making over his life, in severing all connections to his past, Larry would never let him forget where he'd come from. The man was convinced, irrespective of the facts of the matter, that Evan had gotten his professorial job because of his infamous last name, because of his father's notoriety in the art world—and passed up no opportunity to remind him of that.

The point was that Larry would never darken the door of Wanda's. Too plebeian for him.

The ordinariness of Wanda's Diner didn't seem to matter to Emmy, though. They might as well have been at a Michelin-starred bistro. She had been continuously delighted by everything from the friendly Great Dane tied up outside to the hand-lettered menus.

When their breakfasts came, Emmy poured a ridiculous amount of maple syrup over her waffles and took a bite. "Unnnhhh," she moaned through a mouthful. It was like she'd been sprung from prison and was tasting and experiencing life for the first time—which, he supposed, might not actually be that far off the mark.

God. She was so *pretty*, even in her ridiculous getup. Her fake brown eyes had widened when she'd tasted the first bite of waffle.

"So," she said, before taking a second bite. "Why don't you paint anymore?"

He'd been angered by her questioning last night, and annoyed by its renewal this morning, but really, it wasn't her fault. He'd be curious, too, in her shoes. "It's hard to explain," he said, adopting her line from last night and stuffing a bite of his eggs Benedict into his mouth.

"Try," she said, adopting his and waiting, eyebrows raised, for him to finish chewing.

Reprieve up, he sighed. He'd never actually tried to explain it to anyone before. No one in Dane knew that he had ever painted, unless they'd dug way back in Google. As far as they were concerned, art was a topic of research and teaching for him, not something he *did*. And he wasn't in touch with anyone from before, except his mother, who was too busy with her new husband to worry much about him, and his brother, who had always called painting a "pansy-ass pastime" anyway.

"You must know about my father." At the wedding, they hadn't spoken about the trial, or about his father. That had been part of Emmy's appeal: she'd seemed interested in him as him, not as a member of his rich and infamous family. But she had to have known.

"Yeah. I'm sorry about that. Sounds like he was..."

"A grade-A asshole?"

He'd meant to make her smile, to signal that she didn't have to tread lightly on the topic, because it wouldn't be possible for him to respect a person less than he did his father, but she only furrowed her brow. Man, she wasn't going to let him off the hook, was she? He put down his fork and turned to her, preparing to surrender, though he did pause for a second to contemplate how alarmingly easily he was doing so.

"I don't paint anymore for two reasons. One, if I ever had any talent to speak of, it was all built on lies."

She blinked. "Excuse me?"

"My family's fortune was made on stolen and counterfeited art, with a great big Ponzi scheme thrown in for good measure. My father bankrupted hundreds of people. He ruined families."

"Yes. I read about that. But I don't see what that has to do with you."

"Art lessons. Supplies. Weekend trips to the Louvre. My childhood was a lie. Any talent I developed was paid for with blood money."

"Blood money? Isn't that a little overly dramatic? I mean—"

He cut her off. He would tell her his tale of woe, but he wasn't soliciting her opinion. "I don't deserve to paint, Emmy."

She blinked again, several times in rapid succession, no doubt shocked by the declaration. He was, too, in a way. He'd never voiced it quite like that—*I don't deserve to paint*—but as soon as the words were out, he recognized the truth in them.

"Okay." She fiddled with a packet of sugar. "What's reason number two?"

"A more practical one," he said, grateful that she wasn't

going to protest anymore. "My father disgraced our family name in the art world. Who would buy a painting from Evan Winslow junior when Evan Winslow senior is in prison for crimes against the art world? Who would rep me? Show my work? I'm a pariah by association."

"But—"

Something in him snapped. He had told her the truth despite the fact that he didn't owe her an explanation. That she had gotten one at all was pretty unprecedented, actually. So he let his hand fall to the counter, swiveled on his stool to look her in the eye, and spoke slowly, over-enunciating every word. "I. Don't. Paint. Anymore."

She reared back a little, almost as if he had slapped her, which made him feel like an ass. But she needed to understand, even though she was only going to be here for a few days. He didn't need her meddling, thinking she was doing a good deed as she poked and prodded at a wound that had scarred over quite nicely.

It was a hard-won scar, and he was keeping it.

"I want to hear one of your songs," Evan said as they walked up the path to his house after breakfast, arms laden with groceries. Emmy had been marveling to herself over the fact that there were places in this world where people just walked to the grocery store and bought things with no plan, no list, when the request landed like a punch to the gut.

"All right," she said, walking through the door he held open for her and making her way back to the kitchen. Dumping her bags on the table, she fished her phone out of her pocket. "What are you in the mood for? A 'boys suck' power anthem or a 'boys suck' heartbreak ballad?"

He dumped his bags next to hers. "No. I want to hear you."

What?

"I listened to a bunch of your stuff last night—you have some great turns of phrase—but I want to hear *you* sing. In the flesh."

Her instinctive reaction was panic. But… *You have some great turns of phrase.* Evan didn't seem like the kind of person who gave false praise.

"You said you're writing a new album this summer," he went on. "I heard you fiddling around yesterday after dinner. Let me hear what you're working on."

She didn't do that. No one heard her songs before they were done, except Tony, and, of course, her co-writers. Tony was like a cross between her best friend and the supportive dad she'd never had, and he'd been witnessing her create songs since she was a teenager. The co-writers were harder, but she didn't have any choice there. To be fair to Brian and Claudia, they had hooked her up with some great writers, but it was still painful to play something that felt half-baked in front of an audience. It was almost as bad as all the tabloid humiliation—it was like baring some tender, ambitious part of herself that she was half ashamed of, half protective of.

"Okay."

As soon as the word was out, she clasped her hand over her mouth. It was like her body was agreeing with him without her brain having signed off. But he liked her turns of phrase. And, oh, she liked that he liked her turns of phrase. Besides, she sort of felt like she owed Evan. He had told her some deep stuff over breakfast, and he was putting her up for a few days. And, honestly, she was on a bit of a high after their successful outing. She had gone out to breakfast like a normal girl, and no one had spotted her. So screw it. This summer was supposed to be about doing things differently, wasn't it?

It didn't mean she wasn't terrified. After running upstairs to get her guitar, she returned, heart pounding, to find him sitting on the porch swing, a glass of Mrs. Johansen's lemonade in his hand and another one resting on an end table next to the wicker chair perpendicular to the swing.

She took a deep breath. It wasn't only the heat that had her wiping sweaty palms on her jeans. But it wasn't like he was a label exec, or a tour sponsor. And after the next couple days— the next couple days in which she would, hopefully, write a viable song or two—she would most likely never see him again. "Okay, I only have one verse and the start of a chorus." She didn't look up or wait for him to respond, just jumped right into strumming the jangly intro before she could chicken out. She'd been trying to evoke the feeling of Dane. The bright blue sky, the rows of corn, the exuberance of the farmers' market. The sense that even though everything was orderly and tidy, this was also, paradoxically, a place where anything could happen.

She stole a few quick glances at Evan as she played and sang. The first time, she found him staring at her with an intense, almost pained look. Like she was a bug and he a collector with a magnifying glass.

Or like he was a painter, and she was his subject.

The second time she looked at him, though, he had let his head fall back on the top edge of the swing, as if he was asleep. But she could tell by the alert nature of his posture that he was still listening.

As she strummed the last few bars of the chorus, she eyed him. He waited a good ten seconds before he sat up. "So that was not Song 58?" he asked.

She smiled. "That was most decidedly not Song 58."

He nodded, thoughtful. "Not bad for a day's work."

It was only a proto-song, but it had felt promising. But what had she expected? Fawning enthusiasm? She'd come here to do her own thing. To get out of the sphere of influence of everyone else. She didn't need his approval. Still, his lukewarm assessment stung.

She was trying to think what to say when he stood and made for the door. "I've got to run an errand this afternoon."

Right. But that was okay because she was immune to his indifference. It was the Summer of No Men, right? She didn't need them in her bed, and she *certainly* didn't need their approval on her creative output. That had been the whole point of coming here. "And I've got an appointment with Mrs. Johansen and OkCupid," she said—to herself as much as to him.

Summer of No Men.

She didn't like how she kept having to remind herself that.

CHAPTER SIX

He wanted to paint the black hair. Unlike natural dark hair, Emmy's drugstore version was solid, black-hole black, lacking any subtle highlighting. But there were sections near her hairline that were lighter—a kind of muddy dark brown—as well as bits of skin near her ears that were stained with the dark dye.

He dumped the tubes he'd bought on the table he'd cleared in the cluttered attic. He wouldn't just use Ivory Black Extra, though that would probably be the best way to capture the extremeness of the black. On canvas, it would look too artificial. He had a hunch that, paradoxically, he would need to naturalize the artificiality of Emmy's hair in order to accurately capture it. It would be an interesting technical challenge.

At least that's what he'd told himself as he'd hauled his bags of newly purchased supplies up three stories and plugged in a box fan in the stifling attic. He kicked aside boxes and half-broken furniture. The attic was even more of a mess than the rest of his house. It was a mixture of shit that had been left behind and his own forlorn stuff that had been layered on top without any consideration for order.

Enough. This was not the moment to find Jesus with the decluttering. What was he doing? Right. Emmy's fake black hair. The "interesting technical challenge."

But as he set up the canvas, he forced himself to face the fact that he was lying. This wasn't an "interesting technical challenge." It was a pre-primed canvas, for God's sake. Surely, a purely technical experiment could have waited for him to properly stretch and prime.

No, he was a junkie, jonesing for his first whiff of turpentine, for the swish of sable against canvas.

He worked all afternoon and evening in a near trance. She was emerging. But he wasn't satisfied. He thought back to something one of his former teachers—one of the men his father bankrupted—always used to say: "Portraits are about essence."

There was no essence of Emmy on that canvas. The proto-person staring back at him wasn't *her*. It wasn't the person who had sat before him and sung a perfect little song that was a perfect little puzzle—seemingly about one thing but really about another. How did she do that? Just create such a song like it was nothing? Pull it out of the air like it was easy? Was she planning to churn out gem after gem like that this summer?

He took a step back and dropped his brush. What was he *doing*?

Because of his father's fall from grace, Evan had been forced to build a new life. At the time, it had seemed impossibly catastrophic, but from this vantage point, he was glad of it. Everything he had now, he had earned—had worked himself to the bone to get. This rickety dump of a house and its overgrown garden. His PhD. His job—though he wasn't so sure he'd still have that after his tenure review.

But regardless, underlying the new life he'd created was a

promise he'd made to himself after Tyrone's wedding. The very next day, the bank had repossessed all his parents' properties—including Evan's condo—and he'd hit the road with a backpack full of clothes and a handful of résumés, determined to find a job to float him through the rest of graduate school at another university, the promise on his lips like a mantra: *no lying.* His father was a liar. Evan was not his father. Hence, Evan did not lie. Especially not to himself. Not even when it would be harmless, when lying would bring him a measure of psychological comfort.

And this? He looked at the painting with disgust. This was a lie. He didn't paint anymore. And yet here was a painting—a crap painting, but a painting nonetheless. Those two facts could not be squared with each other.

He surveyed the attic. The table he'd used for the paints and supplies looked like a small tornado had hit it. At his father's house, he had always prided himself on keeping a tidy studio. Something another of his artist-mentors had drilled into him: "A clean studio promotes creativity."

Between the painting—the mere fact of the painting—and the chaos of the space, it looked like he'd been on a bender of sorts. And like an addict the morning after, shame flooded his gut. He had fallen short of his own expectations. To be disappointed by someone else was one thing. To disappoint oneself? Unacceptable.

He hadn't purchased any gesso. But it wasn't enough to toss the canvas. He picked up the tube of Ivory Black Extra, squirted its entire contents on his palette, picked up a size twelve flat brush, and got started.

He was almost done when Emmy—the real one —appeared.

♫

"What are you *doing*?"

Okay, that had come out wrong. Emmy could hear how shrill she sounded, like she was a mother catching her kid smoking pot in the attic.

Evan whirled, his shirtless chest covered with specks of paint, mostly black. She had watched him for a few moments before asking the question, so she already knew the answer. He was covering up a painting. She couldn't tell what the original image had been, but he'd been making long, globby, angry strokes with a brush loaded with black paint to methodically cover it up. All that was left was an unidentifiable pink-beige thing that looked like it might have been an arm.

"Get out," he said. The command wasn't hurled in anger. Anger would have been preferable, actually, to the eerie calmness with which he spoke.

She did not obey. "Why are you covering that painting?"

"Because I don't paint," he said, voice rising—*there* was some anger suddenly. "Which you would know if you had *listened* to me today."

"And yet you appear to be painting," she said, smiling as the observation he had made about her a day ago—*And yet you appear to be crying*—echoed through her mind.

He stepped closer, putting himself directly under the naked bulb that swung from the ceiling, and she almost gasped. He wasn't angry; he was distraught. There was a wildness in his eyes that she had never seen before. It was different from the intense look he'd leveled at her while she was playing for him earlier, less controlled, even a little feral.

"What's more," she said, teasing him, hoping to puncture the heavy, charged atmosphere, to bring him back to himself, "you appear to be painting in the least well-lit space in your enormous house." Her joking did not have the desired effect: he took a step closer, but did not speak.

Until he did. "Goddammit, Emmy. I don't paint."

"Okay," she started to say. She'd been going to retreat then —know when to fold 'em and all that. It was his house. If he wanted to paint/not paint alone in the attic, that was his prerogative. She'd been headed to bed anyway, after an after-noon of moderately-successful songwriting and very successful OkCupid profile writing with Mrs. Johansen. She'd heard Evan banging around in the attic, and had left him alone all evening, eating some of the leftover tuna casserole alone in the kitchen before finally giving in to the impulse to come up and say goodnight.

He was so fast that she didn't catch up with what was happening until it was *happening*. His hands landed on the sides of her face, warm and insistent, the pads of his fingers pressing down hard as he tilted her head back and crashed his mouth down on hers. And just like that, their stupid confrontation was gone, evaporated, replaced by a spike of need so strong and gritty that she had to grab his shoulders to keep herself upright. Her skin came alive, as if it were made of millions of tiny, dried-out cells that were shifting, clam-oring for the relief that pressing herself against him could bring.

Lifting onto her tiptoes, she parted her lips and sighed against his mouth. The answering groan as he thrust his tongue in made her bold, and she met him stroke for stroke until all she could see was the need he created. It was red. It was blinding. It made her breasts hurt and the low, pulsing ache in her core deepen like he was wearing a groove in her being.

Could he have heard her silent pleas? Because at that moment, one hand fell from her face. She wanted to protest the loss of the steady, anchoring caress, but then his fingers lifted the hem of her tank top. When he found nothing underneath it but her, another groan ripped from his throat. "Fuck, Emmy." He cupped a breast in one of his hands.

"Oh!" She gasped as the first hand was joined by the second, but this one, instead of pressing, grazed her swollen nipple on the other side. The juxtaposition between one hand roughly kneading and the other barely flicking lanced her with a white-hot lust more intense than any she had ever experienced.

And then they were walking, shuffling really—he forward as he propelled her backward, marching her deeper into the dim attic until her butt banged up against the edge of a table. He reached one arm around her and used it to sweep everything from the surface. Brushes and tubes of paint and bottles of liquid she couldn't identify crashed to the ground. He pressed her down and pulled up her tank top in a single fluid motion, stopping only when he'd lowered his mouth to one aching nipple, already made oversensitive by his touch. She hissed when a flick of his teeth was quickly replaced by the laving of his tongue.

"You like that?" he rasped.

Unable to make her mouth form words, she could only nod vigorously. He wasn't paying attention, though. His world —and hers—seemed to have shrunk to the diameter of her left nipple.

She wanted to touch him, to touch his bare skin, so she moved to press back against his hold, only to discover that he wasn't holding her arms down. It had only felt so: his touch, his mouth, everything about him had seemed to immobilize her. It was a shock to realize that she had been lying prostrate of her own volition, while rivers of desire coursed through her limbs.

Almost angry with herself for the lost opportunity, she reached for him. But when the back of her hand brushed against taut abs, he hissed and let go of her, holding his hands suspended above her breasts, frozen in space.

Suddenly, reanimated, he ran his hands through his hair and hissed again, but this time it was a long, slow exhalation, like the air coming out of a pinhole poked into a balloon. Then he pulled her shirt down and lowered his forehead to hers. She tried to grab his head, to position his lips over hers, but he resisted, shaking his head, a silent *no* rubbing their noses together.

"Oh my God." The horror in his voice was unmistakable, and it was a bucket of cold water over her desire. "I'm so sorry."

He pulled away as she shook *her* head, trying but failing to find the words to absolve him.

"I can't do this," he said. "I can't get entangled with Emerson Quinn."

It wasn't lost on her that he'd said "Emerson Quinn" and not "you," like there were two versions of her, and one of them was lethal.

The worst part was, he was right.

"I know. It won't—"

"And you can't do this either." He spoke over her as he paced away, still raking his hands through his hair. "This is your summer of independence."

Right.

And it was so like her to forget that. *Stupid*, she berated herself. So, so stupid. This was how it always happened. She let herself stand in front of a man and just…melt. Subsume all her plans, her goals, her *self* into the feelings he could create in her without a care for how fleeting they were likely to be.

He turned, having reached the far corner of the attic.

Then he said, simply, "Stay."

"What?" She bolted to sitting. "What are you talking about?"

"This summer. Stay for the summer and write your songs. Get yourself back."

When she didn't answer immediately, he crossed back over to her, covering the distance between them in a few big steps. Looking down at her—she was still sitting on the table—he said, "You don't have anywhere to go, do you?"

He must have taken her continued silence for agreement—and it was, wasn't it? She'd all but admitted as much yesterday.

"That song from earlier," he said. "It was amazing. You have to finish it—and others. Are there others?"

"I hope so," she said, her voice appallingly shaky. She was ridiculously pleased that despite his apparent lukewarm reception earlier, he'd actually liked the song she'd played for him.

"Then stay. Work."

She wasn't sure what to say, so she just whispered, "Thank you."

He took a deep breath before offering her his hand. She took it, and he levered her up and off the table.

His face had grown hard, grim. She struggled to reconcile his apparent upset with the generous invitation—and compliment, she thought—he'd bestowed on her. The minute she found her feet, he dropped her hand.

"But this," he said, waving his hand back and forth in the space between them. "I'm sorry again about this. I got... carried away."

"It's okay," she said, smiling sheepishly. "I did too." Understatement of the year.

"This can't happen again," he said.

"Right. I am one hundred percent in agreement. It's my Summer of No Men," she said. Because it *was*.

He softened then, and shot her a half-smile. "Go on downstairs. I'm going to clean up here."

She took herself down the stairs on leaden legs. This had been a weird, ill-advised episode, but she would feel better tomorrow. And she had a place to stay. A longer respite than she'd dared to hope for.

Exactly what she'd been chasing by coming here.

Flipping on the light in the little bathroom that adjoined the guest bedroom she'd chosen, she lifted her eyes to her reflection.

Her face was covered in paint.

CHAPTER SEVEN

Emmy got up early the next morning. It was the damned birds. Her room looked over Evan's enormous backyard, which was verdant with willows and a bunch of other trees and bushes she couldn't name but were apparently home to approximately seven million chirping and hooting residents of the avian persuasion. Her house in the hills was on a fair parcel of treed land, but she had never heard anything like the wild kingdom symphony that was Evan's yard. But of course, she would never dare to sleep with the windows open at home, so who knew?

She checked her phone. There was a string of middle-of-the-night texts from Tony. After her encounter with Evan in the attic last night, she'd been unable to sleep, so she'd continued working on the song she'd started earlier in the day and had sent Tony a crude recording of her progress, as well as the song she'd written the day before and played for Evan, before she had finally forced herself to go to bed around midnight.

```
Holy shit: That's two days' work?
```

If I'd known this was what you were going to
come up with, I'd have dumped you in a corn-
field years ago. Forget L.A., we should have
gone straight to Iowa.

Seriously, Em, both these songs are AMAZING.

Stay there. Keep working. I'll cover for
you. B&C have been calling. I'll think of
something to tell them.

She laughed. That was certainly true. They'd been calling
her constantly since she left. In addition to the texts from
Tony this morning, she had a bunch from her increasingly
agitated managers. Voicemails, too. She went back to Tony's
epic string of texts.

And let me save you the typing: YOU WERE
RIGHT AND I WAS WRONG.

Let me know if you need anything. xo

Warmed by the positive feedback—Tony didn't do false
flattery—she typed a reply.

I need some money. I don't want Brian and
Claudia to find me. Am I paranoid that I
don't want to use my existing credit cards?
Can you send me a new one? Or wire me some
cash somehow? I'm planning to stay the whole
summer.

Then she deleted all the messages from her managers and typed one more to Tony.

```
I'm going to get a new phone, too. I want to
cut out the noise and focus. I'm not going
to put any social media on it. I'll text you
with the number ASAP.
```

Wow. So she was really doing this. Going into hiding for the whole summer. She didn't know if the tingles spreading from her stomach up through her chest were exhilaration or fear. Or hell, maybe it was just residual lust from last night.

Right. Time to think about something else. She glanced at the clock radio on the nightstand. Five in the morning. What did normal people do at five in the morning?

Well, she was pretty sure that most normal people were asleep at five in the morning, but that was not happening— she was too excited to sleep. She looked around her room as if it would provide a clue to what her next move should be. There was a still life on the wall that she suspected had come with the house, a classic fruit bowl.

"Breakfast!" she exclaimed. All right, then. Time to get some shit done.

After rummaging through Evan's pantry and finding a carton of old-fashioned oats, she looked up "how to make oatmeal" on her phone and was delighted when following the directions yielded a bowl of hot cereal that was actually edible. She ate some and left the rest on the stove in case Evan wanted some.

High on her culinary triumph, she did the dishes and wiped down the kitchen. Then, on a whim, having spotted a broom in the pantry, she moved on to sweeping the cracked linoleum floor. Evan, it seemed, was the quintessential absent-minded professor when it came to his house. It wasn't that things were terribly dirty, more that everything was dull and dusty and in need of a little TLC. And clearly he had only half unpacked, judging by the number of unopened boxes stacked in pretty much every room.

It was kind of heady, actually, doing domestic stuff. She didn't know how to cook. In her starving artist phase, which she'd gone through in lieu of college, she had subsisted on ramen noodles and cheap take-out. These days, she was always on the road, but somehow healthy, organic meals appeared when she wanted them. But cleaning? She was embarrassed to admit that she couldn't remember the last time she'd cleaned anything. She had forgotten how satisfying it could be to do something simple with your own hands that led to an immediate improvement in your environment.

"Emmy."

Startled, she looked up from her sweeping to find a sleep-disheveled Evan wearing nothing but a pair of boxers. Not that she, in her tiny sleep shorts and camisole, was particularly modestly dressed either. It needed to cool off in this town so they could wear some actual clothes. Evan's whole "this can't happen again" thing was going to be *a lot* harder if he was going to parade around nearly naked.

"You don't have to do that," he said, eyeing her broom and running a hand though his hair, which was sticking up at all angles.

He was adorable, but also something else. Something more like…dangerous. It was harder than it should have been to drag her gaze from his sculpted pecs. There was something about the juxtaposition between his persona—the art professor with the horn-rimmed glasses—and his unexpectedly buff body. Her skin tingled. An awareness crackled between them that hadn't been there before. Of course, it was last night's kiss. Last night's more-than-kiss. "You must work out."

Oh, shit. Had she said that out loud? She clamped a hand over her mouth. She *knew* he worked out—she'd seen his home gym in the basement when he'd given her a tour of the house two days ago.

He didn't respond, merely raised his eyebrows, grabbed a hoodie that was hanging over the back of one of the kitchen chairs, and shrugged into it—never mind that it was seven hundred degrees in the kitchen.

She cleared her throat and didn't even bother hoping she wasn't blushing—if it was seven hundred degrees in the kitchen, it was seven thousand degrees on the skin of her face.

"I know I don't have to," she said, gesturing toward the broom she still held. "But I wanted to make myself useful." It was the truth. She was so grateful he was putting her up for the summer. But more than that, it felt good to do something tangible.

"You're not Cinderella. You don't have to earn your keep."

"You said you had all this work you wanted to do on the house, but you hadn't found the time. Let me help with that."

He cocked his head and regarded her silently.

"I can't write songs all day long," she argued. That's how things would have been at the Beverly Wilshire. But she wanted this album to be…different. Less forced, more organic. "I got a second song roughed out yesterday, but it'll be better if I have something else to do. And apparently I'm going to get up at five every day. How do you sleep through those birds in the morning?"

He chuckled. "It did take a while to get used to it."

"Come on," she said. "You have your classes and this big tenure bid to worry about—you're gonna have to explain that to me. I don't really understand it. But the point is, if I'm going to be rattling around this house all summer, you might as well put me to work." When he didn't answer, she said, "I made oatmeal." He didn't know that was akin to saying, "I aced the SATs."

He moved to the stove and served himself some. He leaned against the counter and took a bite. "This is good."

She thrilled at the praise, as if he'd awarded her a Grammy rather than said a kind word about porridge.

"I mushed up a banana in it and added some cinnamon," she said, not telling him that twist had been straight out of the list of "variations" on the wikiHow "How to make oatmeal" post she'd consulted and not the product of her own culinary genius.

"Mrs. Johansen keeps me in casseroles," Evan said, "but I have to say, sometimes a guy just wants, I don't know, a burger or something. Or a fresh vegetable." He flashed her a self-deprecating smile. "Unlike you, I'm not much of a cook."

She beamed back at him. "Burgers! I'll make us burgers for dinner tonight." How hard could it be? "And back to the house. Let me help you with it. There are boxes everywhere, but I'm not sure if they're yours or if they came with the house."

"A mix. Some of it was here. I brought all my shit from Florida, but once I got here, I realized I didn't miss half of it, so I never really bothered unpacking. And I really only use the kitchen and my bedroom. I grade papers here." He tapped the kitchen table.

"But what about the little living room in front—with all the art?" Not his art—he had made his stance on painting *quite* clear last night—but that room had been full of art he *owned*, judging by how different those pieces were from the florals and landscapes that dotted the rest of the house.

"Yeah, I had this idea that I might keep the furniture that

came with the house, for now at least, but swap out the existing art with my collection. I only got as far as that room, though, which is kind of embarrassing given that I've been here seven years. All my other pieces are still packed in moving boxes. There are also pieces lying around in that front room that are submissions for this town art show that I'm supposed to be curating at the end of the summer—over in that barn we saw at the farmers' market. I need to sort it all out—figure out what's going in the show and what I want to hang here in the house."

"I can do that!" Surely there would be a wikiHow article on how to hang art. "Let me help," she added. "It will make me feel better about imposing on you. You can direct me as it relates to the art, and as for the rest of it, I can help sort though it—donate what you don't want to keep and organize what you do."

Damn him, there was that silent staring again. Emmy realized how profoundly unused to that she was. Normally, when she was with other people, they talked a mile a minute. Everyone had an agenda, a case to make, an urgent question. Everyone wanted something.

To be fair, Evan also looked like he wanted something, or like he was trying to figure something out. She just wasn't sure what it was.

"All right," he finally said, hoisting his coffee mug in a toast. "You got yourself a deal. I've gotten so used to walking around all the crap in this house, but it *would* be nice to put it to order." Then he turned. "I'm going to hit the shower."

"Great!" She lifted her mug in return, and as she watched him retreat, she ordered her brain not to think of him in the shower. *Summer of No Men!*

When he disappeared up the stairs, she heaved a sigh.

Now she had to figure out how to make hamburgers and

hang art. In other words, she had to figure out how to be a regular person.

♫

Mrs. Johansen, it turned out, could make more than just casseroles. She could also, for example, make hamburgers.

"I'm so glad you stopped over," Emmy said as she watched Mrs. Johansen beat the patties she'd been struggling with into submission. "I would have had no idea you had to put all that stuff into hamburgers."

"You don't *have* to," said Mrs. Johansen, who had come by for some advice on an OkCupid date she'd set up and, seeing Emmy forming plain ground beef into patties, had run home and returned with an envelope of dried onion soup mix and bottles of ketchup and mustard. "They taste much better this way."

"And here I was thinking people put ketchup and mustard *on* their burgers," Emmy said.

"Yeah, well, I figure if it's going to go on top anyway, why not put it in the meat mixture? It'll stay moister that way." She slapped the final patty onto a platter. "Throw some Saran Wrap on this and stick it in the fridge. Take it out a bit before you plan to throw them on the grill."

"Grill?" Emmy echoed.

"You're not going to cook inside in this heat, are you?" Mrs. Johansen asked. "Isn't that why you're doing burgers in the first place?"

"Uh, yes," Emmy said, following Mrs. Johansen as she made her way to the front door. "Yes it is. Are you sure you can't join us for dinner?" She tried to keep the desperation out of her tone with that last question. *Are you sure you can't help me with this grill thing?*

"You're the one who told me to jump on JollyGent35," said Mrs. Johansen. Then she grinned. "In a manner of speaking."

Mrs. Johansen had been surprisingly forthright with Emmy about her goals for dating when they got together to set up her profile.

"I'm not looking for another husband," she'd said. "I had one of those, and he was the love of my life." Her devotion, so plainly stated, gave Emmy shivers. "But let's face it," Mrs. Johansen went on, "I haven't had sex for eight years."

"You know I meant jump on his *profile*—like, don't let him get away," Emmy teased. "But jump him in the other sense, too, if you want. But I recommend against doing so on the first date." But who was she to talk? She would have jumped Evan that night on the roof in Miami if he hadn't been such a damned gentleman. Or last night in the attic, for that matter.

"What am I waiting for, though?" Mrs. Johansen parried. "I'm not getting any younger."

"You're waiting to make sure he's not a psychopath."

"A psychopath!" Mrs. Johansen exclaimed. "How exciting!" Emmy laughed, and when they reached Mrs. Johansen's door, the older woman stopped and said, "How are you with makeup?"

Emmy thought back to the hundreds, if not thousands, of makeup chairs she'd sat in over the past few years. "I've picked up a few things in my day."

"I'll be over at five thirty."

Emmy found herself looking forward to it. When was the last time she'd helped someone just to help them? Without it being a Big Freaking Deal?

She jogged up Evan's porch humming a tune that had been clattering around in her head all morning as she'd started on the house organization project, moving boxes around and making piles for Goodwill.

Time to find her guitar.

And maybe to root around in Evan's medicine cabinet to see if she could find some condoms for Mrs. Johansen.

It might be the Summer of No Men for Emmy, but at least someone was getting some action.

When Evan arrived home from teaching that afternoon, it was to find Emmy on the porch, applying hairspray to a much puffier version of Mrs. Johansen's usual hairdo.

"There," she said, standing back to admire her handiwork. "You look good."

Mrs. Johansen stood and raised her eyebrows at him. She seemed to be looking for approval, and he gave it freely. "You sure do." She was wearing a blue skirt and a crisp, white, short-sleeved blouse with a glittery blue brooch, and her lips were painted scarlet.

Mrs. Johansen would make an interesting subject to paint.

Whoa. Where had that thought come from? He had been happily coexisting with his neighbor for seven years, and he'd never once had the urge to paint her. But now that the idea was there, he couldn't stop thinking about how he would capture the delicate, crepe-paper skin of her neck, the deep lines around her mouth. The mouth itself, such an unlikely artificial red hue.

Her lips were the same color that Emmy's had been when she'd arrived on his doorstep, in fact. His Google-stalking of Emmy had revealed that red lips were her signature thing. She had kind of an Old Hollywood glamour about her. He liked that look.

But he also liked the fresh, no-makeup, short-shorts and tank top look she seemed to be settling into at his house, even with the black-hole black hair.

He liked all her looks.

Which was a problem.

In fact, it was probably his urge to paint Emmy yesterday that was making him think such crazy thoughts about Mrs. Johansen now. It was like he was hung-over, the residue of last night's painting binge and the subsequent encounter with Emmy still there in his psyche, making itself known.

He forced those thoughts back to his elderly neighbor— the reality of her, not some imagined painting of her. "So where is this hot date going down?"

"Wanda's," Mrs. Johansen said. "Emmy said that in addition to not sleeping with my new friend on the first date, I shouldn't have him pick me up because he might be a psychopath and in that case, I don't want him to know where I live. She said we should meet there."

Trying, and, he feared, failing to hide his shock, Evan glanced at Emmy, who was nodding vehemently, though since she was behind Mrs. Johansen, she was out of the older woman's sightlines. "I'm afraid things have probably changed since you last went on a date, Mrs. Johansen," he said as Emmy's eyes telegraphed her approval. "Emmy's right. It's good to be cautious."

"Well, I overrode her. He's picking me up. I'm pretty sure I can outrun JollyGent35. And that's saying something, because I can't run. The jury's still out on the other matter."

Emmy cleared her throat. "I also told her to have coffee for the first date. That way she's not stuck with a long meal if JollyGent turns out to be less jolly than advertised."

"Yep, and I ignored that advice, too. I gotta go. He's picking me up at six thirty, and I want to go home and sit in the air conditioning for a while so I'm not sweating like an ancient pig when he gets here." She blew them both kisses, and Evan jogged over and gave her his arm, sharing an amused/alarmed look with Emmy as he passed.

It sort of felt like they were in cahoots, sending their kid off on a first date or something. "Emmy sure seems to know a lot about internet dating," he teased, winking at her over his shoulder. After he escorted Mrs. Johansen home, he'd be left alone with her. Teasing might get them back onto more comfortable footing. After all, if he was teasing Emmy, he couldn't stick his tongue down her throat.

"Hey," Emmy protested. "I read!"

But as he and Mrs. Johansen descended the stairs, he *did* wonder why one of the most famous women in the world knew so much about internet dating. As far as he could tell, her romantic history was full of other famous people. He had done some more internet stalking last night after their aborted grope-fest. Surrendering to the knowledge that there was no shower cold enough to break the hold she had over him, he'd delved deeper into those three hundred and seven million pages of Google results. Her last boyfriend had been a musician, and as far as Evan could tell, the douche had been cheating on Emmy with a model, and she'd stumbled across them making out in Central Park. And of course the paparazzi had been on hand to document her humiliation. It baffled the mind how a man could have a woman like Emmy and throw her away like that. A *famous* man, he amended—a man who already didn't mind the limelight that came with being Mr. Emerson Quinn.

"You sure there's nothing going on between you and Emmy?" Mrs. Johansen whispered when they were out of earshot. Evan had a flashback to the feel of Emmy's breasts in his hands, to the sound of her breathing heavily as her nipples pebbled under his fingers.

"No," he said, thankful that Mrs. Johansen was watching her feet as they mounted the steps to her porch, so she didn't see his face, which he was pretty sure was flushed, even in the heat. "We're just friends. And anyway, neither of us is looking for a relationship right now." That much was true. Even if he hadn't been allergic to the idea of fame, he had his tenure bid to focus on, and Emmy was taking a break from dating. All signs pointed unambiguously toward the friend zone.

Mrs. Johansen didn't say anything until she had opened her front door. Then she kissed him on the cheek and said, "That's the dumbest thing I've ever heard," and slammed the door in his face.

Her refrain echoed across the lawns, and he wasn't sure how he was going to explain it to Emmy.

"Oh my God!" Emmy cried from his porch, obviating the need for him to address Mrs. Johansen's outburst.

"What?" There had been genuine anguish in her tone, and he jogged back across the yard searching for something amiss on the porch.

"The burgers!" She was already down the steps and streaking past him, heading for the gate that led to the backyard.

By the time he caught up, she was standing, shoulders slumped, in front of his grill.

His grill which was belching out an astonishing quantity of thick black smoke.

He moved around to take a look. The fact that Emmy had mentioned burgers was the only clue as to what the carbonized, black, vaguely round things on the grate had once been.

"I forgot about them!" Emmy wailed. "I put them on, and

then Mrs. Johansen came over, and they've been back here unattended for like an hour!"

"It's hard to believe they got that burned that quickly." Sure, half an hour would have produced well-done burgers, but they shouldn't be this far gone. "Did you let the coals ash over before you put them on?"

Her eyes darted between him and the dead burgers. "Excuse me?"

"You lit the coals with lighter fluid?"

She nodded.

"And then you waited for the coals to die down and ash over a bit before you put the burgers on?"

After a short pause, she switched to shaking her head *no*.

He burst out laughing. He couldn't help it. She looked so chagrined, and the pucks formerly known as burgers, so pathetic. So he gave in, throwing his head back and letting his eyes fill with the blue, blue sky as laughter rumbled through him. It was a strange feeling.

"I'm sorry! God, I'm so stupid."

That snapped him back to reality. Her tone had been over-the-top critical, like she was disgusted with herself. "Hey, don't worry about it."

"I don't know how to do *anything*," she went on.

"Not that many people have charcoal grills anymore." She still looked stricken, so he added, "And anyway, I'm pretty sure you have other talents."

She raised her eyebrows skeptically.

"Like making multiplatinum records?"

She blew out a dismissive breath. "I don't know how to do anything *real*. That oatmeal from this morning?"

"Yeah?"

"I had to look up how to make it on my phone. I'm completely incompetent."

"So?" He tried not to smile. She acted like she was confessing a mortal sin. "You looked it up, you made it, it tasted good. I think that's what they call competency."

"Just like I had to look up how to grill," she continued as if she hadn't heard him. "And here I was, congratulating myself that I figured out the difference between charcoal and gas. God, I'm *useless.*"

He took her arm. "Hey, I get it. After my dad's fall from grace, I was like a goddamned baby bird pushed from the nest. I *really* couldn't do anything—not even oatmeal." He cringed inwardly now to think of his old self. He'd been so angry for the first few years. Hell, he was *still* angry at his father, but he was glad he wasn't living that way anymore, dependent on his parents for money, his teachers for inspiration, and his friends for entertainment. God, he'd relied on everyone *except* himself. Like the world owed him. It almost made him physically shudder.

But, thankfully, everything was different now. He put food on the table himself—well, Mrs. Johansen put food on the table, really, but he bought her veggies, and he was more than capable of managing on his own. He conducted research and taught classes he was proud of. He had carved out a nice life in this little town, even if "curating the town art show" was what passed for a social life.

It was…kind of awesome, actually. It was a jolt to realize how much he liked the life he'd built, all the more because of how hard-won it was. He just needed to survive his tenure bid to make sure he didn't lose everything he'd worked so hard for.

"Come on," he said. "I've got a freezer full of casseroles. You can take your pick."

"Wow," she said a minute later when they were in his basement standing over his chest freezer. "You weren't kidding."

"She makes me one or two a week. I'm only one person,

and I usually buy lunch on campus, so I get behind. So I decant them into individual portions and freeze them." He chuckled. There *were* a lot of Tupperware containers in there. "So what'll it be?" He started rummaging around, reading the masking tape labels he'd affixed to the containers. "Chicken Divan, tuna, baked ziti, beef pot pie, mac and cheese—"

"Mac and cheese!" she exclaimed. "That tuna last night was amazing, but mac and cheese sounds pretty compelling. I don't know if I've ever had macaroni and cheese that didn't come from a box!"

"Well, your world is about to shift on its axis, then," he said, grabbing two containers of Mrs. Johansen's cheesy goodness and gesturing for Emmy to precede him upstairs.

"Can we eat on the porch so we can check out Jolly-Gent35 when he arrives?" she asked as they stood in the kitchen waiting for the microwave to heat their dinners.

"We can indeed," Evan said, a surge of something that felt remarkably like excitement swirling in his stomach. Which was ridiculous, because being excited about eating defrosted casserole on the porch in order to spy on the comings and goings of his elderly neighbor? He had just been thinking about how much he liked his quiet, small-town life, but, even for him, that was pathetic.

They sat side by side on his porch swing because it allowed them both a clear view of Mrs. Johansen's house. After Emmy's exclamations over the mac and cheese, a comfortable silence settled. He was relieved—and surprised, frankly—that there was no lingering awkwardness from last night's attic encounter. When they'd both finished eating, he took her Tupperware from her and set it along with his on a side table before settling back down and giving a push with his foot to start the swing moving.

Emmy sighed. It was, he thought, a contented sigh. He

felt it, too. There was something so companionable about eating dinner on the porch with someone, united by shared anticipation.

A long, green Cadillac appeared at the end of his street. It moved slowly toward them.

"I bet that's him!" Emmy whispered, the excitement in her tone making him less embarrassed by his own.

"Yep," he agreed, and sure enough, the car inched its way to a stop in front of the house next door, its green hue and slow pace bringing to mind a tortoise.

Its occupant moved just as slowly, taking his time levering himself out of the car, setting his cane on the ground, and shuffling up the walk.

"She can *totally* outrun him!" Emmy whispered, lower this time, right in his ear. Her mouth was so close that he could feel her breath. "Do you think we should offer to get her for him, so he doesn't have to go up the steps?"

"Nah," he said. "Too emasculating."

He felt her nod, and realized they were both leaning forward in the swing, which had stopped moving, as if they were watching a cliff-hanger scene in a movie.

A very slow-moving cliff-hanger scene.

Eventually, JollyGent35 knocked, and shortly after that, Mrs. Johansen appeared. She extended her hand, as if to shake, but her suitor lifted the hand to his lips and kissed it.

"Oooh," Emmy whispered.

"Romantic," Evan whispered in return.

"Maybe," said Emmy, which caused Evan to turn to her with a questioning glance. She shrugged. "Could be romantic, could be a creepy overreach. Depends on context and, like, if there's any insta-attraction."

Insta-attraction. Evan thought back to Emmy-the-brides-maid. He had been so marked by the years that followed that wedding, as he worked to claw his way out of his father's shadow. Those years loomed large in his mind. Or they had. But all of a sudden, it felt almost like they hadn't happened at all, like he and Emmy had met on the roof in Miami yesterday, and today they were sitting on the porch on a fine Iowa evening. Like Emmy somehow had the power to contract time, to collapse all those years between their first meeting and this night so they felt like a barely-there filling in a sandwich made of thick slices of bread.

"Should we say hello?" she said, startling him a bit. "Is it creepy that they don't realize we're watching them?"

"I don't know," Evan said. "Not sure how to play it."

Their uncertainty kept them silent as the pair next door descended the steps.

"I can seat myself," Mrs. Johansen said curtly when Jollygent35 tried to open her car door for her.

"Creepy overreach," Emmy said, presumably firming up her stance on the earlier hand kiss.

Evan had to agree. Mrs. Johansen's tone had been annoyed. And though his neighbor was definitely feisty, and sometimes ornery, she had a big heart and always gave people the benefit of the doubt.

He held his breath as the car pulled away. Emmy must have been doing the same, because she audibly exhaled when the car was twenty or so yards away. "I almost wonder if we should follow them!" she said, the sound of her voice at full volume jarring after all their furtive whispering.

"I gave her my cell phone and showed her how to use it," Evan said. All that innuendo and talk of psychopaths had made him nervous. He had wondered recently why he still bothered with a landline. He'd told himself that it would come in handy someday, which was probably an excuse designed to cover the fact that he had been too preoccupied with work to bother getting rid of it—the same reason the rest of his house was such a disaster zone. He had never imagined his landline "coming in handy" would take the form of waiting by the phone for his seventy-nine-year-old neighbor in case she needed to call in the cavalry.

"You did?" Emmy's eyes widened with surprise.

"Yeah," he said, turning his gaze back to the road where the car had been a moment ago. "She promised she would call my home line if she wanted me to come get her."

Feeling the pull of Emmy's regard, he swung his attention back to her. She was still watching him, the surprise on her face having given way to a kind of quizzical thoughtfulness. But then, before his eyes, a smile blossomed, as slowly as the Tortoise Cadillac had approached. "You are a good man, Evan Winslow," she declared, untucking a long, bare leg—she had been sitting cross-legged on the swing—and pushing her foot against the porch to start them moving again.

You are a good man.

The words sounded strange, like she was speaking a foreign language he was only partially fluent in, and his comprehension was delayed.

But once the meaning of her words sank in, settling on him like an ill-fitting garment, he smiled. He was pretty sure no one had ever called him a good man.

He didn't hate it.

They stayed on the porch for hours, waiting, as if by unspoken agreement, for Mrs. Johansen's return.

Emmy could almost feel something inside her chest loosening, something hard and coiled and heavy slowly expanding, like a dry sponge in water. She had gone inside for her guitar and was playing snippets of songs, the evening having evolved into a kind of musical blast from the past game as Evan called out song titles and Emmy played bits of them. Of course, he knew pretty much nothing from recent years, but he did turn out to have an affection for American jazz.

"Damn, is there any song you *don't* know?" he said as she wrapped up "Lullaby of Birdland." He stretched his legs out and nodded up at the moon, which was almost full. "How about 'Moon River'?"

She laughed at the perfection of the request. There was a shimmery white full moon hanging in the sky like a giant ripe grapefruit, and the light streaming down from it did indeed call to mind a river.

Emmy had never loved her voice. It was fine. It got the job done. But it didn't have the deep, rich tone of some of the singers she most admired. More than one critic had harped on her lack of vocal chops. It had never really bothered her in the early days, because back then she'd thought of herself as a songwriter first. Her voice wasn't incidental, but it wasn't the most important thing. But lately, on the last tour especially, when she wasn't playing any instruments, she'd become more self-conscious about it.

Tonight, though, somehow her voice sounded…perfect. It was strong and even, if soft—you didn't need to belt out a song like "Moon River" when you were sitting on a porch swing in the deepening twilight.

But it was the song itself, too. It was cheesy, yes, but as the cicadas began their nightly chorus and the first stars started to pop out, it also felt…true. Like they really were setting out on a great adventure together.

She cleared her throat and let her hand fall from her guitar. That was enough Name That Tune. Getting all moony—no pun intended—over a man and starting to associate songs with him was a well-trodden path for her, and not one she was going down anytime soon. Evan didn't want her anyway, she reminded herself, letting the shock of him pulling away from her last night in the attic come back to her. She'd thought they were at the point of no return. *She* had been at the point of no return—she would have slept with him right then and there, thrown all her carefully crafted pledges about staying away from men out the window. The fact that he could simply disengage like that was a useful reminder of where she stood with him.

Time for a new subject, and she really did have a question she wanted answered. "What about this tenure thing? You keep talking about it, but I don't really get it. Tenure is one of those words you know, but you don't really know what it means."

"It's job security, essentially. In academia, you do a probationary period of five years. You have to amass enough research and get good teaching reviews to earn tenure. The idea is that tenure protects academic freedom. If you're tenured, you can't be fired for studying or saying something controversial."

"Like 'the earth revolves around the sun'?" Emmy asked.

"Exactly. Or, you know, that a certain drug doesn't work. Obviously, nothing I'm doing is that important, but if you don't get tenure, you're essentially condemned to a lifetime of cobbling together poorly paying sessional teaching, and you can kiss your research ambitions goodbye."

"So it's like your do-or-die moment," Emmy said.

"Yeah, and for me, with all that shit that went down with my father...well..." He fiddled with his empty beer bottle, picking at the edge of the label. "I had to start over with my life."

She got it. He had built this life from scratch, and he didn't want to lose it. She wouldn't either if she were him.

There were rivers of moonlight in Dane, Iowa, for heaven's sake.

She did, however, think he was going too far by drawing such a distinct line between his old life and his new life as it related to his own painting, but she'd learned her lesson on arguing with him. "So what actually happens?" she asked. "Is there some formula, and if you meet it, they award you tenure?"

"I wish it was that objective. It's done slightly differently at different schools, but at Dane College, a committee is assembled to rule on your case. The members look at your tenure file, which is a dossier you put together detailing all your accomplishments, and they commission reports from peers at other institutions—that's like an objective outside voice weighing in. But ultimately your fate is in their hands. They get to decide if you've done enough. My file is due at the end of the summer, which is why I've been working so much, and they'll make their decision early in the new year."

"Wow, okay. So time to start delivering casseroles to the committee members?"

Evan huffed a bitter laugh as he let his head fall back on the top of the swing. "Again, I wish."

"So, what? Have you not done enough?"

He shook his head, still looking at the ceiling of the porch. "I have worked my ass off. I have lived and breathed that college and my research. I have done impeccable work."

Emmy wasn't surprised. Hence the unhung art, the unrenovated, falling-down house. He was pouring everything into his job. "Why so fatalistic, then? What's the problem?"

"The problem is that the chair of my committee, who is also the chair of my department, is out to get me."

Emmy wanted to ask why. It was hard to imagine anyone having it in for Professor Winslow. As far as she could see, he was the full package. His students obviously adored him, if Kaylee—not to mention the carload of oglers—had been any indication.

But she didn't have enough time to muster an argument because the Tortoise Cadillac chose that moment to appear at the top of the street.

"Our girl is back," Evan said, looking at his watch. "Almost nine thirty. It must have gone well."

"I wouldn't count on it," Emmy said as Mrs. Johansen opened her door and stepped away from the car before Jolly-Gent could make his way around to the passenger side to help her. As her date approached, she extended her hand for him to shake, a clear signal if ever there was one.

"Son of a bitch," Evan said, standing as JollyGent ignored Mrs. Johansen's body language and moved in for a kiss. Then he called, "Hello!" His tone was forced and the volume overly loud, but his greeting had the intended effect of drawing their attention. Emmy watched as he jogged down the steps and across the lawns, then stuck his hand out so aggressively that there was no way JollyGent could ignore it. "Evan Winslow," he said. Then he puffed up his chest like a cartoon Chip or Dale facing down a predator. "Neighbor," he added, his lip curling as if he had actually said, "Assassin."

"Well," said JollyGent, clearing his throat as he shook Evan's hand, "it's been a lovely evening, Midori."

Mrs. Johansen's given name on the lips of her unwelcome suitor sounded strange. If Evan, her close friend and neighbor, called her "Mrs. Johansen," Emmy didn't think this dude should be using her first name.

"Perhaps we can make a second date for tomorrow night."

"I'm not available tomorrow night," Mrs. Johansen said, and the fact that she hadn't couched her refusal in any sort of apology or excuse told Emmy all she needed to know.

"Saturday, then," said JollyGent. It was a statement and not a question, which riled Emmy. She stood, too, though she wasn't sure why, given that since she was still on Evan's porch, no one noticed her gesture.

"I'm not available Saturday, either," Mrs. Johansen said, taking a step back even as JollyGent took a step forward.

"I have that cup of tea waiting for you, *Mrs. Johansen*," Evan said, stressing the formal address as if he, too, had heard and disapproved of her suitor's familiarity. Without waiting for a response from either of them, he moved to stand between them and took Mrs. Johansen's elbow. "Goodnight," he said in a short, clipped tone, not even bothering to look at JollyGent as he dismissed him.

Dang, he was sexy when he was all bossy and protective like that.

"What a loser," Mrs. Johansen said, taking Evan's arm as the Tortoise Cadillac pulled away.

He led her across the lawns up the porch stairs and to a wicker chair, it being more steady than the swing, Emmy supposed. But when he sat next to his neighbor in the matching chair, Emmy had to suppress a ping of disappointment as she returned to the swing by herself. "What happened?" she asked.

"JollyGent happened," Mrs. Johansen retorted. "He talked about himself nonstop. Initially, I tried to actually hold a two-way conversation, to get a word in, but eventually I surrendered. I stopped asking questions or even really responding. It didn't seem to make any difference. It was like I was a prop. I'd rather have been at home listening to NPR. Even though Ira Glass doesn't respond to anything I say, I learn something."

"Ah," said Emmy, hit with a flare of vicarious annoyance. "I know the type. Did he try to order for you?"

"Yes!" she said. "And he lives two towns over, so if anyone

should have been ordering for anyone at Wanda's, it should have been me for him!"

"What did he order?"

"Does it matter?" Evan asked. "Isn't the fact that he did it to begin with gross enough?"

"Yes," said Emmy. "It's more than enough. But it does matter what he ordered. It will tell you a lot."

"What will it tell you?" Evan asked, clearly perplexed. "Are there degrees of entitled douchiness?"

"Yes." Emmy was something of an expert on degrees of douchiness, in fact. "Like, if he ordered her filet mignon, that's one thing—"

"Wanda's doesn't have filet mignon," Evan said.

Emmy ignored him. "But if he ordered her, like, the broiled sole, then he is utterly irredeemable."

"He ordered the garden salad with grilled chicken," Mrs. Johansen said.

"Oh my *God*!" Emmy said, punching the air in a fit of rage. "I cannot even."

"But I overrode him. I told the waitress—it was Wanda's niece Chloe, so it's not like she didn't know I didn't want the garden salad—that I'd have a burger and fries."

"Yesssss!" Emmy exclaimed, jumping up and getting into position to give Mrs. Johansen a high five before she realized she was probably a little too invested in the outcome of this date than was seemly. It was just that she was so tired of shitty, entitled men, and it was somehow extra aggravating to find that they were everywhere. She could tell herself that her sample, based as it was in Hollywood and the music industry, was skewed. But to learn that not only was chivalry dead among twentysomething Hollywood insiders, it was also dead among elderly Midwesterners, well…it made her want to punch something besides the air. Or write a revenge song.

Actually, a revenge song that wasn't about *her* life…that wasn't a bad idea. The garden salad could be in it. She got that happy-jumpy feeling that always signaled the beginning of a good song. It was kind of astonishing how easily ideas were coming to her here.

Evan cleared his throat, and Emmy realized she was still standing there like an idiot, crouched in front of Mrs. Johansen with her hand out like a stop sign while she plotted her musical revenge by proxy.

But as she was about to retreat in embarrassment, Mrs. Johansen high-fived her back and looked around at the scene unfolding on the porch—at the abandoned guitar and the empty beer bottles. "I think I'll have that tea now, Evan," she said, causing her host to jump to his feet to do her bidding. "Except make mine beer."

CHAPTER EIGHT

Stage fright was a real thing. Emmy had learned to manage it over the years, to harness it, even—a little adrenaline could make for a better performance. And these days, it was nowhere near as bad as it had been earlier in her career. She'd shaken like a leaf before her first gig at First Avenue, the "it" club in Minneapolis, which, at the time, had seemed the pinnacle of achievement. She didn't get that scared anymore.

Or at least she'd thought she didn't.

Turned out facing a room full of teenagers was pretty freaking scary.

"I don't think I can do this," she said as Evan pulled his car into Dane's community center. What had she been thinking agreeing to his proposal that she help him with the arts program for kids he ran once a week?

Well, she knew what she'd been thinking. It was like the cooking and the art-hanging. She wanted to be helpful and accommodating—to earn her keep, so to speak.

And when he'd explained that a couple of the kids weren't interested in visual arts, and he was having trouble reaching them? And when he'd suggested that music might be just the thing, especially to help a kid named Jace who kept coming but never spoke and seemed like he had no support system and was at risk of flunking out of school?

Of course she had crumpled like a piece of sheet music in his hands.

But now she was wishing she'd been made of something stronger than paper. "I'm afraid they're going to know who I am," she said, jogging after him as he headed for the front door without acknowledging her little freak-out.

"We've been over this," he countered, when she caught up with him. "You look *nothing* like your famous persona." He was so adamant she almost wondered if she should be offended.

She was dressed in more of the clothing she'd bought on her trip to buy hair dye. She'd grabbed a handful of really big shirts on that trip, rationalizing that their size and, well, frumpiness, made them a far cry from her usual wardrobe. Still, she was vain enough that she didn't want him to think she was outright ugly.

"You know I'm the last person who wants you to be discovered," Evan went on. "But people see what they expect to see. *No one* expects to see Emerson Quinn in Dane, Iowa."

"Yeah, but—"

"Emmy," he said, turning to her and placing his hands on her shoulders. The physical contact was at once jolting and calming, which should have been a contradiction but somehow wasn't. He hadn't touched her since that night in the attic last week, which she'd been doing her best to forget about. Even when they sat side by side on the porch swing, which they'd taken to doing in the evenings regardless of Mrs. Johansen's social calendar, they carefully maintained a respectable distance, like a courting couple from centuries past. "It would be really great if you could help me with this.

And you know what? I think it would also be good for you to get out of the house. You've been cooped up for a week." He paused and frowned. "But if you can't do it…you can't do it."

Whoa. Emmy's body almost recoiled physically from the shock. It was almost like Evan was…expressing disappointment in her? That wasn't something that happened. Ever. Another thing that never happened was people challenging her when she said something. In her regular life, if she expressed a desire to do something—or not do something, as in this case —the people around her automatically made it so, arranging the world to her liking.

"Okay. Let's do it." She swallowed. "I'm crazy nervous, though. I've never taught anyone anything before."

"Don't think of it as teaching. Have a conversation about music."

"Okay." Nodding to convince herself more than anything, she followed him past a gym that was hosting a pick-up basketball game and into a room with a bunch of folding chairs and several large tables covered with art supplies.

They were met inside the entrance by Kaylee, the student who had intercepted Evan outside his house on Emmy's first day in Dane.

Evan performed introductions, referring to Emmy as his "friend," which made Kaylee's eyes dart back and forth between Emmy and Evan several times. "Kaylee is one of my students, and she helps me out with this group."

A smile appeared on Kaylee's face as she shook Emmy's hand, but Emmy could tell it was fake. "I like your hair," Kaylee said. "It's really…bold."

Los Angeles had schooled Emmy in the fine art of recognizing shade. And Kaylee, with her peaches-and-cream complexion and strawberry blond hair, did not like Emmy's horrible trailer park goth dye job. Or Emmy. But even though

Emmy was pretty much incompetent at regular life, she knew enough to know that getting into some kind of girl war with a twenty-year-old college student with a crush on her professor was unseemly. So she surveyed the room. There were six kids sitting in a clump toward the front of the room talking, a pair huddled near the back in what looked like a private confab, and a boy sitting by himself off to one side.

"Hey, everyone," Evan said, and the conversation among the main group stopped. Most of its members returned his greeting, but the lone boy remained silent. "This is my friend Emmy."

Emmy waved.

"Emmy plays guitar," Evan said, "and I thought she could jam with those of you who might be interested." He looked at the sullen boy off to the side as he spoke, but the boy's eyes stayed on the floor where they had been glued since Emmy and Evan arrived.

"Jam with those of you who might be interested?" she echoed, purposefully amping up the incredulity in her voice. "Thank you, Professor Winslow. Are you, like, sixty years old? I don't think anyone actually calls it 'jamming' anymore."

That got a laugh from much of the crowd, and the boy looked up, though he did not smile.

"I don't know, you guys. I brought my guitar with me. We can play some music if you like. What are your favorite songs?"

"'Crush Me'!" one of the pair of girls at the back shouted, naming a pop song Emmy detested that was currently ruling the charts.

But hey, she aimed to please. So she opened her guitar case, strapped on her trusty Gibson, and played the trite opening chords of the song. Funny to think, here she was, one of the most successful women in the music industry, intimidated enough by a bunch of kids to cheerfully play crap for them.

It worked. The previously chattering girls fell silent. Emmy was tempted to sing the first verse, but she was afraid they would recognize her voice so she said, "You guys will have to sing. I don't know the words."

After a plodding and somewhat painful rendition, Evan stepped in. "Okay, those of you who are working on paintings come over to this table, and Kaylee and I will nose around and help anyone who needs it."

After a few minutes, everyone except the boy she suspected was Jace, the kid Evan had told her about, was involved in the art. He sat, unmoving, absorbed in his phone.

Well, here went nothing. Emmy ambled over to him with her guitar. "Not a 'Crush Me' fan?" she asked.

"Nope."

"Me either," she said.

That got his attention. He looked up with eyebrows raised before schooling his face back into its default bored expression. He wore cowboy boots, faded jeans that were too old to be on trend, and an equally faded T-shirt. All that was missing was the ten-gallon hat, and he'd be a perfect baby cowboy.

"You're more of a country fan, maybe?" she said.

He shrugged and said, "Yeah, and classic rock."

She strummed the opening bars of "Stairway to Heaven," a song that appealed to sullen teenage boys across time immemorial.

Bingo. He perked right up.

"You know it?" she said, handing the guitar over. "Evan— Professor Winslow—said you play?"

"Not really," he said, coloring a little. "My dad gave me a guitar. I try to teach myself from YouTube tutorials."

She pushed the guitar closer to him, and he took it. "Your dad plays?"

He shrugged. "He's not…around anymore."

Right. Sucky parents. She got that.

He took a long time arranging his fingers for the first chord. She nodded her encouragement as he started strumming. He struggled with the change from D to F major.

She crouched in front of him and arranged his fingers. "I usually find it easier to place my ring finger first and use that as a kind of anchor for the rest."

He was a quick study. It was a bit clunky, but he picked up the pace as he progressed through the song, and Emmy was quick to praise him when he was done.

They settled into a rhythm after that and actually started having fun. Jace had some talent, and by the end of the session, she'd planted the idea in his mind that he should write his own song.

"I don't think I'm good enough," he said, still strumming her guitar.

"But that's the cool thing about music," she said. "There is no good enough. It's not like you're in competition with anyone. It's just you and your guitar. You write a song. The end. There doesn't have to be an audience. You can write for yourself." She thought of the song she had almost finished last night, with the working title "Garden Salad." Both it and the songs she'd written earlier in the week felt like that. They were songs she'd written for *her*, not because she was trying to create a hit, but because she simply wanted to write them. She hadn't done that for *years*.

"That's true," he said, his forehead wrinkling. "It's not like normal people like us are ever going to, like, get a record contract."

Evan chose that moment to stroll over, and Emmy glanced

up at him. He was standing behind Jace so only she could see his face—which he appeared to be trying very hard to keep neutral. His amusement was contagious. Emmy had to press her own lips together hard to keep from laughing, and the "Right" she issued in agreement with Jace came out sounding slightly strangled.

"But what should I write about?" Jace asked. "My life is boring."

"Don't think of it in crude terms like boring or exciting," Emmy said. "Songwriting is about…details." Like the garden salad. She had never had to instruct anyone in how to write a song before, and she was struggling to articulate her approach. "You start with a detail, then you telescope it into something bigger. Your jumping-off point can be totally mundane. What are you doing later today?"

"Fixing a fence." He made a face like he'd tasted something bad.

"Okay," she said. "But what does that mean, specifically? How are you going to do it? What is the fence for?"

"It's a chain link fence. We have dogs. Well, they were my dad's dogs…"

He trailed off, and she suppressed a surge of excitement. An absent dad, left-behind dogs—this was going to be easier than she'd thought.

"So your dad left these dogs behind when he left you," she prompted, feeling no need to sugarcoat the situation. Evan's eyebrows shot up. Shit. Maybe she shouldn't have spoken so frankly. Evan was the one with teaching experience. It was just that she thought most kids appreciated being spoken to like adults. And she was pretty sure this kid in particular didn't need people tiptoeing around, using euphemisms to talk about what had happened to him.

"Yeah. Two of them. Pit bulls." His voice had gone raspy,

and he cleared his throat before continuing. "My mom wanted to get rid of them once it became clear that my dad…wasn't coming back. I wanted to keep them. I'm not even really sure why. They're kind of miserable dogs."

Jace blushed as he spoke, embarrassed that he had hung on to the dogs.

"They were something you had left of your father," Emmy said matter-of-factly. "They're a tie to him."

"Anyway," Jace said, shrugging as if brushing off her interpretation, "my mom and I struck a deal that I could keep them if I built a pen outside, which I did. But I used this shitty, old chain link because it's all I could get. It's gotten a bunch of holes, and it needs patching." He rolled his eyes as if the chore was a familiar lodestone around his neck. "It always needs patching."

Emmy glanced around, noticing that Evan was the only one left in the room—the other kids had gone, as had Kaylee. Which was probably why he'd strolled over to eavesdrop on her conversation with Jace. She'd been so tuned into the kid that she hadn't noticed the session was over, hadn't heard them cleaning up all the art supplies. And in fact, the room was filling up with middle-aged women dressed in workout gear.

All right, then. She stood and brushed her hands together. "So, Jace, you have a father who abandoned you. You have holes to patch. Holes you're *constantly* patching, it sounds like, to keep your connection to him. I'd say that song is pretty much going to write itself."

"Huh?" he said, looking so genuinely befuddled that she almost laughed.

"Metaphor," she said. "Metaphor. And this isn't even a very subtle one."

"Zumba starts in two minutes, ladies!" said a perky brunette dressed in a leotard and miniskirt.

"Broken fences. Broken hearts." Emmy patted Jace on the shoulder as she picked up her guitar. "Metaphor. Google that shit. Then think: verse, chorus, verse, chorus, bridge, chorus."

Emmy was spectacular.

It was the only word Evan could think to deploy. He had spent an entire year leading the after-school arts group, and Jace had spent an entire year sitting in the back row looking at his feet, which had always mystified Evan, because it wasn't like attendance was mandatory. The school district identified kids in need of enrichment, and the community center provided a bus from the high school. And now that it was summer, the program was extra-optional since the kids had to get themselves there. And yet there was Jace, every week, scowling and silent.

Why are you here? Evan wanted to shout at him sometimes.

And then Emmy strolls over there, and within minutes Jace is playing her guitar, which was no doubt some kind of priceless Cadillac of guitars, and looking at her like she's the fucking sunrise. Well, Evan could maybe understand the sentiment, but what the hell? Then she starts getting all in his face about his problems like she's in a cage baiting a grizzly bear or something, except she actually thinks it's a cuddly bunny. Oh, and then she finishes it all off with a dollop of "metaphor." Like Jace would know a metaphor if it bit him in the ass.

And, eff him, it works.

He shouldn't have been so surprised. He'd invited her for this very reason. He had assumed, though, that it would be harder. He'd imagined a montage from a movie in which the earnest but out-of-touch teacher is tested by her jaded students, but reaches them in tiny increments, week after week.

But, no. For Emmy, it was easy.

But then that shouldn't have surprised him, either. He'd been living with Emmy for a week and a bit, but he still couldn't understand how it was possible for someone to go through the world with such...effortlessness. No, "effortless" wasn't the right word. He'd heard Emmy working. She spent hours fiddling around with her guitar. He could hear the same musical snippets being played over and over. And music aside, the amazing progress she'd made on his house—she'd expanded on his original to-do list—hadn't been the result of a magic wand or a Mary-Poppins-like immunity to the laws of physics.

No, it wasn't effortlessness so much as it was competence. Complete and utter competence.

It was an incredible turn-on.

"Why are you so good at everything?" he asked before he could think better of it.

She shot him a questioning look as she walked through the door he held for her, preceding him into the hot, sunny afternoon.

"What was that in there?" he pressed. "You're like the sullen teen whisperer or something."

She shrugged and donned the hat and wraparound sunglasses she always wore outside. "He's got it inside him, I'm pretty sure. He only needed a nudge."

He wanted to tell her she didn't need the hat and glasses. Her tent-like shirts—this one sported a picture of a cat saying "Check Meowt"—not only hid her body, but it was like they hid her essence or something. She'd met a bunch of teenagers this afternoon—her core demographic—and no one had recognized her. The hat and monster sunglasses were overkill, he was pretty sure. In fact, paradoxically, these tools of disguise actually served to call attention to her. The punny, frumpy T-shirts worked, but no one wore her brand of big, floppy hat around here. This was ball cap territory, and you proclaimed yourself town or gown depending on whether yours had a sports team or a fertilizer brand on it.

But mostly he wanted to be able to see her eyes. Even though they, too, were disguised with color contacts.

He kept his mouth shut.

"Anyway," she went on. "I don't know how you can say I'm good at everything. I'm good at maybe a small subset of things." It was his turn to raise incredulous eyebrows. "Hello, burgers?" she said. "The burger inferno?"

"So you're not a natural chef. There's always more casserole."

"That front bedroom!" she said with an urgency that made him laugh. It was like she was arguing a case in court—against herself. "Do you know how many coats of paint I had to do?"

He shook his head. He had tried to talk her out of painting one of the guest bedrooms, but she had proclaimed its peeling peach walls an affront to humanity, made him choose a new color from among a handful of paint chips, and gotten to work.

"Six!" she cried emphatically, as if resting her case in front of a jury. "Why? Because I did not use primer. It seemed like an unnecessary step, but primer—who knew?"

He grinned and shook his head. She was adorable in her indignation.

"Like, I googled everything, and I learned about taping and all that, and then I just *skipped the primer*. Because apparently *I thought I was smarter than the Home Depot website*."

Evan's grin boiled over into laughter, and it felt good. Strange, but good.

Also good? The thought that if the pattern of the past week held, they would go home, go their separate ways for the rest of the afternoon—he to his grading and lesson planning and she to her music—and then they would come together to defrost some casserole and sit on the porch to eat. Mrs. Johansen had a date with a new man, so they would undoubtedly be up late waiting for her to come home. Sitting on the swing, shooting the breeze, maybe singing some songs, watching the stars and the fireflies come out.

The prospect was almost painful in its perfection. So at some point his laugh changed. He'd been laughing at her self-deprecation because it was funny. But now, it seemed, he was laughing for the pure, stupid unhinged joy in doing so. It was almost like—

"What, pray tell, is so amusing?"

That voice. It was like in old silent movies when the villain comes on screen and the score takes a menacing turn. It was also a surefire way to put an end to the laughter it was asking about.

Shit.

But, he reminded himself, this was merely an annoyance. Not the end of the world. If Kaylee and the kids hadn't recognized Emmy, a middle-aged academic certainly wouldn't. Evan was completely confident in Emmy's disguise.

Completely.

Mostly.

It was just that if he had to pick out the last person in the world he wanted to know he was harboring one of the most famous women in the world in his house, it was—

"Professor Larry Williams." Larry stuck his hand in Emmy's face. "Chair of art history at Dane College," he added, like he thought his job title was as important and impressive as "brain surgeon" or "president of the United States." When he added, "Bellows scholar," Evan had to work very hard to prevent his eyeballs from rolling out of his head. God. He had to get tenure, if only because once he had job security he would no longer have to stand around listening to this arrogant prick.

"Emmy Anderson," Emmy said, shaking his hand. "Civilian."

Ha. She'd picked up on Larry's self-important tone and was subtly mocking it. No wonder she was such a talented songwriter and performer. She had a way of putting together words, and pitching her delivery of them, that was masterful.

"Emmy's an old friend of mine," Evan said. "From Miami." Which was not untrue, exactly.

Larry's eyes brightened. He was forever trying to pry into Evan's previous life, always asking about the trial, and Evan always doggedly stonewalled. Evan was polite—he had to be—but they both knew that his past wasn't relevant to his job performance, so he *never* gave Larry an opening.

"Well, Emmy," Larry said, turning all fake-chummy. "Evan here is Dane College's most famous professor." He winked at her, and Evan was surprised by the sudden, overwhelming need to put his arm over Emmy's shoulder, to physically mark her as off-limits or some caveman shit like that. "Or should I say infamous? But I guess you know all about his dark past, if you're an old friend."

"Well, I know about his father's troubles," Emmy said, placing slight emphasis on the word "father's."

"You mean his father's *crimes*," Larry shot back.

"Yes," Emmy said, "His *father's* crimes." There was nothing slight about the emphasis this time.

"Well, looks like you've got a loyal little gal here," Larry said, turning his fake friendly tone on Evan, though as usual there was nothing friendly about his narrowed eyes.

The annoyance that was ever-present when Larry was around hardened into something less benign. "Emmy is a grown woman, Larry, not a 'little gal.'"

She's not "mine" either. But he didn't say that part. For some reason. Just gazed evenly at his boss.

Larry put his hands up in an exaggerated pose of surrender even as he said, "I've signed you up as our departmental rep on the facilities committee, Evan." Which had nothing to do with anything other than that it was a way for Larry to swing his dick around and assert his dominance.

"I'm already on two committees," Evan said. They were supposed to devote twenty percent of their time to "service," and split the rest between research and teaching, and Evan was already doing a lot. He'd been warned by sympathetic older colleagues not to take on too much committee work, as it tended to expand to fill time that would be better used for things that would count when it came to tenure.

"Yes," Larry said, one of his nostrils twitching. "I forgot that you're keeping score. I'll ask Charles to do it. He's always happy to help the department."

Evan refrained from pointing out that Charles was sixty-five years old, hadn't published anything in two decades, and routinely garnered miserable teaching reviews. He arranged his features into something he hoped resembled neutrality and said, "Facilities committee. Great. Let me know when the next meeting is."

"I hate to interrupt," Emmy said, laying her hand on Evan's arm. He'd wanted to touch her so badly before, but he hadn't allowed himself to. Now *she* was touching *him*, and it was like a drug sending calming sedation through his veins. "Mrs. Johansen will be waiting for us, won't she?"

"Yes," Evan said. Mrs. Johansen needed her hair done.

That was way more important than this bullshit. "See you later, Larry."

Emmy was silent until they reached his car. Once they'd pulled away, she turned to him and whistled. "Holy crap, is the chair of your department actually Satan?"

Evan chuckled. It was nice to have some external validation of Larry's awfulness. "He's pretty terrible, isn't he?"

"Um, *yes!*" She shook her head. "The way he announces himself in a social interaction as a Bellows scholar." She made a dismissive noise.

"It's his way of asserting dominance. Pissing on his territory, if you will."

"But that presumes that I know—and care—who Bellows is." She flashed an apologetic smile. "I mean, I'm sure Bellows is great, but…"

He waved off her apology. "George Bellows. He painted working-class New York City in the early twentieth century. Larry, who, I must point out, is from a wealthy California winemaking dynasty, fancies that he identifies with the hardscrabble manliness of Bellows. Anyway, it wouldn't matter if Larry was a Van Gogh expert. The point there was to intimidate you."

"Well, it didn't work."

And that, in a nutshell, was what Evan loved about Emmy. *Liked.* What Evan *liked* about Emmy. She was so firmly herself.

"And I can see now why this tenure thing is such a big deal," she went on.

"Nothing like having your fate in the hands of a sociopath," Evan agreed.

"It would actually be better, I think, if he was overtly evil. At least you would know where you stood. But he's so slippery."

She was right. "Yeah, the minute he gets a clear opportunity, he'll stab me in the back, I'm pretty sure."

"So why did he hire you to begin with?"

"He didn't. The chair at the time has since retired. Larry was on the hiring committee, and I've heard through the grapevine that he lobbied hard against my hiring."

"Why do you think he hates you so much? And why is he obsessed with your father? I'm right about that, yes? He is obsessed with your father?"

"Yeah, but I think it's an excuse he's seized on. This is going to sound conceited, but I think it's as simple as Larry feels threatened by me. I've published in better journals than he has, my courses are more popular, and I've won a bunch of early-career awards. Again, I don't want to sound like a jerk, but…"

"Owning your accomplishments doesn't mean you're being a jerk." She tilted her head and stared out the window like she was suddenly thinking of something else.

"What?" he asked.

"Oh, nothing. I was just thinking that's something I need to learn, too."

Evan wanted to ask her what she meant. She had a slew of awards, including Grammys. She had platinum records and sold-out world tours under her belt. Everything she touched turned to gold, basically. How could she be implying that she was anything less than aware and proud of all that?

But he didn't get a chance because she turned the conversation back to him. "Anyway, it sounds like you've hit the nail on the head. Mr. Manly Man is threatened by you, so he's going to try to sabotage you. And since he can't do it by legitimate means, he's seized on this stupid bullshit about your 'infamy.'"

"Pretty much. I, of course, am not an apologist for my

father, but it's like Larry thinks we're an organized crime family or something. He's constantly harping on how our little college doesn't need this kind of attention. I transferred here to finish my PhD, so I was a student here before I got my faculty job. I admit that when I first arrived, the media coverage of the trial was still going strong. There were reporters here covering the fact that Evan Winslow's son had fled to the boondocks. But that eventually calmed down, and I've never done anything to draw attention to myself here. Quite the opposite—I came here to get *away* from that attention, to leave it behind."

She turned in her seat so she was facing him. "So what will you do?"

He shrugged. "What can I do? Hope the rest of the committee talks some sense into him."

"Is it a vote? Like, democracy?"

"Ostensibly. The question will be how much power Larry has over the other committee members."

She nodded and went back to staring out the window. He kept glancing at her, though, and caught her nod again, quite decisively, at the cornfields passing by their window.

It was like she'd come to some kind of conclusion he wasn't privy to.

CHAPTER NINE

While Emmy did Mrs. Johansen's hair later that afternoon, she added a few items to her mental to-do list.

Well, actually it was one big, honking item: defeat Larry the Bellows scholar.

It came with several sub-items, though. Tactics of sorts, the first of which was kiss the hell up to the other tenure committee members. She just had to figure out how to do that.

"How did those hamburgers work out last week?" Mrs. Johansen asked.

"A barbeque!"

"Excuse me?" Mrs. Johansen said.

"I think we should have a barbeque," Emmy said as she wove a braid across Mrs. Johansen's forehead. "A party. For Evan's colleagues, and we'll make sure the members of his tenure committee have a great time."

"That is an excellent idea," said Mrs. Johansen. "But he won't go for it."

"I'll handle that part." Negotiations would be easy, relatively speaking anyway. The food part was what terrified her. "What do you serve at a barbeque?"

"Burgers, brats, potato salad," Mrs. Johansen said. "I like a green salad at a barbeque, too, to counteract all the junk. Then you can make some cookies or brownies, or do s'mores over the coals."

Emmy frowned. "Is there any way I can get all that stuff catered?" But even as she asked the question, she realized the answer was no. Not if she was trying to show Evan as a down-to-earth member of the department. Someone who belonged in Dane and was not just an interloper from a rich and famous family.

Evan chose that moment to come out to the porch where she'd set up their makeshift hair salon, and Emmy frantically mimed zipping her lip in Mrs. Johansen's direction.

"Whatcha got there?" she asked as she tied off the braid— Evan was carrying a stack of papers—hoping her voice didn't sound too fakey.

He flopped down on the swing and sighed. "These are my notes for the town art show. I've been in denial, but I've got to get the programs done. They need to go to the printer next week, so I have to figure out what the hell I'm doing. And then actually hang all the stuff—that's going to take forever."

"I'll do that part," Emmy said, and when he started to protest, she kept talking over him.

"Doesn't she look great?" She made a Vanna White gesture toward Mrs. Johansen's head. "I watched a bunch of YouTube tutorials on this braiding technique, and I think I did a pretty kick-ass job if I do say so myself."

"She does look great. But Emmy, you can't hang the art show."

"Why not?"

"Because, I'm not—"

"Seriously," she interrupted. "I'm an art-hanging expert now." She had sorted through all the art in his house and hung most of it. Really, there was nothing you couldn't learn from YouTube. "You curate. I'll hang. The show's what? In a month and a bit?" Evan didn't realize that the art show was another opportunity to impress the tenure committee, to demonstrate his devotion to Dane. She would make sure it was perfect.

The mental list gained an item: kick-ass town art show.

"Are you sure this isn't bothering you?" Emmy asked, drawing Evan's attention from his work. He looked up to see her setting her guitar aside and standing and stretching. The evening had advanced without him realizing.

She'd been working on a song that was pretty far along. It was amazing to hear some of the snippets that had been floating through his house—and his mind—start to get stitched together. A song was being born, right in front of him, like it was no big deal. She was even humming a little, like she was thinking of where lyrics might go, and he was dying of curiosity to learn what they would ultimately be.

"Not at all," he said. "It's helping me." Evan usually needed silence when he worked, but for some inexplicable reason, having Emmy around fiddling with her guitar made him extra productive. His hands had been flying over his laptop keyboard, and he had a pretty good draft of the art show program roughed out. It was a task he'd been dreading, and it was finally done. He had moved on to grading a stack of midterm essays from his summer course, and was making good progress through those, too.

"I usually don't let people hear a song before it's done," Emmy said. "I'm kind of obsessively private about it."

"I'm harmless," he said.

Emmy deepened her stretch, reaching her hands to the sky and arching her back, her breasts straining against the tight fabric of her tank top. She was wearing what Evan had come to think of as her "home" uniform—shorts and a tank top—rather than the baggy shirt and jeans she armored herself in when they went out. Her home uniform was a lot more… unsettling. The bright moonlight amped up the lightness of her white tank top against the darkness that framed her. She was so lean, you could see the outline of all the muscles of her torso and stomach through her shirt. He'd read interviews where she professed not to like her tall, slim build, where she called herself "gangly" in a disparaging way. But to Evan she seemed just right, like she was the way she was supposed to be. She inhabited her body—and her entire being—in a way that…well, in a way that cried out to be painted.

When she was done stretching, she put her hands on her hips and regarded him, tilting her head. He was still sitting, so he had to look up at her. "You are a lot of things, Professor Winslow, but *harmless* is not one of them."

"So SilverCEO seemed like a better prospect than Jolly-Gent," Evan said to distract himself from her body and the almost all-consuming itch to paint it.

It worked. "He sure did!" She wiggled a little like the idea was so exciting she had to move her body. It was not helping on the distraction front.

"It would be great if she could find someone," Evan said. "I worry about her all alone in that big house. What if she falls?"

"How long has she been widowed?"

"Eight years."

"No kids nearby?"

"They never had kids."

"That seems kind of unusual for someone of that generation," Emmy said.

"She told me once that they tried for a while but after several miscarriages they gave up."

"Huh."

"Her family was interned during World War II. In California. She was five when they went in." He didn't think Mrs. Johansen would mind him telling Emmy. It wasn't something she talked about a lot, but it wasn't a secret, and it had certainly shaped her worldview.

Emmy gasped and sat back down next to him on the swing. While she'd been sitting across from him on a chair before, he'd been thinking her presence was good for productivity. But now that her thigh was mere inches from his own, "productivity" no longer seemed like the right word.

"Yeah," he said, clearing his throat to get rid of the raspiness in his voice. "She doesn't talk much about the actual experience, but she said after it was over, her mother was determined to appreciate every moment of life, and not to harp on what she didn't have or fixate on what had been done to her. She taught Mrs. Johansen the same outlook, I think."

"That's amazing. I would think an experience like that would make you angry—or at least bitter. How do you carry on like that when your own country locked you up?"

"I wouldn't say she wasn't angry. But it's like she cultivated the ability to let go of anger and be in the moment. Mrs. Johansen looks like a standard-issue old lady." Evan chuckled thinking about how he'd come to that erroneous conclusion shortly after meeting his neighbor. "But in actuality, she's kind of a Zen master or something. She's always saying, 'Live the life that's in front of you.'" He glanced over at her house. It was bigger than his—three stories, and he knew she had trouble with stairs. "But I don't know what the endgame is.

She gets along okay for now, but she can't live by herself in that house forever."

"Maybe we need to find her a younger man," Emmy said.

Evan laughed, and Emmy scooched against the back of the swing, rested her head on its top, and gazed up at the sky. He watched her face change as she retreated into her mind. Her eyes narrowed like she was thinking intensely about something. He could practically see the cogs turning in there, and he was overcome with the urge to know what was going on in that clever brain of hers. "A penny for your thoughts."

She sighed. "Oh, I don't know. I was thinking about what a fine line it is—living in the moment and embracing experience like Mrs. Johansen versus... I don't know, whatever is the opposite of that. Living a programmed life, I suppose." She blew out a breath like she was frustrated with her own words.

"A programmed life," he echoed. It was an interesting phrase. "I don't think Mrs. Johansen is advocating anarchy. We all live programmed lives to some extent, don't we? We have to."

"Sure." She turned her head to him, the rest of her body still lounging back against the swing. "But the question is, who's doing the programming?"

He'd seen the misery in her eyes that first afternoon, when she'd appeared on his doorstep and said she'd run away from her managers. It's why he let her stay when every instinct toward self-preservation had been screaming at him to do the opposite. "But you got away from them. You came here."

"I'm not talking about them." She waved a hand dismissively. "Well, I am, but the hard part is thinking about how did I get to that point? It's not just them. It's *me*. I make bad choices, and then I react by overcompensating, by trying to dictate what I'm going to say or do or how I'm going to behave. I get overly worried about my image. I have to be, to some extent, I guess. But there's always this internal struggle. Is that any way to live?" She huffed a bitter laugh. "It's very un-Zen."

She was obviously struggling, but she was speaking so abstractly, he didn't really understand what she was trying to say. "Can you give me an example?" From his vantage point, it didn't seem like she'd made bad choices. Hell, she'd had a dream and set her mind to making it come true. It was damn impressive.

"Okay, like, remember when we went to the farmers' market?" He nodded. "Until I got recognized, that was the best time I've had in years."

Warmth pooled in his stomach at her words. He thought of all the pictures of her in ball gowns, at galas and award ceremonies, on the arms of famous men, on red carpets in Cannes.

"Riding a bike!" she exclaimed. "Propelling yourself through space in order to get somewhere. It's so simple, but I was so scared!"

"You were scared?" She'd objected, but he hadn't realized she'd been genuinely afraid. He wouldn't have been so pushy if he had. A protective urge rose in his chest, as strong as it was tardy.

"Terrified," she said, smiling at him. "It's like I have this inner critic. She's always telling me not to do stuff. She's very good at imagining the worst-case scenario. Like, a bike crash, the paramedics come, the paparazzi arrive." Her smile disappeared. "So she tells me not to do stuff."

"She?"

"Maude. I call her Maude."

He barked a laugh. "You have an imaginary friend!"

"I don't have an imaginary friend. It's more like I've named part of my subconscious."

"So you have an imaginary imaginary friend?"

139

It was her turn to laugh. "I guess I do."

"Maybe you need an imaginary Zen master. Maude doesn't sound very chill."

"Right, but here's the problem. I need her. Left to my own devices, I have this tendency toward impulsiveness."

He raised his eyebrows, thinking of the utter shock that had hit him when he'd opened his door to find her on his porch. "You don't say?"

She didn't get that he was teasing her and answered earnestly. "Yeah, it's like I get tired of living in such a conscribed way, and I act out. Claudia and Brian—those are my managers—plan everything. I can tell them I need more downtime or I want to do something specific—I could even tell them I wanted to take a bike ride—and they'd make it happen. But they schedule it in, you know? Between other things I have to do. Somehow, even though they're giving me what I say I want…"

"It's a programmed life," he finished for her. It sounded awful. His family's time in the spotlight leading up to and during his father's trial had been excruciating.

"Yeah, and it's not that I don't get it. I know I can't just get on a bike and go. I understand that's the price I pay for the life I've chosen. But sometimes it's…too much, and I try to rebel against it. But that always turns out to be a mistake."

"Like the time you climbed out of Kirby Carson's window in the middle of the night?"

She bolted to a seated position. "You know about that?"

"Doesn't the entire internet know about that?"

"But you didn't even know who I was when I showed up a week and a half ago!" She leaned closer. She had recovered from her shock and was grinning. "Professor Winslow, have you been Google-stalking me?" She wagged a finger to punctuate the fact that she was teasing.

He probably should have been embarrassed to have been caught out. But instead he decided to ignore the question and address her first statement. "I did know who you were." Then, acting on an absurd impulse, he grabbed her finger—wrapped his fist around the protruding index finger and held it there.

"But," she whispered, "you said—"

"I didn't know Emerson Quinn," he interrupted, his throat growing oddly tight. "But I knew *you*."

She regarded him silently for several heartbeats, and he was afraid for a moment that she might cry. "Yes," she finally said. "The time I climbed out of Kirby's window in the middle of the night was one of my little rebellions." It took him a minute to get her meaning, to understand that she was picking up their earlier conversation even as he, for no rational reason, continued to hold her finger. "And as usual, it completely backfired. I thought I was seizing the day, but I was totally humiliated that night—both publicly and privately."

She looked like she was remembering something painful. He wanted to ask her to elaborate. Hell, he wanted to get on a plane to L.A. and hunt down that boy-band dudebro and kick his ass.

He let go of her finger, which was harder to do than he would have liked, and settled for asking, gently, "What happened?"

"The same thing that always happens. I got my hopes dashed." She shook her head. "Anyway, the point is, I shouldn't have been there to begin with. I should have listened to Maude."

"Maude told you not to go?" He was torn between bemusement at this whole Maude thing and anger at the entitled shithead who had dared to disappoint Emmy.

"Maude told me not to go," Emmy confirmed. "Just like she told me not to get on the bike with you."

"But that worked out," he pointed out, disconcerted by the prospect that she might be thinking of that outing as a mistake of the same ilk as her encounter with Kirby Carson. Not to mention that he seemed to be arguing with Emmy's imaginary voice of reason.

"Yes. But only because…"

Only because I kissed you.

He heard what she wasn't saying.

"Anyway, that's sort of my point. I want to do what Mrs. Johansen says, to live the life in front of me, but my carpe diem is broken. I traded it for success, I guess. Every time I try to be unfettered, I end up all over the tabloids, and sometimes I get my heart broken, too, as an added bonus. So then I over-compensate and get all cautious, and it…infects everything. Maude infects everything."

He suddenly understood that she had come here to get rid of Maude. She probably didn't realize it herself, but some part of her, some part deeper than Maude that didn't have a name, had known that in order to achieve her stated goal—creating a bubble of normalcy and independence—she not only needed to get away from her managers, she needed to get away from Maude. But to ditch Maude without it backfiring, she needed to be somewhere safe, somewhere where she could seize the moment but be assured that her every move wouldn't be documented.

The instinct that had gotten her here had been right on. She was in search of Mrs. Johansen's Zen. It was like that utter competence he always observed in her, despite her protesta-tions to the contrary, ran deep. It was the core that powered her.

And eff him if the idea that she'd come to him specifically to try to access that core, to protect herself from the tug-of-war that was happening all around her, didn't make him prouder than any painting back in the day ever had. Christ, the idea that she'd thought of him, after all those years, as a haven, as a place where she might enjoy enough protection to…live—well, shit. He loved listening to her make songs, but now something else rose in his chest, something powerful and protective.

She sighed and let her head fall back on the swing again, then, slowly, she rolled her head to the side so she could see him. "I'm a total mess, actually," she whispered, like she was letting him in on a secret.

He shook his head and lowered his voice to match hers. "You're really not." She was completely and utterly sane, in fact. She was also one other thing: close enough to kiss.

It was the opposite of last time, in the attic, when their kisses had been frantic, panicked almost. He couldn't get enough of her then, had wanted to devour her, to somehow climb inside her. But tonight was different. She was already all around him, had been for hours, with her song snippets and languorous stretches. The way she stared into the sky when she was thinking hard, either about her song or about something they were talking about. She permeated the space around him, so much so that to lean forward slightly—he only needed a couple inches—and gently press his mouth against hers seemed like nothing more than the logical extension of their evening.

Yes, the softness of her lips, the almost-inaudible sigh as they parted for him, lit him up inside, made his dick jump to attention, but it wasn't an axe to his chest like last time. It was inevitable. She was all around. She was inside his head. She was everywhere. So why shouldn't she be here, sighing against his mouth?

Like a bubble floating on the breeze, the kiss only lasted a few moments before its pure, clear perfection popped. He made himself pull away. Slowly, though; he didn't want her to interpret it as a recoil. Because it *had* been there, the kiss-bubble, hanging in the sky reflecting moonlight, and almost certainly he would come to regret it, but right now he couldn't make himself. He was so full of her that there was no room left for regret.

He wasn't recoiling, but, he realized belatedly, she was. She'd stood and was on her way to the chair across from him, the one she'd been in before, but she stumbled. He was up in an instant, grabbing her elbow to steady her. But she kept recoiling, once she had found her feet. "Sorry," he said, letting go and wondering if he should specify that he wasn't talking about the kiss, even if, later, he *would* be sorry about it. No, right now he was issuing an awkward apology because she was falling and he'd had to help her. Or something.

"It's okay," she said. "I just…can't do that this summer."

Shit. She had misinterpreted him. He opened his mouth to clarify but then shut it again because that would only make things worse. And, more to the point, she was right.

Holy shit, was she ever right. Belatedly, alarm bells started screeching in his head. Yes, there was suddenly more than enough room for the regret that had been absent before. What was *wrong* with him? She was Emerson Freaking Quinn. He had to quit kissing her.

And, more importantly, he had to quit feeling responsible for her. Yes, she'd sought refuge with him, and fine, maybe that was a little flattering, but that's all it was. A fleeting emotion. He couldn't make it his job to protect Emerson Quinn.

The slamming of a car door drew their attention.

"I didn't even hear them drive up," Emmy whispered, echoing his thoughts exactly as she sat back down and affected a casual pose that was so obviously fake that he couldn't help but smile. "Look normal!" she whispered urgently as she grabbed her guitar. "She can't think we're spying on her."

Evan was pretty sure Mrs. Johansen knew they were spying on her, but, grateful for something else to do besides ruminate on that ill-advised kiss, he did as he was told and grabbed his red pen and an essay off his ungraded stack, never mind that it was too dark to credibly be grading papers.

"What's happening?" Emmy whispered. She'd sat down across from him instead of next to him on the swing, so her back was to the action. "Is she waiting for him to come around to her side of the car?"

"She is," he said, squinting to try to see through the darkness. He glanced at his watch. "They've been gone five hours." He wasn't really sure where the time had gone.

Well, that was a lie. The time had been absorbed in work and absorbed in Emmy.

Emmy performed a comically exaggerated stretch so she could twist around and see what was going on next door.

"Subtle," he said.

"Shut up," she whispered, sliding off the chair, crouching on the porch, and turning around to peek over its edge.

He laughed. He couldn't help it. "Remind me to remind you never to become a spy."

"Shhh!"

SilverCEO was walking Mrs. Johansen up to her door. Emmy was so riveted, she looked like she was watching a crime show.

With her back turned to him, he could study her unobserved. She was kneeling with her legs tucked under her, and moonlight painted her bare shoulders, making them almost shimmery. She looked like she was in church with the light of the heavens or some such shit shining on her. Or like she was a mischievous fairy from *Midsummer Night's Dream* spying on the simple mortals. Maybe that would explain his odd behavior this evening, too. Maybe she'd put the otherworldly whammy on him.

Dammit. He understood that he couldn't get drawn into the fame-web of Emerson Quinn, but he still wanted to paint her. Wanted it so bad, his teeth hurt.

She sighed, which drew his attention to the scene playing out next door. Theirs hadn't been the only kiss happening this summer night.

They were both silent as Mrs. Johansen allowed SilverCEO to peck her on the cheek. But as he was pulling away, she grabbed his cheeks and planted one on his lips. Her back was to them, so they couldn't see her face as they separated, but she waited on the porch as her date made his way back down the stairs and into his car, lifting her hand as he drove away.

"Oh my God!" Emmy breathed, just as Mrs. Johansen turned to them and said, "I see you two."

Emmy hesitated, like she wasn't sure if she should keep hiding.

"Busted," Evan said, waving.

Emmy popped up. "How was it? What happened? Are you seeing him again?"

Mrs. Johansen was silent for a moment. Evan couldn't see her smiling—the moonlight wasn't that bright—but he could imagine it happening. Then she said, "Night night," went inside, and shut her door.

Emmy turned to him, mouth open in surprise, the moonlight that he'd been admiring on her shoulders illuminating her perfect face. The face he couldn't have, either in reality or on canvas. "Is that all we're getting?"

He huffed a laugh he hoped sounded less bitter than it felt. "Yes," he said. "That's all we're getting."

CHAPTER TEN

Holy crap. Jace was a songwriter. Emmy didn't even bother trying to play it cool at Evan's after-school arts group as Jace played her the song he'd written in the week since their first meeting. The whole fence/holes/heartbreak thing had the potential to be pretty heavy-handed, and she would have expected no less from a first-time effort. The point with Jace, she'd thought, had been to get him making the connections, get him started on putting melody and lyrics together, even if his first effort was clunky.

But the kid had produced a clever, subtle, catchy song. There were a few improvements she would suggest when he was done—after she picked her jaw up off the floor.

Shockingly, Jace was also a *singer*. As with last week, he'd been moody and withdrawn, staring at the floor instead of making eye contact as they'd talked. But once he started singing, he was different. He still didn't look at her, and his voice was soft. But it was clear. It didn't shake, as hers had during her first few gigs—hell, during her first few *dozen* gigs.

When he finished, he set his guitar aside and resumed staring at his shoes.

Emmy started clapping, and she wasn't alone. She wasn't sure who was more startled, Jace or her, when the entire room erupted into applause. She turned and caught Evan grinning from ear to ear. They hadn't really spoken since last week's porch kiss. Well, they hadn't *not* spoken, to be fair. They talked logistics. *Emmy was going next door. Did Evan want another cup of coffee?* But things had been different between them. More distant. A little awkward. Which was fine—or so she'd told herself. After their kiss, she'd hoped to avoid the whole "reasons we can't make out anymore—for real this time" discussion. She didn't need any convincing on that front. Well, her brain didn't, anyway.

But now, it was like all that awkwardness, all that unease, had been sloughed off, thanks to Jace. Evan caught her eye, raised his eyebrows and mouthed something that looked like *holy shit*. Emmy's cheeks were going to split from smiling. And it wasn't only because of Jace. She realized with a start that she had missed Evan. He'd been right there, under the same roof with her, but she'd *missed* him.

But okay, she could examine that thought later. Or not. Jace was looking pretty uncomfortable as a bunch of the girls, who she suspected never gave him the time of day normally, swarmed him. "All right, you lot." She made shooing motions to the kids who had crowded around him and ordered herself to be cool. "Off with you now. Jace and I have work to do."

An hour later the session was wrapped up, and she and Evan had made it to the privacy of his car.

Which meant it was finally safe for her to lose her shit.

She turned to him. "Oh. My. God." She couldn't help herself from making a stupid jazz-hands motion.

He hadn't started the car, didn't appear to be making any movement to do so, just angled himself toward her and said, "Holy *shit*, Emmy. That was incredible."

"You should have heard it by the time we were done."

"I kind of did," he said, looking sheepish. "I got that you were trying to shield him from everyone's attention, but I did my very best to eavesdrop."

She sighed and flopped back against the seat. "This teaching thing, man. I can see why you like it."

He smiled and started the car. "It has its moments."

"I can't button my shorts. I need to go shopping."

"What?" Evan tried not to laugh as he looked up from the porch swing to see Emmy standing in the doorway. She looked the same to him, dressed as she was in her tank top and shorts outfit—her usual "home" outfit.

"Oh, Mrs. Johansen. Sorry, I didn't realize you were here," Emmy said, grimacing. Evan tried not to be chuffed by the fact that while she was apparently embarrassed to reveal her pants-buttoning problems to Mrs. Johansen, she had no such qualms around him.

"So what about SilverCEO?" she asked. "I knocked on your door yesterday to see how your second date went, but there was no answer. Spill it."

"There was no answer because Mrs. Johansen was having lunch at Wanda's on her *third* date with SilverCEO," said Evan, wagging his eyebrows.

"Seriously?" Emmy said, her face lighting up as she sat next to Mrs. Johansen on the swing. Evan instructed himself not to look at the waistband of her supposedly too tight shorts.

"I like him," Mrs. Johansen said.

Evan looked at the waistband of Emmy's shorts.

"And?" Emmy prodded.

Her tank top was pulled over it, so he couldn't see the button. To hear her tell it, it would either be undone, or it would be buttoned but straining to hold.

"I like him." Mrs. Johansen said again.

The idea of her casually sitting there, on his porch, with her shorts unbuttoned… He shifted, his own shorts suddenly less comfortable than they had been.

"So what's this about your shorts?" Mrs. Johansen asked, clearly trying to change the subject and talking loudly enough to drag his attention back up from the gutter.

"They're all too tight—too much tuna casserole," Emmy said.

"I can try to make a…lite casserole," Mrs. Johansen said with about as much enthusiasm as she had displayed when prompted to open up about her date.

"Absolutely not," said Emmy. "I just need bigger shorts. So I need to go shopping. Is there a mall around here?" She fixed her gaze on him. "I want to get…different things than I got at Walmart that day." He got the message: she wanted to go somewhere else to buy more "home" clothes. Because surely her baggy "away" clothes still fit.

"I'll lend you my car," Evan said. "Let me get the keys."

Emmy's face contorted into a pained mask.

"What?" he said. "The Subaru not fancy enough for you?"

"No. Actually, um…" She winced and fidgeted almost like she was nervous. "I don't know how to drive."

"Oh, okay." He was surprised, but given the strength of her reaction, he'd been expecting something more dramatic. "I can drive you. I don't have to go into the office today. I'll work from home, and you can text me when you're ready to come home." Come *back*. He meant to say "come back." Because Emmy didn't live here. This wasn't her home. But no one seemed to notice, so better to not call attention to the slip by correcting it.

"I actually got my learner's permit back in the day," Emmy said, her tone having gone completely flat, "but then I never took the test." He sensed there was more to the story but also that she didn't want to go there. Regardless, in her life as Emerson Quinn, there were, no doubt, people around her who drove her wherever she wanted to go.

"You need to learn to drive," said Mrs. Johansen. "You can't live in Iowa without knowing how to drive."

"I don't live here," Emmy started to say, but trailed off when Mrs. Johansen raised her eyebrows. Maybe his "come home" slip hadn't gone unnoticed.

"You don't drive, either," Evan said to Mrs. Johansen, trying not to sound peevish.

"I'm seventy-nine," Mrs. Johansen retorted before turning to Emmy. "I get a pass. But I know how. And I do have a car." She turned to Emmy. "I'll teach you."

Evan didn't know whether to laugh at the prospect of Mrs. Johansen teaching Emmy to drive in her giant, mothballed Buick, or to forbid it.

"You know what? I can just call a taxi," Emmy said, standing up and heading toward the door.

"Nope," said Evan. "It's really no problem. Let me get my keys and we'll be on our way."

Three hours later, Evan pulled up to their designated meeting point outside Dane's only mall. Emmy skipped down the sidewalk toward him, laden with bags and grinning from ear to ear.

"What?" he said, smiling as he got out of the car—her goofy excitement was contagious.

"The mall!" she said after he'd thrown her purchases into the trunk.

"What about it?" he said, opening her door for her and then coming around to the driver's side.

"It's full of stores, and you can just go in and buy things!"

Her eyes were wide and her tone tinged with awe. He bit his lip to keep from laughing. "That's pretty much how malls work."

She rolled her eyes. "I know that's how malls work. I haven't been to one in a while, though."

"I suppose fancy designers send you clothes so you don't have to lower yourself to mingling with the masses at the Gap."

"Pretty much," she confirmed.

"The idea of not having to shop is pretty damned appealing. Clothes simply show up on your doorstep? Sign me up."

"And, of course, the other beautiful thing about a mall is that you can get everything! My assistant sent me a new credit card, and I went a little crazy." She reached into a bag and pulled out...a giant jigsaw puzzle of a hot air balloon? He hadn't seen that coming.

"A puzzle of a hot air balloon counts as crazy?"

"I love puzzles." She dug around some more in the bag and, with a flourish, produced a newspaper.

The *National Enquirer*. "Where is Emerson Quinn?" screamed the headline, which was accompanied by a grainy photo of her in a headscarf.

He read the subhead aloud. "'Singer hasn't been seen in public in weeks. Social media feeds dark. Reps deny rumors that star has been stricken with cancer.'" He blinked rapidly, almost unable to believe what he was reading. "Holy shit!"

"Ha!" She pumped a fist in victory. "That photo is from a trip to the beach like two years ago. It was windy, so I stuck that scarf on my head."

"Well," he said, "I still think it's possible you're a little too thrilled with a crappy mall in Dane, Iowa."

"I am exceedingly thrilled. I did all this stuff I usually don't do, and as we have previously discussed, I am basically incompetent as a normal human being."

"Hey, that's not true!"

"Said the guy who's picking me up from the mall because I can't drive." She rolled her eyes.

"So what's up with that?" he asked. He sensed there was a story there, and even though it was none of his business, he wanted to know what it was. "You said you got your learner's permit, but then you never got the actual license?"

She deflated a little. "Yeah. With a learner's permit you have to have a parent in the passenger seat with you, you know?"

She was fidgeting as she spoke, so he started the car and pulled away, reasoning that it would be easier for her to tell the story if he wasn't staring at her. "In theory, yes," he said, thinking back to his teen years behind the wheel. "My parents outsourced it to a driving school, though. In retrospect, I suppose my father was too busy cheating hardworking people to spare the time."

"Well," she said, "my parents refused to outsource it or to help me themselves. So I did all the classroom stuff, but then I had no one to actually supervise the behind-the-wheel stuff." He glanced at her. She was looking out the window as she spoke. "I was sixteen, and I had just signed with this guy Tony, who was my first manager—he's my assistant now. He was booking me into local clubs. My parents were *furious*."

"Not into the idea of their daughter hanging around clubs, I suppose," he said, pulling out of the mall lot.

"Not into their daughter doing music *at all*. So they were trying to use driving as leverage. Like, quit your stupid music, get some serious ambitions, and then we'll teach you to drive."

"Wow, that's kind of a dick move."

"You know what else is a dick move?" He felt her turn to him, and it only took a quick glance at her to see the hurt in her eyes.

"What?" he asked, returning his attention to the road. He was pretty sure he wasn't going to like her answer.

"Kicking your daughter out of the house, which they did later."

His hands flexed, and he gripped the steering wheel tighter. Okay, so now he had to add Emmy's parents to the list of people he wanted to pummel on her behalf. Her *parents.* Jesus. Immature boy band members were one thing, but the people who were supposed to love you unconditionally? At least he had been in his mid-twenties when his own family fell apart.

"But they've come around now, I suppose," he said, hoping for a happy ending. "I imagine that seeing your daughter win a Grammy Award has that effect."

"Nope," she trilled with false cheer. "They still think what I do is immature and unseemly. My grandma is the only person in my family who would have been happy about my musical career —but she died before she got to see it happen." He was about to tell her what he thought of that when she said, "Anyway!" in a loud voice, signaling that she wanted to end the conversation. "The mall was *awesome*! It sounds dumb, but a successful shopping trip is like solving a problem, and I don't get to do that very often. I needed clothes. I bought them. Just like a real girl."

"You are a real girl."

"Anyway!" she said again, "the *main* reason I'm so thrilled by my little mall excursion is this." She produced a flyer from her bag and let it flutter to his lap.

"I can't read that while I'm driving."

"It's a regional songwriting contest for teens!"

"Hang on now." He knew where she was going with this.

"It's like it's meant to be," she said, talking animatedly over him. "Finals are at the Minnesota State Fair, and the prize is a college scholarship! It's perfect!"

"Final round at the Minnesota State Fair?" he echoed. He appreciated her enthusiasm, but she was getting carried away. There was no way that Jace the near-mute sixteen-year-old was winning a songwriting contest at the huge fair their neighboring state held at the end of every summer.

"Yeah, there's a preliminary thing at the mall next week— they're going on all around Minnesota and northern Iowa apparently. So when he wins that—"

"Whoa. Emmy. Stop."

She did, but only for a moment. Then she said, "Evan." And the *way* she said it, all low and sort of exasperated, startled him. She'd been so excited a moment ago, the furious pace of her words keeping her voice high. This was…something different. He wondered if that's how she would say his name in bed.

Which was a hypothetical question. *Hypothetical.* As in: not being tested in reality. God damn. What was wrong with him today? Probably just that he'd gone through more emotions in this short car ride home than he had in the past year. Delight at Emmy's infectious enthusiasm, anger at her parents, incredulity at the idea of Jace entering a songwriting contest. And now…this. He shifted in his seat.

"You know how good he is," she went on, still using the sultry voice.

"He is, but—"

"We're not that far from St. Paul, are we?" she asked as he turned onto his street. "What is it? Three, four hours?" When he didn't answer, she sighed, the fight seeming to leave her, and said, "I was only thinking that this might be a way forward for him. I don't get the impression that his mom has a lot of money. She waits tables at Wanda's, right? A college scholarship would be amazing—it would let him develop his skills but still get an education to fall back on. But even if he doesn't win, it seems like…"

It was Evan's turn to sigh. "It seems like what?"

"Like it would be a big deal to him. To make it to the state fair. To be good at something. To have adults believe in him."

Well, shit. He couldn't really argue with that. And he was the one who was supposed to be the teacher, the one helping these kids. He did have one final objection, though. "Well, all right. But you can't take Jace to the Minnesota State Fair, Emmy. It's one thing to hide in plain sight in Dane, but there will be tens of thousands of people there. And you're from Minnesota."

"Well, okay, maybe I can't."

He pulled the car up in front of his house, cut the engine, and turned to her. Finally, she was seeing reason.

"But *you* can."

CHAPTER ELEVEN

Things spiraled from there. Emmy, even though she was clearly trying to be useful and to stay out of his way, was invading his life. His very being.

Exhibit A was a week later, when Evan arrived home on Friday night to find the house empty.

It was an odd feeling, made more so by the fact that he only realized she wasn't around *after* he had burst through the door calling "I'm home!"

What did he think? That they were Ozzie and Harriet and she'd be waiting for him, casserole freshly microwaved, excited to hear about his day? That because it was Friday, maybe they'd bike into town for a piece of pie at Wanda's?

It was just that he'd gotten the programs back from the printer for the art show, and he wanted to show them to her. Despite the fact that he'd been thinking of the event as a monkey on his back, he was getting excited. It was her doing. After he'd agreed to let her help with the execution, she had thrown herself into planning. She'd made a map and had him mark where he wanted each piece to hang, and she was working with Jerry, the barn's owner, to get the walls properly prepared. She'd even stood over Evan, cracking the whip while he made a poster design that she then reproduced and had the community center kids plaster all over town.

But, he reminded himself, Emmy wasn't his wife. She wasn't his assistant. She wasn't his *anything*. And more to the point, he didn't *want* her to be. She didn't owe him an accounting if she'd chosen to go out. Or if she was working on her music upstairs in her room.

"Evan?" came a voice, wafting in from the backyard through the open kitchen windows, and damned if his heart didn't do a little jig. "We're out back."

We.

And damned if *that* didn't temper his excitement a little.

He didn't want to share her with Mrs. Johansen.

Or... "Jace?" The screen door almost hit him in the ass as he stepped into the yard. The teenager and Mrs. Johansen were sitting at the old picnic table in the yard, eating potato chips.

And so was...SilverCEO?

"Burgers!" Emmy announced from her perch at the grill, snapping her tongs as if in victory. "I made burgers, and I didn't carbonize them this time!" She was looking at him the way some of his kids did—both the college ones and the younger ones at the community center—when they craved positive reinforcement.

He was about to give it to her despite the fact that he personally didn't think she needed to make burgers or buy shorts or learn to drive to be a "real girl," but Mrs. Johansen interrupted, trilling, "Practicing for the big barbeque!"

Emmy shot Mrs. Johansen a quelling look, and Evan spoke the line that had basically been fed to him. "What big barbeque?"

Emmy ignored the question. "Evan, this is Mr. Widmer, Mrs. Johansen's friend." She angled her head so that only he could see her face when she said, "friend," and the slight raising of her eyebrows that accompanied the word warmed his insides. When was the last time he'd conspired with someone? "And Jace came over to play us the latest version of his song." Since getting Jace and his mom on board with the idea of competing in the songwriting competition, Emmy had stepped back from helping, insisting that the rules, which specified that the young songwriters could have "adult advice but not co-writers" be respected.

"Okay," Evan said, letting Emmy lead him to a spot at the table and accepting a beer. "But what big barbeque?" He asked the question a little louder this time, as if volume would help extract an answer.

"The barbecue next Saturday where all your colleagues are invited," Mrs. Johansen said.

"*Excuse* me?" He nearly choked on his beer. Evan thought of himself as a solitary person. Well, he hung out with the seventy-nine-year-old next door, but that was about it. He certainly didn't have his whole goddamned workplace over for burgers. "You are insane if you think that's happening," he said to Emmy, allowing some of his annoyance to come through in his tone. It was one thing for Emmy to overhaul his house, but she needed to stay far away from his job. Larry didn't need any reminders of Evan's so-called fame.

"But also the barbecue next Saturday where we'll celebrate Jace's performance in the preliminary round of the songwriting competition," Emmy said with an artificially bright smile, as if she hadn't heard his objection.

"*Emmy*," he said, infusing his voice with warning.

"*Evan*," she countered, and she was using the sultry voice. Whatever. He wasn't backing down here, so he raised his eyebrows at her. He would wait her out. The barbeque was not happening.

The barbeque was happening.

"See," said Emmy, filling up the sink for dishes after everyone left. "That wasn't so bad, was it? Consider it practice for next week."

"Yeah, but your little multigenerational menagerie is one thing. My entire, mostly hostile department is another."

She laughed as she immersed a stack of plates in the soapy water. "My little multigenerational menagerie! Ha!"

Evan wasn't sure what had happened to him.

Well, that wasn't true. He knew exactly what had happened to him. He and Emmy had faced off, and he'd lost. She'd followed his initial objection with a laundry list of reasons why it was, in fact, not the worst idea in the world to have his colleagues—and his boss—over. *Show them another, more casual side of you*, she'd said. *Ply them with drinks. Relax a little. We can totally change their hearts.*

He had held out, he really had, until Jace had joined the argument on Emmy's side. He'd had to pause then, and let it sink in that in a few short weeks of exposure to Emmy, Jace was not only making eye contact now, he was voluntarily engaging in conversation.

We can totally change their hearts.

Part of him thought then, *hell, maybe she's right.* Maybe she could wave her magic Emmy wand, extend her quiet competence to the morass that was his professional life, and, through some kind of alchemical voodoo, deliver him the greatest wish of his heart: tenure. Job security for life, which would mean he had finally and fully broken from his past.

And he could not deny that once he'd stopped objecting and relaxed a little, he'd had fun this evening. In addition to

Jace being as engaged as Evan had ever seen him, it had been great to meet Mrs. Johansen's…boyfriend? Suitor?

He picked up a towel and started drying the dishes that Emmy had set in the drainer. "I guess we can't keep calling Mr. Widmer SilverCEO now that he actually has a name,"

"Well, not to his face," Emmy said as she handed him a pot to dry. "But I don't know how long he's going to stick around anyway."

"Really?" Evan had been meaning to have a dishwasher installed since he moved in, but there was something satisfying about doing the dishes by hand. Or, to be honest, there was something satisfying about doing the dishes with another person as you gossiped, a party of two in cahoots.

"Yeah," Emmy said. "Mrs. Johansen has been messaging with this other guy, Dave344."

"Dave344?" Evan echoed, the incredulity in his voice suggesting that he was maybe a little too invested in the internet dating adventures of his elderly neighbor. "What kind of screen name is that? Even the dreaded JollyGent was more creative."

Emmy shrugged. "The heart wants what the heart wants, I guess."

"And what about SilverCEO?" Evan walked across the kitchen to put away a pile of cutlery he'd dried.

"She says he's looking to get too serious."

"And she wants to, what? Have a friends-with-benefits type thing?" Okay, it was official. He was getting too invested in the love life of his elderly neighbor.

Emmy paused with her hands in the sudsy dishwater and cocked her head as she looked out the small window above the sink. "That's exactly what she wants."

Evan coughed to cover his shock.

"She told me that her husband was the love of her life,"

Emmy went on, still staring out the window, dishes forgotten. "She says she's not looking to replace him."

Evan wasn't sure what to say. Emmy seemed to be almost in a trance, to have left the kitchen behind and gone somewhere else in her mind. But then she snapped out of it and turned to him. "Have you ever been in love?"

Evan almost dropped the dish he was drying. "I, ah, had a pretty serious girlfriend for a couple years back in Miami."

She nodded, and didn't call him on the fact that he hadn't actually answered her question. "What happened?"

"She took off when everything blew up." He snorted. "Or, more to the point, when I went from riches to rags. Dumped me a couple days before Tyrone and Vicky's wedding, in fact. I got in trouble because they'd already paid for her meal."

"Bitch."

Evan reared back a little. He'd never heard Emmy speak so forcefully. In fact, he'd never really heard her say an unkind word about anyone, come to think of it.

"Sorry," she said. "I just…hate that." The way she spoke made him wonder if they were talking about more than him. She shook her head. "But okay. What about now? Kaylee's in love with you, but there must be some actual adult women in this town, too."

"Kaylee is not in love with me," he said, and when she was about to protest he added, "Anyway, I'm too busy for a relationship." It was the truth. "Tenure is what's important right now."

Maybe if he said it enough, it would stick in his goddamned head.

"Come on," she said, passing him the last dish and drying her hands on a towel. "We have a puzzle to finish."

Exhibit B on the "Emmy invading his life" front was later that night when, after they'd finished the stupid hot air balloon puzzle she'd bought at the mall and she'd gone to bed, he went up to the attic again.

He told himself he wasn't going to paint Emmy. And at first, he hadn't.

He started with Mrs. Johansen, going back in his mind's eye to the night she'd been getting ready for her date with JollyGent. He'd wanted to paint her then. The idea had reasserted itself earlier this evening as they'd all eaten Emmy's burgers. And when Jace had played the latest incarnation of his song for everyone, Evan had taken out his phone ostensibly to record him but really to get a snapshot of Mrs. Johansen.

So it wasn't like he could even pretend that this was an impulsive move. He'd planned it. Premeditated. He'd waited until Emmy went to bed, and he'd snuck up to the attic like a delinquent kid.

And he'd painted Mrs. Johansen's date face, complete with the red lips Emmy had painted on her.

And then he had stared at those red lips for a long time. So long and so intently, in fact, that his eyes started to water. So long that they took on an almost holographic quality, changing from the image he'd actually painted—Mrs. Johansen's lips, which were somewhat on the thin side and stained a deeper red where the pigment had settled into her wrinkles—and another one. Another set of red lips. Also thin but not as thin as Mrs. Johansen's. Smooth and curled up into a knowing half-smile.

He started with her mouth on the second canvas, ignoring the beating of his heart and the dryness of his mouth as he methodically broke one of the rules that governed his life. A rule that was the line in the sand between then and now. Between the life he'd been handed and the life he'd earned. A rule that made him the man he was—the man he wanted to be: *he didn't paint.*

And, worse, when he was finished with one incarnation of Emmy's mouth, he did it again.

This time he painted her mouth with smudged lipstick, the way it might be after kissing.

He worked until he heard the birds start chirping.

Standing back, looking at two Emmys and one Mrs. Johansen, he tried to make himself destroy the canvases like he had last time. He could still go back. He could still be a person who didn't paint because he didn't deserve to, because he wasn't coasting on entitlement and ill-gotten gains. A person who didn't capitulate when his presumptuous houseguest started meddling in his professional life.

He heard the first chords of her new song, as clear in his head as if she were standing in front of him playing.

He moved the canvases to the far corner of the attic, taking care to make sure they didn't touch anything so they could dry properly.

CHAPTER TWELVE

"Are you sure this is a good idea?" Emmy asked as she came to a careful stop at a traffic light outside the gates to Dane College's leafy campus, which was an island of sorts in the middle of farm fields on the north end of town. "I mean, do you think I'm ready? Am I good enough?"

"Ready for what?" Mrs. Johansen asked from the passenger seat. "Are we picking up the pope?"

"I know, but he's—"

"Right there," said Mrs. Johansen, cranking down the window of her ancient LeSabre. "Evan!" she called.

The emotions that passed over Evan's face were almost comical. Confusion when he caught sight of Mrs. Johansen on campus. And then, ultimately, bewilderment when he saw Emmy driving.

But there had been something else in there, in between, Emmy was pretty sure.

And it had looked a heck of a lot like happiness.

The idea that he was glad to see her, that her unscheduled appearance on his turf made him happy, if only for an instant before his better judgment took over? Well, that was a pretty great feeling.

But she didn't get to enjoy it for very long, because she had to concentrate to park. On previous parallel parking attempts —Dane's downtown was all street parking—she had ended up either scraping the curb or parked two feet from it. To be fair, though, Mrs. Johansen's Buick was a tank.

"How'd I do?" she asked as Mrs. Johansen opened the passenger door to inspect her work.

"A-plus," Mrs. Johansen said.

"Yes!" Emmy pumped her fist, enjoying a surge of triumph. Only then did she look back at Evan. "Hey, stranger. Want a ride to the mall?" Emmy and Mrs. Johansen were getting some driving practice in before Jace's preliminary song-writing contest. Evan, who'd ridden his bike to the office to get a few things done on a quiet Saturday morning, had planned to meet them at the mall for the performances. But when she and Mrs. Johansen had found themselves near campus, they'd impulsively decided to look for him.

Evan had a weird expression on his face. She was about to assure him that it was fine, that he should bike to the mall as planned—having him in the car would make her nervous anyway—but then he said, "I'd love a ride," and hopped into the back seat.

Evan thought he was an old hand at faking enthusiasm over the questionable artistic output of teenagers. The community center program had honed his poker face abilities. But this. This was awful. Seeing bad art with your eyes, it turned out, was nowhere near as painful as hearing it with your ears.

To wit, the awkward, bespectacled girl of about fourteen

tunelessly lurching her way through a song that Emmy whisper-informed him was a blatant rip-off of "Anaconda" by someone named Nicki Minaj.

"Do you think she really has a gun in her purse?" he whispered. "Because I would like to use it to put myself out of my misery."

"Shhh," Emmy said, but she was suppressing a smile. "This one looks more promising."

Another girl of about fourteen, awkward but less so than the plagiarist, was playing the opening notes of a song on the piano. And Emmy was right—the tune was catchy. And when the girl started singing, he realized with a sinking feeling that the lyrics were, too. It was a song about looking up to but also hating her older sister, which seemed to him perfectly relevant subject matter for a kid. "Uh oh," he whispered, just as Mrs. Johansen leaned in from his other side and said, "Well, shit."

Emmy nodded, lips pressed into a severe line and gaze riveted to the girl. She stayed that way through the whole performance, clapping along with everyone else, but not with the enthusiasm of the rest of the audience. The juxtaposition between her grim visage and her applause was actually kind of funny, as was her "disguise," which today featured a shirt that said, "Did I Roll My Eyes Out Loud" in her usual tent size, along with the jeans and hat. The only concession she'd made was to remove her sunglasses in the dim mall.

They watched the next two performers in silence. Neither of them seemed to Evan to be real contenders. Jace, thanks to a random draw, was up last. By the time he ambled onto the stage in new jeans and a crisp white T-shirt, Evan's stomach was a little heavy. But he had nothing, it appeared, on Emmy, who was pressing one forearm into her stomach as if she might be sick. The other hand covered her mouth entirely, like she was the "speak-no-evil" monkey.

He wondered how many music industry bigwigs would get this invested in the fate of a sixteen-year-old poor kid from Nowhere, Iowa.

When Jace started strumming, Emmy started nodding. They were little nods at first, but they gradually gained scope and speed, and about halfway through the song she lowered both arms and her gaze darted around. Everyone was smiling and clapping along—because Jace was killing it. Evan watched Emmy realize as much. A smile blossomed, and she joined in the clapping, alternating between looking at Jace and looking at the crowd.

When it was over and the crowd went wild, she found his gaze. Her eyes glistened and her mouth had fallen open in an *O* of happiness. That huge shirt concealed a great deal, not the least of which was an equally huge heart.

They shared a moment as everyone around them leapt to their feet, whistling and carrying on. He was going to say, "You did it," but he stopped himself when he realized he wasn't sure exactly what he would be referring to if he said that. The fact that Jace had clearly won the competition, sure, but also that she'd learned to drive. That she'd mastered burger-making. That, judging by what he'd heard over the past month or so, she had half a dozen amazing songs done for her new album.

She broke eye contact, but not before flashing him a huge, unguarded grin. She jumped to her feet, then kept jumping as she clapped and whistled and waved at her prodigy.

Jace was a lucky sonofabitch.

CHAPTER THIRTEEN

Emmy was pretty sure she knew what the word *collegial* meant. It came from "colleagues," right? A bunch of friendly people with a joint interest in their shared environment?

But this group... Well, to be fair, maybe it was impossible to be collegial when your leader was basically Voldemort. But still, the barbeque was worse than a junior high dance. Larry was holding court with Evan's male colleagues, while the women stood in two separate clumps—cliques, Emmy couldn't help thinking—at the far end of the yard. Emmy had made the rounds trying to chat with people—chat with them about *anything*, forget her original plan of trying to make Evan look good. But her appearance in each group had pretty much shut down the conversation entirely.

"I think maybe more alcohol is the answer," Mrs. Johansen said, coming to stand next to Emmy in the kitchen, where she'd retreated to catch her breath.

"The answer to what?" Emmy said, though she knew perfectly well what Mrs. Johansen was getting at. "Wait, let's play Jeopardy. The question is, 'How can we take the collective stick out of this party's collective ass?'"

"Yes," said Mrs. Johansen, "and I think we should start with Larry. I suspect he's a mean drunk, but that would at least spice things up."

"Good plan," said Emmy, picking up her phone to google "extremely alcoholic drinks."

Mrs. Johansen swatted her away, though, and stood, hands on hips, eyeing the assortment of alcohol that had appeared on Evan's kitchen table thanks to the BYOB aspect of the evening's invitation. After a moment of silent contemplation, she nodded decisively, grabbed a few bottles, and said, "Give me a bowl."

"Oh my God, this is actually amazing," said Emmy a few minutes later, sipping from a Dixie cup full of the concoction, which, as far as she could tell from observing Mrs. Johansen's mad bartender skills, seemed to be thirty percent vodka, thirty percent chocolate liqueur, and thirty percent Kahlua—and one hundred percent alcoholically delicious.

"Wait!" said Mrs. Johansen, emerging from Evan's refrigerator with a spray can of whipped cream and depositing a dollop on the surface of Emmy's drink.

"Mrs. Johansen, you are a genius," Emmy said, tipping her head back and chugging the sweet, strong concoction. "An evil genius. Now, let's set up an assembly line."

Whitney Davis was drunk. It took Evan a while to come to that conclusion, but once he did, it was painfully obvious. He had been chatting, or trying to, with his famously taciturn colleague. Though she was one of the world's foremost experts on Diane Arbus, a photographer who had managed to capture humanity in a way no one before her ever had, Whitney wasn't known for her people skills. Or her humor. Or anything that might give a clue that she was an actual human being and not an art-history robot. She was on his tenure committee, and he had no earthly idea how she would vote.

But when she burst out laughing at a lame pun he'd made, he started to get suspicious. He eyed her cup. It was empty.

As if on cue, Emmy appeared bearing a tray. He'd seen her passing out drinks but hadn't paid much attention as they looked like the kind of frothy monstrosities he hated. "Another drink, Professor Davis?" she asked, beaming.

Whitney hesitated.

Emmy said, "And then when I'm done passing out this batch, will you tell me a little about your work? I've heard such great things about it!"

Whitney smiled. It was a strange look for her. "Oh, twist my arm!"

Emmy made an exaggerated arm twisting motion, handed Whitney another drink, and started to spin away, throwing Evan a wink as she did so.

He interrupted her progress by grabbing one of the drinks for himself.

"Oh, I don't think these are really your—"

When he started to down it, she stopped speaking midsentence and fled.

"Oh my God," he sputtered, coughing to clear the sickly sweetness from his throat. He was pretty sure Emmy was serving up straight booze disguised as liquid candy.

"Isn't it delicious?" Whitney said.

"Yes," he said, his eyes following Emmy as she flitted around the party, plying the guests with her lethal drinks. He started to register, then, that the entire tenor of the party had changed. The usual clusters had broken up. A couple people had cracked out the old croquet set that had come with the house. And Larry. Larry was *laughing*.

He watched Emmy give away her last cup and head back into the house.

Well, hot damn.

♫

"I don't know if I should be thanking you or..."

Emmy's whole body tightened as Evan materialized behind her, speaking low into her ear, which wasn't necessary given that the only other people in the kitchen were a couple of his colleagues, and they were having a loud debate over the origins of the typography on the Beefeater gin bottle.

"Or what?" she said, pitching her voice low to meet his. She was almost baiting him, which wasn't wise, but she was a little drunk, and her body wanted him to fill in the rest of the threat.

"Evan, man, great party," said one of the Beefeaters, a man of about forty.

Emmy felt the loss of Evan's body behind her as he pulled away, which was ridiculous because he hadn't even been touching her.

"Yeah," agreed the other, a thirtysomething woman she thought might be named Melissa. "Hey, do you hike by chance? A few of us are going hiking next weekend. You free?"

Evan started to answer but Emmy intervened. "He is not free." Evan started to say something, but she talked over him. "He's taking one of his community center kids to the Minnesota State Fair to compete in a songwriting competition," she said, smiling brightly.

"Community center kids?" Dude Beefeater echoed.

"Yep," said Emmy. Her brain was fuzzy from one too many whipped cream Dixie cups, and she couldn't remember if Dude Beefeater was on Evan's tenure committee. But it didn't really matter, because they all talked to each other, right? Or at least they did after this party. Hopefully. When they got over their hangovers. Heh. She laughed at her own thoughts, but then, realizing everyone was looking at her, remembered that she was supposed to be talking. "Evan runs an arts group at the community center for underprivileged kids." He started to object, but she moved—lurched, really, though she'd tried her darndest to be graceful—in front of him to keep control of the conversation. True, she had no idea if those kids were underprivileged. Jace certainly was, but she didn't know about the others. But she was laying it on thick here. Like a layer of whipped cream on top of the truth. "He mentors them," she went on.

"I wouldn't really say—"

"And there's one kid with this crazy musical ability," she went on, dimly aware that she was practically shouting. She made a concerted effort to tone it down before continuing. "His mom can't get off work to take him to the fair for the competition, so Evan is doing it."

There. She'd gotten it all out. Triumphant, she smiled and crossed her arms over her chest.

The Beefeater who might or might not be named Melissa was smiling indulgently. "Can I say I think it's so cute that you have such a supportive girlfriend, Evan? She's your biggest cheerleader, isn't she?"

"She's not my girlfriend," Evan said as Emmy was about to say the same thing. It was just that her lips wouldn't move as fast as his.

Maybe Melissa's eyes narrowed. "You look familiar," she said to Emmy. "Did you go to Dane College?"

That sobered Emmy right up. "Nope!" she trilled as the brain fog lifted, replaced by adrenaline-spike-induced clarity. "Just visiting. Evan and I are old friends. Our families are intermarried. Sort of." Never mind that it wasn't technically true, since it was only Evan's friend who had married Emmy's cousin. "So we're kind of like in-laws. Sort of."

All three of them—the Beefeaters and Evan—were looking at her strangely.

"Okay!" she said, trying to be subtle as she searched the kitchen for her abandoned hat. "Nice to chat with you guys. I'm going to head out and do some cleanup."

What she actually did was hide in the garden. She dragged a chaise longue to the very far back corner of the yard, where she was mostly obscured by large lilac bushes, and looked up at the star-studded sky.

…And woke up who knows how much later when she sensed someone's presence looming over her.

She opened her eyes. "Evan," she said, sleepy and happy. The fear that she'd been in danger of being discovered had been borne away by her little nap, leaving her in a pleasant buzzy state. She wasn't drunk like she'd been before, just uncharacteristically loose. Relaxed.

It wasn't a familiar feeling, but it was an awesome one.

Part of it was the satisfaction of a task completed. She'd planned the party. She'd executed the party. It had gone well. But part of it was something else. This place. This summer.

"Is everyone gone?" she asked, rubbing her eyes.

"Yep," he said, and as she pulled her legs up and gestured to the extended part of the chaise, he lowered himself to sit. But then he surprised her by reaching for her legs and guiding them back to where they had been, which meant they extended over his lap. It was the way a couple of long standing would watch TV, one reclining, half draped over the other.

Except she needed to revise that analogy, because she was pretty sure that couples of long standing vegging out in front of *Homeland* didn't do it sporting boners. Or lady boners. His she could feel clear as anything under her calf, and he either didn't realize that her leg was there or didn't care. Hers, as he rested his hands lightly on her bare shins, was intensifying—moisture gathered between her legs and her nipples hardened to almost painful peaks.

God damn it. Her defenses were down, thanks to the booze and the contentment. It was going to be hard to enforce the Summer of No Men thing in this state.

"Thanks for the party, Emmy," he said, his voice gravelly, which wasn't helping. "You are insane, but thank you. I think your evil aims were achieved."

She was sober now, so she couldn't blame booze for what she said next. "And here I was, going to vote for Option B."

"Pardon me?"

"What you said before—you didn't know if you should thank me or…"

"You don't even know what Option B was," he said, sounding almost angry.

She shrugged. "I'm feeling lucky." She was treading on dangerous ground, but that boner under her leg…it made her brave.

"Fuck, Emmy," he muttered before turning and straddling the chaise. It had the effect of removing any contact between them, and she was about to register her displeasure when he pressed a hand on each of her ankles. Grabbed them. He was still for a long moment with his hands around her ankles. It was too dark to read his face. His hands, heavy and hot, were shackles. She wanted them to stay there, but she also wanted them to move up, up toward the center of her body, to her core, which was on fire, throbbing as surely as the pulse in her throat, which was beating so frantically she had to press a hand to her neck and will herself to breathe. She would have been embarrassed at how obvious her desire no doubt was, but she was protected by the darkness, and he was breathing hard, too.

How to break the standoff? Who would move first?

Him. She was surprised there wasn't a burst of steam when he finally took his hands off her ankles. She moved forward to meet him halfway, except…

He wasn't there. He'd stood and moved away, hands on his hips, staring into the dark yard of his back neighbor. There was another whispered, "Fuck," but this one was different than the first. Dismay had replaced desire.

He didn't say anything else, and after several long moments she had to conclude he wasn't going to. She got up and started for the house. She knew how to take a hint.

"I'm sorry," he said. His back was still to her, but he sounded so tortured that he stopped her in her tracks. "I'm so sorry. I don't know why I keep doing this. I know this isn't what either of us wants." Then he turned. It was still too dark to see his face, but she could feel his eyes on her.

She was tempted to object, to raise her hand, to say, "I do. I want it." But of course he was right, elementally, even if he hadn't used exactly the right word. She might want him, but this summer was supposed to be about what she *needed*—freedom, independence, a break from her usual patterns.

So she shrugged, affected a light tone, and said, "It's okay. We both had a fair amount to drink." Which had absolutely nothing to do with what had happened, and they both knew it.

"Right," he finally said, the urgency drained from his voice. "Well…thanks for the party, Emmy."

CHAPTER FOURTEEN

By the time they set out for Minnesota the next weekend, things were almost unbearable. Evan wasn't sure how he had fucked things up so badly. Well, that wasn't true. He knew exactly how: he'd practically rubbed his dick on Emmy's leg, shamelessly letting her feel what she did to him, and then he'd done some kind of weird caveman-possession thing with her ankles. He'd been thinking only of touching every part of her skin. Of starting at her feet and working his way up. He'd wanted—needed—to put his hands all over her, like she was a statue he had the power to animate or some shit.

But he'd forgotten—*again*—the critical context: they were living in a bubble. Yes, they could have a one-night stand, or a one-summer stand or whatever, but the key point was that bubbles always burst. She wasn't going to hide out in his house forever. Hell, he didn't *want* her to. They were playing with fire. They'd been lucky so far in that she was mostly lying low, and when she did go out her disguise seemed to work. But it was only a matter of time. There was also the equally important point that the bubble wasn't about sex for her. It was about songwriting. Finding her feet again.

It was Emmy's Summer of No Men. And how did he respond to that? By putting his hands all over her? God, he was an asshole.

Despite his self-flagellating, Emmy had been acting normal. Or trying to. She had developed a new pattern: she would get up early, make breakfast, and leave him a portion before heading out on a walk he was pretty sure was designed to minimize face time with him. Often, when he arrived home from the office, Mrs. Johansen was at his house or Emmy was at Mrs. Johansen's. Gone were the cozy evenings spent on the porch, working side by side. When they did have to be together, she was perfectly friendly, and so was he, but it felt like they were actors playing parts. There was an artificiality about their interactions that felt weirdly formal.

But, amazingly, the odd stiffness between them wasn't enough to extinguish the *attraction* between them. It was still there, underneath everything else. It was there all the time, like a third person in the house. No, like a ghost. A relentless motherfucker rattling his chains and howling, intent on dogging Evan's every move.

And he was painting. Every night.

He couldn't stop. Was no longer sure he even wanted to. While he was painting, the ghost went away, allowing him to channel all his restlessness, all his anxiety, all his lust, into his work. He was still overcome with disgust at the end of a session, though, like a junkie coming off a bender. It wasn't like he was ever going to show any of the paintings, so what the hell was his endgame? When would it stop? When the summer was over, and Emmy left, he hoped. At least that's what he told himself every time he mounted the stairs to the attic.

So even though he hadn't initially been crazy about the idea of their field trip to the Minnesota State Fair, by the time he pulled the Subaru around from the garage in back to the front of the house so they could load it up, he was all in. Sure, it meant a long drive with Emmy in the car and then two days with her in close proximity, but they had their teenage chaperone—Evan and Jace would share a hotel room—and he hoped everyone's focus on the competition would let some of the pressure out of his relationship with Emmy. And more importantly, he couldn't paint at the Marriott Courtyard Minneapolis. So maybe he could use the time to calm the fuck down and get out of his own head.

As Evan got out of the car, Jace, whose mom had dropped him off that morning, popped the trunk and threw in his guitar and backpack. Evan added his stuff—a gym bag and a computer case. As if on cue, Emmy appeared at the front door, decked out in her usual "going out" attire: "Not So Basic," this shirt said. He was pretty sure that was a joke he wasn't getting. She had her guitar slung over her shoulder and was pulling her suitcase with her other hand.

"What is *in* here?" Jace asked, making a face as he took the suitcase from her and hefted it down the stairs. "We're only going for two days, you know."

Emmy glanced at Evan, and then away.

Of course, he hadn't thought of it, but she only had the big suitcase she'd come with. "I can loan you a backpack," he said, "or a carry-on-sized suitcase."

"That's okay," she said, jogging down the steps from the porch and taking over management of the suitcase from Jace.

He watched her struggle with it for a moment as she tried to get it started rolling over the uneven cobblestones of the path that led from his house to the street. "Let me," he said, easily overcoming her resistance when she tried to object.

"Man, this *is* heavy," he said as he hoisted it into the trunk. What did she have in there? A hundred baggy shirts?

"Actually," she said, looking at the ground like Jace used to do, "I'm going to stay in Minneapolis for the rest of the summer."

"What?" he said, blinking. The question had come out neutrally, which was kind of amazing given that the corresponding "*What?!?!*" inside his head had been shrieked by a chorus of indignant banshees.

"Yeah, I figured it was time to get out of your hair." She opened the rear passenger-side door and said to Jace, "You sit in the front. You have much longer legs than I do."

Evan was on her in an instant, grabbing her elbow before she could get in the car. "You don't have to leave."

She looked at him sadly for a moment. "I kind of do."

"But…you haven't finished—"

She coughed, and the sadness on her face turned to admonishment as she hitched her head slightly toward Jace.

Right. He couldn't ask about the album in front of Jace.

But what could he have said anyway? *Please stay even though I can't seem to stop mauling you? Not to mention the fact that I didn't want you here to begin with?*

"Anyway," she said, her voice dripping with artificial enthusiasm, "I'll get to spend some time with my parents! It's gonna be great."

It *was* great. Surprisingly. Emmy had expected the ride to Minnesota to be as uncomfortable as the last week in Evan's house had been, but having Jace with them made all the difference. Emmy had made a playlist for the trip. Jace hadn't heard most of the songs—she'd put some obscure stuff on there—and he wasn't shy about sharing his opinions. They alternated between talking about the upcoming competition—it felt like a shared sense of mission was kicking in—and listening to the songs. The miles went by much more companionably than she'd expected.

"Have you ever heard anything by Emerson Quinn?" Jace asked as the last song on Emmy's playlist wound down.

Adrenaline surged through Emmy, and she whipped her head up to meet Evan's alarmed eyes in the rearview mirror. "Um," she began, and then had to pause and clear her throat because she sounded like a chipmunk. "Yeah, I've heard some of her stuff."

"What about you, Professor Winslow?"

"Can't say that I have," Evan said, and damn him, he thought this was *funny*. He was pressing his lips together like he was trying not to laugh, and his eyes were twinkling like he was in a contact lens commercial. "But I'm notoriously not plugged in to pop culture." He turned to Jace. "What do you think of her? Are you a fan?"

Was he kidding? Was he insane? Was he trying to give her a coronary? Emmy started to scooch down in her seat.

"I used to think she was kind of fluffy," Jace said, "but I got her last album, and it's actually really good."

"I have to go to the bathroom!" Emmy shouted.

Evan dutifully exited the highway, and Emmy breathed a sigh of relief that the interruption succeeded in derailing Jace's critique of…her.

When she emerged from the bathroom a few minutes later, neither Evan nor Jace was at the car, so she took a moment to collect herself, walking over to the vending machines. She was mindlessly staring at rows of candy when Evan appeared behind her. She felt him before he spoke.

"Do you have the album done?"

"I've made a great start." It was the truth.

"A great start is not enough."

She turned. "What's it to you?"

He took a step back, like she'd slapped him. Instead of answering her question, he said, "Your parents disowned you when you decided to pursue music. And now you're skipping off to see them like it's no big deal? You think that's going to be a good environment to finish the album in?"

"What's it to you?" she said again, as if repeating the same question might actually get him to answer it. She didn't mean it in a confrontational way, just to point out that he, especially given his extreme aversion to her fame, wasn't invested in her decisions.

She'd been hoping to end her time with Evan on a not-sour note, to slink away and not make a big deal of it. She was going to be eternally grateful to him for creating a haven for her these past six weeks. Even if he was right, even if she didn't manage to write a single note in Minnesota, she'd written eight pretty damned amazing songs at Evan's, and no one could take that away from her. Hell, she'd also learned to drive. And cook. And perform various household tasks. She felt a little bit bad about—

"Who's going to help me with the art show?"

That. She sighed. Abandoning her work on the art show was the one thing she couldn't square with herself when she'd decided to leave Iowa early. She knew the show was a big deal, both because Evan cared about it and cared about his town, but also because it was a tool to impress his colleagues and help bolster his tenure bid.

As bad as she felt about bailing, she couldn't stay. Couldn't sit on the porch working side by side with him, watching the fireflies emerge, and pretend that there was nothing between them. She wasn't supposed to want him. *He* didn't want *her*. There was no way out but to save herself. She had to listen to Maude. She could only hope she was capable of continuing to write when she *wasn't* sitting on the porch with him. "Look, I—"

"Hey guys, can we go to the fair this afternoon when we get to town?" Jace ambled up to join them. Saved by the adolescent cowboy. "You know, to get the lay of the land?"

Evan huffed a frustrated-sounding exhale, but he pasted a smile on his face as he turned to Jace. "Fine by me." Then he looked at Emmy as if in search of her agreement.

She hadn't been planning to go to the fair with them. Being from Minnesota, she ran the real fear of being recognized not only by fans but by actual people she knew. She'd been planning to hang out in the hotel room. Maybe make Evan FaceTime her Jace's performance. She hadn't yet figured out a way to tell Jace that she wasn't going, though.

"Also, I want to say thank you." Jace reverted to his old, shy self, shuffling his foot on the pavement and not making eye contact. "To both of you, but mostly to you, Emmy. You know, for helping me so much."

Wow. It was a day for high emotion, apparently. "Oh, Jace—"

He held up a hand, apparently not done speaking. "And even if I don't win—even if I come in dead last—I don't care. I'm glad I get to perform in public with you in the audience. I just want you to see me, and I want to make you proud."

Emmy sniffed. Well, fuck it. Her disguise had worked perfectly this summer. And her Iowa retreat was over regardless, so what did it matter if she was spotted in Minnesota? In a warped sort of way, it would be the perfect ending to this summer. If she was discovered, Evan would run for the hills, and that would be that. A decisive break.

She hugged Jace. "There's nowhere else I'd rather be."

CHAPTER FIFTEEN

"Deep-fried cheese curds?" Evan liked to think of himself as an adventurous person, and that included eating, his usual diet of casseroles aside. But…blobs of cheese covered in some kind of breading and dunked in a vat of boiling oil? Wanda had them on her menu in Dane, but he'd always steered *way* clear of them.

"Just *try* it," Emmy entreated. She was literally bouncing up and down, buzzing with happiness. The weirdness between them at the rest stop had evaporated. Erased by the magic of the Minnesota State Fair? He had no idea, but hell, he'd take it.

So he played it up, popping the disgusting orange-brown blob into his mouth, and… "Oh my God."

"Toldya," she said, gloating.

"Wow," he said, hoovering curd number two, "that is inexplicably, amazingly delicious." He looked around, suddenly panicking. Where was Jace? Had he fallen down on his chaperone duties because of deep-fried cheese?

"He's in line over there for candied bacon donut sliders,"

Emmy said, reading his mind and pointing to a concession stand fifty or so yards away.

He breathed a sigh of relief. They'd established with Jace's mom that she was okay with the almost-seventeen-year-old being on his own a bit, but Evan wasn't sure he was. Jace was talking animatedly (Jace was talking animatedly!) with a teenage girl who was also in the line. Evan narrowed his eyes.

"Oh, calm down," Emmy said, apparently still reading his mind. "He's *right there*."

Evan watched the girl laugh at something Jace said, and then when they got to the front of the line, Jace bought the girl one of the deep-fried monstrosities. He turned to Emmy, his eyebrows raised. "And that's why his mom works sixty hours a week? So he can buy some girl he hardly knows an overpriced meat donut?"

"Shhh! He's coming over!"

"All right," Evan said, clapping his hands together once the boy reached them. "What's next?"

"Seed art," said Emmy decisively.

"Huh?" said Evan, momentarily distracted from his mission to protect Jace's purity.

"Yeah, like portraits of famous people made out of seeds. You know, like Lucille Ball or Abe Lincoln?"

"We are going to make pictures of I Love Lucy out of seeds?" Evan said. Now he'd heard everything.

"No!" she scoffed. "We're going to *look* at the pictures. In the fine art building!" She grabbed his arm, and he hated how much he liked it. "It will be right up your alley, Professor Winslow."

"Yeah, um, actually…" Jace began, reminding Evan anew that he was there. Shit, he *sucked* at this chaperoning thing. Both he and Emmy turned to their charge. "I was thinking I might split off from you guys for a bit?"

Evan was about to answer with a "Hell, no," when Emmy said, "Who's your friend there?" Evan followed her gaze. The girl Jace had been talking to was still hanging around the donut stand, and she was doing it in a very obviously fake casual way.

"Her name's Brianna. She's showing her cow here."

"She's showing her cow here?" Evan repeated. The Minnesota State Fair must have either messed with his hearing or lowered his IQ or both, because he was apparently reduced to repeating everything Emmy and Jace said. But in his defense, phrases like "seed art" and "showing her cow" weren't things that easily computed in his brain.

"Yeah, it's a 4-H thing," Jace explained, and Evan didn't even bother asking what 4-H was. "She's raised a Jersey and now she's part of the 4-H Dairy Showcase."

The 4-H Dairy Showcase. Yet another mystery phrase.

He opened his mouth to object, but Emmy said, "You have to bring her over here for us to meet her first, and you have to keep your phone on."

"But—" Before Evan could get a full sentence in, Jace bounded off to fetch his dairy date.

"Oh come on," Emmy said. "He's nearly seventeen. And I think it will be good for him. It's not like he ever talks to anyone, let alone girls, at home. I mean, in Dane."

Evan didn't miss the way she corrected herself. Didn't like it, either. Of course, Dane *wasn't* her home, but still, it grated on him. And it grated on him that it grated on him.

So, basically, he was turning into a cranky old man. He might as well start shaking his fist and yelling, "Get off my lawn!" Knowing Emmy was right, he swallowed his fear and smiled through introductions and listened as Emmy extracted information from Jace's new friend. She was from Owatonna, which he gathered was a rural Minnesota place. She had been raising cows since before she could walk. She was in town for the duration of the fair with her parents. She was going to give Jace an insider's tour of the livestock barn.

It was all very on the up-and-up. For God's sake, given what he knew about the social lives of some of his college students, who were only a couple years older, Jace and Brianna's date was practically taking place in the fifties. So after extracting one more promise to check in via text periodically, Evan reluctantly watched the teenagers depart.

"It's going to be fine," said Emmy, and when he didn't respond right away, she grabbed his hand and said, "Come on, we have seeds to marvel over."

Evan was, as Emmy had predicted, really into the seed art.

She watched him make his second round of the exhibit, getting right up close to the display panels like he was a detective looking for evidence.

She tried not to check out his ass while he did so.

She sighed. She was going to miss him so much. Honestly, she'd never met anyone like him. She couldn't really put it into words, but he felt like…protection. Not in a gross, sexist way, but more like he stood between her and the grasping world that always wanted something from her. He was a buffer, which had been such a profound relief.

"This is extraordinary," he said, coming to stand by her. "Folk art at its finest."

"Hey!" she exclaimed. "Maybe you could study this."

"I just might," he said. Then he pointed to one of the creations. "Who is that?"

She laughed. "Katy Perry."

"Right," he said.

"You have no idea who that is, do you?"

"I do not."

She took his arm. "Come on. Next stop, the midway."

"I'm not really a ride person," he said.

"Too bad." She tugged to get him moving. "We lost Jace, and I need someone to go on the Ferris wheel with me."

Twenty minutes later, they were ascending said wheel.

"When you said 'Ferris wheel,' I was imagining something...gentler," Evan said as they rose toward the top of the ride.

It was true. The ride was actually a double Ferris wheel, or at least that's what everyone called it, and it consisted of two wheels that rotated both on their own and around each other, like a binary star system.

"We're at the top!" she said. They had slowly been working their way up, pausing every few feet as a new car on the bottom was loaded. Man, she loved this view—she'd forgotten how much. "That's the St. Paul campus of the University of Minnesota," she said, pointing to the experimental farm fields that abutted the fairgrounds. "And look at the fair! It seems so huge when you're down there, but you can see everything from up here. Everyone looks like ants!"

She turned to him and was startled to find he wasn't looking at anything she was pointing out. He was looking at her with a strange, intense expression.

"Come back to Dane with me, Emmy. Finish your album."

"I can't," she said. "I—ahhh!"

The deceptive thing about the Ferris wheel at the fair was that once it got going, it went *fast*. This was no mild county fair kiddie ride.

"Ahhh!" she shrieked again, no longer able to focus,

through the exhilaration, on mustering an argument as to why she couldn't return to Iowa.

Maybe this was what Mrs. Johansen meant. *Live the life that's in front of you.* As they spun faster and faster, there was no room for anything else, for the past or the future, or for worries that someone would recognize her. All she could do was hang on and enjoy the ride—literally. *Live the life that's in front of you.* This was an extreme example, in that circumstances were forcing that stance. But why couldn't she, in theory, do this every day?

She looked at Evan again. He was still staring at her, but the intensity that had been in his gaze earlier was gone. He was grinning from ear to ear, his wide smile looking like it was in danger of cracking open his face.

She laughed, and he did, too. They laughed like there was nothing to worry about in the world, not now or ever again.

It was over too soon.

But, somehow, its effects lingered.

As they made a dinner of Pronto Pups, lemonade, and warm chocolate chip cookies, they talked and laughed easily, delighting in the sights and sounds of the fair. They visited the refrigerated building where the fair's dairy princesses were having their likenesses sculpted in butter, had their skulls read by an old-fashioned phrenology machine, and lost a ridiculous amount of money playing skee-ball.

"Oh, hang on now!" said Evan, pointing to a darts game where players tried to pop balloons pinned to a board at the back of the booth. "I don't like to brag, but I am actually a killer dart player."

"You are?" Emmy said, delighted by the idea. It seemed so at odds with his serious persona.

"Yep. I think I spent more time playing darts in the grad student pub during my PhD than I actually did studying."

"*Really?*" said Emmy, still unable to picture it.

"Yep." He reached into his back pocket for the wad of game tickets they'd bought. "It was my escape from all the shit that went down with my dad." He huffed a bitter laugh. "I used to pretend the dartboard was him, and later, the goddamned photographers who stalked the trial."

She chuckled. "Oh, I know *that* impulse."

He pointed at the prizes that were hung from the booth's ceiling. "So pick one out, my friend."

"Aren't these things always rigged?"

In response, Evan cracked his knuckles and accepted the five darts the operator handed him in exchange for his tickets.

Then, one by one, he lined up his shots, flicked his hand, and popped five balloons.

"Yay!" Emmy was surprised at how happy his victory made her.

When the operator asked Evan if he wanted to pick a small prize or play again for the possibility of trading up for a larger one, he silently handed the guy more tickets.

And popped five more balloons.

She couldn't pretend it wasn't ridiculously hot. There shouldn't have been anything inherently attractive about a man popping balloons with darts, and yet… The focus. The competence. The confidence. Damn, she was going to miss him.

"Ha!" Evan pumped a fist in the air, having completed his last round and scored a prize of the highest order.

"Take your pick." The operator gestured toward the huge stuffed animals hanging from one end of the booth.

Since it appeared her choices were a giant Bart Simpson, a giant Dora the Explorer, and a giant Care Bear, she went with the Care Bear. "I'll take the pink one with the rainbow on its belly."

"Cheer Bear," the grizzled carnival operator said—someone less kind would have called him a carny—and she laughed in delight, both at her prize and at the fact that this man knew Cheer Bear's name.

As Emmy was turning to thank Evan, his phone rang. He picked it up.

"Where are you? Okay, but I don't think—wait. Jace! Jace? Oh, hello Mrs. Kendall. Yes, I'm Evan Winslow, Jace's chaperone. Well, I don't want him to be any imposition." There was a long pause while Evan nodded and furrowed his brow. "Are you sure, because really—" More furrowing. "Okay, if you're sure." Nodding. "All right. Let's meet at the front gate, then."

Emmy grinned as he hung up. "Jace and Brianna, sitting in a tree!"

He rolled his eyes. "That, as I'm sure you surmised, was Brianna's mom. They've invited him to dinner. Apparently Brianna has three sisters. We're going to the front gate now to do the meet-and-greet."

Emmy hit the restroom before they arrived at the front gate, leaving Evan to meet Brianna's parents. It was better for her not to talk one-on-one with people if she could avoid it.

"They're dropping him off at our hotel around nine," Evan said when she emerged. He paused and looked at his watch. "That will mean we'll go four hours without having him around. Man, do I suck as a chaperone or what?"

She patted his arm. "What's going to happen with her parents around?"

Evan looked almost pained. "He showed me a text from his mom saying it was okay."

"Then stop worrying. I'm sure that defense will hold up in a court of law."

"What?" he said, looking stricken.

"I'm kidding!" She hoisted Cheer Bear higher on her hip.

"What do you say we go back to the hotel and consume a vegetable that has not been deep-fried? I'm beat." It had to be ninety degrees, and she was wearing the baggy T-shirt and jeans uniform that she'd developed in Iowa. It had proven reliable as a disguise but it was hot as hell. She looked around and lowered her voice. "And I kind of want to quit while I'm ahead. I almost can't believe I got away with this."

Evan took the bear from her, tucked it under one arm, and offered her his other one. "You got it."

CHAPTER SIXTEEN

Evan knocked on the door connecting his and Jace's room with Emmy's. "Food is here," he called. They'd ordered salads and a bottle of wine from room service but had it delivered to him in order to reduce the possibility of anyone knowing that Emerson Quinn was in the hotel.

She swung open the door, and damned if she didn't take his breath away. She had showered—as had he—and her hair was wet, starting to dry in waves around her face. And she was wearing her indoor clothes. The tank top and shorts were nothing remarkable. Hell, the shorts were one of the pairs she'd gotten at the mall in Dane. But the overall look was so familiar, so...*her* that it made his heart twist.

And she was holding that stupid, giant bear.

"Hey," she said softly, smiling.

He had to stifle a gasp. She'd taken her colored contacts out, and the true blue of her eyes was a jolt to the system, like it was every time he saw them. He stepped back and gestured for her to come into his room, feeling a little like he should bow or something, like he was a footman making way for his queen.

She threw the bear on one of the beds and moved toward the table room service had laid. "After everything I consumed today, there is no way I should be hungry now."

"And yet," he said, his own stomach growling at the sight of the two Caesar salads and accompanying bread basket.

"And yet," she agreed, lowering herself into a chair.

"It must be a relief to have all those clothes off," he said, sitting across from her. Wait. Did that sound pervy?

"It so is," she said, twisting the corkscrew into the bottle of Sauvignon Blanc he'd ordered. She poured them both generous glasses and lifted hers in a toast. "To Jace." Then the corners of her lips curled up like she had thought about a secret pleasure. "To romance."

He knew she was talking about Jace and Brianna, but there was some empty part of him that those words fell into, and once there, they clattered around uncomfortably.

She took a drink of her wine, then lowered her glass and looked right at him. Looked at him so intently he felt like she could see into that hollow, unpadded, vulnerable place that kept getting poked by her words. "So things have been kind of weird between us lately."

He opened his mouth to respond, though he wasn't sure if he should agree or object. Before he could decide, she held up a palm to silence him.

"You know it's true. Anyway, bear with me. I'm going somewhere with this." He nodded, and she continued. "Do you remember when we were talking about Mrs. Johansen's Zen outlook on life?"

"I do."

"And how I made this probably mostly incoherent speech about how I keep trying to live the unexamined life or whatever and it keeps backfiring?"

He chuckled. "To listen to Maude or not to listen to Maude, that is the question."

"Yes," she said, nodding vehemently. "When I was on that Ferris wheel, I suddenly got it."

"Got what?" he asked, sitting up straighter. She had leaned forward so much and had such a serious look on her face that he felt like a kid under the scrutiny of the principal.

"Live the life in front of you," she said. "That's what Mrs. Johansen says, right? When I was on that ride, that's all I could do. You know what I mean?"

He nodded. "There wasn't room for anything else." He'd felt it, too. It wasn't like they'd been in any real danger, but the ride had been just fast enough, just thrilling enough, that he hadn't been able to do anything except let the exhilaration course through him. He didn't tell her that he thought part of the effect, though, had been her. Maybe the lion's share of the effect. Watching her mouth fall open, listening to her shriek in delight, shivering when she grabbed his arm. It had been like that night on the porch—she was all around him, and there had been no choice but to lose himself in the experience. Lose himself in her.

Suddenly, she picked up her fork and started pushing her salad leaves around her plate. She'd clearly been working up to some kind of question or announcement or something, but now she was nervous. Not knowing what else to do, he picked up his own fork.

It was halfway to his mouth when she looked directly at him. "I don't really know how to say this, so I'm just going to say it."

"Okay." He speared a crouton.

"Will you have sex with me?"

The fork clattered to his plate, bounced off it, and both fork and crouton went flying a very impressive distance.

She smiled. "Hear me out."

He blinked rapidly, nodding. Talking wasn't something he could do right now anyway.

The smile turned into a giggle. "You should put your hand down."

Huh? Oh, right. His arm was still suspended in midair, holding a now-imaginary fork. He managed to lower it even though it felt like it belonged to someone else entirely, like it was no longer attached to his body. Perhaps because most of the blood in said body had traveled south in response to her bold question.

"The thing is," she went on, "I never get to have sex, unless I'm in a relationship."

He cleared his throat.

"I can't do a casual hookup. It's too risky. Is there a hidden camera somewhere? Am I going to—"

"*Wait. What?*" he interrupted, suddenly finding his words.

She looked startled. "Yeah, people filming you without you realizing?"

He knew what a hidden camera was. He just could not fathom the epic assholery that would compel a man to secretly film his sex partner. In general. But the idea of someone doing it to *Emmy* in particular? Jesus Christ, his poor body. Now the blood felt like it had rushed out of his dick and into his arms. His fingers flexed. He wanted to punch someone.

"I'm always afraid I'm going to wind up on TMZ the next day. Or not even that. Sometimes they take a picture of you while you're sleeping—especially the not-famous ones. They might not even be planning to do anything with it. Maybe it's merely a trophy of sorts. But you have to demand their phones before you leave." She blew out a bitter breath. "I got that piece of advice from a female rock legend who shall remain nameless. And I only had to do that once—find a picture of me half-naked on this guy's phone. He seemed like a nice guy, but… Yeah, so, that was my one and only post-fame casual hookup with a civilian."

Evan blinked rapidly. It was almost impossible to just sit there and listen to this.

"So you restrict yourself to other famous people because you both have something to lose," she went on, her speech picking up speed. "There's an unspoken pact. Everyone has careers to protect. But then…" Her voice caught, and she swallowed hard.

"Then what?" he prompted, probably too gruffly, but he needed to know.

She made a resigned, almost self-deprecating face. "I end up with a broken heart. The press thinks I'm all calculating. Like I'm using men for material for songs. But I swear to God, every single time, I think it's going to be different."

"And it never is," he said.

"That's right," she answered, though he hadn't meant it as a question. "When I look back, I can see clearly that most of them were using me."

"How do you mean?"

"I don't mean this to sound conceited, but I'm more famous than most other celebrities."

"That's not conceit. That's the truth."

"So, yeah, even if there was genuine affection there, I think most of my exes were using me, too, at least partially, to bring attention to their movies or their records. Like, most of them would *try* to get photographed by the paparazzi when we were together." She pinched the bridge of her nose like she was in pain. "But mind you, these great insights are always after the fact. At the time, I go all in, and because I'm *stupid*, I fall for these guys. And then when the inevitable heartbreak gets served up, I get gun-shy and all closed up for a while. Until it happens *again*."

He suddenly knew what to do with the robotic arm, the one that had gone from not feeling like his to feeling like it belonged to the Incredible Hulk. He would give it to her. It was *hers*. So he slid his palm across the table, right into her space, so there could be no mistaking the invitation. He stopped short of actually grabbing her hand, because he didn't want to be another entitled jerk taking shit from her. "You're not stupid," he said softly.

She rested her hand over the top of his, which he took to be enough of a green light for him to flip his own hand and squeeze hers. She smiled—a little bitterly—and said, "Yeah, so, it's hard to find people to have sex with, is the point. And we're parting ways after the show tomorrow." She bit her lower lip, her smile turning a little embarrassed. "And there seems to be um…" She waved her free hand back and forth in the space between them.

"A wild, unquenchable attraction between us?" he asked. He was teasing, but it was the truth. Trying to ignore it after the barbeque was what had make things so weird between them recently. It was a relief to have it out in the open.

She laughed again. He loved seeing her laugh. He loved *making* her laugh. "Yeah," she said. "But also trust. I *trust* you. I trust you unreservedly." Her expression turned quizzical. "I'm not sure that's ever happened. Even…before."

It was like a lance to his chest, and also, to be honest, to his dick. He'd never have thought that the concept of trust could be so lust-inducing, but here he was, holding Emmy's hand over uneaten Caesar salads and feeling like the fucking king of the world.

"I'm not gonna get all starry-eyed on you, I promise," she said. "I wouldn't be going into this like I usually do, with my expectations ratcheted way up. I know we can't be together, not really. That's sort of the point. We're parting ways tomorrow anyway…and, well…here we are now with some time to kill." She giggled at that last bit.

God. If she didn't stop with this strangely paradoxically innocent come-on, things were going to be over before they even began.

And they were *going* to begin, because honestly, what man could resist her proposal? Her argument was airtight. They would probably never see each other again since she wasn't coming back to Iowa with him. They'd pulled off their crazy caper. Emerson Quinn had lived in his house for a good chunk of the summer, and no one had found out. By the end of the day tomorrow, the threat of being caught up again in the whirlwind of fame would be gone. He'd be back to his quiet, normal life.

And, more urgently, he wanted her so very, very badly. His body practically vibrated with it. A man could only stand so much pent-up desire, and he had wanted her since she'd shown up on his doorstep a month and a half ago. Hell, he'd wanted her since she was a too-young-for-him bridesmaid seven years ago.

And now there was absolutely no logical reason to say no. She'd methodically torn down every barrier that stood in the way of him finally, finally getting what he wanted, what he'd thought he could never have, what it felt like he'd spent his whole life resisting.

But he also wanted to do this *for* her. He wanted her to feel safe. He wanted to give her pleasure that was truly no-strings attached, because he was pretty sure no one ever had.

He squeezed her hand even tighter as he looked at his watch. "We have an hour till Jace gets here."

She took that for the assent that it was, and pressed her

lips together like she was trying not to grin. "An hour is a long time."

He licked his lips. "An hour is not a very long time for what I plan to do to you."

Her mouth fell open, but he merely shrugged. It was the simple truth.

"Do you have any condoms?" he asked.

Her gaze whipped up to meet his. "Shit. No! Do you?"

He shook his head and looked at his watch, mentally calculating how long it would take him to go down to the hotel gift shop to buy some.

"I have an IUD, though," she said. "And I got tested before the Summer of No Men. So if you're clean..." She trailed off half hopefully, half seductively.

This negotiation should have been awkward, but it wasn't. It was like now that they had established their mutual attraction and their intent to act on it, the details had lost their power to embarrass. "It's been a bit of a dry spell for me," he said. "I haven't wanted to get entangled with anyone in Dane. Half the town is connected to the college, and—"

"You never know when you're going to run into a nineteen-year-old who isn't being totally upfront about her age?" she teased.

"Ding, ding, ding." He pointed at her. "Yeah, so when I go to conferences in other cities, which is maybe twice a year, I usually hook up with someone on Tinder. I've always—"

She held up her hand. "You don't have to give me your entire sexual history."

"I disagree." He spoke sharply, causing her eyes to widen, but it was because he felt strongly about the matter. "I think if you're going to have sex with someone, Emmy, they most decidedly do owe you their sexual history." She blushed. He had shocked her. "I always used condoms. I didn't with my last girlfriend, the one I told you about, in Florida, who bailed when my dad's trial started. She was on the pill. I was tested at my last physical, which was six months ago, and there hasn't been anyone since."

She took a deep, shaky breath. "Why was that little speech so hot?"

He laughed. "Regardless, I will happily go downstairs for condoms." In fact, despite the fact there was virtually no risk, that was the responsible thing to do. He stood. Or tried to. She didn't release his hand as he tried to raise himself, which left him sort of awkwardly slouching while she remained sitting at the table.

"I trust you," she whispered. "That's the whole point here, isn't it? *I trust you.*" She spoke with amazement in her voice, and damn, it went straight to his ego. And possibly other places.

He was still holding her hand, so he tugged on it, bringing her to her feet. He hitched his head toward the connecting door. "Shall we retire to your room? In case Jace is early?"

"Definitely my room." She glanced at his phone on the table and added, "And set an alarm or something." He did as she asked, then led her across the room and held the door for her, instructing himself not to lunge at her when they were on the other side. He didn't want to do anything to puncture the trust she had in him.

She lunged at *him.*

Threw herself into his arms, full-out leaping off the floor.

And he laughed and caught her, like it was the most natural thing in the world.

Because it was.

She wrapped her legs around his waist, put her nose to his, and said, "You must work out," a joking reference to the other time she'd awkwardly said that.

"Yeah," he rasped, letting his mouth move over hers as he spoke. "Especially this summer. I've had a lot of shit to sublimate."

"Oh, yeah?" she said, tipping her head back, a clear invitation for him to pay some attention to her neck.

So he pressed some open-mouthed kisses against the smooth skin there before saying, "Yeah, this ridiculously hot woman showed up on my doorstep, and she's been in my house all summer."

"Mmmm," Emmy said. "Tell me more."

He took a couple steps toward the bed, and she tightened her legs around his waist.

"She walks around all day wearing these tiny little shorts—that is, when she's not wearing muumuus with funny sayings on them—and she has legs that go on forever. It's hard not to look at them and imagine what they'd feel like wrapped around you."

She moaned, and he took it as encouragement to continue, as well as to take a few more steps toward the bed. He was tempted to add something about how she made everything easier, working and eating dinner and…being in the world, but he was pretty sure that wasn't the vibe that was called for here, so he would stick with his laundry list of lust. "And she has these perfect little tits. I'm pretty sure she doesn't wear a bra, and even though it's been hot as hell, her nipples seem like they're always at attention."

"She sounds like a little tease," Emmy choked out.

He continued their slow march to the bed. "That's the thing," he said, moving his hands down from where they were clasped around her back so he could grab her ass. "I don't think it's intentional. I don't think she knows how sexy she is."

Emmy gasped, and he continued his verbal assault.

"I'm sure, for instance, that she has no idea how much I

want to taste one of those cheeky little nipples." He rubbed his face against the skin of her collarbones, probably too roughly because he hadn't shaved this morning, so he was sporting two days' worth of stubble. "Because I have a feeling they would taste like cherries or something fucking ridiculous like that."

"Cherries?" She was panting and laughing at the same time, and the combination shouldn't have been so potent, but it made his dick even harder. "That's a pretty tall order."

His shins hit the edge of the bed, and he lifted his head to meet her gaze. He grinned and shrugged. "I don't know. Maybe strawberries?"

She stared back at him with an insolent expression. "So why don't you find out, then?"

He paused for a moment, their eyes locked as he instructed himself to savor this moment, this point at which he stood on the brink, about to devour her. She felt like…his muse. An astonishing thought he shoved away for later examination as he dropped her on the bed. She squirmed and laughed uproariously, and he lifted her tank top, exposing both her breasts. He pinned her hands down and straddled her. He didn't put all his weight on her, but he did let her feel what she did to him. It was the same strange impulse as the other night in the garden. He'd been almost angry then, wanting her to know how much she tormented him. The impulse to show her was still there, but the anger was gone. He cocked his head and contemplated her beautiful breasts. They were small and pert and perfect, handfuls of white flesh topped by pink nubs that did really call to mind berries. To tease her—God, he loved teasing her—he said, "Hmmm… raspberries? Loganberries?" But then he thought seriously for a moment about them. What color paint would he use? Permanent Rose? No, not on its own. Maybe mixed with a little Cadmium Red Medium, though.

"Loganberries?" she echoed. "Do you even know what loganberries taste like?"

"Yes," he said, composing his face into a parody of seriousness. "I may be hopelessly ill-informed when it comes to pop culture, but I'm one of the world's foremost experts on berries." She burst out laughing. "You probably didn't know that because I don't like to brag," he added, marveling that such silliness could ensue yet not even remotely be a boner-killer.

Still, it was time to get this show on the road, to do more than look at her like she was sitting for a goddamned painting.

So he made good on her invitation/threat, set his glasses on the nightstand, and lowered his mouth to one of her nipples. He didn't waste any time teasing, simply took the whole thing into his mouth.

"Oh!" she cried out, and he circled his tongue over the sharp little nub, trying to make her do it again.

She did, and it went straight to his dick.

Then she tried to push him off. She was laughing, so he held her down, pulling back just enough to check that she didn't really want to escape, and satisfied that she didn't, said, "Hmmm, maybe not loganberries, but lingonberries."

"Like at Ikea?" She grinned. "Take your shirt off."

He obeyed, relishing the little intake of breath that resulted. "I think so," he said, going back to the berry question. "But I am going to need more data." He sat up and leaned back against the headboard of the bed, then swung her onto his lap so she was straddling him. "Unnnh," he groaned when they made contact. He pulled her tank top the rest of the way off, grabbed the cheeks of her ass to anchor her, and lowered his mouth to her other breast.

God. He had been teasing. She didn't really taste like berries, but she tasted So. Damned. Good. She was tarter than a berry, almost salty, and as he was level with her neck, the scent of her surrounded him.

"Jesus, Emmy," he said as she started grinding on him. "I want to taste you everywhere."

"I don't think we have time for that," she said. "Alas." Panting, she lifted herself off his lap. He was about to object but shut his mouth when he saw that she was taking off her shorts. She must have pulled off her underwear with them too, or else she wasn't wearing any—*Christ*. She had a small patch of blond hair but was otherwise bare.

"Emmy," he growled. He let his eyes roam up and down, taking in the whole sight of her. She was lean and graceful and… "Gorgeous," he whispered, hurrying to shed his own shorts.

"Oh," she said, and he followed her gaze to his dick. "It's big," she whispered.

He laughed. It was big—not porn star huge, but he'd assembled enough commentary from women to know that he was larger than average. "We don't have to—"

"Hell, yes, we do," she said, interrupting his attempt to reassure her.

He grinned. Honestly, never before had he had a sexual experience so infused with joy, with laughter.

"Pronto pup," she said, and his mind struggled to grasp why she was suddenly invoking a corn dog, the iconic state fair food they'd indulged in hours ago.

"No, wait." She giggled. "Maybe corn on the cob?" He felt his brow furrow, and she said, "I'm trying to figure out what *you'll* taste like."

Aww, hell. He let his head fall back against the headboard at the same time that he said, "Get over here, Emmy."

But then the goddamned phone beeped.

"What is that?" she wailed, just as she was about to climb onto his lap.

"Fuck," he ground out, grabbing the phone to silence it. "It's eight thirty. I set an alarm for eight thirty and another for eight forty-five, which I figured was as late as we could go." They were going to have to speed things up, and the injustice of it practically gutted him. "So what do you want to do?" he asked.

"I wanna taste you," she said, sliding down the bed.

It took all he had to stop her. "And I want that too, but seriously, we only have fifteen minutes, if we want to make sure we don't get caught. We have to prioritize here."

She burst out laughing. "We have to *prioritize*?"

He grinned. "Yeah. Triage sex. So tell me what you want, most of all."

She turned a little pink, and when she spoke, her voice was soft. "I'm not good at talking about this stuff."

He took her hand and pulled her back onto his lap. She buried her face in his chest. "About what stuff? About sex? Because it seems like you've been doing a fine job so far." He tipped her chin up. "So tell me. Because I want what you want."

She took a deep breath and said, "Then I want you to fuck me—fast and hard."

He had them flipped in an instant. "Good choice," he growled, spreading her thighs and drawing his fingers experimentally across her folds. She was wet. She moaned. "Do you like that?" he asked, and she nodded vigorously. "Tell me what you like about it," he exhorted her. If she was usually shy talking about sex, he wanted to be the man who made her shameless. And if they only had this one time together, he wanted her to *remember* it.

"I like the pressure," she said. "Of your fingers."

He increased the pressure, and she drew in a sharp breath. "What do you like about the pressure?" he prompted her, taking a long, slow breath to try to beat back the familiar tension growing in his lower back.

"I like how your fingers are hard against where I'm soft."

"Yeah?" he said, putting his mouth back on one of her nipples.

"I like how they tease me, like they're a preview of this."

A hand snaked around his dick and he groaned, then nipped her breast in return.

"A preview of what?" he asked, almost taunting her. The time for teasing was done, and he wanted to hear her say it. He liked the dirty-mouthed Emmy.

"A preview of your cock," she answered immediately. "Of what it's going to feel like inside me, stretching me out."

They were almost out of time, and not only because the clock was ticking. She had moved her hand around to gently squeeze his balls, but he batted it away and took himself in hand. He paused at her entrance, raising his eyebrows in a silent question.

"Yes," she said.

They both cried out as he breached her hot, tight channel. He started moving, attempting to go slowly, but she was arching and grinding against him, and after a few strokes, on the brink of losing his mind, he started slamming into her and using one hand to rub her clit. He watched her closely, trying to gauge what kind of pressure she liked, to learn what made her gasp the loudest. He would have been embarrassed at how quickly his orgasm came barreling down on him, except for the fact that she beat him to it, freezing for a moment in her writhing to stare at him in silent, wide-eyed astonishment before her inner muscles started fluttering and clenching around him.

"Oh my God!" she whispered.

Then the alarm went off.

She lifted her head, which looked like it took a lot of effort, and started laughing.

He wrapped his arms around her, holding her tight, and laughed, too.

CHAPTER SEVENTEEN

Emmy was rather pleased with herself as she lay in bed that night waiting for sleep to come. Well, fighting off sleep, to be more accurate. She was exhausted, but she wanted to spend a few moments basking in the aftermath of the best day she'd had in a long time. And it hadn't been just the sex. She hadn't been prepared for how much flat-out fun the fair had been. She'd been there every year as a kid, but seeing and experiencing it anew through Evan's eyes had been exhilarating. And bickering good-naturedly with him about Jace going off with Brianna had all felt so deliciously, joyfully... *normal.*

But okay, who was she kidding? The basking she was doing? It was ninety-nine percent about the sex.

God, it was almost like that had been her first time. But honestly, it had been like nothing she'd ever experienced before. The absence of the fear that she'd told him about—that someone she was sleeping with would compromise her—had created a safe space. She had suspected she would be more comfortable with him—that's why she'd propositioned him to begin with—but she'd had no idea how much power that fear had held over her all these years. Because *holy shit.*

Maybe it wasn't only the absence of that fear, though. Maybe it was Evan in particular. Everything he did made her feel safe. The importance he placed on discussing their sexual histories, the way he encouraged her to say specifically what she wanted.

And the laughing. She also hadn't known that sex could be so funny but simultaneously be so hot. She'd never laughed like that with a man.

All of that had swirled together to create some kind of alchemical magic that, to be crude, had resulted in her coming harder than she ever had.

Or ever would again, she feared.

God, she was getting hot thinking about it, despite her exhaustion. Sighing, she rolled over and wrapped her arms around Cheer Bear. Maybe she'd have some good sex dreams.

Oh my God, she *was* having a sex dream. She sighed, luxuriating in the sensation of him stroking her back.

"Emmy," he whispered.

"Mmmm," she purred, but she was waking up. She fought against it. She hadn't even got to the good parts yet. So she kept her eyes closed and concentrated on the deep breaths she hoped would lull her back into full sleep, trying to grasp at the tendrils of the dream, to use them to lever herself back into it.

"Emmy." His voice, though still a whisper, was a little louder this time, and all of a sudden it wasn't just his hand against her back, it was all of him. She burrowed back against the hardness of him—his solid chest, his erection nestled up against her bottom.

She smiled in the darkness. "You're real?"

He reached a hand around and threaded it up her shirt

and lightly stroked her stomach, whispering, "As far as I know."

"I thought I was dreaming," Then reality, unwelcome as it was, truly hit her. "Where's Jace?" she whispered urgently. They had all watched some TV together when Jace got home, she and Jace forcing Evan to watch the shallowest show they could find, which had been a rerun of *Real Housewives of Orange County*, and teasing him as he treated it like an archaeological expedition. Then she'd taken her leave and retreated into her own room.

"He's asleep. It's three in the morning."

She tried to turn to face him, but he banded an arm around her, keeping her back snug against his front. "What are you doing here?"

"I need to borrow a cup of sugar," he said without missing a beat. "What do you think I'm doing here?"

The words, hovering somewhere between a whisper and a growl, went straight to her core.

"Being with you earlier was amazing, but it was too damned rushed," he went on. She was going to argue, to tell him that sometimes rushed was exactly what the doctor ordered, but when he said, "I can't stop thinking about how much I want to take my time with you," slid a hand down under the waistband of the stretchy sleep shorts she was wearing, and teased her clit, she shut her mouth.

Shut it over his fingers, to be precise, because she used one of her hands to grab the arm that had been keeping her prisoner, stuck his first two fingers into her mouth, and sucked on them.

It made his dick pulse against her, which, in turn made her bolder. She took his fingers deeper, and he used his other hand to enter her. "Jesus Christ, Emmy, one hand in your mouth and one hand in your…" He moaned, and so did she.

Letting his fingers come out of her mouth with a pop, she tried to turn over again, and this time he let her. She kissed him, opening her mouth the moment their lips met, accepting the deep sweeps of his tongue into her mouth and licking into his in return. They sank into each other for a long time, kissing and letting their restless hands roam and stroke. For his part, he would tease her clit for a while, start getting her ramped up, and then he'd back off, and move to stroking her collarbones, or her hair. It was both delicious and maddening, and it went on and on. He hadn't been kidding about taking his time.

Just when she was about to tell him she couldn't take it anymore, to use her newfound directness to order him to get on with it, he pushed her onto her back. It was a sweet relief. She couldn't wait. She was still a bit sore from last time, but she craved that delicious burning sensation of being breached by him, and— "Oh my God."

He was going down on her.

"Evan!" she cried as he licked across her slit. She didn't know whether she meant to encourage him or to stop him, but either way, she'd spoken too loudly. Jace was on the other side of the wall, and though she assumed Evan had locked the connecting door, their teenage charge *couldn't* discover them like this.

Evan slid back up Emmy's body, holding himself over her with one arm and clamping his other hand over her mouth.

"We're going to play a game," he said. "Are you ready?"

She nodded, trying to calm her heart.

He kept his hand over her mouth as he spoke. "This is what's going to happen. I'm going to eat you out. I'm going to feast on you, actually." An involuntary whimper escaped, even with his hand over her mouth. "And you're going to lie there and take it, and you're not going to make a sound." He stared at her silently for a moment, and she was sure she was blushing so intensely that she was glowing red, even in the dark. "Okay?" he asked.

She nodded vigorously, because she wanted that, too. Oh, how she wanted that, and she wasn't going to risk even a whispered *yes* that might endanger the likelihood of her getting what she wanted.

He removed his hand slowly, like he wasn't sure he could trust her. She forced herself to meet his gaze unflinchingly, even as her heart beat a crazy rhythm she could feel directly between her legs. It was like her body, having heard him state his intentions so boldly, had decided to light the way for him. When he still didn't move, merely remained where he was, like he was trying to memorize her or something, she used the toe of one foot to catch the top of her shorts and panties, which he had only shoved down as far as her knees.

The movement seemed to jolt him, and he came to life, pushing himself back down her body and finishing the task of undressing her from the bottom. Then, suddenly, they were back on the lounge chair in his backyard, because he banded his hands around her ankles like he had that night. It was quieter here, though, their hotel room lacking the soundtrack of cicadas and leaves rustling in the wind, so she could hear his labored breathing. And he didn't stop at her ankles this time. No, his big hands moved slowly but decidedly upward, exactly as she'd wished they would that night. She felt like she had a fever; her body didn't know whether to be hot or cold, to shiver or shudder. She wanted to yell, to curse him, to exhort him to move faster, but she bit down on her lip, hard. She hadn't shaved her legs since yesterday morning, and the hotel's air conditioning was powerful, so as he made his way up her shins, he encountered stubble. She had enough non-stunned brain capacity left to spare a thought that maybe she should be embarrassed. Certainly if anyone had a picture of her leg right now, tomorrow she'd find a horrible zoomed-in version in a "Celebrities—they're just like us" feature in some rag.

But instead, inexplicably, it was the single most erotic thing that had ever happened to her. The room was so silent, his hands made a slight scratching noise as they traversed her legs, the little prickles providing drag.

He didn't have his mouth on her—yet—but his face was tracking closely behind his hands as he made his way up her legs, close enough that his hair flopped into his face and tickled her skin as he went. She exhaled a shaky breath, and finally, *finally*, he reached the top of her thighs. He hooked his thumbs in the crease where her thighs met her hips and rotated her legs outward, so they fell open for him.

She squirmed, hot, restless, aching. He responded by pressing down hard on her thighs, immobilizing her. Then he stretched out his legs. He had crawled up on his hands and knees as he'd made his way up her body, but now he lay flat on his stomach with his head between her legs.

And then, oh God, he lowered his mouth to her. He didn't move it at first, just exhaled a couple times, the heat of his breath coming through lips that rested unmoving against hot flesh, like he was breathing life into her. She tried to lift her hips, to rock into him, but he continued to pin her to the bed. He waited a moment, ignoring her silent plea, before he finally began moving his mouth. He licked her outer folds, and she swallowed a gasp. He used his nose—his entire face—to nudge them open to reach a deeper part of her, and she swallowed a scream. When he plunged his tongue inside her, she couldn't do it anymore—a whimper escaped.

She was surprised he didn't stop, didn't scold her, but one of his hands did come off her, floated up a few inches, and then came back down on as much of her butt cheek as he could reach in their position, a little slap of admonishment.

Oh shit. She grabbed Cheer Bear and stuffed his ear into her mouth. She was going to come.

He must have sensed it because he moved his mouth to her clit and sucked on it gently, and that was the end.

She came and came and came, with a teddy bear in her mouth and *her* in his mouth.

♫

He didn't want to leave.

Evan extricated himself from Emmy's arms enough to crane his neck to see the digital clock on the nightstand. It was four thirty.

Shit.

He'd been lying in Emmy's bed for fifteen minutes, and he was nowhere near recovered from what had been the most intense orgasm of his life.

Emmy. He had forced himself to stay awake after their encounter, promising himself he'd stay only long enough to catch his breath. But she had fallen right asleep, exhausted, he flattered himself, after two orgasms. And maybe also—still flattering himself here, probably—because she knew she was safe. Safe with him like she hadn't been with anyone else. He didn't want to go back to his room. He didn't want to walk around the fair all day tomorrow and pretend there was nothing between them.

He wanted more. He wanted her to swallow his cock again, like she had earlier, nearly causing him to have a nuclear meltdown, but he wanted to do it at high noon, with the full force of the Midwestern sun beaming down on them so that he could see *everything*, her pink lips stretched around him,

JENNY HOLIDAY

that little ring of gold in her blue eyes peeking up at him from behind her lashes. And, as hot as their little silence game earlier had been, he wanted to hear her moan. No, he wanted to hear her *scream.*

But—fuck—he wanted more than that, even. He wanted to be able to fall asleep with her. He wanted to wake up with her in his arms. *In his house.* Then he wanted to eat her oatmeal and go grade some fucking exams while she fiddled around on her guitar. He wanted her to finish that goddamned album.

But he was an adult. An adult who had learned, better than most, he suspected, that you can't always get what you want.

So, with the last vestiges of his will, he climbed out of bed.

She looked younger when she was asleep, more like the nineteen-year-old he'd met so long ago. Or maybe it wasn't younger so much as less guarded. He understood, from being with her and from listening to her stories, how hard she had to work to keep her guard up. How it had to be up all the time. How elementally alone she was.

Her bear had fallen onto the floor, so he bent over to retrieve it, then tucked it into bed with her.

He had almost made it out of the room when she stirred.

"Evan?" she whispered, and he knew—feared—that in that moment he would do anything she asked. Give up anything.

"Yes?" he answered, heart pounding.

"You really do suck at chaperoning."

CHAPTER EIGHTEEN

Evan was sheepish in the morning. He didn't regret anything. He shifted in a booth at the hotel restaurant as memories of last night washed over him. No, a man would have to be insane to regret the best sex of his life.

Just that he was a bit embarrassed over the strength of his emotional reaction, how nearly unhinged he'd become simply watching her sleep. But, he reminded himself, *sleep* was the key word there. No one had witnessed his little gushfest. No one had heard his interior monologue about how exposed she was, how in need of haven and protection. He just didn't know what it was going to be like when—

"Hey."

Emmy, bundled back up in her baggy armor, slid into the booth across from him and nodded her thanks when a server appeared offering coffee. "Jace will be here shortly. He fell back asleep after you left." She upended a creamer into her coffee. "He sleeps like the dead, which turns out to be kind of handy." She shot him a playful grin. "Retrospectively, I mean."

He breathed a sigh of relief. Okay, so it wasn't going to be awkward. That would make it much easier to say goodbye after the competition tonight.

When the server came back, Emmy declined to order any food. He raised his eyebrows. "I'm going to my parents' for brunch," she said, and like that, the impish light in her eyes went out.

Unsure how to respond—other than to curse her parents —he raised the eyebrows higher.

She sighed. "I know. I just…"

"You want them to love you," he finished.

The way her eyes widened and filmed over with moisture told him he had hit the mark. He couldn't say he understood. He maintained a cordial relationship with his mother and brother, but some things were too wrenching. Sometimes the past—and the people from it—had to stay in the past. But she was kinder than he was.

"Even though they threw you out," he added. He didn't want to make her feel worse, but he did want to remind her of the context.

"Isn't that dumb?" she said. She'd been trying for cheerful self-deprecation, but it hadn't worked—she deflated right before his eyes. "I don't know why I keep trying. I guess because I want them to understand that doing music…wasn't a mistake."

"How can they not understand that?" he said, trying—and probably failing—to temper his anger. "For God's sake, look at you."

She shook her head. "It's more like…I want them to understand that I love it. *Why* I love it."

"I'll come with you," he said, suddenly determined. She was making a mistake, but he wasn't going to let her make it alone. Even if they only had this last little bit of time together, he still felt protective of her. Still saw it as his job to try to create a safe space for her to…be her.

She smiled, and for a moment it looked like the tears that had been threatening were going to spill over, but she beat them back, staying true to her declaration from earlier that summer that she was not a crier. "Thanks, but I'll be okay. My assistant Tony, who's also a great friend, is coming with me."

"Well, then it will be three against two," Evan said, because now that he'd decided, he wasn't backing down.

He could tell she was about to protest, but he could also see Jace entering the restaurant. He waved the teenager over.

"Hey," he said, when Jace slid in beside Emmy. "Slight change of plan. We're going to drop you at the fair for the rehearsal and then catch up with you later. I need to help Emmy with something."

Emmy was about to object, he could tell, but Jace cracked a smile, and said, "What happened to Mr. Overprotective?"

Evan looked at Emmy as he answered Jace. "I'm over it."

Or, to be more accurate, he'd transferred it to someone else.

Emmy had made arrangements to meet her assistant at a coffee shop near her parents' house.

"Tony!" she said as they entered. A tall, slim man sitting near the door stood and moved toward Emmy with his arms open. She stepped right into them, and they held each other for a long time. Then Tony wordlessly handed her a coffee that was no doubt doctored exactly to her specifications. Evan had no idea how Emmy took her coffee.

When Emmy and her assistant parted, Tony's gaze

whipped to Evan. It was an unimpressed gaze. He might even go so far as to call it openly hostile.

He stepped forward and offered his hand. "Evan Winslow."

Tony didn't reciprocate, so Evan, feeling like an idiot, retracted his hand. "And what, pray tell, are you doing here, Evan Winslow?"

"The same thing you are, I imagine," he said, allowing his tone to grow as skeptical as Tony's.

Tony's eyebrows shot up. Probably, as Emmy's assistant, he wasn't used to sass. "And what might that be? Humor me."

Evan gave up the pissing contest and answered honestly. "Showing up for Team Emmy duty."

That must have been the right answer, because Tony smiled and stuck out his hand, and they shook.

"So what's going on with Brian and Claudia?" Emmy whispered. Then she turned to Evan and said, "My managers."

Tony shrugged. "They're freaking out, of course. But they don't have your new phone number. You have your new credit card. Don't worry about anything else. I'm handling it."

Evan found himself glad that Emmy had Tony in her life.

Selfishly, he was also glad that Tony was around, because whereas Emmy had spoken only generally about her parents, and reluctantly so, Tony had no compunctions about filling Evan in on exactly what Emmy's parents were like.

"You should have seen them the day we told them we were moving to L.A." Tony was driving—they'd decided to leave Evan's car at the coffee shop and go together in Tony's—and he kept glancing over at Evan, who was in the passenger seat, as he talked. "They accused me of seducing their daughter." He laughed uproariously. "I think I was wearing a Louis Vuitton scarf over a rainbow T-shirt. I assured them that I was gay as the day was long, but somehow that didn't help."

"What did they do?"

"There was nothing they could do. She was nineteen. She hadn't lived at home since she was seventeen."

Evan turning around to look at Emmy. "You never told me you were *seventeen* when they kicked you out." He knew it had happened after her aborted driving lessons, but somehow he'd imagined it happening…later. "Where did you live?"

"With friends," said Emmy. "I couch-surfed while I finished high school. I didn't think it was a good idea to move in with Tony until I was eighteen. I was afraid my parents might actually get the cops involved. So I spent a year with friends, then a year with Tony, then we moved."

Evan whistled. This was a lot more sinister than he had imagined.

"Yeah, it was harsh," Tony said. "They thought it was tough love, but they didn't understand that their kid was tougher than they were."

"Or that she was talented enough to blow the lid off the music industry," Evan said. He could understand a little parental reluctance, but honestly, anyone who paid any attention to Emmy and her songs, even back then, he imagined, would have had to see the potential there.

"I like you, Evan Winslow," Tony said, though he was looking in the rearview mirror at Emmy as he spoke. At the next red light, he turned his attention to Evan. "You should have seen her when she came to me. She had this proto-riot-grrl look—you know how teenagers sort of try on different personas? But her music was tending toward rootsy-Americana. Not heavily, but you could see that's where it wanted to go. It was the damnedest thing."

"I can imagine," Evan said as Tony turned off the arterial road they had been on into a neighborhood of suburban McMansions.

"Um, hello? I can *hear* you guys." Evan could practically hear the eye-rolling going on in the backseat.

He twisted around. "So is all this to say that you haven't seen your parents since you left?" Christ. He'd had no idea. Was doubly glad he'd insisted on coming.

"No, no," she assured him. "I usually come by when I'm in town for a show, and we have a stilted conversation—like we're about to have now!" She was trying to make a joke, but he knew her. Self-deprecating humor was her defense mechanism. He could sense the hurt behind the smile.

"Which is how often?" he asked, wanting to get a sense of whether she put herself through this ordeal regularly.

"She's seen them six times since the move to L.A." Tony said, answering for her. "She's played big arena shows in Minneapolis four times, and they've come to one."

Though Evan wasn't going to proclaim it out loud the way Tony had, he liked this guy. The fact that he knew exactly how and how often Emmy had interacted with her parents suggested that he was paying attention, and not just to things like record sales and red carpet outfits.

"All right," Evan said as Tony slowed down in front of a house that looked like someone had plunked a southern plantation down on a one-acre lot in suburban Minnesota. It had a grand staircase leading to a veranda studded with four huge columns. "Wow." Then, "Hey, is this where 'Plantation in the Snow' came from?" One of the songs Emmy had been working on that summer talked about suburban alienation and isolation, about people searching for—and falling far short of—some kind of authentic connection.

"Wait till you see the back," she said. "It's the antebellum south in front, but it's Japan in back—all cherry trees, koi, and rock gardens."

Tony, who had stopped the car, turned to Evan with his eyebrows raised. "She let you hear a song in progress?"

Evan wasn't sure what to say. Was he not supposed to hear her songs? Were they embargoed or something?

"Let's go," Emmy said, getting out of the car before Evan could answer.

Silently, the men followed Emmy up the fake cobble-stoned path. Unlike his own, which was bumpy as hell and missing stones, this one was actually, upon further inspection, made of concrete poured to look like cobblestones, which pretty much summed up the whole place. It was a collection of signifiers of wealth. What his parents, back in the day, would have sneeringly called new money.

At the enormous double doors, Emmy raised her hand to knock but then paused and turned to him. "Thank you for coming with me," she said, her face impossible to read.

"Anytime," he said, and he meant it. Because apparently he was addicted to doing whatever he could to protect this woman, to ease the way for her. He could only wish this wasn't his last chance to do it.

The visit went about as well as Emmy could have expected. No worse or better than they always did. She wasn't even sure why she persisted in coming when she was in town. Did she honestly think that one day she would show up and her parents would hug her and say, "Oh my gosh, we were wrong all along"? Or even "We missed you"?

No, they went through their usual routine of coffee and painful conversation. Emmy asked about her parents' accounting firm, at which they'd both made partner in the years since Emmy had left, and about the horrible house, which they loved, and which Emmy was thankful she'd never had to live in. At least they weren't money-grubbing stage parents, she consoled herself, coming out of the woodwork after she'd risen to fame. They had plenty of money and had never expressed interest in any of hers.

"Oh! I almost forgot!" she said, after the conversation, which Evan had been trying valiantly to keep alive, started to dwindle. "I got you a present, Dad." She took out her phone and pulled up an image. "I randomly met this koi breeder." She almost laughed, thinking back to the party where she'd met him. It had been after a show in…Houston? Orlando? She couldn't remember. It seemed like a lifetime ago, like it had happened to some other version of her. "We got to talking, and it turns out he breeds Tancho koi." She shuffled closer to him on the sofa. "Do you know them? Their only markings, apparently, are these single huge dots on the back of their heads." She'd thought they were so strange-looking, and, knowing her dad was getting more and more into the koi pond, she'd ordered two for him. "They're supposed to be ready to go by mid-September, and they'll arrive via UPS. Can you imagine that? UPS ships live fish!" Not to mention that two stupid goldfish could cost thousands of dollars, but she didn't say that.

"That's very kind of you, Emerson," her mom said, "but we don't need any more fish. The pond is well-stocked."

Emmy looked at her dad. He had seemed into the picture, but now he was scooching away from the phone.

"And, you know, we're trying to restock only with black-and-white breeds," her mom added.

"Black-and-white goldfish?" Evan said. She could tell he was not impressed.

"Yes," said her mother. "They're not as common, but they're really rather striking. I think it will make quite the statement. Your father can't bring himself to dispose of the ones with the orange markings." Her mom pursed her lips as if this display of compassion was distasteful. "So we're left waiting it out."

"Waiting for the orange goldfish to die so you can replace them with black-and-white goldfish, which are more striking?" Evan repeated, as if he couldn't believe that his interpretation was correct.

"Well, they're *koi*," Emmy's mother said.

"So…big goldfish," Evan said, and Emmy almost burst out laughing. His incredulity, and to be honest, his obvious annoyance at her parents, was gratifying.

"I think we should get going," Evan said, "The later it gets, the harder it's going to be to find parking around the fair."

"You're going to the state fair?" her mother said, eyebrows lifting.

Emmy was wearing her normal clothes—she hadn't wanted her parents to see her in her schleppy disguise. "Yeah, I discovered that if I wear really baggy clothes and a hat and glasses, I can pretty much go incognito."

"So that explains that…" Another sniff. "Hair."

Emmy knew her hair was awful, but the disdain in her mother's tone still stung. She didn't want it to. She wanted to be the kind of person who didn't get her feelings hurt when her parents rebuffed her overtures. But every single time, she ended up sitting in front of them, a lump growing in her throat.

It was always the same.

Except when it wasn't.

A hand came to rest on her arm. A familiar, strong, warm hand. She was playing out the same old scene with her parents, but that hand was a new addition.

She turned to him, and his face was hard, almost angry,

but she knew it wasn't directed at her. "We're done here," he said, and she wanted to throw her arms around him. Of course, Tony was always on her side, but that was different. Their fortunes had been intertwined from day one. But to have Evan so overtly in her court? Well, it was powerful. She admired him so much, this smart, determined, self-made, *gorgeous* man, and he was here for her. *With* her.

For one more day, at least.

And he would get her out of here. Already was, in fact. Without her really realizing it, they'd made their way to the door, and Evan was picking up her purse from the floor of the entryway. She barely had to do anything but murmur goodbye to her parents. They usually exchanged awkward, robotic hugs, but apparently that wasn't required this time, because she was already being herded out onto the porch and ensconced in the passenger seat of Tony's car. She tried to protest that Evan, with his longer legs, should take the front, but he had already folded himself into the back.

"Let's get the hell out of here," he said once everyone else was in, too. "We have some cheese curds to eat before the show starts."

Tony turned to her with his eyebrows raised. She was about to say, "What?" when he started the car, looked in the rearview mirror and said, "I *really* like you, Evan Winslow."

"I like you, too, Tony. Want to come to the fair and watch this incredible kid Emmy turned into a songwriter win the junior songwriting showcase?"

If you had plucked Evan out of his life two months ago and put him here, in the crowd at an outdoor amphitheater at the Minnesota State Fair, and told him he'd be watching Jace, the silent, unreachable kid who always sulked in the back at the community center, stand in front of an audience and perform an original song, he probably would have expired from shock.

But, like a lobster being slowly boiled in a pot, he'd had time to get used to the idea.

Which he supposed made Emmy the chef in that unfortunate metaphor, because if watching Jace was gratifying, watching Emmy watch Jace was better.

He was starting to understand how she did it, her magic alchemical songwriting ability. She watched things very carefully; she took note. She was like him that way. If he had an eye that translated things into paintings, she had one that translated things into songs. But she also opened herself up, so utterly and unreservedly, to emotion. It sounded clichéd, but it was like it flowed through her, and she transformed it into songs. That feeling he had when he painted in the attic, in secret? It was like she let herself feel that way all the time. She was radically open to experience. Somehow, unlike most people, she hadn't built up any armor.

Like now, for instance, she was sitting next to him watching Jace, who was giving a flawless performance, with her hands clutched beneath her chin, her whole body tense.

When Jace finished, and the crowd erupted into applause, she turned to Evan with a look of utter astonishment, like she was surprised it had gone so well. Like she'd been expecting a disappointment. Like she'd grown so accustomed to heartbreak that she wasn't sure what to do with the opposite.

There was a downside to her talent, to her extreme openness to experience and emotion, and that was that she couldn't turn it off. So people could hurt her. Men who wanted to take advantage of her. Managers who didn't understand her aims. Her own parents, for fuck's sake. That was a perfect example. There was her eye for detail: the perfectly-thoughtful gift, which Evan swore her father had actually been into before her mother had shut things down. There was her vulnerability, her openness, which kept her coming back for more of the same freeze-out from her parents, who were apparently robots.

She leapt to her feet, joining the crowd, which was giving Jace a standing ovation. She turned to him again, and briefly hugged him, hard, harder than her thin arms should have been capable of. Then she turned her attention back to the crowd, screaming so loud he was sure she was going to be hoarse tomorrow.

Tomorrow. The word arrived in his body like it was made of iron and sank to the bottom of his gut. Tomorrow she would be gone. He and Jace would be on their way back to Dane and she'd be…somewhere else. Staying with Tony? Surely she wouldn't go back to her parents' place. Maybe she'd give up on hiding out and head back to L.A.

No. And that word, the *no*, was stronger than the terrible knowledge that had settled in his gut.

There was no way she could go back. Not yet. She wasn't ready.

He wasn't ready.

So he waited until the applause died down, and *he* hugged *her*. She thought it was another celebratory hug, and as he picked her up off her feet and gathered her close, she said, "Wasn't he so amazing?"

"Come home with me," he said, speaking over her. "Stay for the rest of the summer. You're not done yet." He squeezed her tighter. "*We're* not done yet."

She squirmed out of his embrace and searched his face, eyes wide.

"What does it matter if we say goodbye now or we postpone it for a bit?" he said, shoving down the surge of emotion that had prompted him to ask in the first place and preparing to deploy logic. "Classes don't start until the second week after Labor Day—that's still two and a half weeks away. I've heard you. You can get a lot of songs done in two and a half weeks. And we can—"

"Okay," she said.

"What?" He hadn't been prepared for such easy capitulation.

"Okay, I'll come back with you. But what were you going to say?"

He had to fight through the fuzzy cloud of happiness that materialized in his chest to follow her meaning.

He must have looked confused because she prompted, "You started to say, 'We can…' Fill in the blank."

He thought about making up a lie, of saying something like, "We can get the art show hung," but he decided to tell her the truth. "We can have sex in every room in my enormous house."

CHAPTER NINETEEN

When Evan emerged from his house onto the porch and handed Emmy a beer, she had the astonishing thought that she didn't think she'd ever been happier. Yes, she'd had sharp, wild moments of joy-mixed-with-pride at certain milestones of her career: her first record deal, her first gold record, her first Grammy. But this was different. After a morning of bone-meltingly great sex with Evan, she'd spent the day working alternately on a new song and on the last upstairs bedroom she had yet to tackle. She assumed Evan had spent the day working, too, though she hadn't seen him until he'd emerged from the basement in his workout clothes. And now, fresh from said workout and a shower, damp and bare-chested—he was doing that to bait her, she knew, and it was working—here he was. And soon, Mrs. Johansen would be leaving for a date. He lowered himself to sit in the swing next to her. She sighed happily as he settled an arm around her shoulders. To have done good work…and now the rest of the evening stretched ahead of them like it was a feast and she was starving. It was a delicious feeling.

And Jace had won the competition—and, more importantly, the scholarship that came with it. She was still practically bursting with pride.

"You eat already?" he asked.

"Yep. Chicken spaghetti," she said, because in addition to being metaphorically starving, she'd worked up quite the appetite moving boxes around. "I was too hungry to wait." And in truth, she loved the fact that they had established a routine that allowed them to be together but also to do things on their own without it being a big deal.

In the three days they'd been back from the fair, they had managed to weave in and out of each other's routines seamlessly. They would wake up together. Evan was an insomniac, which Emmy hadn't realized before, and he often got up in the night, but he always made his way back to her arms before dawn. Then they would eat breakfast together. Well, technically, they'd have sex and *then* eat breakfast together. Her face heated thinking about it. Then they would mostly go their own ways, she to her songs and her house tasks, he the kitchen table or to his office at the college. Then they would come together again for dinner on the porch, though she'd eaten without him this evening. After dinner, they would shoot the breeze until…well, until they had to take it inside. Evan had made good on his promise: they'd had sex in every room in the house. And then, if Mrs. Johansen was out on a date, they would come back outside afterward to wait up for her.

"I'm glad you went ahead and ate," Evan said, looking at his watch. "I got on a roll with…stuff, so I kept going."

And then he'd lifted weights. She knew his habits—after an intense session of professoring, he always went for a run or lifted in his basement gym. She took the opportunity to shamelessly ogle his naked chest—that was one of the "benefits" of this whole "friends with" arrangement—she didn't have to be subtle about checking him out. Honestly, the juxtaposition of the big brain and the big muscles—it was almost too much.

"Oh, you made it just in time!" Emmy said to Evan as Mrs. Johansen came out of her house. She looked up the street for IveGotYourBach, Mrs. Johansen's latest suitor. Mrs. Johansen and Dave344 had parted ways while Evan and Emmy were in Minnesota, and the classical music enthusiast she'd replaced him with seemed to have really captivated her.

"Don't wait up for me tonight," Mrs. Johansen called across the yards.

"We never wait up for you," Emmy said, though the lie was so obvious she cracked up as she told it.

"Well, you'll be waiting a long time if you do," Mrs. Johansen said. "Until tomorrow."

"Holy shit," Evan muttered. "Is she saying what I think she's saying?"

Emmy flashed Mrs. Johansen a thumbs-up and whispered to Evan, "She is indeed."

"Okay, no way." Evan started to get up.

Emmy motioned him back to his chair. "She's fine. Honestly. She's taking her own advice about enjoying life, and she's pretty much the smartest person I know."

"Let me give you my phone!" he called, trying not to sound as discombobulated as he felt.

Mrs. Johansen pulled something out of her bag. "I got my own!"

"I gave her condoms, too," Emmy whispered.

"Well, hot damn," Evan muttered. "I guess everyone's getting some this summer."

Even though they didn't have Mrs. Johansen to wait for—

Evan was trying to be open-minded and not ageist, but honestly, seeing her off for her date had felt like sending his grandmother into a sex dungeon—they stayed outside, as was their habit, until the fireflies, and then the stars, came out.

After an hour or so of sitting side by side in their usual spots on the swing, each working separately—him on grading some quizzes, Emmy humming to something only she could hear and scribbling what he assumed were lyrics, she set her notebook aside and sighed. He took it as his cue to stop, too, and closed his laptop and turned to face her.

She didn't even have to say anything.

"Let's go," he said, offering his hand, which she took with a cat-that-ate-the-canary grin.

His dick rose immediately to the occasion. He laughed at himself. It was like he was fifteen instead of thirty-three.

He would have been embarrassed by his near-constant state of horniness, if it hadn't seemed like she was right there with him.

Which she demonstrated at this particular moment by slamming his front door behind her after he led her inside, shoving him back against it, grabbing the waistband of his shorts, and taking them with her as she fell to her knees.

"Emmy," he groaned, taking his glasses off and trying— but not very hard—to pull her back to standing.

"What?" She looked up at him after she'd finished the business of taking his dick out. "I realized today that we haven't done the entryway yet. Put your glasses back on. They're hot." She grinned. "Plus, you're going to want to see this."

His next groan was an inarticulate mess of sound, because he was beyond language. The sight of her paused like that, looking up at him from her knees, knowing what she was going to do... Well, it was a good thing he *wasn't* fifteen anymore. He'd learned some control—at least he had that going for him.

Okay, he corrected himself as she took him into her mouth, it wasn't the sight of her pausing, *about* to suck him off, that did him in so much as it was *this* sight, her lips in their natural, non-scarlet state, bobbing up and down on his cock while she sighed and purred deep in her throat like she was feasting on the most delicious meal. He had to close his eyes against it, to let his head fall back against his front door, so the fun wouldn't be over before it started.

He let her go on like that for a few minutes, losing himself in the warm wetness of her mouth. But when she stroked his balls at the same time she took him in as deep as she could, and the pressure in his lower back ratcheted way up, he gently pushed her off him. Then, in a repeat of her earlier move, he turned them, pushing her back against the door, reaching for her shorts and unbuttoning them.

He only needed one exploratory touch to know that she was ready—when he stroked her with his fingers, she was as wet as her mouth had been, and she gasped, the big exaggerated inhale she always made when she was close to coming. So he positioned himself near her entrance, and, as she whispered, "Please," drove home. But once inside her, he paused.

He hadn't been waiting for her to give him the go-ahead, but she must have thought he had been, because she repeated her exhortation of a moment ago.

"Please, Evan, please."

No, it was nothing so chivalrous as him waiting for her to stretch to accommodate him, to get used to opening her body to him. It was the reverse, actually. He needed a moment, as he so often had the last few days, to adjust to the idea that he was inside Emmy. That he was welcome here. That she trusted him so utterly. Sometimes, the enormity of it bore down on him so hard that he...well, he needed a moment.

But he could not deny her, so he began moving.

And when she said, "Harder," he went harder. When she wrapped her hands around his neck and hoisted her legs around his waist, he went harder still, pounding into her over and over, never wanting it to end even as he knew it was going to, and soon.

When she came, clenching around him and shuddering in his arms, he was helpless to do anything but follow her.

And as they slid down the door and landed in a heap on the floor, he was helpless against the knowledge that later, much later, when she was asleep, he was going to go back up to the attic, where he'd spent the better part of the day, and paint her again. He'd been up half the night the last few nights, painting. And if the movement of him slipping out of bed disturbed her enough that she sleepily asked him what was wrong, he claimed insomnia.

"Oh my God, poor Cheer Bear!" she said, suddenly.

Huh? He looked between her and the bear, which she'd left perched on an antique bench on the side wall of the entryway, across from the coat hooks.

She scrambled to her feet, and, naked from the waist down, loped over to the oversize cartoon bear. "You shouldn't have had to see that, Cheer Bear." Then she turned him around so he was facing the wall, drawing a laugh from Evan.

"Come back here," he said, too wrecked to get up but not willing to be without her. When she opened her mouth to form what was probably going to be an objection, he growled, "Don't sass me. Get your pretty ass back here."

"Do you remember when you were teasing me about my nipples being like berries?" she asked, pasting herself against his chest and laying her head on his shoulder.

"Mmm-hmmm." He nodded against her hair.

"And do you remember when I was teasing you about what your penis would probably taste like?"

"I do. I think you suggested corn on the cob."

She laughed. "Yeah, so I have enough experience with the matter now that—"

"With the *matter*?" he interrupted, unable to resist teasing her. "You sound like you're talking about a legal briefing."

"Well, what do you want me to say? I have enough experience with your dick in my mouth?"

"That works for me."

"Anyway," she said, nuzzling his neck, "I figured out what you taste like. Cheese curds. The most delicious state fair cheese curds. Tangy and salty and decadent."

He burst out laughing. "Did you just compare my dick to deep-fried cheese?"

"It's the most delicious thing in the world," she protested, defensive. "And anyway, it would have to be a big curd. Like, a single, enormous one. On a stick."

Evan had no idea how this had all happened. How he had ended up here, sprawled on the floor of his house with Emerson Quinn in his arms, turning her writer's eye for detail to the nuances of his dick.

More critically, he had no idea how he was ever going to live without it.

The next morning, it was too quiet in the house—Evan had gone to the college for a meeting. Emmy set down her guitar, frustrated with her inability to get the bridge right on the song she'd been working on.

She wasn't sure why she missed him so much. It wasn't like

they were together during the day much anyway, except of course for the occasional…quick interruption. She smiled, her cheeks heating at the dirty slide show playing in her head. But the point was that since they didn't spend most of the daylight hours together, it shouldn't have mattered that he wasn't here now. But somehow, she felt his absence.

Everything was flowing so smoothly this summer, song-wise. Hell, life-wise, too. It sounded so clichéd, but she could feel herself…blossoming. Part of it was learning to do the "real girl" stuff like driving and cooking. Part of it was the great big inside joke that she had managed to play on everyone by hiding in plain sight.

But part of it, she feared—a bigger part than she was really comfortable with—was him.

She worried that she had become too dependent on him, like a hockey player superstitious about not shaving during playoffs. In addition to being the giver of mind-melting orgasms, Evan felt like Emmy's lucky charm.

Which begged the question: what was she going to do without him?

She shook her head. The answer to that question was that she was going to take her new songs, go back to L.A., and record them. That had been the point of her crazy jailbreak, right? So: mission accomplished.

She was also going to go back to L.A. and press the reset button on the "no men" thing. At least this affair had not been conducted in the public eye.

She sighed. What she needed now was a change of scenery, so she set down her guitar and headed for the stairs. On the second floor, she drifted from room to room, looking for something that could be a mini-project, maybe an hour's worth of work to take her mind overtly off the song and allow it to marinate in the background. Evan was always telling her she didn't have to work on the house, but she'd meant what she said about it being an essential part of the creative process. It was like when her hands were busy, her subconscious was free to churn away at song-problems. Maybe that was the answer to what she would do in the post-Evan era—maybe she should buy a fixer-upper. Become a house-flipping songwriter.

She opened the door to the last room on the second floor —it was a guest room she'd converted into a little TV den. Not that Evan owned a TV. It was a theoretical TV den.

There was really nothing more to do house-wise. She was rather proud of herself, actually. The work itself had been so satisfying. Like her revelation about cleaning the kitchen on her first day here, it had been gratifying to do something concrete, to expend effort and create a real, physical outcome. And she'd truly transformed this house. It retained its original character, but having cleared out boxes, applied a fresh coat of paint in rooms that needed it, and rearranged the furniture and added a select few new pieces, the place felt like it had undergone a gentle face-lift. It was usable and cozy and…there was really nothing more to be done.

And there wasn't any more work to be done on tomorrow's art show, either. Everything was ready.

She eyed the stairs to the attic. Evan had never told her explicitly not to go there, and she hadn't dared since the night she'd caught him painting up there. But why was she so gun-shy? Whether he wanted to paint or not was his business. She thought he was wasting his talent, but she'd made her views clear, and it was his life. But for heaven's sake, it wasn't like this was *Jane Eyre*. There was no crazy wife locked up there. She could take a peek, and if there was anything up there that seemed private, she'd turn back. But if it was more boxes and junk, that would give her a task. The completist in her would get a thrill out of the idea that she'd cleared out the whole house.

Emmy opened the door and ducked under its smaller-than-average frame, shoving down any moral twinges. The stairs were creaky, and her heart pounded even though there was no one in the house to hear her trespassing. At the top, she reached blindly for the string attached to the overhead light bulb.

She found it, pulled it, and blinked again, this time in shock, because the space had been totally transformed. Big pieces of furniture had been pushed to one side. Gone were the boxes and clutter, and they'd been replaced by a worktable littered with paint, brushes, knives, and bottles of stuff she couldn't identify.

And there were paintings *everywhere*.

Oh my God. He wasn't an insomniac. This was where he'd been disappearing to at night.

Struggling for breath, she walked to one side of the room, where finished canvases rested against a wall. She counted ten of them.

Many of them were of her.

And they were gorgeous. Exquisite. Her hands started shaking. His signature style seemed to be to put his subject in a fantastical or unlikely background, which made for an interesting juxtaposition, sometimes hinting at the supernatural, sometimes introducing a sense of unease into the beauty he captured. There was one of her in a forest, another where she was surrounded by rows and rows of corn. There was one of her and Mrs. Johansen, floating above their neighboring houses and sporting matching red lipstick that really drew the eye against the blue sky background, and one of Mrs. Johansen by herself against a backdrop of barbed wire and rubble, which must have been intended to evoke her World

War II experience. You only had to look at any one of them for a lump to grow in your throat. It was hard to say why, exactly, just that there was something beautiful about them, made more so by the touch of terribleness they also possessed.

She moved aside the last one in the row to reveal the painting behind it.

It was her, and unlike many of the other paintings, her hair wasn't its harsh dyed black and she wasn't wearing baggy clothes. She was back to her normal look. In fact, she looked more like...*herself* than her own reflection in the mirror did. That should have been impossible, but it was like he'd captured the essence of her somehow, latched onto some inner part of her that was beyond naming, and painted it. She pulled her real gaze from the intense blue painted one that stared back at her, and examined the rest of the painting. She was standing in...a meadow? It was hard to say because the bottom of the canvas was a riot of flowers and they were almost up to the top of her thighs. But, no, it was actually water. A lake covered with flowers, and they were on fire.

I will wade out till my thighs are steeped in burning flowers.

She burst into tears.

CHAPTER TWENTY

Evan had managed not to think very much about Larry and the whole tenure thing since they'd come back from Minnesota. He'd reached a kind of peace with the whole process. He'd done the best work he'd been capable of, had put together a pretty damned good tenure file. The rest was out of his hands. Maybe all the talk about Zen had actually had some impact.

The other thing that had made some impact? That party Emmy had given where she'd gotten everyone drunk. Not on the outcome of his tenure, he hoped—he didn't like to think the process was so vulnerable to outside influence—but on his day-to-day life. To wit: he'd just spent an hour chatting in the faculty lounge, which was usually a pretty barren space, with Ken and Melissa, whom Emmy had charmed at the party. They'd commiserated about college politics, but then they'd started talking about projects they had in mind for the future, and had actually found a promising avenue on which to collaborate. It was astonishing, really. It was like the department was Narnia during the thaw. People were coming out of hiding, making academic and social connections. Which he supposed made Larry the White Witch and Emmy Aslan in this little analogy. Hmm. An idea for a painting popped into his head.

His phone buzzed. Ah, speak of the devil. Or the magical Christ-surrogate lion.

Emmy: I'm going early to make sure every-thing's looking okay.

He'd spent so long talking to Ken and Melissa that he'd lost track of the time. He needed to get home and change for the art show.

Evan: I'm sure it's all great. But, yeah, I'll meet you there.

He'd stopped in yesterday, when she was done with ninety percent of the hanging, and, as with everything she touched, she'd done an impeccable job. He'd decided to go with a show featuring contemporary artists from the Upper Midwest, so there wasn't a lot of thematic coherence, but she'd hung every-thing exactly as he'd instructed and had even made a few suggestions that were spot-on.

Emmy: I think it's better if you come, say, at seven? Make a grand entrance of sorts.

He laughed. She was overthinking this. He was the cura-tor, not the artist, and this was the town art show in Dane, Iowa, not the Guggenheim. But okay, she'd worked so hard on this—he wouldn't have been able to pull it off without her, not even close—so he'd let her have her dramatic entrance.

Evan: Sounds good. See you at seven.

He got up and headed back to his office, surprised to find he was actually excited about the show. How had Emmy managed to turn this thing he'd been dreading all summer into something he was looking forward to?

Maybe she really *was* magic.

There were *a lot* of cars parked outside the show. Evan's excitement was joined, suddenly, by a twinge of nerves. But, he reminded himself, Jerry's barn conversion had turned out great, and probably many of tonight's attendees were here to see the barn that would become the new community center arts annex as much as they were the show itself. And it wasn't like he had to impress anyone; it was only the town art show.

"Evan!" It was Melissa and Ken, whom he greeted warmly. They'd mentioned earlier that they were going to stop by, so it wasn't a surprise to see them, but still, he was touched by the gesture. His department had never been particularly collegial, and he hadn't really known what he was missing until, suddenly, he wasn't missing it.

But before he could get too carried away on a warm, fuzzy cloud of Oprah-style gratitude, Larry pulled up. Well, hell, for every action there was an equal and opposite reaction, right? So much for "it wasn't like he had to impress anyone." And the bar for impressing Larry, would, of course, be high. It would be unreachable, in fact, because his boss would keep moving it, ensuring that it stayed perpetually out of Evan's grasp.

"Couldn't miss your little show," Larry said, getting out of his car.

Evan watched as Melissa and Ken fled inside, leaving him

alone with Voldemort, as Emmy called him. "Good of you to come," said Evan evenly, forcing himself not to rise to the bait Larry had set with his snarky "little show" comment. God, he needed to get tenure, if for no other reason than he would be done walking on eggshells around this asshole.

Once inside, he calmed down a bit. The place looked amazing. He had seen it almost all done, but the addition of the guests, the festive bar set up in one corner, and the gentle, warm lights installed in the rafters of the former barn painted the art—the whole space—with a lovely glow. It was really something.

"Hi."

So was Emmy. "Hi," he said, his pulse kicking up a notch as she smiled at him.

And there she was, the magician. The woman who'd made everything happen. And by everything, he didn't just mean the show. She'd fixed his house and his professional relationships. She'd…thawed him somehow, even though he hadn't realized he was frozen. She'd pushed her hair back from her face with a headband, so she was looking a little less shaggy puppy dog than she generally did in public. And she was wearing a dress, though it was loose-fitting. He spared a momentary thought for whether she looked too much like herself but told himself he was being paranoid. If she hadn't been discovered at the densely-populated Minnesota State Fair, she certainly wasn't going to be at an obscure art show in Dane.

"Everything is amazing, Emmy," he said, and she blushed at the praise. "*You're* amazing," he added, wanting to see if he could make that blush deepen. It did. Damn, how long till they could get out of here?

"Evan!" Melissa sidled up holding a plastic cup of wine and wearing a huge grin. "You have been holding out on us!"

Evan frowned, unsure what his colleague was talking about.

"Don't be mad," said Emmy, taking his arm.

Foreboding uncurled in his gut. "Don't be mad about what?" He let her lead him through the crowd, his eyes scanning the space as they went. Nothing seemed out of place. He tried to keep up with the greetings that were being lobbed at him, nodding to well-wishers. But he couldn't hear what they were saying. He couldn't hear anything, actually, over the buzzing in his ears. It was like locusts getting louder—an ominous soundtrack inside his head. He kept twisting around. Something was wrong, and he needed to see what it was.

Emmy stopped suddenly, near a corner. There was an odd little alcove inside the barn. It was effectively dead space, and when planning the exhibition, Evan and Emmy had discussed what to do with it, ultimately settling on hanging a bulletin board with some information about the community center's arts programming.

"What did you do?" he said in a low voice, but he knew, suddenly, with a terrible certainty, what he would find when he turned that corner.

"People should see what you can do," she said, her voice low to match his, but resolute.

He rounded the corner, his whole body shaking.

And came face to face with one of his paintings of Mrs. Johansen.

His knees almost gave out. He had to put his hand on the wall to steady himself, so he wouldn't crumple in front of the whole town. In front of his tenure committee, for fuck's sake.

"I told you I don't paint anymore," he said, still staring at the painting. It was a good painting, and she'd had it well framed. Those facts, though, weren't enough to counteract the crush of…betrayal.

This was what betrayal felt like. He knew this feeling.

There was also panic. The hot tendrils of panic crawling up his spine, like they had all those years ago in Miami, when he'd had to run a gauntlet of reporters on his way in or out of court.

He turned to her. He knew this feeling, too: standing there in front of someone you loved and watching them hurt you.

"I don't understand how you could do this," he whispered, unable to get the volume of his spoken words to match the scream in his heart.

"You can't just hide your talent," she said. "Who cares about how it was nurtured? I'm sorry you went through some shit, but you can't let it derail your whole life. Life is too short not to do what you want to do, not to make the kind of art you want to make. I'm forcing your hand. I know you think you're angry, but—"

"I *think* I'm angry?" How could she be so presumptuous? "I guarantee you, I *am* angry."

"She's right, Evan," said Melissa, who must have followed when Emmy came to fetch him. "If there's more like this, you need to let your work find an audience."

There was a crowd gathering, and suddenly everyone was talking over everyone, Emmy defending herself like she occupied some sort of moral high ground, Melissa praising his work, lots of other voices weaving over and under each other.

"Evan, you need to listen to your friend," Melissa said. "She's right. This painting is marvelous."

"I don't know," said another voice that Evan recognized right away. Larry. Approaching with a sneer. "I'm not sure Miss…" He sniffed and turned to Emmy. "Anderson, is it? I'm not sure Miss Anderson is any kind of expert on art, either as it relates to quality or to marketability."

Emmy took a step forward. "Hold on."

"I won't hold on," said Larry. "Art—well, great art, which this most decidedly is not—is about truth. Beauty. It communicates something besides ego. What do you"—he let his eyes run up and down Emmy—"know about that, Miss Anderson? Who are you to decide what is great art?"

"Oh my God!" came a voice from the crowd.

Evan whirled, trying to pinpoint who had spoken, but it was impossible, because the crowd started shifting, surging, closing in on them.

Emmy's eyes darted around frantically, perhaps sensing, as he did, that the shit was about to hit the fan.

Don't move! he wanted to yell at her, but his mouth wouldn't obey. Even as everything was ratcheting up inside him, a cacophony of volume and discordance, his voice was drying up. So he tried to reach for her to…what? Shield her? He wasn't sure, just that he had to get to her, to try to stop—

"Holy shit! Is that *her?*"

Emmy turned toward the voice, and Evan, who had reached her side, went with her. The way he'd grabbed her, lunged toward her, really, had tangled them up together, one of his arms across her shoulders, the other resting on her forearm. He'd made them into a unit, and there wasn't time to undo it before…

"That's Emerson Quinn! Emerson Quinn is here!"

Emmy gasped.

And a series of flashbulbs went off.

CHAPTER TWENTY-ONE

Three days later – Los Angeles

"All right," said Martin Eklund, Emmy's producer. "That's good enough for now. Let's break for an hour. Let me fiddle with this a bit."

Emmy took off her headphones and made her way from the recording booth to the control room. Martin held his hand up for a high five, which Emmy reflexively gave him. This made Brian, one of her managers, do the same thing, so she high-fived him, too. Claudia was in the background talking a mile a minute on the phone, but she hustled over, grinned, and gave Emmy her own high five, yammering the whole time. Emmy felt like an athlete working her way down a line of opposing players, slapping each other's hands and saying, "Good game."

The next person in line was Tony.

Tony did not offer to high-five her.

He didn't say anything. He didn't have to. He'd made his views known. Disapproval practically radiated off him.

"I think we'll be able to wrap this track tomorrow," said

Martin. "We should figure out what you want to record next. Do we want to plan on some writing time?"

"Emerson has a bunch of songs ready to go," Tony said.

This wasn't news to her team. She'd played them the songs she'd written this summer.

Their response had been...underwhelming.

But it had only been three days. The album would take months to put together. The first step was to record a bunch of stuff. They could battle it out later in terms of what stuck.

Maybe. Because right now, all Emmy knew was that working on Song 58 was at least forward motion. It gave her something to do, a reason to keep putting one foot in front of the other. Something to focus on so she wouldn't cry.

Because she had turned into a crier. In some ways, that was the worst part of the fallout from the summer. After Dane, and the beautiful illusion she had created there, she couldn't stop crying. She wanted so badly to get back on her no-crying streak, but her eyeballs wouldn't cooperate with her brain. She cried in bed at night, reading e.e. cummings so many times that she had all his absurd poems memorized. It was like some higher power was pouring water through her eyes and she was incapable of stopping it.

Except when she was working. When she was working, she wasn't crying. It was like Mrs. Johansen said: *Live the life in front of you.* Thirty-six hours ago, she'd been in Iowa. Now she was here.

Being here was all she could do right now.

And, to be brutally honest with herself, she wasn't sure anymore that they weren't right about the song. Song 58 was good. It was clever and catchy. And, after all, she had chosen Brian and Claudia because they knew what they were doing, and her career had gone stratospheric after she'd signed with them. So when they said it wasn't a good idea to totally change her sound in one fell swoop…well, maybe they were right. She had a formula, and it worked, Claudia had gently suggesting that they include one or two of the new songs on the new album rather than all of them.

"I'll be back an in hour," Emmy said. If they were breaking, she was going to take a walk. She needed forward motion. If she stopped moving, she would cry. Hell, right now it felt like if she stopped, she might *die*.

Tony was at her heels as she pushed out of the studio into the hallway. She just wanted some goddamned peace. Was that too much to ask? For the first time in Emmy's life, she was questioning whether having Tony around was a good thing. Like, maybe things would be easier if he just…wasn't here.

"You're making a mistake," he said in a low voice when he caught up with her.

She punched the button for the elevator. "Do we have to have this conversation *again*?"

"I'm not talking about the song."

That stopped Emmy in her tracks. He wasn't talking about the song? Song 58 was *all* he'd been talking about since they landed in L.A. and Brian and Claudia suggested they start recording it. They had lined up Martin and studio time, had everything arranged so all she had to do was show up. "Well, you could have fooled me," she said, a little astonished at how mean she sounded. "Because you seem obsessed with Song 58."

"I mean, yes, I think you should be recording the songs you wrote this summer, but—"

"Tony, you know it's not that simple."

"It *is* that simple! You're falling back into exactly what you were trying to escape. It's Song 58, and pretty soon, Martin will have another one ready, and then it will be Song 59.

You're starting to think that Claudia is right, aren't you? Song 58 is the thin end of the wedge."

"I thought you said it wasn't about the song." She braced herself for more of his onslaught.

It didn't come, and that was somehow worse than if he'd kept yelling at her. He shook his head, looking so utterly disappointed with her. It was unsettling. From day one, Tony had believed in her unwaveringly.

"What was I supposed to do, Tony?" she said, deciding to finally address the real issue, the one she'd been stubbornly avoiding in favor of mindless forward motion. "He didn't want me, not for keeps. I was going to have to leave in a couple weeks anyway. What does it matter?"

"You know it matters."

The elevator arrived. She stuck her hand in the door to hold it open and said, "Tony, look at me." He met her eyes, and she saw steely determination in his. It was what had propelled them up and out of Minneapolis, and now it had turned on her. "Are you with me or are you against me?"

His eyes softened, and he sighed. "You know I'm with you, Em. I'm always with you."

She pressed her lips together and swallowed. She'd be damned before the crying was going to spill out into her professional life. "Then we are done talking about this. Not just today, but forever. Do you understand me?" She was shaking. She never spoke to Tony like this, like she was his boss. They had always been partners in everything, despite his current job title. But if he didn't let up, she was going to have to…make some changes.

He nodded stiffly, got on the elevator, and looked at the floor. Like Jace used to do. Sweet Jace, who'd written her a letter confessing that Brianna, his state fair girlfriend, had been pestering him about whether Emmy was Emerson Quinn.

After the art show where Emmy had been exposed, Jace wrote, he'd confronted Brianna and she'd admitted to tipping off TMZ about the uncanny Emerson Quinn lookalike in Dane, Iowa, who was mentoring a young songwriter. He'd been abject, and she had reassured him, via an old-fashioned paper letter, because she didn't want to open the lines of communication in an ongoing way, that it was okay.

She'd been living on borrowed time in Dane anyway.

She put on her sunglasses so Tony wouldn't see her tears.

Evan kicked his sneakers against the edge of his porch, trying to dislodge the grass clippings that had accumulated on them from mowing the lawn. If only he could dislodge the heavy dread that had taken up permanent residency in his chest as easily.

"Thank you!"

He turned and lifted his hand. It was Mrs. Johansen, who'd opened her front door and called to him from across the yards. He'd cut her lawn, too. "No problem."

"Come in for some lemonade."

He shook his head as he grabbed his mail from the box mounted next to his door. "Thanks, but I can't. I have a ton of stuff to do." He couldn't see her, but he could feel her raising her eyebrows at the lie. He hustled inside.

He felt bad blowing her off, but honestly, he was annoyed at her. One of the things he'd always loved about Mrs. Johansen was her realism. Emmy would have called it her Zen. She took life as it came and made the best of it. So he wasn't sure why she had been riding him so hard about Emmy.

Even after he'd told her everything about his past, explained the origins of his allergy to the spotlight, she wouldn't let up. Which was grossly unfair. She of all people knew how hard he had been working toward tenure. She should understand how important this life was to him, how it was worth any sacrifice.

For God's sake, there were *paparazzi* in Dane. An *Entertainment Tonight* truck was parked outside the new arts annex. Some of the community center kids had been talking to the media, enthusiastically telling stories about their time with Emerson Quinn in disguise. His only consolation was that they hadn't found him, hadn't ferreted out his role in the story. Yet.

He hoped they would clear out soon. And even after Emmy left—and hell, she'd left fast—the media had stuck around, like they couldn't believe she was actually gone.

He shared the sentiment. As he went inside, his eyes moved automatically to the bench in the entryway, Cheer Bear's former home.

When she'd run away from the show—he still had no idea how she'd gotten back to his house—he hadn't been that far behind her. He'd had no idea what he was going to say to her. He'd been left reeling from the one-two punch of her having displayed his art and then watching her cover be blown so spectacularly. Clearly, she couldn't stay, and they'd been planning to part ways in a couple weeks anyway, but he hadn't wanted her to leave without…what? Some kind of closure? He didn't even know. So he'd followed her blindly, hoping that when he saw her, he'd find the right thing to say.

But when he'd come barreling in the front door that night, the first thing he'd seen was that empty bench.

And if he knew one thing for sure, it was that if Cheer Bear was gone, so was Emmy.

It had been for the best. He told himself that then, and he told himself now.

But to make matters worse, he feared that he hadn't just lost Emmy, he'd lost Mrs. Johansen, too. Because he was resolved to avoid her until she let up about Emmy. And since it didn't seem like she was ever going to do that, he feared that his closest friendship in Dane had been another casualty of the summer.

What did she expect him to do, though? Pick up and move to Hollywood? It wasn't like Emerson Fucking Quinn was going to up and move to Iowa. And regardless, he wasn't about to throw away everything he'd worked for and voluntarily walk back into the media spotlight that he had so vehemently fled after his father's crimes came to light. No. He and Emmy had been distractions for each other. Lovely, useful distractions, but distractions nonetheless. They had run their course. Whatever was between them, it had never been permanent. It had been designed with an expiration date.

He glanced at his watch. Three thirty. Was it too early for a beer?

Hell, who cared. It was the end of summer vacation. His summer class was done, and fall classes were still two weeks off. He popped the cap off a bottle and headed to his living room. The porch was another thing he'd lost since everything had blown up. If he went out there, Mrs. Johansen would descend.

He picked up his phone, intending to read the newspaper while he drank.

There was a text from a number he didn't recognize.

`This is your fault`

Then there was a video, and after that, two more texts.

Listen to what she's recording. This is Song
58. Do you know about Song 58?

This is Tony, btw

What the hell?

Beer forgotten, Evan hit play on the video. It wasn't a
video per se—the image was the back of a sofa, but he could
quite clearly hear the audio.

It was her. Of course it was her. What had he been
expecting?

He hadn't been expecting a full-body meltdown, that's for
damn sure. He'd never had a panic attack, he didn't think,
even back in the courtroom days when reporters had been
getting all up in his face while he watched his entire world
crumble in slow motion.

But now. Now, with her voice all around him. He was
sweating and cold at the same time, and his lungs felt like they
were shrinking. That voice was so familiar, so...*beloved*? *Fuck*.

And worst of all, if Tony was to be believed, she was
singing Song 58.

He listened to the whole thing. Then he sat there in
stunned silence.

Another text arrived.

She's recording Song 58 instead of this.
This got vetoed.

The text was accompanied by another video. It took him
several tries to get it to play; his fingers had become shaky and
clumsy. Once again, there was no meaningful visual. He got
the sense Tony had made his recordings without Emmy's
knowledge, but the audio was clear enough.

Her voice was quiet, but strong. She sang the first line unaccompanied: "It's all straight lines around here, he said." It was like a lance to his chest, her voice a thin, lethal, metal edge working its way in under his sternum. After the first line, she started playing an acoustic guitar. The first strum was startling, but also felt inevitable as the song gained momentum.

The song was about a girl who lived carefree in a castle surrounded by corn. She used fairy-tale imagery, describing a moat surrounded by densely packed crops. The song crescendoed, and it had her signature catchiness, the magic, ineffable ingredient that made even a hermit like him want to get up and dance. But then it turned, gradually becoming overlain with something else. A sadness, maybe, though that didn't seem like quite the right word. There was a weariness under the happiness. It was like the song was a crystal, and she'd picked it up and tilted it slightly, and suddenly you were forced to look at it in a new way, in new light. Fall came and the moat froze over and the corn died, and the girl had to come down from the castle.

Listening to the song evoked the feeling of being a kid at the end of summer, when pools and popsicles give way to structure and stiff new jeans.

Or, you know, the way it feels when the summer ends and you let the best thing that ever happened to you slip through your fingers.

When you let the woman you were supposed to protect run straight into the wolves' den.

Evan had tried, this past summer, to make a space for Emmy to feel safe. Safe to write unaccosted, safe to have sex with no fear, safe to live without constantly looking over her shoulder. To be a "real girl," to use her phrase.

But, he suddenly realized, when shit got real, when she'd really, really needed him, he'd failed her. He'd thought their parting was inevitable, that her discovery had merely forced their hand by a couple weeks. But he'd been wrong. So wrong. He should have been working overtime on replanting the the corn, not letting the princess just…walk away.

He'd thought of her as his muse all those years ago. And maybe she was. Hell, she *definitely* was. But now that knowledge was joined by a new and utterly astonishing thought: maybe *he* was also *hers*. Maybe a muse wasn't someone you were attracted to, or compelled by, someone who inspired you just by being. Maybe a muse was someone who, somehow, in a way that only that person could do, created space for you to do your thing. Made you safe.

He hadn't felt safe for so long. Maybe ever, actually, if you considered the fact that what he had thought of as safety before, back when he was younger and living with his family, had actually been an illusion, a mirage. A lie.

He didn't lie to himself in this life that he had so painstakingly created. That was the promise he'd made to himself when he'd packed his shit up and driven a U-Haul across the country. If he didn't get tenure, if everyone he knew forsook him, if something happened that was worse than what his father had done, that was the one thing he could count on: he would always be honest with himself.

So what the fucking hell had he been doing since Emmy left?

The song ended, and there was a momentary pause before a man's voice he didn't recognize started talking. "Well, that was cute, Emerson."

Cute? That wasn't *cute*. It was fucking genius.

"A bit of a departure, though, don't you think?" said a second voice, a female one. "Maybe too big of one?"

"Well, I don't know, I—"

The recording ended there.

Hell, no.

He sat up, almost knocking the phone to the floor. His panic coalesced into focused certainty.

No more lying.

♫♪

"Thank you all for coming on such short notice and so early," said Claudia at eight the next morning as Emmy's team assembled in the boardroom at the offices of her record label. Wow, Claudia really had gotten everyone. Brian was there, of course, and Tony, and Martin as well as her A&R rep from the label. They'd been joined by a stylist Emmy often used, and a couple of social media people and publicists from the management company.

"I have some amazing news," Claudia said. "I didn't want to say anything before I was sure, but I just got confirmation." She pressed her hands against the table and stood, like she was preparing to deliver a sermon. "I got us the opening slot on the MTV Video Music Awards. We'll debut the new song." She flashed a self-satisfied smile. "They've bumped Bieber."

"But the MTV awards are…" Emmy had lost track of time, what with the all-consuming work of putting one foot in front of the other.

"In four days," Tony said flatly.

"Right," said Claudia. "Which means we're going to have to get our shit together. Martin, we need a band, and we need them rehearsed. Emerson can join them after they've learned the song."

"Done," said the producer.

Wait. *What?*

Claudia turned to the stylist. "And we need a dress."

"Hold on," said Tony. "*If* Emerson is going to open the

MTV Awards, I think she should do 'September,'" Tony said, naming her fairy-tale song about Iowa. It was her favorite of the songs she'd written over the summer.

The room went silent for a long moment, then Claudia said, "We don't even know if that song is going to be on the album."

"We *don't*?" Tony turned to Emmy with an exaggerated expression of incredulity.

"Well," she hedged, "I'm not sure we know any of the songs that are going to be on the next album."

"Except Song 58," said Brian.

"Which is now called 'Walk Away,'" Claudia said. "Even if 'September' makes the new album, it isn't a show opener. You don't open the MTV Awards with a quiet song like that, Tony."

"Why not?" Tony said. "Is it against the law?"

Claudia pursed her lips. Brian did this subtle "I'm rolling my eyes but I'm not rolling my eyes" thing that only he could do. Then they looked at each other for a beat before Brian said, "Anyway, it's moot because we've recorded 'Walk Away.' We'll need to get whatever she plays wrapped and up on iTunes as soon as humanly possible after the show."

He looked at Martin, who said, "I'll do my best."

Then Brian continued, "So, realistically, 'Walk Away' is the only option."

Everyone looked at Emmy. When she didn't say anything, Claudia started talking again. "I know this is happening fast, but this is a huge opportunity. After your...disappearance and all the accompanying drama, it's a chance to normalize things."

"She can normalize things—whatever that even means—with 'September,'" Tony said. "You can spin it as the product of her summer hiatus. That will make a great story."

"It's not recorded yet," Claudia said with exaggerated patience, as if she was talking to a child.

"If we bust our asses the next few days—"

"Stop." Emmy shot Tony a quelling look. It wasn't that she didn't appreciate his loyalty, but he needed to lay off. They were right. It would be stupid to pass up an opportunity to open the MTV Awards. And she should play the song that was the most ready. The sure thing. She'd be foolish to do anything else. And really, so what? Song 58 was a fine song. It wasn't like having it on the next album would be a terrible mistake. "Where are the awards being held this year? Madison Square Garden?"

"Microsoft Theater," said Brian, naming an L.A. venue.

"Perfect," she said.

"Perfect," Tony echoed in a tone that suggested it was anything but.

Emmy glared at him again. She didn't need Tony aggravating the powers that be right now. They were already telling her in private that they thought he was overstepping, hinting that maybe she should consider getting a new assistant. Emmy always defended Tony, but it was all so…exhausting.

"Okay, onto the dress," said Claudia, turning to the stylist. "What can you get on short notice?"

"For Emerson Quinn? Whatever you want. I saw a Stella McCartney the other day that would be perfect."

"Fine." Claudia waved a hand in the air dismissively. "But make sure it's not too stuffy. Nothing like that Valentino from the Grammys last year."

"We *are* trying to skew older," Brian said.

"But you don't want her to look like she's *trying* to skew older," said Claudia.

"Point taken."

Emmy was listening, but she was staring at the walls of the

conference room, which were hung with her awards, so she didn't notice at first that they'd all turned to her. She was a few beats behind, which pretty much summed up the last few days. It was like everyone else was in real time, and she was in slow motion. Or like she was looking at everything through glasses with an out-of-date prescription. Everything was fuzzy and muffled.

But that was fine with her, because she didn't really *want* everything to be crisp and clear. She had a hunch that her evening weeping-with-poetry sessions were a preview of what would happen all the time if she could really see and hear and feel everything in real time, at full intensity.

"What do you think, Emerson?" Claudia asked.

She didn't know what she thought. She turned to the stylist, a beautiful, effortlessly stunning woman. "You choose. I trust you."

"Great! So that's settled." Claudia looked down at her agenda. "I think that's all for today. I'll email everyone their marching orders. Let's meet again tomorrow morning to check in."

CHAPTER TWENTY-TWO

One day later

"I'm not sure why you were so hesitant. These are amazing. I would be honored to show your work."

Evan would have liked to pretend that the gallery owner's words didn't thrill him to his core. He had prepared himself for rejection, even as he had gone through the motions of contacting one of his former painting teachers and asking for some introductions to galleries in Los Angeles.

He had told himself, as he started with his teacher's first recommendation, to the Riel Gallery, one of the city's most exclusive, that he would be dismissed out of hand once he said his name. He would have been okay with that. He was prepared to move down the list, facing as many rejections as he needed to. Hell, he would have rented a storage space and mounted the show himself if it had come to that. After watching Emmy put on the community center show in Dane, he even kind of knew what he was doing.

He hadn't been prepared for Jean-Claude Riel, one of the

art world's most famous dealers, to say, "I would be honored to show your work."

"I just…" He cleared his throat. It was important to project confidence, even if he didn't feel any. "I assumed that my father's crimes would reflect poorly on me."

"I admit that I was a bit taken aback when you called." Jean-Claude furrowed his brow. "But if I recall the coverage correctly, and your testimony at the trial, you weren't involved in any of it."

"I wasn't involved, but I benefited from it."

"As did I from my wealthy upbringing," Jean-Claude said calmly.

Evan took a deep breath. "How quickly can we get this show together? Because there's something else I need to tell you."

Three days later

Evan hadn't worked this hard since his grad school years, when he'd go to classes all day, work in the evenings, and then paint all night, subsisting on junk food and fumes.

He was exhausted, but, as he looked around the space that Jean-Claude had rented for the show and took in the finished tableaux, he was suffused with a sense of hope. The art dealer had fallen for Evan's tale of woe, and instead of making him wait until a show could be properly mounted at the main gallery, had rented a dedicated space for it. And then they'd gotten to work. And work, and work, and work. He was exhausted.

But it was worth it. *She* was worth it. To have a chance to make things right meant everything. Because he wasn't going to blow this. A person didn't let Emerson Quinn go and then show up on her doorstep with mere words. And he didn't mean Emerson Quinn the pop star—he didn't care about that—he meant Emmy. His bridesmaid. His muse. His love.

Evan's first solo art show was to open tomorrow in a converted industrial space in Echo Park that Jean-Claude was calling Riel Annex, which tickled Evan because his last show had been at Jerry's barn, aka the Community Center Annex. Evan did a quick mental double check of everything. The paintings Mrs. Johansen had couriered from Iowa were hung, the postcards were printed and distributed, Jean-Claude had arranged staff.

It was all ready to go. Everything was perfectly set up for his Hail Mary pass. Which meant shit was about to get real.

He got out his phone and pulled up the contact he'd created for Tony. His finger hovered over the call button.

Please let this work.

"Hello?"

"Tony? This is Evan Winslow."

There was a long silence on the line, so long that Evan feared Tony had hung up on him.

"I'm here," he added. "In town."

Tony let out a slow breath. "And why are you in town?"

"I'm in town because I made a mistake and I want to make it right."

"Bullshit," Tony said. "If you can't say it to me, how are you going to say it to her? Try it again. Why are you in town?"

He didn't even hesitate. "I'm in town because I love Emmy, and I have to tell her. Because that song was amazing, and she should be recording it, not Song 58."

"Do you know what day it is, Evan?"

He had no idea what day it was. The past few days—and

nights—had blurred together as he'd worked frantically to put things in order for the show. "Tuesday?" he guessed.

"It's the MTV Video Music Awards," Tony said, exasperation in his voice.

"Okay," said Evan. "I'm not very up on this kind of stuff, I guess. Does that mean—"

"It means you're too late, you jerk. She's going to debut Song 58, and Song 58, my friend, is not your song."

"My song?" He'd known, of course, when he'd heard the song back in his living room, but to hear Tony say it like that made his breath catch.

"Yes, you idiot. Your song. Which is decidedly *not* the song she's opening the show with in thirty minutes."

Too late. The implications of those words sank in. Evan didn't give a fuck about which song opened the MTV Video Music Awards, but he did care that Emmy was about to step back into what she had once called her golden cage. Maybe he even cared about that more than whether she forgave him, whether she wanted him.

But maybe they were one and the same thing, all hopelessly tangled together.

"No," he said. "It's not too late. I don't accept that. Tell me what I have to do."

Tony paused for an uncomfortably long time, but then he said, "Meet me at the corner of Pico Boulevard and Flower Street. Now."

Emmy was glad she was opening the show because it gave her an excuse not to walk the red carpet. Normally she was fine at these kinds of things, but today she was relieved not to have to smile and twirl and talk to reporters about "who you're wearing."

Instead, she could chill out backstage for a bit, confident that the last rehearsal and sound check had gone flawlessly, and do her usual pre-show routine. Except where was Tony? She looked around the room. Actually, where was everything? She didn't generally have a lot of diva-esque demands. Her rider was full of food items her touring band liked, and she never made anyone pick out the yellow M&Ms or anything crazy like that. But Tony always made sure she had a new puzzle at hand before a big performance. He knew puzzles calmed her nerves. They had an ongoing joke, in fact, where he tried to find the most obnoxious puzzle he could—puzzles featuring TV shows she hated, or inspirational quotes and frazzled-looking kittens—and they'd work on it together. On tour, he'd get big ones, and they'd do them on a big board, which would make its way from city to city with them. For one-off shows like this, he usually got her a small one, and she always looked forward to seeing what he'd come up with. And if she was wearing a gown, like tonight, he always had some kind of standing table set up so she wouldn't rumple herself.

Because Tony thought of everything.

She got up and looked into the cabinet in the corner. No puzzle.

Crap. Maybe he'd left her. He'd helped her get ready this evening, wrangling the hair and makeup people and the bodyguards that came with the diamonds she'd waved off, not wanting the extra pressure of wearing millions of dollars' worth of jewels on her person that evening. But maybe he'd gotten her ready for the appearance he disapproved of, and he now he was done. Could she really blame him?

Maybe he was such a good assistant—no, such a good *partner*—that he knew she'd been questioning whether their relationship should continue, and was fading away so as to spare her the pain of having to fire him.

"Miss Quinn?" One of the stage managers stuck her head in Emmy's open door. "We're ready for you."

Right. "Okay," she said, forcing herself not to dwell on the fact that she'd been abandoned by her oldest friend. This was live TV, and the audience would be in the millions. This was no time for interpersonal drama. She followed the woman down the hallway past the dressing rooms, trying to catch some excitement from the buzz of focused activity all around them—people talking into headsets, presenters who would be on stage after her number having the finishing touches of their makeup done.

"Emerson," said Claudia, who was waiting in the wings. She held her hands out and cocked her head, like a proud mama examining her daughter. "The McCartney was definitely the right choice." Then her face fell. "But no jewelry?"

"No. I didn't want to deal with the bodyguards."

"You're on in fifteen seconds," said the stage manager.

Brian appeared, and Emmy nodded at him. "Hey, do either of you know where Tony went?"

"Emmy!"

She whirled, her question answered. God, it was good to hear that voice.

"Don't do this!" Tony arrived at her side, panting.

"What are you talking about?" Emmy said, anger and relief at war inside her. She was so happy he hadn't left her, but what the hell was he thinking doing this now? She only had—

"Ten seconds!" the stage manager said, voice tinged with alarm.

"That's enough, Tony," Claudia snapped, nodding at one of the venue's security guards, who started to move toward Tony.

"You don't have to do this," Tony said. "You don't have to do anything you don't want to." He spoke calmly, like he was oblivious to the fact that she was about to go live—or that he was about to be forcibly thrown out of the venue.

"Get him out of here!" Brian roared, as the stage manager said, "You have five seconds, Miss Quinn!"

"We'll speak afterward," Emmy said, because whatever else happened, it wasn't okay for them to treat Tony like that.

"Places!" said the stage manager. "Go!"

Emmy could see her band coming in from the opposite side, finding their marks in the dark. That was what Tony didn't understand. It wasn't about what she wanted or didn't want anymore. There was a whole show depending on her now.

"Evan's here!" cried Tony, shrugging out of the security guy's grasp. "He's here in town, and he loves you," he added, his eyes filling with tears. "He just couldn't get here in time."

"*What?*"

The stage manager hissed, "We come off commercial in seven seconds." Emmy was supposed to have been out there for a full thirty seconds, in the dark, ready to go when the lights came on and the cameras rolled.

"Don't do this," Tony whispered, and she could hear him even though Claudia, who was speaking much louder, was saying "So help me, Emerson Quinn, get on that stage."

Emmy's mind reeled. What did Tony mean Evan loved her? How did he know?

It didn't matter, at least not now. Because she couldn't let everyone down. She couldn't embarrass herself. Again.

Just before she stepped out of the wings, Tony thrust something in her hand. She stumbled out in the dark, but righted herself and aimed for the piano. She was to start this song seated at the piano and rise partway through to finish it at a mic stand downstage. When she reached the bench and sat down, she looked back to where she'd come from. It was too dark to see anything.

"Ladies and gentlemen, to kick off the MTV Video Music Awards, please welcome Emerson Quinn!"

The lights came on, and the crowd went wild. The heat of the lights converging on her was a jolt to the system. She hadn't done this for so long. She had literally spent the summer out of the spotlight. The song was meant to start with a couple bars of her on the piano alone, before the band kicked in. Realizing she was still clenching her fist around whatever Tony had given her, she dropped it on the keyboard in front of her. It was a piece of paper, and as she was about to brush it aside, something familiar about it snagged her attention.

Oh my God.

She was aware of time passing, of the attention of the whole auditorium. She could imagine the attention of twenty-five million TV viewers, too. But she couldn't not look.

It was her. The one with her standing in the flaming lake of flowers.

STEEPED: PAINTINGS BY EVAN WINSLOW, JR.

The paper was a printout of an advertisement for an art show. An art show that, judging by the address, was happening right here in L.A.

She looked closer, at some of the smaller, thumbnail images under the large one, and was startled by several more pictures of her, some she'd seen in his attic that day, others that were unfamiliar.

September 5 – 7, 10 am to 5 pm or by appointment.

Evan was having an art show in L.A., and it opened *tomorrow*.

All of a sudden, she got it. She got what Tony had been trying to say. Hell, she'd said it herself, to Evan, when she'd forced his hand on showing his art. What the hell was she doing? Why in heaven's name would she, arguably one of the most powerful people in the music business, not write, record, perform, *whatever the hell she wanted*? Her skin started tingling. All over. Every inch of it.

She looked back over her shoulder. It was still dark in the wings. She couldn't see anyone, but she could hear frantic whispering back there.

"Emerson!"

Frantic whispering from up here on stage, too. It was Trey, a bassist who'd done a lot of session work with her, the band member standing closest to the piano, and he was looking at her like she was crazy.

Which, to be fair, maybe she was.

She grinned, a big wide one that felt like it was going to crack her face, and maybe her soul, open.

She was about to blow the lid off this place.

The entire bar held its breath, but no one more than Evan. He hadn't made it inside the venue. He'd given it everything he had, running through the streets like a crazy man when his cab had gotten stuck in gridlock, following the directions Tony shouted at him through the phone. But when he'd reached the arena, there was no way in. Even though the stars were already inside, crowds thronged the red carpet. When he'd attempted to jump a fence around a big, white tent that looked like it might lead, on its other side, into the venue, he was chased off by security and had to actually sprint away for fear they'd call in the real cops.

Which left him, sweaty and dirty and on the brink of insanity, in a bar a block away from the show, yelling at the bartender to turn the volume up on the TV behind the bar.

He had no idea what, if anything, Tony had told her—or if Tony had even reached her. They'd hung up when Tony had decided Evan wasn't going to make it, Tony promising to do his best to intercept her.

Something was clearly going on, though, because she wasn't starting. She was just sitting there on stage, illuminated by spotlights, looking at something on the piano as her band stood in awkward silence.

"Oh my *God*," said a twentysomething woman sitting next to him at the bar. "But I guess that's Emerson Quinn for you," she added. "Always with the drama."

"Shut up," said her companion, also a young woman. "I love her."

Shut up. I love her.

That made two of them. Fuck, looking at her, even just through the TV, nearly killed him. She was so beautiful, so *herself*, that she took his breath away.

Everyone in the bar seemed to lean forward on their bar stools. No one spoke as Emmy got up from the piano and walked over to her guitar player. She spoke in his ear, and then the guy handed over his guitar.

Then she walked over to an empty mic stand at the front of the stage. Hoisting the guitar over her shoulder, she said, "Sorry about the confusion, but there's been a slight change in plan." She smiled.

Then she looked right at him. Well, she looked right at the camera, but he knew she was looking at him. "I'm going to play you a new song called 'September.' I wrote it this summer."

♪♫

"Are you sure he's going to wait for me there?"

"Yes, Emmy," Tony said, sounding exasperated but smiling as he held the car door for her. "For the millionth time, I'm sure. I'm also sure that you could have told him to wait for you at the freaking North Pole, and that's where he'd be right now."

"It's just that I want to see the art," she said, buckling her seat belt. I want everything to be..." Ahh, it sounded so stupid. She probably should have gone running out of the theater after her song and hunted Evan down on the street. But she didn't want their reunion to be public. And, more than that, he had heard her declaration—she assumed—and now she wanted to *see* his. Her art for his—an even swap.

Tony shoved his phone in her face, showing her a text from Evan, time-stamped thirty minutes ago.

On my way. I'll be there when she gets there.

She looked out the window and tried to calm her nerves as the high rises of downtown L.A gave way to the lower-rise landscape of Sunset Boulevard and on into Echo Park. The driver slowed in front of a commercial building covered by a colorful mural, then turned the corner and came to a halt next to a side entrance. There was no sign on the building, but the main floor had a huge window, and the lights were on inside.

"Oh!" she gasped, because she could see him. He was in there. She stumbled on her way out of the car and lurched toward the door. It was heavy, and her palms were sweating. It took two tries to push it open.

Just as she stepped into the light, he turned.

There he was, her muse.

If she'd been unsure of his intentions, or worried about her reception, she needn't have been.

Everything fell away—the past few days and all the loneliness and fear they had contained. So did that night at the gallery in Dane. It was almost like now, here, in *this* gallery a world away from Iowa, they had a chance for—

"A do-over," he said, his voice cracking. He was on the other side of the large space, and between them were paintings, so many paintings. Lots of them were of her, but there were also portraits of other people, of Mrs. Johansen and Jace, and some people she didn't recognize. They all shared that magical, almost-supernatural quality she'd seen in his work in the attic.

"Yes," she said, her own voice wobbling. "A do-over."

He opened his arms, and she ran to him. He scooped her up, and she was crying again, but it was okay this time because it was a different kind of crying. It was a shedding of pain, of the past, of all that heavy stuff she didn't need anymore. She hadn't needed it for years, really, but it had taken Evan, and the space he made for her to rest in, for her to see that.

He spun her around, like in the movies, and they laughed, but after a few twirls, he lifted her higher, his arms under her bottom, and she wrapped her legs around his waist.

"I'm glad I didn't catch you at the awards show," he said. "This is better. This is what should have happened that night in Dane. I get to see my paintings and you…together."

"They're beautiful," she said, knowing full well that the word fell short.

"If that's true, it's because their inspiration is beautiful," he whispered. "She was this girl—this real girl—who taught me to paint again."

She couldn't hear any more. It was too perfect; it hurt to keep listening to him. So she planted her palms on his cheeks and kissed him.

He responded immediately, opening his mouth on a groan. They kissed and kissed, like they were making up for lost time, licking deep into each other's mouths. Eventually, he started to lose his grip on her, and she began to slide down his body. She whimpered in protest, and tightened her legs around him. She'd fallen low enough that his erection pressed against her core. She rocked her hips into him, and he grunted, staggering backward. There was a bench behind him, nestled against the wall underneath a painting of her on that bridge in the sculpture garden at the farmers' market. She remembered that day, that moment, when she'd looked at the wide blue sky and the miles and miles of corn, and it had felt like the world was expanding before her, like anything was possible.

He sat down with a thud, with her crosswise over his lap. She tried to straddle him, but the wall behind the bench was in the way.

So they sat there and kissed some more, like horny teenagers who couldn't get enough of each other. And since his hands were free now, he wasted no time reaching for her breasts. He couldn't reach her actual breasts, though, because of the dress, and though his hands felt good as they kneaded her through the silk, she wanted more. She squirmed off his lap and turned her back to him. "Unzip me."

Nothing happened. "Hello?" She looked over her shoulder. He'd stood up and was moving toward the other side of the room.

"I'm just getting the lights," he said, and as if to punctuate the point, the room dimmed. "I don't want anyone to look in and see you here."

Right. After he flicked the switch, there was enough ambient light from outside that they could still see each other, but they wouldn't be visible from the street unless someone was pressed right up against the window. The thoughtfulness of his gesture, the protectiveness, nearly undid her. She was safe with this man. She always had been.

He came back to her, took her hand and slowly, too slowly, lowered her zipper. Then he turned her around and continued to move maddeningly slowly as he drew the unzipped dress down her body. She wasn't wearing a bra, and he made a hissing noise she was pretty sure was approval. She jutted her chest out to encourage him to touch her, but he kept going with the dress. It was form-fitting, so he had to work it over her hips.

"What the hell is that?"

She looked down and burst out laughing. She'd forgotten about the fact that she was wearing the world's most unattractive undergarment. She'd also forgotten how, with him, laughter and lovemaking were not mutually exclusive. "That's Spanx."

"I beg your pardon?"

"Spanx. They keep your jiggly bits in when you've had too much casserole."

"You don't have any jiggly bits."

She jiggled her boobs at him as she stepped fully out of her dress, leaving her clad only in the monstrous beige compression garment.

He laughed. "I stand corrected. Those are some very nice jiggly bits, indeed." He ran a finger around the waistband of the biker-shorts-style Spanx. "How does a person remove these?"

"It's not very dignified," she said, starting to wiggle out of them.

"Hey, I tried to break into the MTV Video Music Awards." He gestured at himself. "So I think we're post-dignity, you and I." She only just registered that he was wearing sweatpants and a paint-splattered, holey T-shirt.

She wagged a finger at him. "Those clothes are entirely inappropriate for this occasion."

"I totally agree," he said, and he was out of them before she'd finished working off her stupid girdle.

And then the laughing interlude was over.

Oh, how she'd missed him. The safe space he created for her, yes, but also *him*, the way he filled that space.

He ran his fingers over the indentations in her skin where the edges of her Spanx had been, and she shivered. He continued skating his fingers lightly up one side of her torso. When he reached her breast, he paused, then took a small detour to caress her nipple. It wasn't long enough, though, and she huffed a frustrated breath as his fingers continued up over her shoulder, circled there briefly, then started down her arm. By the time he reached her hand, and grabbed it, she was shaking with need. Moisture bloomed between her legs, and she ached deep inside. He stepped back, holding her hand high between them like they were doing an old-fashioned dance, and she, picking up his cue, took a step after him. He led her like that for a few steps until his back reached a wall. Then he sat down, but kept hold of her hand, so by the time he was seated, his arm was over his head and she was hunched over him.

He wanted her to come down with him.

So she did.

"Oh, fuck, *Emmy*," he ground out when he realized what she was doing, which was lowering herself directly onto him.

She didn't want to wait. There would be time for slow lovemaking later. Right now she needed him inside her. She started moving, levering herself up on her knees a little, then letting herself fall back onto him, taking him as deeply as she could. He thrust up to meet her every stroke, cursing every now and again like a sailor, but still holding her hand like a gentleman.

"I'm not going to last," he panted.

"Good," she said, not only because she wasn't either, but because she wanted to claim him as quickly as possible. He was *hers*.

He pressed a thumb against her clit as his thrusts became irregular. She cried out and bucked wildly, and in a moment they were both splintering apart.

It was only after a few minutes had passed and their breathing slowed, that the question occurred to her. He was supposed to turn in his tenure file at the end of the summer. She bolted to a sitting position. "Did you get tenure? Did you turn everything in?"

He smiled and pulled her back down, tucked her up against his chest, and banded a heavy arm around her. "I did turn everything in, but I don't know the outcome yet. I probably won't find out until early in the new year."

There was laughter in his voice, as if this thing, this goal he had structured his whole life around for so many years, was nothing. And then, as if to ratify her interpretation, he said, "Either way, it doesn't matter."

She struggled against him until he released her. She didn't sit up this time, but she pulled back enough that she could see his face.

"I'll get it, or I won't. We'll work it out."

"We?" she echoed, warmth spreading through her body like a blanket from the inside.

"Hell yes, *we*," he said, kissing her softly. Then he asked, "Are you going to release Song 58?"

She chuckled and repeated his own phrase back to him. "Don't know yet."

"What does that mean?"

"Probably not, but really, I have no idea. It's not that bad a song. But I do know that things will be different from now on. I need to make a change in management, and then I'll worry about the next album." She turned another phrase back on him. "We'll work it out."

She could feel him smile against her forehead. Then her stomach growled, and it echoed through the silent gallery.

"Let's get dressed and get you some food," he said. "What are you in the mood for?"

She didn't even have to think about it. "Casserole. But I'm not sure where to get that in L.A."

EPILOGUE

Nine months later

Evan breathed a sigh of relief as the applause at Jean-Claude Riel's main gallery died down. He'd given brief remarks, as was expected from the artist at an opening, and now the attention would be off him for a while.

It would be on the woman standing in the back sipping a mimosa as the morning sun shone down on her like she was on loan from heaven, for fuck's sake. His painting hand twitched.

But it wouldn't be overt attention, because it turned out that the L.A. art crowd liked to pretend it was above gaping at famous pop stars. So Emmy could circulate around the brunch party celebrating his second show with Riel as the recipient of sideways glances rather than pleas to autograph body parts. He met her eyes, and she inclined her head toward the door.

He nodded. Yes. *Hell, yes*. Time to blow this pop stand.

A young woman stepped into his path. "This is amazing, Professor Winslow!"

He turned to smile at Kaylee, the newest art history MA student at UCLA, where he held an adjunct appointment.

He had not gotten tenure at Dane College.

And he didn't give a shit.

He almost laughed aloud. It hadn't even been a year since Larry had let the axe fall, but it felt like a lifetime ago, and it still sort of amazed him how *much* he didn't give a shit. How you could spend years of your life laboring toward a goal and then it could just...not matter anymore.

The reason it didn't matter? Because when you broke it down, he had everything he'd ever wanted. More than he'd even thought to dream of—the parts added up to way more than the whole he'd been working toward all these years. He had an adjunct appointment at UCLA that scratched his professorial itch—he got to do a little teaching and as much research as he liked on the side. But he spent most of his days painting. And that was like being given a second chance at life, like breathing on his own after years on a ventilator. His return to the art world had not been without its controversies. The reviews of his first show had been mixed, many of them focusing more on him and his familial legacy than the actual art. But it had sold out, which was enough for Riel to order up a second show, and now Evan was selling steadily.

He met Emmy at the door, Kaylee trailing behind him.

"Kaylee," said Emmy. "You finished your first two quarters of grad school—congrats!"

Kaylee grinned. "Thanks."

"You gonna be okay this summer?" Emmy asked.

Emmy had adopted Kaylee as a sort of surrogate daughter-sister hybrid when Kaylee had arrived to start her studies, inviting her to dinner and taking her as her date to industry events—Evan wasn't much of a red carpet guy and usually sat out those sorts of things. If Kaylee had ever had a crush on him—Evan still wasn't convinced by Emmy's take on the situation—she had long since gotten over it. Hell, judging by the way she was beaming at Emmy, she'd probably transferred it to his girlfriend. Not that he blamed her.

"You remember to call Tony if you need anything," Emmy said, kissing Kaylee on the cheek, then putting on her hat and sunglasses.

Evan peered out the gallery window. There was a long black car waiting for them. As had become their custom, he went outside first. In a stroke of luck, the sidewalk was empty. He, the infamous hermit, had learned a lot about the celebrity ecosystem. It turned out that if you put a little planning into it, you could lead a semi-normal life. Sure, there were places you couldn't go if you wanted to avoid the paparazzi, but if you were smart, you could move around more freely than he might have expected. And she had a huge-ass wall around her house in the hills. *Their* house in the hills, he should say, because they'd bought one together, a fixer-upper that Emmy was slowly transforming.

"Hey," Tony said as he held the car door for Emmy. Tony had a mobile office set up in the car because he and Emmy had some last-minute business to attend to before she disappeared for the summer.

"Oh my God, it's Emerson Quinn!" Shrieks echoed from down the street, and he sighed as Emmy first froze, then turned to assess the situation. It was only a handful of teenage girls, so she smiled.

It wasn't always easy being Emerson Quinn's boyfriend.

But it was so, so worth it.

He leaned against the car and watched the girls exclaim over how much they loved her last album, which she'd ended up calling, simply, *Summer*. They weren't alone because the album had outsold all her previous efforts, even though she'd fired Claudia and Brian and co-produced it herself. The short tour she'd embarked on to support it had raked in so much money that he'd started calling her Sugar Mama.

"Sir!" trilled one of the girls. "Sir, can you take our picture?" She thrust a phone into his hands, and he pushed off the car to perform his duties.

"Wait!" said the other one as he was handing the camera back. "Aren't you, like, that guy who paints Emerson Quinn?"

That guy who paints Emerson Quinn.

He grinned. He was actually totally okay with that.

Six hours later the taxi pulled up in front of Mrs. Johansen's house.

"We'd better go right to the back, don't you think?" Emmy said, checking the time on her phone. "We're late."

"Sure," he said, content in the knowledge that they were home—or close enough.

A cheer went up in the backyard when they appeared.

Mrs. Johansen, her latest suitor, Jace, Jace's mom, and Evan's former colleagues Ken and Melissa all abandoned their burgers and brats and swarmed Evan and Emmy. Hugs and kisses and greetings were exchanged.

"How did the show go?" Mrs. Johansen asked.

"Swimmingly," Emmy said, beaming at him. "I lost count of how many little red dots there were on the captions."

"And look at you, you jet-setter," Ken said, clapping Evan on the back. "An art opening in L.A. in the morning, a barbeque in Dane in the evening."

"Hey!" said Emmy, moving to embrace Jace. "Graduation next week!"

Jace rolled his eyes, but Evan knew he secretly relished the fact that Emerson Quinn would be attending his graduation ceremony. "Yeah, and I don't know why Tony won't take my calls," he grumbled.

"Because we all agreed you're going to college first," said Jace's mom, who, judging from the number of pies on the picnic table, had come directly from work bearing goodies.

Tony, who devoted most of his time to managing Emmy, had selectively taken on a couple up-and-comers as clients, and he'd agreed to manage Jace's career—after he finished his degree at the University of Minnesota, which would be paid for by the scholarship he'd won at the songwriting contest.

"Everything fine here?" Evan asked no one in particular, once they'd all settled in with pie and ice cream.

"There were some photographers in town earlier this week, but Wanda chased them off. She told them you guys had bought a house in Miami."

Evan laughed. Given his background, it was a plausible story. He could imagine the paparazzi spinning their wheels in Miami, looking for them. The people of Dane, it turned out, were actually pretty chill when it came to Emmy. It was like the town had collectively decided that she was one of theirs, and hell if they were going to throw her to the wolves. In fact, they seemed to enjoy going to elaborate lengths to put the media off the scent. And, in a miracle he didn't expect to endure but would enjoy while it lasted, no one in the media had found out his address. Tony had overseen some kind of data wipe that made any evidence of Evan Winslow in Dane magically disappear.

So, for now at least, they had their haven. Their "summer home," Emmy liked to call it, which, even with the indoor refresh she'd overseen last summer, was a rickety, leaky old bag of bones that was such a far cry from their life in L.A. that it was laughable.

But that was the point.

As the fireflies and stars started to pop out in the darkening sky, he met her eyes over the campfire that Jace had started.

She raised her eyebrows and did the same slight jerk of her head that she'd done that morning in the gallery, but this time toward the house next door.

Hell, yes.

He was on his feet in a flash, and he didn't care that they left rather abruptly.

He didn't care that everyone probably saw him grab her ass as they crossed the yards.

He didn't care that the house was hot as Hades. He'd been going to retrofit for central air this summer, but she'd talked him out of it, and, frankly, given the image of a summer spent sitting on the porch with her in her little tank tops and shorts, she didn't have to do much convincing.

She dropped her purse on the table in the entryway and kept walking.

"Hey," she said to the giant bear sitting on the bench at the back of the entryway. She patted its head. "It's good to be home."

Then she twisted to look at him over her shoulder and performed one more questioning twitch of her head, this time toward the stairs.

"Hell, yes." He said it out loud this time, and then he, the guy who paints Emerson Quinn, followed his girlfriend up the stairs.

ACKNOWLEDGMENTS

Thanks to Tracy Montoya for working her usual editing magic and to Julia Ganis of JuliaEdits.com for the thoughtful copy editing. Carmen Pacheco's eagle eyes saved me from some embarrassing last-minute typos.

Sandra Owens, Audra North, Erika Olbricht, and Gwen Hayes provided extremely helpful feedback on early drafts. Also: friendship, well-timed jokes, pep talks, and all that jazz.

Laurie Perry straightened me out on a bunch of Los Angeles details. (Emmy is now shopping at the correct Whole Foods thanks to her.)

Alexis Hall provided tagline help. (Meaning he basically came up with it.)

My agent, Courtney Miller-Callihan, contributed a lot of brainpower to this project and remains amazingly supportive of her hybrid clients' indie adventures.

Thank you to all!

CONNECT WITH ME

Sign up for my newsletter at jennyholiday.com/newsletter. I send newsletters when I have a new release or a sale, and I sometimes include giveaways and access to freebies only for subscribers. Or you can find me on Twitter at @jennyholi or Instagram at @holymolyjennyholi. (I'm technically on Facebook, but I'm rarely actually there.) Visit my website at jennyholiday.com.

Reviews really help authors, not only because they help us find new readers but because more reviews means more favorable treatment by retailers' algorithms. If you're moved to leave an honest review of this book or any of my others on the retailer's site where you bought it, I'd be most grateful.

ABOUT THE AUTHOR

Jenny Holiday started writing at age nine when her awesome fourth grade teacher gave her a notebook and told her to start writing some stories. That first batch featured mass murderers on the loose, alien invasions, and hauntings. (Looking back, she's amazed no one sent her to a kid-shrink.) She's been writing ever since. After a detour to get a PhD in geography, she worked as a professional writer for many years. Later, her tastes having evolved from alien invasions to happily-ever-afters, she tried her hand at romance. Today she is a USA Today bestselling author of all sorts of romance novels: contemporary and historical, straight and gay. She lives in London, Ontario.

www.jennyholiday.com
jenny@jennyholiday.com
Twitter: @jennyholi
Instagram: @holymolyjennyholi
Newsletter: jennyholiday.com/newsletter

BOOKS BY JENNY HOLIDAY

THE FAMOUS SERIES

Famous

Infamous

BRIDESMAIDS BEHAVING BADLY

One and Only

It Takes Two

Merrily Ever After

Three Little Words

THE 49TH FLOOR

Saving the CEO

Sleeping With Her Enemy

The Engagement Game

His Heart's Revenge

NEW WAVE NEWSROOM

The Fixer

The Gossip

The Pacifist

REGENCY REFORMERS

The Miss Mirren Mission

The Likelihood of Lucy

Viscountess of Vice

AN EXCERPT FROM INFAMOUS

FAMOUS #2

Available everywhere ebooks are sold, and in paperback from Amazon. Read on for an excerpt.

Is he brave enough to face the music?

All that up-and-coming musician Jesse Jamison has ever wanted is to be on the cover of *Rolling Stone*. When a gossip website nearly catches him kissing someone who isn't his famous girlfriend—and also isn't a girl—he considers the near miss a wake-up call. There's a lot riding on his image as the super-straight rocker, and if he wants to realize his dreams, he'll need to toe the line. Luckily, he's into women too. Problem solved.

After a decade pretending to be his ex's roommate, pediatrician Hunter Wyatt is done hiding. He might not know how to date in the Grindr world, how to make friends in a strange city, or whether his new job in Toronto is a mistake. But he does know that no one is worth the closet. Not even the world's sexiest rock star.

As Jesse's charity work at Hunter's hospital brings the two closer together, a bromance develops. Soon, Hunter is all Jesse can think about. But when it comes down to a choice between Hunter and his career, he's not sure he's brave enough to follow his heart.

CHAPTER ONE

At the last second, Jesse changed his mind and sat next to the hot guy instead of the middle-aged businesswoman.

It was a breach of the rules. Jesse had been taking the Sunday afternoon Montreal-to-Toronto train once a month for the past four years, and he had a system, a well-honed methodology developed from painful trial and error.

And by *painful*, he meant, for example, *five hours trapped next to a young mother holding a teething baby.*

Most people liked to rush onto the train as soon as possible, and they aggressively went after empty rows, seating themselves alone. But this route always sold out. Since the train was going to fill, it was smarter to hang back a bit, to bide his time and get onto a car that looked like it was about half-full. That way, he could choose his seatmate, whereas all those hasty people alone in two-seater rows had to resign themselves to a journey with whoever happened to plop down next to them.

No, it was infinitely preferable to be in control of one's own destiny.

And Jesse was nothing if not in control of his destiny.

So whenever Jesse got on a train, the first thing he always did was start profiling the hell out of potential seatmates.

Middle-aged women were the best. Even better if they looked like they were traveling on business. If they *also* wore wedding rings? Jackpot. Women in general tended not to initiate conversation and left him to pass the time in peace, the aforementioned mother-of-teether being emblematic of an exceptional subcategory: mothers desperately in need of adult conversation.

Another subcategory to avoid regardless of gender? The elderly, God bless them, were not ideal seatmates.

Neither were teenagers, the ultimate undesirables. They were starting to recognize him. Some people in their twenties and thirties did too, but they usually couldn't remember from where—or if they did, it sparked a brief conversation and then they picked up on his not-so-subtle cues and left him alone. But if a teenaged girl recognized him, he was doomed. He generally didn't like to think of teenagers as the band's target demographic, but you never had any idea what the record label was going to do with your stuff. Before you knew it, you'd be appearing on Spotify playlists called "teen heartbreak" or some shit.

He was beginning to think it was time to arrange alternate transportation for his monthly trips back from Montreal. Things were happening faster on the career front than he'd anticipated. By the time he was on the cover of *Rolling Stone*, he wasn't going to be taking the train anymore anyway. And what do they say? "Start as you mean to go on"?

Today, he ambled down the aisle, scanning the rows until he spied the perfect target: midforties, hair blown out into a perfect dark-brown helmet, business suit, laptop already fired up.

As he approached, he surveyed the rest of the car. The row across from the businesswoman was occupied by a man reading a book. He was dressed in an aqua button-down shirt and dark jeans. Salt-and-pepper hair, which was clearly premature—the guy couldn't have been more than thirty-five—

swooshed back into a messy pompadour that was shorter on the sides. His most prominent facial feature was a chiseled jaw dusted with a few days' worth of beard growth that was more salt than pepper.

Well, shit. A baby silver fox.

The poor bastard would probably end up with some clingy woman sitting next to him, projecting all her hopes onto him for the duration of the trip.

Jesse should do a good deed and sit next to him.

He usually tried to ignore men who weren't obviously working on something. You never knew with men. It was harder to make snap judgments about them. Sometimes they kept to themselves, but sometimes the newspaper they'd seemed so engrossed in would turn out to be a prop and they'd want to buddy up with you.

Someone was coming up the aisle behind him. Jesse was holding everyone up.

The woman was safer. Infinitely safer.

He set his bag down on the seat next to the man.

Jesse rummaged through it to pull out the items he'd need during the trip—phone, bottle of water, the latest issues of *Billboard* and *Rolling Stone*. It was hard not to sigh over the talentless, manufactured boy band on the cover of the latter. But he would have his turn someday.

As he reached up to stash his bag on the overhead shelf, the man looked up and caught his eye.

Jesse nodded as he sat. The man's eyes were striking—a kind of light brown flecked with gold, bright enough to be visible behind his black horn-rimmed glasses. The silver hair and the almost-gold eyes were a weird but compelling combination, like clashing jewelry.

The man gave a slight smile and said, "Hey," before returning his attention to his book. A second later, though, his phone dinged. He picked it up and eyed the screen. Jesse watched him key in his passcode and read a long text. His eyes seemed to darken in real time, becoming a little less gold, like the sun dimming. He dropped the phone carelessly into the seat pocket in front of him, closed his eyes, and mouthed, *Fuck.*

Some part of Jesse's brain could sense some other part of his brain gearing up to speak.

Don't do it.

They had a five-hour journey ahead of them.

Don't do it.

"Everything okay?"

Damn it.

The man's eyes flew open as the rational part Jesse's brain railed at the mouth-controlling part, which had apparently gone rogue.

"Sorry," Jesse said, and what was he *doing*? This way lay ruin. Or at least the possibility of an excruciatingly tedious five hours, because who knew if he'd been brainwashed by this guy's good looks? "You just seemed…upset all of a sudden."

The man opened his mouth, then closed it, like maybe he was at war with himself too.

"Sorry," said Jesse again, which was weird because *Spin*'s review of the band's last record had called it "unapologetic," and never had Jesse been more satisfied with an adjective. "I'll leave you alone."

You know the best way to leave someone alone? Leave them the fuck alone.

"I'm a doctor," the man said, kind of woodenly, like he was trying out this talking thing for the first time. His voice was all gravel and velvet, which should have been a contradiction, but apparently a guy with silver hair and gold eyes didn't have to hew to the rules that governed the rest of the slobs in the world. "A pediatrician. I have a patient who got some bad news."

"Yeah?" Jesse prompted, because suddenly, he could no longer imagine anything he'd like to do more for the next five hours than listen to Baby Silver Fox talk about his job. Also: what the hell?

"He needs a new liver. We were testing his brother as a possible donor." He looked out the window at the passing scenery as he spoke. "It was this kid's best hope. That was one of the nurses texting with the news that the brother is not a match. Now he's got to sit around on the waiting list biding time—and time isn't something this kid has a ton of." He ran his hands through his hair, scraping his fingers against his scalp in frustration as he turned his attention back to Jesse. "Sorry. That was probably a longer answer than you wanted."

Christ. That put things into perspective, didn't it? Here Jesse was, his biggest problem that he wasn't making enough money to fly back from Montreal after his visits with his sister but he was starting to be recognized on the train. "You know what? I'll be right back." He popped up and hunted down the porter, who hadn't begun food and beverage service yet and, by dangling an enormous tip, managed to procure two tiny bottles of whiskey.

When he plunked them down on Baby Silver Fox's tray, it occurred to him that maybe whiskey wasn't the best answer to *liver problems*, but the man grinned and said, "It's noon somewhere?"

"Exactly," said Jesse, a fierce sort of satisfaction lodging in his chest at the idea that he'd made this man smile. "Nothing like a little midmorning whiskey to take your mind off your problems." He twisted open one of the bottles and handed it over, belatedly wishing he'd gotten something classier than whiskey. This guy probably drank martinis.

"Thanks." Baby Silver Fox clinked his bottle against Jesse's and then took a sip.

He wasn't sure what to say. "So you're a pediatrician? That must be rewarding." As soon as it was out, though, he regretted it. *The guy tells you a kid is on the verge of death, and you say, "How rewarding"?* "On the whole, I mean. Making kids well," he added, because why stop while he was behind?

"I wish. Most of the kids I see are really sick. I work at Toronto Children's Hospital. I'm a hospitalist. You know what that is? Most people don't."

"I would be one of those people."

"It's sort of like a general practitioner, but for patients in the hospital. I oversee their care—many of them are being seen by lots of different kinds of specialists and technicians. I make sure everything is integrated optimally and…" He trailed off and sighed.

"And that kids who need new livers get them?" Jesse finished softly.

Baby Silver Fox—make that *Dr.* Baby Silver Fox—rolled his eyes like he was disgusted with himself. "In theory."

"Hey, now. It's not your fault this kid's brother wasn't a match."

"I know. I'm just… I don't know. I moved to Toronto from Montreal three months ago. I thought about changing things up when I decided I was going to move—joining a regular pediatric practice. Giving out vaccines and fixing tummy trouble and referring on the hard cases. You'd think stuff like this would get easier, but it doesn't."

"I don't imagine dying kids ever gets easy."

The doctor made a vague noise of agreement. "Sometimes I wonder what I was thinking. The point of moving was to make a fresh start. And here I am doing the exact same thing I was doing in Montreal…and, Jesus, listen to me. I don't even know you, and it's like I think you're my therapist or something." He held up his now-empty bottle. "I'm a bit of a lightweight, I'm afraid. And also a chatty drunk, so…"

"Hey, it's okay." And, amazingly, it was. This was exactly the kind of conversation he normally bent over backward to avoid, but somehow, this time, with this guy, he wanted to know more.

"Let's change the subject," said the man. "What about you? What brought you to Montreal? Or is Montreal home?"

"Nope, headed home to Toronto. I'm in a band. We have a monthly gig in Montreal."

"A band that travels by VIA Rail?" He smiled. "You guys should make a commercial."

"No, the gig's on Friday, and the rest of the band heads back afterward in a couple of vans. My sister and her son live in Montreal, though, so I usually spend the weekend with them and make my own way home on Sunday."

"Would I know your work?"

"I doubt it."

"Try me."

"The band's called Jesse and the Joyride."

"Alas, I don't think I know it. Are you Jesse?"

"Yep. Jesse Jamison." He stuck out his hand.

"Hunter Wyatt."

Hunter Wyatt's hand was soft. Or maybe it was only Jesse's guitar-induced calluses that made it seem so.

Jesse held on a heartbeat too long, lulled for a moment by the rocking of the train and the warm flesh against his own.

Hunter quirked a smile as he pulled away. "It's not every day you meet a rock star on the train. Especially a rock star taking the train because he's so dedicated to his sister. You're a regular saint."

"I'm not a saint. Or a rock star, for that matter." *Yet.* "But, yeah, it's just me and my sister and my nephew—he's three. Our parents are gone. My sister's had a rough couple of years. She's mostly on her own with my nephew."

"Husband left?"

If only he *would* leave, once and for all. "Something like that."

"That's tough. We've all been there." He huffed a bitter laugh. "Some of us more recently than others."

"Ah," Jesse said. "The fresh start. The move to Toronto."

"Officially I came for the job, but…yeah."

"How long had you been together?"

"Eight years."

Jesse whistled. "Wow. I don't think I've ever even made it eight *months* in a relationship." Not even close to eight months, truth be told, but he didn't want to admit that in front of this guy who so clearly had his shit together.

"Not so impressive, really," Hunter said, "given that I have literally nothing to show for it."

"So you were back for a visit this weekend?"

"Yeah, the dog died. My ex called and said this was it, so I came up to…say goodbye, I guess."

"Man, harsh."

"Yeah, the worst part is that the dog died before I got there."

"Your girlfriend leaves you and your dog dies? It's like a country song—a bad country song."

The doctor didn't laugh, just screwed up his face like he was trying to decide something. Then he said, "It's, uh, not a girl."

"The dog is not a girl?"

"The girlfriend is not a girlfriend. He's a boyfriend. *Ex*-boyfriend."

"Right."

Right.

Jesse had been afraid of that.

This was the part where the rock star would freak out.

Which was fine, because Hunter's dog was dead, his sickest patient was going to keep getting sicker, and his ex, Julian, was still a closet-case bent on sucking all the life out of Hunter.

So a little straight-boy panic induced by accidental proximity to a homo was nothing.

He wasn't into pretending to be anything he wasn't—not anymore, anyway—so the testosterone-oozing musician in the next seat could just feel free to panic.

And he *was* panicking.

But apparently not over the fact that Hunter liked dick.

"Holy shit."

His phone had chimed, and he'd picked it up and was scrolling through what looked like an article illustrated with pictures. Whatever it was, it wasn't good news.

'Twas the season, apparently.

"Holy *shit*," Jesse said again, closing his eyes and letting his chin fall to his chest.

"What's the matter?" Hunter asked, because it seemed rude to check out now.

Jesse opened his eyes and blew out a long, slow breath. "Well, it's nowhere near as bad as your news. That's a good perspective to remember."

"Less-bad bad news. That sounds delightful right about now. Hit me."

He didn't answer, but he handed over his phone.

It was an article on a website called *GossipTO*, headlined

Jesse Jamison making out with mysterious blond—and she isn't Kylie Cameron.

He read on. Apparently his seatmate was notorious for his stereotypical rock star ways. Before his current girlfriend—this Kylie person—Jesse had enjoyed the groupie lifestyle, if this site was to be believed. Everyone had been shocked when he'd gotten together with Kylie, the story reported. There was also something in there about a trashed hotel room incident.

"I thought you said you weren't a rock star," Hunter said.

"I'm not. Not really."

Hunter chuckled and read part of the article out loud. "'We all know Jesse likes his sex, drugs, and rock and roll, but'—"

Jesse cut him off. "I mean, I have a band. We're doing pretty well in Canada. No one knows our name in the States. Yet. This"—he gestured toward the phone—"is a sensationalistic, B-list Canadian gossip website. But damn, they're out to get me. I can't do anything without them all over my ass. So I enjoy having a little fun from time to time. It's not like I'm breaking any laws." He quirked a grin. "Mostly."

"So they got you making out with this woman who isn't your girlfriend?"

"Yep."

"And your girlfriend is also some kind of celebrity?"

"She's a model."

Hunter couldn't really see anything about the person Jesse was kissing in the blurry shot. Jesse had his back to the camera, and his companion was leaning against a brick wall. She was as tall as Jesse, and models were tall, right? All that was visible of the kiss-ee was shoulder-length, dirty-blond, almost-messy hair—which also seemed kind of model-esque, in that way that models sometimes seemed to strive to look bad in the name of fashion. "So there's no way this could be her?"

"You don't know Kylie Cameron?" Jesse asked.

Hunter searched his mind. "I don't think so?"

"She's Asian. She has long black hair."

"Ah," Hunter said. "I guess you're busted."

"Yeah, and in addition to that not being her, Kylie is like, Canada's sweetheart. She was on *Degrassi* as a kid—before she moved into modeling."

"I'm kind of out of the pop culture loop," said Hunter, though of course he did know the iconic TV show. Everyone who grew up in Canada knew *Degrassi*. Hell, Drake had been on *Degrassi*.

"Yeah, well, everyone loves her. Now I'm the asshole who publicly broke Kylie Cameron's heart."

Hunter squinted at the phone again. If the Kinsey scale was a reliable measure—as a medical doctor, he had his doubts—Hunter was a solid six. Unambiguously gay. And usually he was ruthlessly adept at not developing crushes on straight guys. (Gay guys who pretended to be straight in certain circumstances were another question. Unfortunately.) So the image of Jesse Jamison kissing Ms. Anonymous should have had no effect on him. He should have been immune.

But damn, there was something about that picture. The way Jesse was crowding his not-girlfriend up against the wall. The way he was framing her face with his hands. That was why only her hair was visible—Jesse's hands were clamped possessively on her face.

And if Jesse had this much to lose by being spotted, the fact that this kiss had gone down in public must have meant they'd both been pretty carried away. Hunter shifted in his seat.

"What's her name?" He handed the phone back with an odd reluctance.

"My girlfriend? You mean her real name? It's Kylie—she never used a stage name. And I should probably start calling her my *ex*-girlfriend. 'Cause she is not going to stand for this shit."

"No." Hunter gestured to the phone. "What's the other woman's name?"

Jesse paused before answering. "It doesn't really matter."

"You don't know it!" Damn, this guy *was* a rock star, or at least well on his way to becoming one. Hunter cracked up; he couldn't help it. Jesse certainly looked the part. Choppy dark, messy hair hung around his face. His forearms—he wore a ratty flannel shirt with the sleeves rolled up—were covered with tattoos. He had that kind of sexy-sleazy look.

That was not a look Hunter went for.

Historically.

He liked a more polished look.

Usually.

"Haven't you ever made out with someone whose name you didn't catch?" Jesse asked.

"Not for a really long time." Not since before he'd met Julian. And even before Julian, Hunter had been a serial monogamist. He could count on one hand the number of casual hookups in his past.

Maybe that was what the move to Toronto had been missing so far—some casual sex to break him out of his slump. The prospect was kind of terrifying.

"Well, you should try it," Jesse declared. "Quickest way to get over your loser ex."

"Why do you assume my ex was the loser? Maybe I was the loser."

"Nah."

Hunter wanted to ask how Jesse could possibly know this, but he didn't want to make it seem like he was fishing for compliments.

Jesse's phone buzzed. He picked it up again. "And there it is."

"What?"

Jessie scrolled for a moment, then said, "The breakup text." He sighed resignedly.

"Really?" Hunter was taken aback by the idea of breaking up with someone via text, but he supposed that was part of the jet-set, rock star life his seatmate lived. "Jesus, I'm sorry."

Jesse shrugged. "It's okay. Saves me having to do it. The writing was already on the wall."

"The writing on the wall being something *other than* you making out with someone else against the wall? It seems like your whole problem here is the wall."

All he got in response was a chuckle.

Clearly, Jesse was not the type to invest his heart and soul and the better part of a decade into a relationship.

Hunter should learn from Jesse.

He was downloading Grindr as soon as he got home.

"The more important question is whether my *manager* is going to dump me over this."

"You're more concerned about getting dumped by your manager than your girlfriend?" Hunter asked, though he wasn't sure why—the answer was clear.

"I have a bit of a work-life balance problem?" Jesse shrugged. "And also a manager who basically has me on probation."

"Wow." Who *was* this guy? Hunter had never seen anyone so…unapologetic.

"What are you drinking?" Jesse asked.

"What?" Oh, the service cart was making its way down the aisle.

"I'm guessing whiskey isn't your preferred poison."

When Hunter didn't answer right away, Jesse dropped his magazines into the seat pocket in front of him and said, "Fuck career-ruining photographs." Then he did the same with his phone, holding it between one finger and a thumb like it was contaminated. "Fuck dying kids. Fuck *everyone*. We're single and free. We should toast that shit."

♫♪

Four hours later, as the conductor announced they were ten minutes from Union Station, Jesse was feeling good.

Eight mini-bottles of red wine could have that effect on a guy.

"We should hide the evidence," Hunter said, slurring a bit and then laughing. He'd only had four mini-bottles. The handsome doctor *was* a bit of a lightweight.

It was adorable.

Jesse had procured most of the aforementioned mini-bottles by sweet-talking a young woman porter after the older man assigned to their car responded to Jesse's request for bottle number four by looking down his nose and saying, "There's only an hour left on your journey, sir."

Hunter reached toward the small garbage bag the train provided, his bottles in hand.

"Hey, no need to 'hide the evidence.'" Jesse grabbed Hunter's arm near the elbow to halt his tidying instinct. Maybe Jesse was an entitled rock star asshole, but he planned to leave a pile of tiny bottles on the seat for the snotty porter to deal with.

Hunter was wearing one of those shirts that looked like

An excerpt from Infamous

flannel, but were actually made of some kind of unbelievably soft mystery material. It was hard to take his hand away. It was hard to do anything but let his hand slide down a forearm that was softer than…all the soft things. A cat? A cloud? A—

—hand.

He'd reached the bare skin of the back of Hunter's hand, and the change in texture was so jarring, he snatched his own hand away as if he'd touched a hot stove.

"No need to hide the evidence, because there was no crime," he said firmly. "These baby boozes were procured with cold, hard cash."

"Cold hard cash and a boatload of charm," Hunter said, and Jesse didn't have an argument for that one. "What about public drunkenness?" Hunter went on. "Isn't that a crime?"

"You might have me there."

Except not. He wasn't nearly drunk enough to plug back into reality. He fished for his phone, dread in his gut. He knew what he would find. Outraged tweets from the public that he had dared to cheat on their beloved Kylie. Incredulous texts from the guys. Anger from his manager, who had read him the riot act about his out-of-control behavior only a month ago.

And there it was.

His second breakup text of the day.

He'd been fired by his manager. Cut loose by the woman who had plucked the band out of the club scene and deftly shepherded them to the next level—they were now routinely selling out midsize venues, and she'd been talking about a major-label deal when they were done with their current indie contract.

It stung like hell. *Way* more than Kylie.

He glanced at Dr. Wyatt the Baby Silver Fox, who was shrugging into his coat.

Since they were approaching the station, Jesse stood and moved into the aisle.

"Well, thanks for the...boozy chat." Hunter stood too, but he lost his footing, and Jesse had to grab him to steady him.

"Whoa," Jesse said, liking the feel of the scratchy wool of Hunter's coat under his fingers. Hunter, with his fuzzy coat and his cottony soft shirt, had Jesse on tactile overload. "Maybe there was too much booze in that chat."

"No." Hunter flashed an impish, satisfied smile. The kind of smile Jesse could imagine coming up in...other contexts. "That was the *perfect balance* of booze and conversation. You made me forget all about my dead dog and my broken heart."

Broken heart. Hunter had been vague about his breakup earlier. It was hard to imagine someone as confident, as obviously accomplished, as *solid* as Hunter getting his heart broken.

It was hard to imagine any man giving him up.

Any man who was in the stage of life and career that promoted being settled and monogamous, that was.

And out.

Which was not Jesse. Not even close.

Which was why he couldn't explain why the next thing he did was dig around in his bag until he found a receipt and a pen, scrawled his email and phone number on it, and said, "Keep in touch."

"Give me one reason I should sign a punk like you?"

Jesse blinked. He was hungover, and his mind was slow. He had gone home last night after that surreal train ride and graduated from mini-bottles of booze to a full-size one. And, in a state of drunken overconfidence-mixed-with-defiance, he'd emailed Matty Alvarado, Canada's most famous artist manager. The guy oversaw a handful of successful musical exports, youngish pop stars mostly, who'd made it big south of the border and beyond. He was known as a rainmaker.

There was no way he'd take on a medium-time rock-and-roll band like Jesse and the Joyride.

Or so Jesse had thought.

But here he was twenty-four hours later, having been summoned to the dude's palatial office, which was decorated with a weird mixture of Catholic paraphernalia and photos of Matty with some of the world's most popular acts.

"You have quite the reputation, you know," Matty went on when Jesse didn't answer fast enough. "The Canadian music scene is small. People talk."

"We've been steadily building momentum for the last couple years." Jesse started in on the speech he'd been rehearsing in his head on the way over. "We've been playing midsize venues. I'm getting better and better as a songwriter. We have one more record left on our contract. After that, a major-label deal is within reach—I know it."

Matty waved a hand dismissively, like all of Jesse's painstaking, incremental work was nothing more than a bit of lint to be brushed off. "There's no shortage of acts in your position. Wannabe rock stars with big dreams are a dime a dozen, so you—"

"We're good," Jesse said, daring to interrupt the famed tastemaker, because why not? This wasn't going well, and he had nothing to lose. "No, we're fucking *great*."

Matty sighed. Drummed his fingers on his huge lacquered desk. "You are," he finally said, as if it pained him to admit it. "But you're also a fucking mess. Look at you—hungover, splashed all over the tabloids every couple of months with some drama or other. That's what I expect from the teenagers I sign, Jesse, not from grown men. What I do is brand people. I *make* them. I can make something from nothing, no problem. But I don't know that I can make something from…a big pile of shit."

Jesse winced.

"Coming back from cheating on Kylie Cameron might be impossible," Matty said.

Might be.

Those two words surged through Jesse. They were a thin edge of crowbar he could use to pry open this door.

Jesse had spent his entire life striving to get where he was. He'd had to beg his parents for piano lessons, for second-hand guitars. Later, when he'd been a bit older, he would have moved into the band room in his high school if his teacher had let him. It had literally been his happy place. Some days, it had felt like his *only* place.

Music was his life. It had been from the start.

And, just as importantly, it was his *living.* He was making a living as a musician. Or he had been, anyway.

All he wanted—the dream he'd had since he'd been old enough to dream—was to be on the cover of *Rolling Stone.*

And he could get there. All the ingredients were in place.

The only thing standing in his way was him.

That's what Matty was saying, and suddenly, Jesse *got* it.

"The way I see it," he started slowly, thinking through his argument with a mind suddenly cleared of cobwebs, "is that the *GossipTO* article was a blessing in disguise."

Matty raised an eyebrow. "That's the first interesting thing you've said since you got here."

"Kylie told me something once. She said that everyone performs who they are to some degree. Despite having gotten her start on a TV show, she had no aspirations to cross back over into acting, but she said she was an actor all the same.

'We all are,' she said. 'All of us whose livelihoods depend on being in the public eye. We perform who we are, consciously or no. The trick to success is to understand this and to learn to exploit it. Learn how to control the performance. Be in control of your own narrative.'"

He had dismissed her approach as too Machiavellian, but he saw now that she'd been right.

"Smart woman." Matty made a "go on" gesture.

"The way I see it, I have two choices. I can live like a rock star—partying, coming in late to recording sessions because I'm hungover, slutting around with anything that moves."

Which was exactly what he'd been doing. He'd been too busy with his degenerate life lately to prioritize what mattered: the music.

"Or…" he continued, trying to formulate his thoughts into a coherent argument. "I can *act* like a rock star."

"What does that mean?"

"I don't know. You tell me. You sign me, and I'll do whatever you tell me to do. But only on the surface. Underneath that, I'm keeping my head down. Cutting way, way back on the booze so I'm clearheaded enough to make kick-ass music and smart business decisions. Keeping my dick in my pants."

Matty was silent a long time, then he said, "Do we need to send you to rehab?"

We. He'd said, *We.* Adrenaline started frothing in Jesse's veins.

"No. Let me give it a shot, and if it doesn't work, I'll go without argument." He was pretty sure now that he'd had his come-to-Jesus moment—maybe all that Catholic stuff on Matty's walls had put the whammy on him—making the necessary lifestyle changes was going to be easy.

"Drugs?"

"Not really. The odd joint to relax after the show if

someone offers, but I'm not buying the stuff. And I'll drop that too, if you want."

"No one wants their rock stars to be saints," said Matty. "It's a fine line."

"I get that," said Jesse. That was kind of what he'd been trying to articulate with the whole *live like a rock star versus act like a rock star* thing.

"Fuck me, but I think you do," said Matty. "The question is, are you all talk?"

Jesse smiled, feeling some of his old swagger returning. "There's only one way to find out."

"This is how it's going to work," Matty said. "You and I sign a contract for six months. Consider it a probationary period. A tryout. You know that whole three strikes, you're out thing?"

Jesse nodded and tried not to grin too overtly.

"With you and me, it's one strike. You do the music. I do everything else. You do exactly what I say. I tell you you're going on Howard Stern, you're going on Howard Stern. I say you're going on the Mickey Mouse Club, you're going on the Mickey Mouse Club. I get you a girlfriend, you've got a girl-friend. I tell you to break up with her, you break up with her. I say you're playing a show at the North fucking Pole, you're out shopping for snowsuits. After six months, we regroup. If we both want to continue—and if you've behaved yourself—we sign for real. Got it?"

"Yes." Jesse refrained from babbling about how grateful he was. Matty didn't seem like the kind of guy who appreciated empty words, and Jesse respected that.

"Is there anything else I need to know about? Any other scandals brewing? If I don't know about it, I can't fix it."

Jesse hesitated. As much as he hated to do it, it was prob-ably wise to lay all his cards on the table.

"What?"

"That...person in the photo from *GossipTO*..."

"She going to talk to the press?" Matty did the dismissive waving thing again. "That's no problem. We can spin that to our advantage."

"I don't think so. It's more that she...wasn't a she."

Matty blinked rapidly.

"But I don't think he actually knew who I was," Jesse continued quickly. "We didn't really talk, and he didn't say anything about recognizing me. I met him at—"

"What are you saying, Jesse? You're gay? Because that is not going to work with the brand I'm envisioning for you."

"Not gay. Bisexual. And not even that much." It was true. Jesse thought of himself as mostly straight but...open to other possibilities. But he figured Matty probably didn't care about shades of gray here.

Matty got up and walked around to the front of his desk. Jesse stood, thinking he was being dismissed. *Fuck.* That picture really *had* ruined his life. He'd had the biggest agent in all of Canada *almost* locked down.

"Sit." Matty leaned back against the front of his desk, like he was a school principal.

Jesse sat.

"I don't want to hear another word about this. From this point onward, you are not...*bisexual.*" Matty spat the word like it was a curse. "You are Jesse Jamison, the bad-boy rock star next door. What does that mean? You're a fucking rock star. As I said, no one wants you to be a saint. You're brilliant and prickly and you live large. Or rather, you give the appearance of living large. You do what you need to do to keep yourself clean enough that your head is in the game, but you are not to speak publicly about having a problem with booze or any of that. Jesse Jamison the recovering alcoholic is not what we're going for here. When you appear at high-profile events, you have a fucking craft beer in your hand. You're single now, and we're going to use that. You are going to date casually. You are going to break a heart or two. All that's the rock star part. But you have a soft side. You're a little vulnerable. A sixteen-year-old girl can imagine reforming you. She can imagine you taking her to the fucking prom. Hell, I might make you actually do that. That's the boy-next-door side."

Jesse could see where Matty was going with this. It made sense. Matty's "brand," as much as Jesse hated that word, picked up on Jesse's natural tendencies and…magnified them.

Well, *some* of his natural tendencies.

"But one thing I need to be absolutely clear about is that both the rock star and the boy next door are straight. Those hearts you're breaking are *female* hearts. Those teenagers fantasizing about you are *female* teenagers. If you don't agree one hundred percent with this right now, we're done."

Something pinged inside Jesse's chest, like a pebble being dropped into an empty box. And for some stupid reason, he thought of Dr. Hunter Wyatt, the heartbroken pediatrician.

Then he thought of the cover of *Rolling Stone*. He thought of what he'd been striving for his whole goddamn life.

He stuck his hand out. "It's a deal."

AN EXCERPT FROM ONE AND ONLY

BRIDESMAIDS BEHAVING BADLY #1

Available everywhere in ebook and paperback. Read on for an excerpt.

Miss Responsibility meets Mr. Reckless...

With her bridezilla friend on a DIY project rampage, bridesmaid Jane Denning will do anything to escape–even if it means babysitting the groom's troublemaker brother before the wedding. It should be a piece of cake, except the "cake" is a sarcastic former soldier who is 100% wicked hotness and absolutely off-limits.

Cameron MacKinnon is ready to let loose after returning from his deployment. But first he'll have to sweet talk the ultra-responsible Jane into taking a walk on the wild side. Turns out, riling her up is the best time he's had in years. But what happens when the fun and games start to turn into something real?

CHAPTER ONE

TUESDAY—ELEVEN DAYS BEFORE THE WEDDING

Jane! I thought you were *never* going to get here!"

"I came as quickly as I could," Jane said, trying to keep the annoyance out of her tone as she allowed herself to be herded into her friend Elise's house. She exchanged resigned smiles with her fellow bridesmaids—the ones who had obviously taken Elise's "Emergency bridesmaids meeting at my house NOW!" text more seriously than Jane had.

Gia and Wendy were sprawled on Elise's couch, braiding some kind of dried grass–type thing. Wendy, Jane's best friend, blew her a kiss.

Jane tried to perform her traditional catching of Wendy's kiss—it was their thing, dating back to childhood—but Elise thrust a mug of tea into Jane's hand before it could close over the imaginary kiss. Earlier that summer, Elise had embraced and then discarded a plan to start her wedding reception with some kind of complicated cocktail involving tea, and as a result, Jane feared she and the girls were doomed to a lifetime of Earl Grey. Their beloved bridezilla had thought nothing of special ordering twenty-seven unreturnable boxes of premium English tea leaves. She also apparently thought nothing of forcing her friends to endure the rejected reception beverage again and again. And again.

"Jane's here, so now you can tell us about the big emergency," Gia said. "And whatever it is, I'm sure she'll figure out a solution." She smiled at Jane. "You're so . . . smart."

Jane had a feeling that *smart* wasn't the word Gia initially meant to use. The girls—well, Gia and Elise, anyway—were always telling Jane to loosen up. But they also relied on her to solve their problems. They liked having it both ways. She was the den mother, but they were forever teasing her about being too rigid. Which was kind of rich, lately, coming from Elise, who had turned into a matrimonial drill sergeant. Jane put up with it because she loved them. Besides, *somebody* had to be the responsible one.

"Well," Jane teased, "this had better be a capital-E emergency because I was in the middle of having my costume for Toronto Comicon fitted when you texted." She opened the calf-length trench coat she'd thrown over her costume at the seamstress's when Elise's text arrived. It was the kind of coat women wore when seducing their boyfriends—or so she assumed, not having personally attempted to seduce anyone since Felix. She should probably just get rid of the coat because there were likely no seductions in her future, either.

"Hello!" Gia exclaimed. "*What* is that?"

"Xena: Warrior Princess," Wendy answered before Jane could.

"I have no idea what that means, but you look hot," Gia said.

Jane did a little twirl. The costume was really coming together. The seamstress had done a kick-ass job with the leather dress, armor, and arm bands, and all Jane needed to do was figure out something for Xena's signature weapon and she'd be set. "It was a cult TV show from the 1990s,"she explained. Gia was a bit younger than the rest of them. But who was Jane kidding? The real reason Gia didn't know about Xena was that she was a Cool Girl. As a model—an honest-to-goodness, catwalk-strutting, appearing-in-Calvin-Klein-ads model—she was too busy with her fabulous life to have time to watch syndicated late-night TV. "It's set in a sort of alternative ancient Greece, but it's leavened with other mythologies . . . " She trailed off because the explanation sounded lame even to her fantasy-novelist, geek-girl ears.

"Xena basically goes around kicking ass, and then she and her sidekick get it on with some lesbian action," Wendy said, summing things up in her characteristically concise way.

"Really?" Gia narrowed her eyes at Jane. "Is there something you're trying to tell us?"

"No!" Jane protested.

"Because you haven't had a boyfriend since Felix," Gia went on. "And you guys broke up, what? Four years ago?"

"Five," Wendy said.

It was true. But what her friends refused to accept was that she was single by choice. She had made a sincere effort, with Felix, whom she'd met halfway through university and stayed with until she was twenty-six, to enter the world of love and relationships that everyone was always insisting was so important. Felix had taught her many things, foremost among them that she was better off alone.

You know we'll love you no matter what," Gia said. "Who you sleep with doesn't make a whit of difference."

"I'm not gay, Gia! I just admire Xena. She didn't need men to get shit done. We could all—"

A very loud episode of throat clearing from Elise interrupted Jane's speech on the merits of independence, whether you were a pseudo-Greek warrior princess or a modern girl trying to get along in the world.

"Sorry." Jane sometimes forgot that most people did not share her views of love and relationships.

"I'm sure this is all super interesting, you guys?" Elise said. "But we have a serious problem on our hands?" She was talking fast and ending declarative statements with question marks—sure signs she was stressed. Elise always sounded like an auctioneer on uppers when she was upset.

"I need to grab my phone because I'm expecting the cake

people to call? So sit down and brace yourselves and I'll be right back?"

Jane sank into a chair and warily eyed a basket of spools of those brown string-like ribbon things—the kind that were always showing up tied around Mason jars of layered salads on Pinterest. She wasn't really sure how or why Elise had decided not to outsource this stuff like normal people did when they got married. The whole wedding had become a DIY-fest. "What are we doing with this stuff?" she asked the others.

"No idea," said Wendy, performing a little eye roll. "I'm just doing what I'm told."

Jane grinned. Although she, Wendy, Gia, and Elise were a tightly knit foursome, they also sorted into pairs of best friends: Jane and Wendy had grown up together and had met Elise during freshman orientation at university. They'd picked up Gia when they were seniors and Gia was a freshman—Elise had been her resident assistant—RA—and the pair had become fast friends despite the age difference.

"We are weaving table runners out of raffia ribbon," Gia said. She dropped her strands and reached for her purse. "Slide that tea over here—quick, before she gets back."

"God bless you," Jane said when Gia pulled a flask of whiskey out of her purse and tipped some into Jane's mug. If the "emergency" that had pulled Jane away from her cosplay fitting—not to mention a planned evening of writing—was going to involve table runners, she was going to need something to dull the edges a bit.

Elise reappeared. Jane practiced her nonchalant face as she sipped her "tea" and tried not to cough. She wasn't normally much of a drinker, but desperate times and all that.

"I didn't want to repeat myself, so I've been holding out on Gia and Wendy?" Elise said. "But there's been a . . . disruption to the wedding plans?"

I love you, but God help me, those are declarative sentences. Sometimes Jane had trouble turning off her inner editor. Job hazard.

"Oh my God, are you leaving Jay?" Wendy asked.

"Why would you say that?" Elise turned to Wendy in bewilderment.

Now, that was a legitimate question, the inner editor said—at least in the sense that it was meant to end with a question mark. The actual content of Wendy's question was kind of insensitive. But Wendy had trouble with change, and Elise pairing off and doing the whole till-death-do-us-part

thing? That was some major change for their little friend group. Jane might have had trouble with it, too, except it was plainly obvious to anyone with eyeballs that Elise was head-over-heels, one hundred percent gaga for her fiancé.

"I'm kidding!" Wendy said, a little too vehemently. Elise looked like she might have to call for smelling salts.

"Take a breath," Gia said to Elise, "and tell us what's wrong."

Elise did as instructed, then flopped into a chair. "Jay's brother is coming to the wedding."

"Jay has a brother?" Jane asked. Though she was guilty of maybe not paying one hundred percent attention to every single wedding-related detail—for example, she'd recused herself from the debate over the merits of sage green versus grass green for the ribbons that would adorn the welcome bags left in the guests' hotel rooms—she was pretty sure she had a handle on all the major players.

"His name is Cameron MacKinnon."

That didn't clear things up. "Jay Smith has a brother named Cameron MacKinnon?" she asked. Was that even possible?

"Half brother," Elise said. "You know how Jay's mom is

single?" It was true. There had been no "father of the groom" in Elise's carefully drafted program. "Well, she split from Jay's dad when Jay was nine. Then a couple years later, she had a brief relationship with another man. Cameron is the product of that—that's why his last name is MacKinnon and Jay's is Smith."

"But he wasn't always going to come to the wedding?" Gia asked. "Were they estranged?"

"They're not particularly close. There are eleven years between them—Cameron was in first grade when Jay left for school—but they're not estranged," Elise said. "He wasn't going to be able to make it to the wedding because he was supposed to be in Iraq. He was in the army. But now he's . . . not."

"That sounds ominous," Wendy said.

"Look, here's the thing," Elise said, sitting up straight, her voice suddenly and uncharacteristically commanding. "Cameron is a problem. He's wild. He drives too fast, drinks too much, sleeps around. You name it—if it's sketchy, he's into it."

"And this is *Jay's* brother," Jane said. Because no offense, she liked Jay fine, but Jay was. . . a tad underwhelming. He was an accountant. No matter what they were doing—football game, barbecue, hiking—he dressed in dark jeans and a polo shirt, like it was casual Friday at the office. To be honest, Jane had never really been sure what Elise saw in him. The girls were always telling *her* to loosen up, but compared to Jay, she was the life of the party.

"Yes," Elise said. "Cameron is Jay's brother, and he must be stopped."

"Dun, dun, dun!" Wendy mock-sang.

"Hey, I can totally switch gears and weave this thing into a noose," Gia said, holding up a lopsided raffia braid.

"I'm not kidding."

Elise's tone made everyone stop laughing and look up. The upspeak was gone, and the bride had become a warrior, eyes narrowed, lips pursed. "He's a high school dropout. He burned down a barn outside Thunder Bay when he was seventeen. He was charged with arson, the whole deal. Jay says his mother still hasn't lived it down. And there's talk he got a girl pregnant in high school."

"What happened?" asked a rapt Gia.

Elise shrugged. "Her family moved out of town, so no one really knows."

"Wow," Wendy said, echoing Jane's thoughts. Jane had initially assumed Elise was being melodramatic about this black-sheep brother—as she was about nearly everything wedding related—but this guy *did* sound like bad news.

"Anyway." Elise brandished an iPad in front of her like it was a weapon. "Cameron MacKinnon is *not* ruining my wedding. And if he's left to his own devices, he will. From what Jay says, he won't be able to help it." She poked at the iPad. "This changes everything. We need to redo the schedule —and the job list."

The words *job list* practically gave Jane hives. Elise had turned into a total bridezilla, but by unspoken agreement, the bridesmaids had been going along with whatever she wanted. It was the path of least resistance. But also, they truly wanted Elise to have the wedding of her dreams. Even if it was painful for everyone else.

But, oh, the *job list*. The job list was like the Hydra, a serpentine monster you could never get on top of. You crossed off a job, and two more sprouted to take its place. Jane had already hand-stenciled three hundred invitations, planned and executed two showers, joined Pinterest as instructed for the express purpose of searching out "homemade bunting," tried on no fewer than twenty-three dresses—all purple—and this Cameron thing aside, it looked like today was going to be spent weaving table runners. And they still had the bachelorette party and the rehearsal dinner to get through, never mind the main event.

It boggled the mind. Elise was an interior designer, so of course she cared how things looked, but even so, Jane was continuously surprised at how much the wedding was preoccupying her friend. She could only hope they would get their funny, creative, sweet friend back after it was all over.

"Cameron is coming to town tomorrow," Elise said. "I don't know why he couldn't just arrive a day ahead of the wedding like the rest of the out-of-town guests, but it is what it is." She let the iPad clatter onto the coffee table. "I don't even know how to add this to the job list, but somehow, we have to babysit Cameron for the next week and a half."

"We?" Wendy echoed.

"Yes. He needs to be supervised at all times until the wedding—until after the post-wedding breakfast, actually. Then he can wreak whatever havoc he wants."

"Hang on," Jane said. "I agree that he sounds like bad news. But let's say, for the sake of argument, he did something horrible and got arrested tomorrow. I don't really see how that would have an impact on your wedding at all, because—"

Elise looked up, either ignoring or legitimately not hearing Jane. "You can't do it, Gia. You're my maid of honor, and I need you at my side at all times."

"Sure thing," Gia said.

Easy for her to say. Gia had purposely not taken any modeling jobs the two weeks before the wedding. She had plenty of time to lounge around braiding dried foliage and looking effortlessly beautiful in sweatpants. Also, there was the part where she was a millionaire.

Elise started scrolling through some kind of calendar app on her iPad. "Now, tomorrow we're supposed to be spray-painting the tea sets gold."

Jane looked around. *Spray-painting the tea sets gold?* Why was no one else confused by that sentence?

"But we'll have to do that in the afternoon," Elise went on, "because—"

"I have to work tomorrow," Wendy said. And when Elise looked up blankly, she added, "Tomorrow is Wednesday."

Jane was about to protest that she had to work tomorrow, too. Book seven of the Clouded Cave series wasn't going to write itself. Just because she didn't have to be in court like Wendy didn't mean her job wasn't important. She had an inbox full of fan mail from readers clamoring for the next book, not to mention a contractual deadline that got closer every day.

Elise continued, seemingly oblivious to her friends' weekday employment obligations. "Tomorrow we also need to do a practice run of boutonniere, corsage, and bouquet making. I finagled a vendor pass to the commercial fruit and flower market, but we need to get there early. So we should do the flowers in the morning and paint the tea sets in the afternoon. We'll meet in Mississauga at five thirty, but someone needs to pick up Cameron and make sure he behaves all day."

"I'll do it," said Jane, mentally calculating that to be at the suburban flower market by five thirty, she'd have to get up at four a.m. Also, there was the part about spending the afternoon spray-painting tea sets. It didn't take a genius to figure out which was the lesser of the two proverbial evils. She could babysit this Cameron dude. She'd treat him like a character in one of her books—figure him out, then make him do her bidding. "Give me the wild man's flight info, and I'll pick him up."

"I thought it would be best if you did it," Elise said, still scrolling and tapping like a maniac. "I mean, your job is so—"

Wait for it.

"Flexible."

But at least she hadn't said anything about—

"And you're so responsible. I feel like this is your kind of task."

Jane stifled a sigh. Everyone always called her responsible, but they made it sound so . . . boring. She preferred to think of herself as conscientious.

"I really, really appreciate this, Jane," Elise said, finally looking up from her iPad and gracing Jane with a smile so wide and sincere that it almost made her breath catch.

Yes. Right. That was why she was voluntarily submitting to this bridesmaid torture-gig. Her friend Elise was still somewhere inside the bridezilla that was currently manning the controls, and she was so, so happy to be marrying the love of her life. That was the important thing. It made even Jane's heart, which was usually immune to these kinds of sentiments, twist a little. A wedding wasn't in her future, and she was fine with that, but all of this planning made her think of her parents' wedding pictures, the pair of them all decked out in their shaggy 1970s glory. Had they been in love like Elise and Jay, before the accident? Maybe at the start, but probably not for long, given her father's addiction. He was never violent, but he wasn't very . . . lovable.

But now was not the time for a pity party, so she smiled back at Elise. "No problem."

"You need to meet his plane, take him to Jay's, and make sure he doesn't do anything crazy. Jay will be home as soon as he can after work, and then you can leave for the evening and we'll figure out the rest of the schedule from there."

"Got it."

Elise reached out and squeezed her hand. "Seriously. Making sure Cameron doesn't ruin my wedding is the best present you could give me."

She waved away Elise's thanks. This was going to be a piece of cake. Or at least better than tea set spray-painting duty. After all, how bad could this Cameron MacKinnon guy be?

Made in United States
North Haven, CT
17 August 2024

56204348R00202